"Is this

Erin saw that he was ⬚⬚⬚⬚⬚⬚⬚⬚⬚⬚⬚⬚⬚ hands in one of his.

"That's why I came to Colorado," she said. "To tell you."

"Glad you got around to it." Abe let go of the soft tiny hand with its miniature fingers and grabbed the stick shift.

Erin knew he had reason to be mad, and her *ifs*, *ands* and *buts* would sound pretty lame. *If you'd just called after Twin Falls. And showed you cared...* "How did you guess?"

"It makes sense." Of something that made no sense otherwise. In March, people came to Alta to ski— not to visit ranches. "I have to tell you," he said, feeling that he wasn't being clever with words. "I'm engaged."

Erin told herself it didn't mean *anything*. Abe drove on, taking her deeper into the snow-swathed mountain valley. "That's okay. I didn't come here to get you to marry me or anything." *I didn't. I really didn't.*

"It would have been natural if you had."

His honesty made her eyes burn. Who had caught this cowboy and how?

ABOUT THE AUTHOR

Margot Early's first Superromance novel, *The Third Christmas*, was published in 1994 and was a RITA Award finalist for Best First Book; *The Keeper*, her second novel, was a finalist for the 1996 Janet Dailey Award. She is profiled in *The Romance Writer's Sourcebook*, published by Writer's Digest Books. *The Truth About Cowboys* is Margot's sixth Superromance title. Her seventh, *Who's Afraid of the Mistletoe?*, will appear this December.

When not wandering the fictional realms of her stories, Margot lives in cowboy country—within sight of Colorado's San Juan Mountains—with her husband and son.

If you would like to receive information about Margot's upcoming releases, write to her at: P.O. Box 611, Montrose, CO 81402-0611.

Books by Margot Early

THE TRUTH
ABOUT COWBOYS
Margot Early

Harlequin Books

TORONTO • NEW YORK • LONDON
AMSTERDAM • PARIS • SYDNEY • HAMBURG
STOCKHOLM • ATHENS • TOKYO • MILAN
MADRID • WARSAW • BUDAPEST • AUCKLAND

ISBN 0-373-70743-6

THE TRUTH ABOUT COWBOYS

The help of many people made it possible to bring this book to its present form.

Mark and Nancy Covington and D'Ann Linscott-Dunham shared their wisdom about cows and horses and read the manuscript for errors on those subjects. Darcy DeVries, Mary Thomas and Sue Steggs recommended their favorite country-western songs and artists. My father, James Early, helped with some tricky research on a copyright date. Brenda Mott and Donny Wilkinson provided information on rodeos and bullfighting. Rebecca Smith told me cow stories, and Ivan W. Martin told me wonderful tales of Colorado winters. My sister, Joan Early Farrell, described Reno to me in exquisite prose. Priscilla Miller-Peters of Cimmaron Books recommended and lent research materials *and* introduced me to the exceptional music of Ian Tyson! Lisa Staton refreshed my memory about one-year-olds. Laura DeVries answered miscellaneous questions about cowboys and cowgirls. My son shared traditional cowboy songs and constructed a mechanical bull from Lego.

Most of all, my editor, Paula Eykelhof, provided the encouragement, guidance and constructive criticism that helped me shape *The Truth About Cowboys* into the book I wanted it to be.

To all of you, my heartfelt thanks. All technical errors in this fictional work are mine.

For my sister Joan, who likes towns where a man
and his dog can enter a bar and sit down and have
a beer together.

> *"History is a vast early warning system."*
>
> —Norman Cousins

CHAPTER ONE

Reno, Nevada
June

NO COWBOYS, vowed Erin Mackenzie.

But the bullfighter clown, the greasepaint matador of the rodeo, had already helped himself to the vacant seat beside her. The clown's face was painted like a dog's, with a black splotch around one eye, and his baggy Wrangler cutoffs brushed the legs of her own not-at-all-baggy jeans as he gazed at her with a look of spellbound adoration. His thick-lashed green-gray eyes were made for pantomime—and unmeant seduction. Erin studied his suntanned knees and the stripes on his athletic socks and the dust on his cleats. Bandannas—red, yellow, orange and shocking pink—dangled from his baggies, fanning out to touch her, too.

Over the public-address system, the announcer said, "Found you a girlfriend, Abe?"

The rodeo clown jerked his chin up and down. Backing from Erin just a little, he shyly offered her some invisible flowers.

Erin took them.

The eye contact was long and awkward.

As though overcome by his feelings, he sprang to his feet and darted away. Seconds later, he settled beside a

Nashville-haired blonde in the next section and regarded her hopefully.

"Now, Abe..." said the announcer.

Erin steadied her breath. Just part of his act. But when he back-flipped over one fence and vaulted over another into the night-lit arena, she admired his agility, the way he moved. Earlier, he'd made her laugh with the antics of his Australian shepherd and with a bareback act on a chestnut gelding. Few of his jokes were new; she'd heard them at rodeos before, but *he* had that rare gift. He was funny.

And according to the program, he hailed from Alta, Colorado.

Erin couldn't ignore that. Couldn't forget it.

His patchwork shirt and suspenders with sunflowers on them transfixed her as he wandered toward the barrel in the center of the arena. When he peered inside, the barrelman, another clown, popped up like a jack-in-the-box and shouted at him. The bullfighter ran away and the crowd laughed. But the mood changed as the man at the microphone promised, "Folks, you are about to see some of the rankest bulls on the rodeo circuit..."

Bull riding. Erin sat up, watching the chutes. The Reno Rodeo was a huge event, with a $175,000 purse. It was unlikely she would run into Abe the Babe—her bullfighter clown—again.

"No cowboys," she whispered into her beer.

Erin was a candidate for the Dumped by Cowboys Hall of Fame. Sometimes she thought her life was a case study in rejection by bull riders and ropers in too-tight Wranglers, with rodeo belt buckles the size of dinner plates and small closed minds. Erin had a broad educated mind. She prided herself on clear thinking, on commitment to all things rational.

So what was she doing at the rodeo?

Partaking of an ancient rite, she told herself, a rite as old as the domestication of animals. Hadn't Theseus ridden into the city of Athens astride a bull? Weren't bulls always considered symbols of virility and cattle a measure of wealth? Wasn't Erin herself descended from people who raised cows, from cowboys?

Nothing, not even an almost completed doctorate in History of the American West from the University of Nevada at Reno, not even her own history of cowboys, could destroy her childhood dreams of snagging a rodeo champion like Ty Murray. She imagined growing old with a millionaire Gold Buckle winner who would never walk right again. He'd raise Herefords; she'd grow prizewinning vegetables for the county fair.

A bullfighter clown would do just as well. A bullfighter from Alta...

As the first bull, a brindle monster as big as a car, plunged out of the chute, bucking and spinning and raising plumes of dust, the clown in the patchwork shirt and his partner danced just out of hoof's range, ready to help the cowboy.

When the bull jettisoned his cargo, Abe withdrew a red bandanna from one oversize pocket. With a mime's grace and a matador's speed and skill, he flourished the handkerchief like a cape. The bull swung its head away from the fallen rider. While the cowboy scrambled over the fence like startled wildlife, the clown crouched on all fours and pawed the ground.

Erin leaned forward.

"I'm not sure that's such a good idea, Abe," said the announcer.

The bull charged. Grasping its horns, the bullfighter vaulted over the animal's muscular bulk—a feat depicted on a wall painting in Crete dated 2000 B.C. Abe landed on his feet, and the bull spun to meet him.

"Abe, you've made him mad now. You just leave that bull alone."

The clown was done for. The brindle beast chased him,

its lowered head committed to the seat of those baggies. Abe the Babe stood to get freight-trained by two thousand pounds of Brahma bull.

As the crowd salivated, the bullfighter swung toward the bull's shoulder, running in a small circle, forcing the bull to turn, too. Breathing deeply, Erin inhaled the rodeo smells—dust and manure and animals, beer and popcorn and hot dogs—all mingling in the dry hot Reno night. It was the modern equivalent of an evening at the Roman Coliseum.

Outmaneuvered, the bull grew bored with his quarry. Spotting the open gate and other animals, he lifted his head and trotted out of the arena, and Abe made a production of dusting off the seat of his pants and twisting around to blow on them, as though they were too hot.

"No cowboys," Erin repeated into her beer.

No cowboy from Alta.

JUST HOURS LATER, she changed her mind. On the grounds that he was a thread to her history, she'd brought him home. Granted, she would never follow the thread to its end, see where it led. But she could wrap herself in this bit of it for the night and try to stay warm.

In his sun-faded red Dodge pickup, he'd followed her to Reno's north side, to the neighborhood of houses all the same. The neighborhood that, for Erin and her mother, represented Success. Triumph over poverty. Security.

The glass patio doors were open. The swamp cooler was broken, and the ninety-degree night was as stubborn as it was rare. Outside, in the compact grass-and-concrete yard, the bullfighter's Australian shepherd sniffed at Erin's mother's cocker spaniel, Taffy. Then, the two dogs wagged tails and sniffed some more and trotted together along the board-and-batten fence.

The cowboy on the plaid sofa gaped at the shoe-box yard as though he couldn't conceive of such closed-in spaces.

His greasepaint was gone and she saw now that his skin was a smooth light golden brown, his lips flushed and sensuous. He had the hard square jaw Erin associated with descendants of those who had settled the West. Too-long Wranglers were stacked over his boots, and his white straw hat shone clean and white, not stepped-on, rolled-in-manure, end-of-the-season battered.

He was *so* cute. The cropped dirt brown hair reminded her of a World War II pilot—or the Marlboro man. So far, she'd learned he was twenty-seven and an Aries. She was a Taurus, just turned twenty-five last month; her belated birthday present to herself was a cowboy and a national-finals chance to break her own rodeo record in Getting Left.

Erin prepared for another hit of Jack Daniel's. Sloppy pouring had left shot-glass rings on the metal-legged kitchen table where she and her mother had sat so many mornings, eating Cap'n Crunch or Shredded Wheat. Now Erin and Abe were passing the bottle.

As a motto, *No cowboys* had lost its effect. Erin had been thinking of the bullfighter from Alta, Colorado, when she came home and showered and dressed after the rodeo. She'd stepped out to the rodeo dance in red Wranglers, a blue-and-red fringed Western shirt and tricolored hand-tooled cowboy boots, looking like the child of the West she'd never quite managed to become, no matter how hard she'd begged her mother for a horse of her own.

Lessons, six weeks each summer, were all they'd been able to afford. They happened only if Erin got straight A's.

Erin had never gotten anything else—except in that life course entitled Resisting Cowboys.

She studied the bullfighter, Abe Cockburn—pronounced Coburn, he'd said, same as Bruce Cockburn, the musician.

What was he thinking?

That second, Abe's thoughts were only whiskey-deep. Reliving the eight-day rodeo, subtracting the money he'd lost in travel expenses and hotel bills from what he'd earned bullfighting. Between performances he worked for Guy Loren, the stock contractor. He'd never get rich this way. But he'd always get by.

A photo above the T.V. showed a girl in a prom dress, probably this woman in high school. How did she stand living here, with just a patch of brown grass for a yard? The two-story house was identical to every other house on the street and on the next street and the next. Long and narrow with vertical cedar siding, it seemed flimsy enough to blow down in a good wind.

He blinked away drunken visions. Hotel rooms. The arena after the kids had gotten autographs and everyone had left—the trampled earth and the empty stands littered with beer cups and popcorn boxes. He imagined his truck on the road, hauling Buy Back in the trailer. Martha always rode in the cab, where Abe could sing Ian Tyson songs to her and she could put her head and paws in his lap while he drove.

The woman—Erin—took another drink. At the rodeo, he hadn't been able to decide if she was pretty or not, and he still couldn't. Her eyes were such a dark brown they seemed to make holes in her white skin, and her light reddish brown hair looked home-cut. The haircut suited her.

Her clothes did not.

He asked, "What do you do here?"

"I'm in grad school at UNR, and I work at the Museum of the American West. Also, I'm a valet." Parking cars at the hotel casinos was the best deal going for students, and Erin took pride in her work. Besides earning large tips, she'd discovered she had a way with small children abandoned in the parking lot by parents who were inside gambling. Like them, Erin understood abandonment. As they and she knew, it was often simply a case of being totally *forgotten*.

For days.

Or maybe for decades.

Now the cowboy would ask what she studied.

"You like rodeos?" he said.

"Of course."

When Abe had first spotted her, at the refreshment stand, she was rooting through a cracked and stained leather purse with dog-shredded fringe, hunting loose change. Seeing her, he'd felt like he'd walked into a post, and he'd been sure he'd never see her again. The rodeo was too big. But her seat was in the fourth row—accessible during the performance. He'd felt nervous, flirting with her. Only the greasepaint made it easy.

They'd met again at the rodeo party at the White Horse Hotel and Casino. Their eyes had caught—or rather, he had seen her staring at him, as though trying to figure out if she'd seen him before. He'd taken the bar stool next to hers and yawped at her just like he had at the rodeo, pretending he was still in his clown face. She'd recognized him then. And said, *Please go away. I don't like you.*

Soon they were two-stepping on a floor growing slick with spilled beer to country rock belted out by a band called the Spittoons.

Abe wished he wasn't leaving in the morning.

"Did you say you live with your mom?" he asked.

Erin nodded, thinking she was crazy to invite a stranger, any stranger, into her home this way. It wasn't safe. But Erin made a career of living dangerously. Hunting down gamblers in the casino to tell them when toddlers were hungry or needed their diapers changed. Frequenting rodeos, stock shows and the kind of cowboy bars famous for table-turning brawls, where people fell asleep in their drinks and no one had heard of line dancing. As a result, she had friends in low places and was often up to her ears in tears. This new friend had asked about her mother. "She's a croupier."

A blackjack dealer. Abe squinted at the croupier's

daughter. Feeling romantic and wanting to *be* romantic, for her, he asked, "Who are you?"

Was he really curious? Erin thought so. As though he cared about her for more than this night. As though, even when he moved on in the morning, he would be thinking about her. As though he might be the one who stayed on—or came back. He would fall for her like Vince Gill for the "Oh Girl" girl. She'd be never alone anymore.

"What do you mean?"

He shrugged, a boyish half-embarrassed gesture, the kind of possibly false shyness she'd learned to distrust.

"I don't know. You seem different."

As his whiskey-glazed eyes searched hers, Erin decided this clown had used these lines before. "Who are *you,* Abe?"

She meant it to be ironic. It didn't work. Abe Cockburn's layers of manhood and cowboy pride were the real McCoy. Erin wondered who he was beneath them and knew she'd never know.

It made him fascinating.

He got up and drew out another chair at the dinette, to sit closer to her.

Erin offered the bottle, but he said, "I'm fine." Then, "Can I kiss you?"

It was inevitable. Why did she do this self-destructive thing?

Erin knew exactly why. She'd passed psychology, after all. "You could talk me into that."

Into feeling his fingers push back her hair. It was a soft kiss.

Afterward, he peered down at his chest. Slowly, he fished an imaginary object from his pocket—a key ring. Finding the key he wanted, he fit it into a lock in his chest, over the left front of his black-and-white-and-green Western shirt, and opened a door Erin could almost see. Removing an object, he blew some dust off it and held it up to his ear to check if it was still ticking.

Then he handed her his heart.

Erin received the imaginary heart, held it. *Boy, I bet this thing has been around.* She set the heart aside, on the table, and picked up the whiskey bottle.

He winced and sank in his chair, dying of rejection. An instant later, he tried to snatch back his heart, but Erin grabbed it from under his hand, and he caught her fingers and their eyes met.

She followed him upstairs to the bedroom he guessed was hers, maybe because of the posters of bull rider Lane Frost and rodeo-cowboy-turned-singer Chris LeDoux on the walls.

ABE TRANSFERRED a stuffed buffalo from the pillow to the desk, balancing it beside his hat on a stack of academic-looking books with thrill-a-minute titles like *The Territories of the United States: 1861-90*. The books wedged between two geodes at the back of the desk, beside her computer, were grim. *If I Die In a Combat Zone. Witness to War: Vietnam. The Battle for Saigon.*

What did she study, anyway? What were her dreams? Abe's own were gone. He did not ask hers.

Above her desk were signs of common ground. Breyer horses like his childhood playmate, Chaley, had collected. Erin Mackenzie was a grad student, but the room told her life story. It was the room of someone who loved horses and rodeo. Of someone who was herself loved. "What's your mom going to say when she comes home?"

"She won't say anything."

Though when it came to cowboys, no one's silence could be more vocal than Jayne's. And cowboys from Alta?

On the discount-house bed, in the glass-washed desert starlight and glow of far-off neon coming through her window, Abe kissed her again. He tasted like mint and whiskey. He smelled like horses, and she liked kissing him.

Don't think, Erin. Not about him leaving.

She'd stopped telling herself stories. He wouldn't love her.

He was scrutinizing her again, as though she mattered to him. Unbuttoning her shirt. A dog came into the room—his dog. Taffy, the cocker spaniel, needed her nails clipped. The Australian shepherd didn't.

"Martha, lie down," he said.

She did, and Erin knew how the dog must feel, that you wanted to please this man. You wanted him to love you.

They took off each other's clothes. She'd known his body would be this way—hard, his chest paler than his face and throat and forearms and hands.

He had his own condoms and was good at hugging, before, during and after sex. Muscle, hair and strength pressed to her, while the bed creaked and the headboard knocked the wall. But even excited, even coming, she stayed distant. She knew cowboys.

After she'd lain in his arms awhile, she pretended to hunt through the covers and drew out an imaginary key on a ring. She unlocked the door in his chest and put his heart away and locked it up again.

That made Abe want to do something funny, to make her laugh, to make himself laugh. But they both knew he would leave. *Maybe I'll see you next year,* really meant, *Goodbye.*

"I'm going to be in Twin Falls—Idaho—the first of August," he said, shocking himself. Even being in her bed surprised him. Picking up women after rodeos wasn't his way; usually he was busy helping Guy care for the stock. But he'd wanted to be with Erin. Because talking to her for five minutes at the White Horse, he'd found out she was smart. She'd made *him* laugh. And when the band played "My Heroes Have Always Been Cowboys," she'd said, in his arms, "It's my fatal flaw."

Abe was still thinking about that. "Do you think you could drive up?" he asked. To Twin Falls.

She looked starry-eyed and wary. "Is it a rodeo?"

"Just bull riding." Guy Loren was providing the stock. Working for the stock contractor was the best way Abe knew to guarantee work bullfighting.

Erin considered. He was from Alta. And she really liked him. Maybe... She lived on maybes.

"Okay. I guess."

He hugged her again, a long sleepy kind of hug like she'd never felt before.

"So—you're from Colorado?" she asked weakly.

"Yeah." The ranch was gone, had been for eleven years. Abe gave his address as Guy Loren's place in Alta, but he wasn't from anywhere anymore.

To Erin, his voice sounded rough. Husky. As though the land was someone he loved, someone he missed. "Do you have any brothers or sisters?"

"A little brother. His name's Lane."

The black shapes of the bull and bull rider on her poster swam in the dark. "Like Lane Frost?"

"Like, but not for. Rides in all the rough stock events, though. Junior rodeo. He's good." He paused. "My folks are divorced."

"So are mine. My dad lives in Colorado, too." It wasn't enough; she had to say more. "He's a cowboy. I've never met him."

That didn't make *any* sense to Abe. He loved his own daddy. Their relationship had its ups and downs and pissing contests, but Abe couldn't imagine life without him. Lloyd Cockburn had shaped who he was. "Why don't you look him up?"

Erin rolled onto her back. "Sometime I will."

"What kind of cowboy is he?"

Erin knew what he meant. There were rodeo cowboys and dime-store cowboys and urban cowboys and ranchers and… Well, there were real cowboys. Real, honest-to-God, home-on-the-range cowboys. Erin knew the answer that would satisfy Abe. She would tell him the work her father did, and he would form a picture that might be right or might be wrong.

But Erin was a little drunk, so she gave the answer she'd held in her heart all her life. So what if it was a mystery, like the truth about cowboys? As a doctoral candidate in History of the American West, she was entitled to an opinion.

"He's a real cowboy."

The night was cooling off. Abe drew her against him. But he wasn't thinking about sex, and he wasn't thinking of her father anymore. Or even how "My Heroes Have Always Been Cowboys" could be a fatal flaw.

He missed his own dad and the brother tagging along where he rode, where he walked. Lane, who looked up to him the way kids at the rodeo did, showing up with their faces painted like clowns.

Most of all, he missed the place that should have been his and the person he had always counted on being.

Erin didn't notice his wandering thoughts, only the way he was hugging her and how loose and sleepy her body felt. It wasn't usually easy to sleep with another person.…

A WHILE LATER, she woke up with him, and the kisses and strokes resumed. It all seemed more intense than sex. Like those hugs, but more than that, too. As his penis nudged her, slid against her wetness, Erin knew it wasn't safe. Cowboys could have AIDS and make babies, same as other men. But it felt good to let him ease partway in and out of her, teasing until at last he sighed and turned to get a condom. This time, the headboard didn't hit the wall. Only their bodies shook.

Abe kissed her to sleep and couldn't sleep himself. But he lingered in her bed, thinking of Buy Back, his horse, in a stall at the livestock arena, thinking of the road heading east. It shouldn't have been hard to let a strange woman go; he would see her in a few weeks.

But his strings were unstrung and "pretty" would never matter again. She read war stories and had a cowboy father she'd never met. She was a graduate student, but Abe had never asked what was worth so much school.

He stole from her bed and dressed with Martha waiting. It was almost dawn, the day waking on a dimmer switch, and the view from her window was a hundred brown houses just like hers.

Abe folded his red bandanna into the shape of a heart and laid it on her desk on top of her opened notebook. On the blank page he wrote, "You can give it back to me in Twin Falls, August 1." He clapped on his hat.

Martha followed him from the room and down the stairs in the stillness. The cocker spaniel tore from the living room to the foyer just as a key turned in the lock. A woman in a black-and-white casino uniform froze in the half-opened doorway. Erin's face in an older portrait, with fewer angles and more curves. Sexy, like a showgirl.

Abe touched his hat. "Ma'am."

Looking suddenly weary, suddenly ten years older, the mother stepped inside and held the door in silent disapproval until he and his dog went through. The latch clicked behind him.

Two weeks later
Gunnison, Colorado

DUST.

The wind was up and they were all picking the dirt out of their teeth. Abe felt it catching in the paint on his face—the white base, the black spot around his right eye, his black dog's nose and mouth, and the brown-and-black spots on his cheeks. It had sifted into his cleats and through the weave of his tube socks and between his toes. The crowd hated the wind, especially with July heat, and it was his job to make them laugh about it, so he'd borrowed a duster owned by three-hundred-pound Marvelous Mark Friday, the announcer. In the center of the arena, Abe donned the coat and let it blow him like a sail on a boat.

He was barrelman this performance, leaving the bull-fighting to Tug Holcomb and a rookie named Chad. Abe was sorry in a way. He loved clowning, and being the man in the can gave him the chance. But almost everyone he cared about was in the audience this afternoon. His father, Lloyd, sat in the stands with Abe's pretty and sharp-tongued childhood friend, Chaley Kay, and her father, Kip, who owned the last family-run ranch in Alta. And Lane, Abe's brother, was hanging out back of the chutes, checking out the stock; Lane was counting the months till he turned eighteen and became eligible to earn a Professional Rodeo Cowboys Association card.

For all four of those spectators but especially for his dad, who thought rodeo was play, Abe would have preferred to be bullfighting.

Saving cowboys.

There weren't many cowboys to save anymore. Old cowboys like his dad and Kip Kay were mostly gone. Soon the only ones left would be wannabes, like the movie stars and corporate bigwigs buying up all the land from Gunnison to Alta and line dancing at the I'm Okay, You're Okay Corral. Them—and rodeo cowboys.

Dark storm clouds tumbled overhead and Abe heard thunder. Yanking the duster over himself, he hurled his body to the ground in a timid quivering mass. Under the laughter of the audience, he peeked out and saw a bull rider wrapping his hand in the chute. *Left hand.* A bullfighter always needed to know which direction to turn the bull. Soon the cowboy would nod for the chute to be opened.

Abe jumped up, produced a whisk broom from his baggies and swept himself off.

"Now this next bull, Belligerence," said the announcer, "has killed a dozen clowns."

Still wearing the oversize duster, Abe ran for the barrel and climbed in, to sweat.

"In the can."

The crowd laughed.

Abe popped his head out, then ducked, jerking on his hat until the flapping crown popped up. As rain tapped the brim and wet his hair, he sprang up again, trying to close the crown. People were laughing, which was good. He was dying of heat and ready for the bull.

Guy Loren was the stock contractor for this rodeo—Gunnison was in his backyard—and Abe knew all the stock. Belligerence was the mean offspring of a Brahma and a Mexican fighting bull. Big brown patches ringed his eyes, and when he burst out of the chute, snorting bull slobber and standing on his head, Abe thought that if he ever saw death it might look like that. Chad, the rookie, tried to make the bull spin, but the rider was already launched.

Line him out. Belligerence had a reputation for charging downed riders, and it was the bullfighter's job to distract him.

The cowboy made it to the fence, and Abe took a bow as though he'd had something to do with it. The bull charged the can.

As Belligerence came, Abe crouched in the furnace of the can, bracing himself for the impact. His barrel was reinforced with steel and old automobile tire casings and painted with the sponsor's logo. One of the bullfighters rolled the barrel onto its side, and then the force came, a hard hit, and Abe was on the worst carnival ride of his life, not rolling on the ground, but spinning through the air with a horn in his shoulder and a bull's bad breath in his face, bracing his body against the sides of the barrel. Pain ripped his body, and the bull tossed free the can.

There was no landing right and lots of ways to land wrong, and later Tug said he heard the crack from outside the can.

Twin Falls, Idaho
August

A HIGH-SCHOOL STUDENT waved Erin to a space in the dirt parking lot. Signs throughout town had advertised the bull-riding event, and Erin had found the rodeo grounds easily. But when she arrived, her instincts said to hit the road again.

That would be futile. No matter how far she drove, this cowboy would be with her.

Anyhow, *he* had suggested the rendezvous. Erin was hopeful enough to wear her favorite black Wranglers and fringed black shirt and her favorite boots, black lace-up ropers, a two-year-old birthday present from her mother. Though Jayne didn't approve of cowboys, she did appreciate Western wear.

Erin had even worn a big silver belt buckle with her name on it—in case he couldn't remember. She didn't *need* a belt. Not now.

It was hot and almost muggy. As she shut the door of her mother's baby blue 1969 Mustang convertible, borrowed for the weekend, a half-ton pickup powered past, and the resulting dust cloud coated her clothing. Blinking and nauseous, Erin groped in her purse for her sunglasses, then headed for the entrance with the regret of those who wear black on August afternoons.

Where was he? As she paid admission—ten dollars—she caught sight of a bullfighter with a green wig and striped shirt. Not Abe. She followed the crowd into the rodeo grounds and past the refreshment booth. *He'll be near the chutes.*

Skirting the track that circled the arena, Erin scanned the bodies. She ignored bull riders in bright chaps, fringe waving with every step, and hunted for clowns. One rolled a barrel into the arena, but he was too short to be Abe—and wearing the wrong costume. Another bullfighter lazed against a rail near the chutes with a grizzled rancher type.

Where was Abe?

The bullfighter inside the fence was tantalizingly close. She could get his attention. Erin contemplated the back of his companion, the rancher. The white shirt stretched across his shoulders was damp under the armpits. His walnut-shell face and weatherbeaten boots marked him as a real cowboy.

Wondering if her father looked like that, if maybe this was her father—it always *could* be—Erin approached the fence. "Excuse me."

Neither man heard at first, and she felt stupid, especially when three passing bull riders smirked at her. *They think I'm a buckle bunny, trying to pick up a man at the rodeo.*

Red-faced, Erin said more loudly, "Excuse me."

The bullfighter turned. A moon-white wig framed his makeup. "Yes, ma'am?"

She hung on to the hot fence. "I'm looking for Abe Cockburn. Is he here?"

The old cowboy ignored her, though he'd shifted so that now she could see his weathered face. He wasn't her father. She had a twenty-five-year-old picture of her father, and this wasn't him.

"I don't know him," said the clown. "Is he riding bulls today? You might ask back in the chutes, but I think those cowboys are all thinking about the performance right now."

"He's a bullfighter. He's supposed to be working here."

"Oh..." His star-painted eyes squinted. "Cockburn.

Yeah, he canceled. I don't know why. I live over in Preston. Stock contractor phoned and asked me to fill in. Maybe you want to talk to him. He might be able to tell you something.''

Erin was afraid she'd throw up. ''That's okay. Thank you.''

''Sure.'' He tipped his hat. ''Enjoy the bull riding.''

''Thanks.''

The stands seemed miles away. As the announcer welcomed fans to the professional bull-riding competition, Erin pushed toward the exit. Heat hung in her clothing.

Being Dumped by a Cowboy was nothing new. She was an expert in the field. But she'd never known till now that it felt even worse to be dumped by a cowboy when you were pregnant with his child.

"Cowboys hide the truth beneath their hats."

—Erin Mackenzie,
"Cattle and Cowboys: The Ancient
Currency of a Modern Enigma"

CHAPTER TWO

Reno, Nevada
March, twenty months since Erin was Dumped by a Clown

PENCIL HOLDERS. Seven days before Maeve's first birthday, Erin was called for jury duty and took her daughter to day care. She was dismissed before noon, and when she picked up Maeve, the older kids were making pencil holders from juice cans.

Driving home, Erin tried to forget this. But some things a person couldn't forget—like the juice-can pencil holder in her own past.

When she reached the house, *Prorodeo Sports News* was in the mailbox, and *he* had the cover.

At six o'clock, still thinking of pencil holders, she picked up the phone.

Her grip on the receiver was like a bull rider's suicide wrap; she'd gotten on, and the only way off was through. Cowboy up and ride. The now cut-up copy of *Prorodeo Sports News* covered the table in the same room where she and Abe Cockburn had drunk whiskey one fateful summer night. On the paper sat a manila envelope stuffed with clippings. Erin had removed a tiny cut-out want ad from the envelope—for reference. He still lived in Alta.

Where a phone was ringing. Not at Guy Loren's ranch, Abe's address, but at a neighboring place. The ranch of Missing Past. The ranch that kept Erin's grail, which was the truth about cowboys.

Between rings, someone picked up with a clatter. "Kays'."

A man.

Maeve sat in her playpen in the living room. While her daughter tried to stuff a square block through a round hole, Erin said, "Hi. I'm interested in coming to visit your ranch. I have a brochure." She supposed that was what she should call the tri-fold black-and-white leaflet.

"When were you thinking of coming?"

"Next week." The contract on the house was pending; she wouldn't hear on any of her applications before the following week was up; the kennel would board Taffy. The timing was perfect.

"We have room," he said, and he sounded like a cowboy, like his voice had been in the wind that day. "It's cold here, though, and we're calving. How many in your party?"

"Just me and my daughter. She's eleven months old." Outside, the sky had darkened from Baskin-Robbins pink to deep gray. Erin stretched the phone cord as she went to draw the curtains. It was seven months since she'd enjoyed a starry night through the glass patio doors. Seven months since she'd felt comfortable leaving Maeve even one room away. Now she shut all the curtains at night and carried Maeve with her everywhere in the house.

There was no reply. Had they been disconnected?

"Hello?" asked Erin.

"We don't have child-care services. You have a baby, you'd best come in June. We'll have a barbecue and a dance after branding's done."

June? If she didn't come now, she'd lose her nerve. The house would sell, she would receive a job offer and move somewhere safer and more wholesome than Reno. The crucial would seem inessential, the matter of juice-can pencil holders...maudlin.

"I'd prefer to come now."

"Well, I guess we can find something for you to do. Make sure you bring warm clothes. It's twenty below out."

The man of the gruff voice might or might not own the Kay Ranch of Alta, Colorado. *Stop shaking, Erin.* "I'd like to make a reservation, then, for next week."

"We'll need a two-hundred-dollar deposit. But we don't take credit cards."

"I'll send a money order." It was what she'd planned. Because of his next, inevitable question.

"That'll be fine. What's your name?"

"Erin O'Neill." It was satisfying to lie to a cowboy for a change, instead of him lying to her.

"Address and phone?"

Erin told him her post-office box and phone number. They agreed that she would arrive on Saturday, March fifteenth, and stay through the twenty-first.

"You'll want to fly into Grand Junction, or Gunnison if you can get a decent fare," he said. "Either way, we'll meet you."

"Thank you."

"You're welcome. We'll be glad to have you."

The sign of warmth let her ask, "And who am I talking to?"

"This is Kip Kay," he said. "Owner."

HAUNTED BY A NAME, by the name *Erin,* Kip returned to the supper table. Only three others were eating tonight— Beulah Ann, Lloyd and Lane. Kip's niece Beulah Ann had come to the ranch the past summer to work as wrangler and cook. Lloyd Cockburn, once his neighbor, was now

Kip's foreman. And Lloyd's youngest son, Lane, was biding his time; his future was rodeo, not ranching.

Kip told them, "We have a guest coming next week. She's bringing a baby."

"We're calving," Lloyd said.

"I pointed that out." Kip picked up his fork, glad that Lloyd, too, had seen the problem. Lately his foreman—who was in his seventies—seemed a little vague. And right now Kip needed every mind and every pair of hands.

Twenty-four-year-old Lucky, who came from Alta to help out, was living on a trust fund and cowboying for fun; Kip found him reliable but inexperienced. Another hand was studying for finals at the college in Gunnison and showed up when he could, which wasn't often enough. That left Wayne, Kip's top hand, who had just accepted a job in Telluride, at a ranch owned by movie people; he'd have his own house and health insurance and fourteen thousand a year. No way Kip could match that.

It was coming down to family. At this minute Chaley and Abe were in the barn with a sick heifer who'd just aborted her calf.

Kip found that thought reassuring—not the heifer's troubles, but Abe's being with Chaley. Their engagement still gave him anxious moments. In fact, he spent hours every day mulling over his future son-in-law.

The question that ate at him was: why hadn't Abe quit his job down the road with Guy Loren and come home to the Kay Ranch? The offer had been made. And what kind of fiancé didn't want to spend as many waking hours as possible with his betrothed?

Seventeen-year-old Lane pushed back his chair. "Good night," he said. When no one responded, he cleared away his plate. Cold came through the kitchen to the dining room as he banged outside, probably heading for the trailer he and his father shared.

"We're all talkative," remarked Beulah Ann, who was

eighteen and, in Kip's estimation, an excellent person in all ways. She had her past, and Kip had taken a risk bringing her on, but so far he didn't regret it.

One day he'd overheard Lane tease her about her weight, which was substantial, and Beulah Ann had said, *So what? I could ride one of those bulls as good as you.* Next day she and Lane were down at Guy Loren's bucking pens, and Beulah Ann stayed on one of his Brangus bulls for eight seconds. So there. Kip still chuckled thinking of it.

Now he winked at his niece. "That's a sign of good cooking."

"Or grouchy men," grumbled Beulah Ann good-naturedly. "You can sure tell the difference when Chaley's here."

Kip felt the same. It had made all the difference to his daily happiness when his daughter, Chaley, had graduated from the university in Fort Collins and come home to the ranch. Chaley was here to stay, and this ranch would one day be hers. Hers and her children's.

And Abe's.

From one brooding notion came another, unrelated. That bitter day twenty-five years past. A day invoked by the speaking of a name, the name of Jayne's child. Kip turned his thoughts to cows.

They crept to mortality, instead.

Things happened suddenly on a ranch, like earlier that week when he'd fallen from the sleigh while hooking hay to the cows. Like when Yule, his horse, had rolled over him last winter. Like years before, when Lloyd's little girl had fallen between the wheels of his tractor.

Life on a ranch was whimsical and he could die at any time.

He could die without ever having known the child Jayne had borne, without ever having seen her face.

And frankly he just didn't care.

HANGING UP THE PHONE, Erin glanced again toward Maeve, then put away her clippings, including the new photo of a bullfighter jumping a whitish Brahma cross. She'd seen the same patchwork shirt and sunflower suspenders at the Reno rodeo and in other rodeo photos since; they were his costume. The caption read, "Bullfighter Abe Cockburn, making a comeback after a broken neck, jumps Big Ugly in Tuscon."

Erin knew about Abe's broken neck. She'd read about it the day before Maeve was born. Somehow, reading about Abe's solid legitimate excuse for standing her up in Twin Falls had made her feel better, had in fact given her permission to go into labor and finally have his baby, who was nine days late. A broken neck was the best excuse she'd ever heard for standing up a date.

Though he'd never bothered to get in touch, either. To explain.

It had left her in limbo, arguing with her mother about right and wrong. Jayne had felt that the existence of a child should supersede "petty grievances." As far as Erin was concerned, the man had shown he didn't care about the fate of his sperm by never trying to see her again.

But what happened to Jayne made her stop thinking about Abe and start thinking about Maeve and how a person with one parent could become a person with no parents.

Meanwhile, Abe had been barrelman for Cheyenne Frontier Days and was featured in *Prorodeo Sports News*. Although bullfighting had itself become a rodeo event—bullfighters spent from forty to seventy seconds in the ring with a fighting bull, smaller and more agile than the stock used for bull riding—Abe did not compete. "'I never wanted to be a competitor,' says Cockburn. 'I just like protecting cowboys—and making people laugh.'"

Erin tucked the photo into the manila envelope, then

picked up the want ad. It was three months old; probably he didn't need to advertise much these days.

ABE COCKBURN, Clown, barrelman, bullfighter. Unforgettable acts. Excellent cowboy protection. Loved by children and dogs.

Then came his phone number and address. Guy Loren Rodeo Company, 10598 Skyway, Alta, CO. Guy Loren was a former National Finals Rodeo champion calf roper and bulldogger, and as a stock contractor he was still a big deal in rodeo.

In July Erin had called for a brochure from the Kay Ranch, also on Skyway in Alta.

And now...

I'm going there.

She closed the envelope. It belonged upstairs. Maeve was trying to put a plastic ring around a cone on a rocking base. The toy had been Erin's when she was a baby; Jayne had saved everything.

Erin scooped up the baby, and Maeve whimpered, reaching out with her ring. But Erin could not go upstairs and leave her daughter downstairs in this house. Balancing Maeve on her hip, Erin took the manila envelope to the second floor, switching on lights, glancing around corners, jumping at the jingling of dog tags as Taffy emerged from her mother's room. Taffy liked to sleep on the bed, as though waiting for Jayne to return.

"Mama," said Maeve, rubbing her eyes and putting a baby hand on Erin's nearest breast. With Maeve crying in her arms, Erin made another trip up and down the stairs, double-checking locks, peering behind coats in the closets, looking for shoes beneath the drapes. At last she carried the baby into her bedroom, to the bed where Maeve had been conceived.

Erin turned on the desk lamp each night to sleep and

turned it off in the morning when she awoke. Nursing Maeve to sleep in its glow, Erin studied a faded color snapshot turned toward her in its plastic gilt frame. Behind the glass, everything was faintly green. Her father's skin and his uniform and the washed-out hills behind him. Erin understood the details. A silver bar meant lieutenant. The weapon was an M-16.

There were no Herefords in Vietnam.

Had he forgotten his wife was pregnant when she left him? Once, Erin had asked her mother, *If he wanted to find me, could he?*

Oh, yes. He knows right where you are.

It would have been better, Erin thought, if he'd never known. And maybe it would be better for Maeve if Abe didn't.

But Jayne had stood up for Abe.

Erin, you shouldn't judge Maeve's father by your own. You don't know your father, and you barely know this rodeo clown. You must tell him about his daughter. It's right and it's fair.

Fair. She'd never told Jayne about the pencil holder. It would have troubled her, which Erin had known even at eight years old.

Maeve stopped nursing; her eyes had long since shut and now she slept. Erin rolled her onto her stomach and covered her with a blanket. A crib was too faraway in the night, in this house.

She recalled her mother holding Maeve in the rocking chair downstairs, playing peekaboo with her. Night was here, and Erin greeted again the foremost uncertainty of life, which was the certainty of death.

IN THE KAYS' BARN, the heifer was wheezing and Chaley was crying. "Dammit, Abe, what are you doing? I've listened to your bitterness—"

"I'm not bitter."

"—and your anger for more than ten years. My dad wants you here, and what are you doing?"

Why answer? He was going to a rodeo—weekend after next. Chaley knew that, just as Abe knew what her father was offering. He'd been a rancher's son himself, and there was nothing finer than knowing the land was his, that he would marry a staying woman and raise children who would love the land and feed cattle from it. Chaley had recovered his stolen dreams and returned them to him.

But they were worn-out, changed like he was.

The diamond on her hand gave off a guilty gleam, and Abe stroked Martha, who offered a cold wet nose and serious competition for the role of main female in his life. "Want to see my new act?" He got to his feet and hunted for a prop. His art was turning tears to laughter.

But Chaley laughed slow and sniped quick. She whipped back her blond braid. She was a lanky woman with strong hands, and could clear ditches and handle livestock. She spoke plain. "Your act is a disappearing act, and I don't like it. I need a husband I can count on, a man who'll help look after cows and mend fences and care about this ranch. This past year, I've thought it could be you. But you won't even quit Loren's place—"

"He and I have worked together a long time, Chaley."

"But you're *marrying* me, and you belong on *this* ranch. Anyone could understand that. Besides, your dad's here, and he's an old man."

"He's not that old."

"Seventy-two?"

"He looks great."

"He forgot to close a gate yesterday."

Abe swallowed. That was serious.

"Six cows got out onto the highway."

"Maybe someone else left the gate open."

Chaley didn't dignify that with a response. Except, "He

needs you. And *you* need a twelve-step program. You've got a problem, and it's called rodeo."

Abe didn't appreciate her point of view, but all he said was, "Stop now, before I command Martha to lick you to death."

She didn't smile. "Someone else would save those bull riders if you weren't there. It costs money to drive all over the country and stay in hotels."

"Sometimes I sleep in my truck. Anyhow, I break even." He loved bullfighting, loved making people laugh, loved how the kids stared up at him when he walked past the stands because he was the bullfighter, the man who put his body between the bull and a fallen cowboy. Most of all, he loved hearing their laughter the way he loved water in the ditches in August; he loved hearing some small voice say, *Look at the clown, Mommy! He's so funny.*

Chaley filled a syringe with antibiotic and injected the heifer. Her eyes were tender. She cared about animals, all animals, and Abe admired her. Chaley's mother had died when she was seventeen, and Chaley had done a good job of going on.

"I hate rodeos," she said. "I can't stand all those buckle bunnies and barrel racers and dime-store cowboys. It's just a big pickup scene. It's as phony as the I'm Okay, You're Okay Corral."

He couldn't take that comparison. Rodeo was nothing like the new dance hall near Alta called the Okay Corral, where rich people from cities tried ranch dressing and line dancing and called themselves cowboys.

Abe stood up. "I've got to get back and check on Missy." One of Loren's mares was due to drop a champion bucking bronc into the world.

Chaley glowered.

Abe said, "Martha. Attack."

The Australian shepherd wagged her tail and slurped a

kiss across Chaley's face, teasing a smile to the corners of her mouth. The kiss that followed—Abe's—fixed it there.

CHALEY'S PROBLEMS simmered on the back burner most of the next week. At Loren's place, they were calving and foaling, and Abe had his hands full with sharp-horned Mexican cows and Brahmas who thought cowboys were for hurting. The pleasure was horses. Besides broncs and bulls, the stock contractor was assembling some good roping horses. And work for Guy Loren had no uncomfortable strings attached.

The strings dangling from Kip Kay's standing job offer weren't something Abe spent time noticing, though he kept tripping on them as a result. He just wanted to do what he was doing and leave it at that and not think very hard about the June evening he and Chaley had ended up engaged.

Early Saturday, as he crossed Guy Loren's snowy yard after pulling a calf, the phone rang in the disabled fifth wheel he and Martha shared. Abe sprinted for the door and blew in with the snow. The clock on the stove read four-thirty.

His dad...

Shivering from the sweat that had cooled on his body, he snatched up the receiver. "Hello?"

Martha came down from the sleeping area, wagging her tail, and Abe stroked her ears, let her sniff and lick at him.

"Abe, it's Chaley. We have a problem."

His heart wouldn't slow down. He waited for her to tell him something had happened to Lloyd.

"That woman's supposed to come today, and the Snowcat won't start. There's three feet of new snow on the road, and we can't get the trucks out, and nobody but Lucky showed up today. We're up to our necks in calves, and every single one of them needs warming up. It's too damned cold."

"I know." He and Guy and Terry, Guy's wife, and

Pedro, their other hand, had been up all night. Kip Kay had more stock and, at the moment, no more hands. Abe didn't mention that he was covered in blood and manure and ready to drop in his tracks. A shower and a cup of coffee would fix him. "I'll ask Guy if I can go. Where'd you say she's coming in?"

Chaley gave him the flight information. "Her name's Erin O'Neill, and she's coming from Reno. No, wait, the flight's from Salt Lake."

Erin from Reno. Erin from Reno.

"Erin who?" He tried not to sound very interested.

"O'Neill. Do you need it *spelled?*"

From the indoor-outdoor carpet, Martha watched him with eyes far more patient and loving than the voice on the phone. "I got it," he said. Erin O'Neill.

Different Erin from Reno.

A few minutes later, stooping down to kiss and hug his best girl, Abe realized he was disappointed.

And what a bad sign that was for him and Chaley.

There were a lot of bad signs.

IT WAS SNOWING in Grand Junction five hours later, and through the terminal window, Abe watched passengers leave the plane and descend onto the tarmac. He saw no woman with a baby. Maybe she wouldn't show up....

That might not be a bad thing. What if the Kays' guest didn't appreciate the unconditional affection of the most beautiful and intelligent dog in the world? Well, Martha might have to ride in the back. That was what the camper shell was for, protecting his dog from the elements.

Oh, damn. A car seat. The baby would need a car seat. *We'll have to go buy one.*

If she showed up.

As he began to plan what he'd do if Erin O'Neill didn't get off the plane, he saw her. She carried the baby in one arm and a bulging black tote in the other. She had dude written all over her, from Stetson to ropers, and looked like she might catch a toe on the hem of her duster. Abe hoped she wouldn't slip on the snowy tarmac lugging all that gear—and the baby.

The arrivals poured in through the glass door of the terminal, and around him people greeted loved ones. Then she passed through the gate with the baby, and he saw her face.

Erin.

Erin Mackenzie.

No, O'Neill.

And she was holding a baby, a baby with curly light red hair and a floppy denim hat with a flower in it and brown eyes like two holes in her face, just like her mother's.

She had a baby.

Then Abe understood, the way a man understands he's been shot.

She had married someone and had a baby.

When she saw Abe, she blanched.

Of course.

Married now, she wouldn't want to be reminded of their one-night stand.

In fact, *he* should hurry up and forget it.

There was really only one thing to do, which was to set her at ease. Make her see that no word or reminder of the night they'd spent together would pass his lips. The incident would never be mentioned. Abe would conduct himself as though it hadn't happened. As though they'd never met before. It was the decent solution.

"You must be Erin," he said. "I'm Abe. I came to drive you back to the Kay ranch."

*"Maeve asked MacRoth if he knew where
she might acquire a bull finer than Ailill's.
MacRoth told her of a magical bull, the
Donn Cualigne, the Dark One of Cooley."*

—The Cattle Raid of Cooley,
Ancient Irish oral tradition, first
recorded in the eighth century

CHAPTER THREE

ERIN DIDN'T NEED a Ph.D. in Cowboys to grasp the
situation. It was Abe. He recognized her. He was pretending they'd never met.

*He wants me to forget it. This is his way of saying it was
just a one-night stand and it's over now. He has someone
else.*

Well, one night together almost two years before wasn't
much on which to build a relationship. Only a candidate
for the Dumped by Cowboys Hall of Fame would think it
meant something.

Abe was acting like a stranger, and he seemed like one.
His black hat and blanket-lined Carhartt made him look like
a real cowboy. His eyelashes and mouth made him look
like Maeve's father.

"Thank you for meeting me." Erin regrouped. "Do you
work for the Kays?"

Abe explained, omitting Chaley. It seemed insulting to

Erin to mention his engagement. Why should she care about his love life?

"But how will I get out to the ranch if they're snowed in?"

"My boss will take his Snowcat up and clear their road." Neighboring ranchers did things like that for each other, like driving home your cows if they got out. Guy Loren had bought his spread just fifteen years earlier with rodeo winnings, but from growing up on a ranch in Oklahoma he knew how things were done; he'd earned the respect and friendship of longtime local cattlemen like his father, Lloyd, and Kip Kay.

"Can I get that?" Indicating Erin's tote bag, Abe stole a glance at the baby. He'd met eyes like those in bed one June night. It took time to get the situation straight in his mind. Erin had been looking at some other man when this child was made.

"Did you check anything?" he asked.

"Yes. One bag."

"Let's get it."

With Maeve on her hip, Erin matched his strides through the airport and couldn't match his grace. The baby began to fret.

A baby, thought Abe. He couldn't get it out of his head that she'd had a baby with someone—so suddenly. But it was a while since he'd driven down the road singing along with Ian Tyson's "Old Corrals and Sagebrush" and thinking of laying his own eyes on Erin from Reno. Usually he sang to Martha, who thought all his songs were for her.

Where was Erin's husband, anyway?

Pieces of nylon webbing hung from the tote bag Abe carried, with toys for the baby tied on. He stopped while Erin untied a rubber pretzel. The baby put it in her mouth, then flung it on the ground and began to cry.

"Oh, sweetheart." Carefully holding the child, Erin stooped to pick up the pretzel.

Abe got it first. It was slobbery, like Martha's toys after they'd been in her mouth. Handing it to Erin, he tried to see her wedding ring.

She wore none.

The baby fussed as an escalator lowered them to the baggage-claim area. The luggage was already on a carousel.

"Do you see yours?"

"The blue duffel bag with black straps."

When Abe turned with the bag, he found her sitting in a corner. She opened her duster, pushed up her flannel shirt and gave the baby her breast. Abe almost tripped. He had grown up around cows suckling their calves. He'd tied the hides of stillborn calves to the bodies of orphaned calves, to trick the mothers of the dead calves into accepting the others as their own.

He remembered his own mouth on this woman's breasts.

He stared too long. At the curve of the baby's cheek around that denim hat as she suckled from a breast he couldn't see. At Erin. As she watched the face hidden from Abe, her expression was loving and sad.

Maybe her husband was dead.

When Abe brought the duffel bag, Erin murmured, "Thanks." She took a bottle of springwater from her tote and loosened the cap. Holding one of the baby's hands in one of hers, she drank.

Abe sat and studied the people milling about near the carousel. "It took five hours to get here from Alta this morning. I'll get you back there soon as I can, but the roads are bad."

Erin remembered his voice. What did Abe remember? The house in Reno? The woman he'd met on the way out at dawn?

This journey, Erin told herself, *is not a betrayal of Jayne.*

Jayne had wanted her to tell Abe.

The Kay Ranch was the problem.

"Also," Abe said, "I didn't think to round up a car seat

for your baby. So we'll go buy one." He was solvent this week, had finally saved enough for a new saddle. Keith Springs in Gunnison was making it, and Abe had already paid half down.

"Oh. Thanks." Absently Erin switched Maeve to the other breast. The baby was limp, eyes shut, and Erin wished she'd changed her before nursing. Maeve shouldn't sit in a wet diaper for the car ride. To the Kay Ranch.

It's for Maeve, Mom. Everything I'm doing is for Maeve.

It was like telling her mother that she hadn't even *liked* Abe Cockburn, that she didn't *want* to see him again.

If Jayne were alive, she wouldn't believe this, either.

SHE HAD TO CHANGE the baby, so Abe went to get the truck. A half-inch of snow candy-coated the red Dodge pickup he'd bought used from an NFR bull rider. Martha stood guard in the driver's seat, and her tail whipped back and forth when she saw him.

"Hi, Martha. Did you miss me?" They exchanged kisses, and he rubbed her mottled blue-gray-and-black coat, stroked the red patches near her face. Martha was the only light in this day.

It wasn't that he hadn't wanted to see Erin again. He'd often thought of Twin Falls, the rendezvous he'd missed.

Maybe he should explain about that.

No. She's Mrs. O'Neill. You're engaged to Chaley.

And this was not a good day.

He thrust Ian Tyson's *Cowboyography* into the tape deck while he warmed up the engine. Whistling to "Summer Wages," he drove around to the arrivals area. She wasn't out front, and he double-checked the airline sign and calculated how long it should take to change a baby. Letting the truck idle, he sang four songs to Martha and thought about Erin till he wondered what was keeping her. He turned off the engine. "Stay, Martha. Good girl."

As he left the truck, Erin emerged from the terminal with

the baby and the tote bag. In her hat and duster, she reminded him of a kid dressed up for make-believe.

When he took her tote bag, she slipped—maybe those new boots. Abe caught her arm. "Okay?"

She nodded, holding her baby tighter.

"Erin…" Oh, shit. He'd thought about her a lot. This was payment.

Her darker-than-earth eyes gazed at him.

"We'll go to Target," he tried at last, "and get a car seat. Can you hold her in your lap across town?"

"Sure."

Abe unlocked the passenger door for her, and Martha leaned forward to sniff the newcomers.

"Hi, Martha," Erin said.

No other words could have made Abe more interested in why she didn't wear a wedding ring.

The baby said, "Da-dee."

"Yes, it's a doggy," Erin agreed.

"I'll put her in the back. Martha, come."

The dog jumped down and sniffed Erin's duster and her boots. While Erin climbed into the passenger seat with her sleepy baby, Abe called Martha around back, let her in the camper shell and told her to stay off the bed.

When he got behind the wheel and started the engine, Ian Tyson's voice filled the cab, singing about his own heart's delight. Abe turned down the stereo. The baby dozed in Erin's arms, dreaming in Hatland. All babies should have hats like that. Red curls like that. "This okay?"

"It's fine."

He pulled away from the curb and joined the light traffic. Slowing at the parking kiosk, Abe eyed the baby again. "She's still suckling." Air. In her sleep.

"I think that's what she dreams about."

It was extremely difficult not to comment. Abe concentrated on digging quarters out of the drink well behind the stick shift. He waited in line, paid the attendant and thanked him, then drove out onto the road.

Silently Erin watched the landscape. Buttes stretched along the horizon, not unlike Nevada, but at their feet were countless adobe mounds, and the angle of the sun made them look like tents. This was a land of big sky, too, but no casinos, and she looked carefully, thinking about safe neighborhoods. Erin had never wanted any kind of neighborhood, had never liked the way she'd grown up. So she'd played make-believe in a real past she hadn't lived. With history books, she tried to close a hole that could only be filled by impossible childhood dreams.

Life on a ranch and a horse of her own. A cowboy father on-site.

"Is Alta like this?" Hotels and restaurants lined the four-lane thoroughfare.

"Not much. You're going to the prettiest place on earth." Belatedly Abe realized he was picturing *his* childhood home, not the Kays' place. He was picturing the land that used to be. Now expensive lodge-pole rails replaced his family's barbed wire, making the new owner the ridicule of every subsistence rancher for miles. Jack Draw called it the Soaring Eagle Ranch, his way of making sense of Charlie Cockburn's hundred-year-old triangle-E brand, chosen in honor of his wife, Elizabeth.

Busy had been named for that same Elizabeth.

Abe blotted out thoughts of that land, of chasing calves for his dad, of summers at cow camp. Chaley and the Kay Ranch were no refuge, just wear and tear on his honor and his pride. He thought of bullfighting, instead.

Of saving cowboys, the noblest work left to him.

"HOW MUCH does she weigh?" Abe read tags hanging from the display car seats.

"I don't know. She's healthy, so I don't take her to the doctor much. She's just gotten her immunizations, nothing else." *You're probably wondering why I'm telling you all this. And, Abe, if you're getting a funny tingling in your veins about standing in the aisles of Target picking out a car seat with me and this baby, well, I could explain it.*

She *was* going to explain it.

Just not yet.

Maeve's head turned to follow the progress of a woman passing with a shopping cart. Another baby sat in the cart.

"Let me guess." Maeve's weight. Abe reached for the baby. For his daughter.

Erin let him take her. A scar on one of his knuckles mesmerized her. His hands were as confident with new life as with cranky bulls and needy women. Strong and gentle and...indifferent. No, indifferent wasn't right.

Abe smelled baby shampoo and baby skin. The small warm body in his hands brought memories. Childhood memories of holding Lane. An earlier recollection of when his mother had let him hold Busy, the new baby. He must have been just four.

Erin's daughter stared right into his eyes. God, her eyes were her mother's. But those dimples...

"Those are some dimples. What's your name?"

"Maeve." Erin saw other dimples—his. "M-a-e-v-e." Again she overexplained. "Maeve is the central character in the oldest recorded legend in Irish history, *The Cattle Raid of Cooley.* She was a queen and a warrior and some say a goddess. She led her men into war to steal a magical bull so that her possessions would equal those of her consort."

"A rustler. I see." Abe tickled Maeve's tummy through her purple sweatshirt. She giggled at him.

You're a heartbreaker, aren't you? Must run in the family. Abe gave Maeve back to her mother. "Twenty pounds? Not twenty-five, anyhow." Exploring the boxes, he asked, "How old is she?"

"She'll be a year old Tuesday." Erin hoped math wasn't his strong subject.

"That's my little brother's birthday." And that day would be the last they saw of Lane. All but Abe. He and Lane would meet from time to time at rodeos.

Eighteenth birthday.

First birthdays were a big deal, too. He had rodeo friends with kids, and usually a first birthday was a three-ring circus, complete with video cameras. *Will your husband be joining you?* he wanted to ask Erin. *And what about your mom?* Surely that mom who'd kept Erin's room for her while she was in college was in love with her grandchild. *That's how grandparents are.* His dad would be tickled pink if he and Chaley...

His father's mortality invaded the Target store, followed by the unsettling thought of himself and Chaley having children.

"First birthday. Wow." He picked a car seat off the shelf. "Let's go."

In the checkout line, when he dug out his wallet, Erin said, "You'll get the ranch to reimburse you?"

He nodded, and their eyes locked. Counting cash for the car seat gave him something else to look at. He remembered to get a receipt for Kip.

But did you ask your future father-in-law to reimburse you? Or did you acknowledge that one day his place would be yours anyhow, that you were all in it together?

Maeve blew a big raspberry and beamed, and the tug on Abe's heart separated today from yesterday, the way losing the ranch had divided his life into before and after.

He didn't want to think why.

THEY HEADED SOUTH on Highway 50 into the storm. Raw desert bordered each side of the road. To the east, toward the Rockies, snow spread like powdered sugar sprinkled over rolling adobe foothills. It was land without vegetation but with an alien beauty. Anyone could see it would yield no crops; still, this place that the pioneers would have shunned seemed desirable at a time when other people grew the food, when City Market was ten miles north. To the west, the rock became swirling humps of reddish sandstone carving out canyons that fell from sight.

"When it's clear," said Abe, "you drive south on this road and you can see the San Juans. They're the most rugged mountains in Colorado."

Near Montrose, more than an hour and a half after they'd left the airport, the storm let up but clouds still hid the mountains. And as they wound east toward Gunnison, up into foothills and snow-covered rangeland, the weather worsened again. Snowfall faded the sagebrush and junipers and the gullies full of bare-limbed trees. Rock outcroppings jutted from the land and were suddenly mountains. The deserted stock pens, isolated gas stations and empty campgrounds were civilization. Maeve woke up tearful and whiny, and Erin fed her applesauce while Abe crossed a bridge over a vast reservoir where steam grew up from the water like grass.

"Need me to stop?" he asked.

"Not unless I'm distracting you."

She was, but he worked at ignoring her and driving. Why had she brought a baby to the Kay Ranch in March? Kip Kay never even promoted his guest business, banking on word of mouth. "You know the Kays?"

"Uh…no."

Maeve gave up eating and turned full-time to complaining. Erin could still remember what it was like to hear a baby cry before she'd had one. It could make you leave a restaurant.

There was no leaving the pickup, and Abe might have been deaf. Except that he sang to Maeve, replacing the music he'd turned off miles before.

I ride an old paint and I lead an old dam,
I'm going to Montana for to throw the houlihan...

Erin rearranged Maeve in the car seat. The baby burped, then quieted, looking about to find the source of the voice.

Git along, you little dogies, git along there slow,
For the fiery and the snuffy are a-rarin' to go...

When he was done, Erin said, "I wrote a paper on the history of cowboy music."

Abe quit pretending they'd never met. "Did you ever get your master's?"

"Doctorate. Yes."

"When did you get married?"

The driver could feel a passenger staring.

"I'm not married."

She must have been, though. Remembering he was engaged to Chaley made Abe stop asking questions. He began counting the miles to Alta.

Erin confronted the problems of her alias. He'd thought she was married. Leaving other men's wives alone was a good trait.

Beside her, Abe checked out fences and stock. "Look."

A bald eagle perched on a cottonwood limb. Erin had never known birds came so large.

"They like it by the reservoir and along the rivers in winter. In summer they head for the high country."

His nearer boot eased on the gas pedal as he slowed for a curve. The back hems of his jeans had faded in ragged half-moons from dragging on the ground against his boot heels. Cowboys wore their pants long so the legs wouldn't hitch up when they were in the saddle. Erin thought about the seat of his Wranglers and how the denim would stretch over his thighs when he rode. She thought about sex in Reno.

It took a while to get smart and ask, "So, you know Mr. Kay?"

"All my life. My daddy's his foreman."

Erin's throat dried up. She'd brought Abe home that June night because he was from Alta; she'd never known Alta was such a small world. It was a prairie-dog colony. Like a military leader gathering intelligence, she asked, "Are they a big family? The Kays?"

"No."

He didn't elaborate. Erin didn't ask. White flakes flew at the window, with a polka-dot field beyond. They hid the world the way other things she couldn't change had hidden what she wanted to know, and they were unfriendly, the way cold is.

"YOU NEED ANYTHING here?" Abe asked in Gunnison. He'd lived on the Kays' ranch, and he knew their guest business. "You'll be staying in a cabin with a refrigerator and a microwave. They serve meals three times a day in the big house, but if you need anything special... Diapers?"

"Thanks. Let's stop." At home Erin used cotton diapers and laundered them herself, but she'd bought disposables for this trip. Still, she could pick up some of Maeve's favorite foods.

He parked in the City Market lot, and inside, when Erin began to buckle Maeve into the cart, the recollection of the baby's soft body, like a sack of warmth, like the best of new animals, made him ask, "Want me to hold her?"

"Oh. Okay. Thanks."

Abe lifted the baby again, smelling her scent and remembering Busy and the lives that had changed when she died.

He and Erin explored the aisles, and people smiled at the young couple with the baby. Hiding beneath her hat brim, Erin chose soy milk and applesauce and bananas for Maeve and tampons for herself.

The cowboy ignored her selections and played with Maeve. He used her hat to cover her eyes, then let her see him again.

In the register line, a white-haired woman behind them fell for Maeve. "She's darling," she told Abe. "You have a beautiful family."

"Thanks." He didn't look at Erin. It was time to get this baby out of his arms.

But her little hands were touching his neck and the collar of his coat, and Abe wasn't eager to let her go. The tabloids and chewing gum and candy grew hazy. Maeve would be a year old on Tuesday.

Abe's mind was a rodeo calendar, and while Erin paid for her groceries, he reviewed the date of the Reno Rodeo. He was used to figuring gestation periods. Cows went 280 days, more or less. So did humans.

He did the math, anyway. Three times, three different ways, his heart pounding harder every minute.

THERE WAS a traffic accident at the main intersection in town. Abe was so preoccupied that seconds passed before he recognized the one-ton blue truck and the cowboy finger-pointing at the driver of a crunched Range Rover. The pickup had won this round. Sort of.

Oh, shit, Dad.

Abe nabbed a parking space outside a furniture store.

"What is it?"

"Please excuse the delay." He got out.

A cop was trying to calm Lloyd, and Abe welcomed a few minutes of not having to think about suddenly having a daughter.

She is. You know she's yours.

We used condoms.

Yeah, but remember the second time, Abe, when you were both just waking up? You actually thought it would be

*really great if you didn't have to use one, so you tried it
out that way.*

It *was* great.

And now he had a redheaded baby named for a cattle-
taking Irish queen.

"He was driving too fast," Lloyd told the policeman as
Abe approached. "Couldn't even see him coming. Going
like a bullet."

"Takes a sharpshooter to hit a speeding bullet." The
driver of the Range Rover wore a long duster, but you
could still see those snakeskin boots. Especially with his
jeans tucked inside.

The street was icy, snow coming down again.

Abe thought about Maeve's hands.

"Abe, did you see it?" demanded Lloyd. "I had the
right of way. That light was still yellow—"

"Red," said the Ranger Rover's driver.

"Let's get out of the street," the police officer suggested,
"and let the tow trucks move these vehicles."

"Mine still runs," said Lloyd. "I'm not paying a towing
fee." But the crushed wheel well spoke for itself. The truck
might run, but it wouldn't go.

Abe stuffed his hands in his pockets and recalled being
inside Erin without a condom.

*Come with me, Dad. I'll introduce you to your first
grandchild.*

Grumbling, Lloyd stalked to the curb and produced his
driver's license.

"We'll need the vehicle registration and proof of insurance, too."

As Lloyd started for the truck, he ordered Abe, "You
wait. You can drive me to the parts store and back to the
ranch."

When his father returned and gave the papers to the cop,
Abe explained, "I've got Kip's new guest and her baby in
the truck."

"What guest? We're calving."

"Chaley called this morning and asked me to meet the lady at the airport." Outside a store across the street, an OPEN banner flapped in the snow-wet wind. Abe huddled in his coat, trying to close the gap between his turned-up collar and the brim of his hat.

"Well, she can come along," Lloyd muttered.

"The seat's all taken up. Look, you'll be busy here for a while. I'll run her up to the ranch, come back and get you."

"Waste of gasoline."

"According to this, your insurance has lapsed," said the cop.

Abe and Lloyd looked up.

"What?" Lloyd examined the card. "I must have another in the truck."

"Where will you be?" Abe asked. Lloyd's insurance would be current. His father never forgot bills, and he paid cash for everything. Same went for Abe. It was the family habit of people whose overextended credit had cost them the ranch.

"Stockman's." The Stockman's Grill was the only place in town Lloyd still ate. He believed a cup of coffee shouldn't cost more than fifty cents and shook his head at the espresso shops springing up all over Gunnison. What was the point? If you wanted high octane, put in more grounds.

"See you in a while," Abe said.

"WHAT WAS THAT ABOUT?" asked Erin when he returned.

"My dad had a fender bender."

He fastened his seat belt and started the truck. He looked like he wished the day was over, and Erin let him have his silence as they headed out of town.

North of Gunnison, the road met mountains. Snow smothered the meadows. Aspens wearing just the gold twigs of winter surrounded a log cabin. Everything was frosted and irresistible, the way Christmas should look, until she saw the deer someone had hit lying stiff on the side of the road.

A sign said Alta was fifteen miles away.

That was where she would learn the truth about cowboys, and if she looked at it that way, she would be all right. She tracked the slushy marks left by the Isuzu Trooper in front of them. There were skis on the roof. Skiers shared places like this with cowboys, but the two did not meet. Erin understood the first group; the second was a closed order.

"There's Guy Loren's place," said Abe. "See that brindle with the big hump? That's Ah'll Gore, 1993 Bucking Bull of the Year."

Erin studied the meadows fenced with barbed wire, the Corriente rodeo steers eating hay, a tractor pulling a sled loaded with bales. This was where Abe worked.

The miles held homestead cabins with fallen roofs, trailers in empty country and the occasional rich man's castle. The snow was everywhere, dangerous, and chimney smoke meant safety.

To the east, evenly spaced pine rails bordered a ranch where cows stood in the snow. A massive stockade gate, like something out of "Bonanza," declared Soaring Eagle Ranch.

A hitch in his throat, Abe recited the sight-seeing information. "That's Jack Draw's ranch."

The television actor was the star of "Rodeo," cowboy culture's answer to "Northern Exposure." His name was a household word. "It's beautiful," said Erin. "Oh, look, he's got those shaggy Highland cows. They're so cute."

The silly-looking Scotch Highlanders were only one of the exotic breeds in the actor's herd. What was wrong with Herefords, anyhow? Abe didn't look—at the cows or the glossy cabins Draw had built for his hands. Draw's own home was over a rise, out of view of the highway, close to the national-forest border.

Abe knew his own privation.

He had a child. And no land and no cows.

"How big is it?"

Draw's ranch. The question felt more personal than it was. When he got over being taken aback, Abe said, "Fifteen thousand acres."

Beside him, a tiny hand touched the sleeve of the dirty Carhartt he'd shrugged off. The coat had fallen across Maeve's little legs in her turquoise pants. *Oh, baby.*

He downshifted and switched on his left turn signal. Chaley was coming across the Kays' pasture with the teams and the sleigh, and Lane and Kip were with her, feeding hay to the cows who fell in behind. Everyone's breath was white.

The simple wooden sign over the swing gate read Kay Ranch. Erin offered, "I'll get the gate."

"Thanks."

She opened the door, and the cold made her want to shut it again. Instead, she stepped down onto the crunchy snow. While the truck blew steam, the icy latch burned her fingers. Pulling her duster sleeves over them, she swung open the gate and held it as he drove through. *I never knew there were places this cold.* Securing the gate was another arctic ordeal; then she was back in the cab, cold-shocked.

The team and sleigh loaded with hay grew larger, raising clouds like Maeve's chariot on the road to Ulster.

"Let's stop and speak to these folks," said Abe.

A figure waded through the white. When he'd almost reached the truck, Erin rolled down her window, letting in the frigid air. The lean-faced rancher removed a leather work glove and held out his hand.

"Kip Kay. You must be Erin."

Her throat felt like there were cracks in it.

He stared at her face, no reaction on his. "Mears Cabin

is ready for you and your child. You'll find the key inside on the table.'' He glanced at the baby as he said, ''Thanks for your trouble, Abe.''

''Glad to do it. I'll take her up to the cabin. Dad had a wreck in town. He's okay, but the truck's not.''

''That right?''

Erin counted smells on Kip Kay's barn coat—hay and manure and the hair of livestock—as he rested an arm on her open window. Under his hat, his earmuffs were faded gray, the pile worn away in patches. She knew his face.

''Well,'' the rancher said, ''Beulah Ann's gone up to the big house to get supper on. Join us, Abe?''

''I'm going to get Dad. He said something about the parts store.''

''The Snowcat. Well, you'll be hungry when you get back. Dinner's at one.''

Abe studied the dash.

The pause stretched.

Never noticing, Erin breathed the rancher's nearness. Lived the moment he was close enough to touch. ''Could I help Beulah Ann in the kitchen?''

Kip Kay started and stepped backward. ''If you like.'' With a nod that encompassed Erin, Abe and the baby, he turned, and his Wellingtons and the legs of his insulated coveralls disappeared as he trudged back through the thigh-deep snow to the sleigh.

A real cowboy.

The truck idled, pouring smoke and steam into the freezing air. Erin rolled up her window.

''Erin.''

Across the cab, Abe's black hat shadowed his eyes, half his face.

''What?'' Erin saw he was holding one of Maeve's little hands in one of his, while Maeve gazed at the dash. Why was he doing that?

''Is this my child?''

"My books are the brooks, my sermons the stones,
My parson's the wolf on his big pile of bones,
My books teach me ever consistence to prize,
My sermons, that small things I should not despise."

—"The Cowboy,"
Nineteenth-century western
folk ballad

CHAPTER FOUR

IS THIS MY CHILD?

Student teaching had taught her to think on her feet. Being Dumped by Cowboys had taught her to think in the cab of his red pickup. "That's why I came to Colorado. To tell you."

"Glad you got around to it." Abe let go of the soft tiny hand with its miniature fingers and grabbed the stick shift.

He had reason to be mad, and her ifs, ands and buts would sound pretty lame. *If you'd just called after Twin Falls. And showed you cared....* "How did you guess?"

"It makes sense." Of something that made no sense otherwise. In March, people came to Alta to ski.

Guiding the truck over the freshly plowed road, Abe tried to plan. His father had wrecked the pickup. Kip Kay wanted him to join the family for dinner. And Chaley had suddenly become more than an object of doubt to be dealt with at leisure. "I have to tell you," he said, with the uncomfortable suspicion that he wasn't being clever with words. "I'm engaged."

It should not have meant *anything*.

Erin told herself it didn't as Abe drove on, taking her deeper into the snow-swathed mountain valley. "That's okay. I didn't come here to get you to marry me or anything like that." *I didn't. I really didn't.*

"It would have been natural if you had."

His honesty made her eyes burn. Who had caught this cowboy and how?

Just when she thought the white road would never end, she spotted buildings and livestock. In the corral, horses shook their manes and blew pale steam against the black trees. Cows—Herefords, Angus and black baldies—huddled in distant pastures. Barns, sheds, a four-square house made of fieldstone, a long pale green trailer and a couple of cabins broke up the white wilderness of the mountain winter.

Abe veered right with the corral. Far past the barn, smoke puffed from a cabin chimney. He parked under the fir trees, released his seat belt and unfastened the harness protecting Maeve.

Nervously Erin watched him lift their daughter from her car seat.

Holding Maeve, Abe raised the brim of her hat to see her face. He cradled her closer, then hugged her against his left shoulder. He felt his own heart and his daughter's little body, and he wanted to ask Erin, *You're sure?*

But she was getting out. And he was sure. Maeve was his. Cold filled the cab as she gathered her tote bag and groceries. Leaving him with the baby, she shut the door and hiked up the shoveled path to the cabin.

Abe sat Maeve on the bottom of the steering wheel and looked at her eyelashes and nose and mouth and carrot-colored curls. He thought he saw family traits. God, she was pretty. She was so pretty.

Maeve peered about. "Mama?"

"Mama went inside. Let's go find her." Setting her in

his lap, Abe shrugged on his coat. He used it to shield the baby from the cold as he opened the door. When he let Martha out of the back, Maeve said, "Da-dee."

With his free hand, Abe grabbed Erin's duffel bag, and he knew the why of that change-of-seasons feeling in Target. This mattered like the ranch, and the moment dividing before from after was right now.

THE CABIN WAS WARM, Erin found, thanks to the woodstove. The bedroom contained a maple crib and a metal-frame double bed. The kitchenette had a fridge, toaster and microwave. She put away groceries, welcoming the heat. Here, heat was safety. She could pretend the cold wasn't right outside, wasn't everywhere else in this place.

But Abe was engaged to someone else and the cold was coming in.

His boots thumped on the rough wood floor. He set down her duffel bag and gave her the baby.

His voice matched the dusky room and the tall dark shape he was. "What about you? Any guys around?"

"No." Why was he asking?

"I have to go get my dad in town. And then I have to go home. But I'll be back."

Cowboys who didn't care were all she knew, and she forgave Abe in advance and spun lies like wool. "You don't have to do anything. It doesn't matter. I just wanted you to know about her."

Had his solemn eyes ever been clown eyes, gazing at her in the Reno livestock arena like a dog hoping for a bone? These eyes belonged to a man living in the promiseland Willie Nelson had described.

"It matters." She smelled the earth smells of his coat, as he repeated, "It matters."

Then he left.

Erin remained motionless, holding a new piece of the puzzle that was the truth about cowboys. His promise to return hadn't set her at ease. The clown had been transformed into a man. A man capable of being a father to Maeve. Or of ignoring her, as Erin had been ignored.

Even of trying to take her from Erin.

Ultimately, of getting his way.

You're so stubborn, Erin, Jayne always said. *You don't think things through; you just charge, and no one can stop you.*

This was where her latest charge had brought her. The logs snapping in the stove spread the heat of burning aspen. She pictured Kip Kay's face—a photo turned alive and then aged to reality.

She'd come for the truth. If she found it, could she make herself look?

Yes. When the black came, there would still be Willie Nelson and Garth Brooks, believing in dreams.

She'd said she would help Beulah Ann, whoever that was, prepare the midday meal. Erin washed in the cabin's bathroom and changed Maeve's diaper and her clothes, which had applesauce on them. She dressed the baby in an outfit Jayne had bought—red pull-on pants, a white top with leg-of-mutton sleeves and ruffly hems trimmed in red. On the front was a soft silk screen of a red house, and the outfit came with a matching floppy corduroy hat.

Oh, Mom, she looks so cute.

Erin had never cried easily, and she had never cried about her mother. She couldn't, except without tears. And it was a lifetime since she'd laughed.

She went outside, carrying Maeve. Sparkling snow heaped the meadows and hills and the cragged peaks of the Alta Range, but as before, the frost penetrated her clothes and bit her skin. Evergreen trees, their needles almost black, broke the white of the mountains. The hay stacked under a shelter and the livestock in the pastures filled out a scene that must have changed little in a hundred years.

A scene that must have looked identical a quarter century ago.

A past Erin hadn't witnessed.

She approached the two-story fieldstone house. Two dogs, a border collie and a blue heeler, watched from the barn but kept their distance. She climbed stairs to a red-painted deck, where plastic shrouded a barbecue grill and folded lawn furniture and snow topped the deck railings. Before she could knock, a female voice called, "Come on in!"

The door opened into a mudroom; jars of preserves crammed the shelves. Juggling Maeve, Erin yanked off her boots.

The voice belonged to a husky blonde in tight jeans and a Harley Davidson T-shirt. She shoved a casserole into the oven and straightened, pushing wispy hairs, ponytail runaways, back from her face. "Hi, there. I'm Beulah Ann Ellis. Wrangler, cook and bull rider. And who's this?"

"This is Maeve. I'm Erin."

"It's nice to meet you. Even up the gender odds around this place. You're here for a week? Tell me where you're from. Tell me if I'm being too nosy, but this is my social life, you know?"

The wrangler/cook/bull rider looked only about seventeen or eighteen, which made Erin wonder how she'd gotten a job on the ranch. *Could I get a job here?* "I'm from Reno."

"Well, I'm from Baton Rouge. That Garth Brooks song 'Callin' Baton Rouge,' I want you to know he wrote it for me. Can I hold your baby?"

Erin surrendered Maeve. "You know how to make friends."

"Not everyone would agree, speaking of which—" Beulah Ann thrust a finger of her free hand toward the back of her throat as a cowboy about her own age tromped up the porch steps.

The window gave a good view. "I don't see anything to make you throw up."

"Just wait till he opens his mouth." As the temperature dropped with a frigid draft, Beulah Ann yelled, "Shut the door!"

"Yeah, yeah, maybe I'll just stay outside and *freeze*." The door shut and the draft stopped.

"You're so cute," Beulah Ann told Maeve.

The cowboy entered the kitchen and paused dramatically when he saw Erin.

"Meet the reincarnation of Lane Frost, Mr. Lane *Cock-burn*," introduced Beulah Ann. "He was too nice in his last life, so no one gave him a heart this time. Kind of like the Tin Woodsman? Lane, this is Erin. And this is Maeve, and she's too sweet to talk to you. You don't appreciate people who are plump and cute."

Erin kept her face straight, the way she had when a student asked if sex could improve his grade. Lane *Cock-burn* must be Abe's little brother. The fair skin was different, but Erin knew that mouth.

He glanced nervously at the baby and began sniffing around the kitchen in his sheepskin-lined denim jacket and the hat he hadn't taken off. "When do we eat? Boss has a calf he wants you to pull, Beulah Ann. You being such a big girl and all, he could sure use your help."

"No, thank *you*. I am not sticking my arm up inside some cow."

The place was crawling with Abe's relatives. *Maeve's* relatives. This was her uncle. Abe's dad was her grandfather. And Kip Kay—

Breathe, Erin. This is where you find the truth. "Can I help with dinner, Beulah Ann?"

"Well, you're so nice! Thank you, Erin. You want to make a salad?"

"Sure."

"Everything's in the big fridge in the pantry, except the

dressing, which is in this one. Now, you just make yourself at home. Whenever you get hungry, help yourself to whatever you want to eat.''

"Yeah, take a lesson from Beulah Ann."

"Shut up, loser. Erin, just make yourself at home."

A draft cooled the room again, the door banged shut, and a blond gazelle sailed inside. In sheepskin jacket, jeans, riding boots and a good beaver cowboy hat, she was all long legs and competence. She registered faces. "Where's Abe?"

Abe. Erin's heart turned hot and hurting, the Dumped by Cowboys way. *It's her.*

She saw Lane and Beulah Ann shrug and almost missed the glances they exchanged that no one else was supposed to see. The cowboy opened and closed the refrigerator, and Beulah Ann said, "Chaley, this is Erin, and this is Maeve. Look how cute she is. She has these little hands, don't you love them? God, I love babies."

"Pity no one'll ever have one with you," said Lane, his head in the refrigerator.

Chaley's heel shot up and struck his rear end.

"Ow!" The refrigerator door slammed.

"Why don't you get out with the cows, brat?" Chaley said. "Maybe one of them will have *you.*"

"I don't think they will," Beulah Ann said frankly. "Him being so little and all."

Chaley tugged off her gloves, and Erin saw the diamond ring with its heirloom look.

Abe's fiancée was everything Erin herself could never be. And everything she wanted to be. Chaley was strawberry blond rather than true blond, with freckles and blue eyes and angular features. There was hay on her clothes, and her boots were worn. Who was she on the Kay Ranch?

The blue eyes swept over Erin and dismissed her— *Dudette, no threat.* "Abe brought you, didn't he?"

Chaley inspired attention and speedy answers. Erin explained about the traffic accident and the truck that wouldn't go.

"Is he coming back for dinner?"

"This meal," clarified Beulah, like a bright student helping a slower classmate.

"I don't think so," Erin said.

Chaley made a face, and Beulah and Lane exchanged another glance as the blonde snatched a cordless phone off the kitchen counter and went into the other room.

Whistling to himself, Lane moseyed toward the hallway to listen.

Beulah Ann handed Maeve to Erin. "I'll get back to you in a minute, Maeve. There's a fly I gotta kill." She plucked a flyswatter from a wall nail.

"Leave me alone, woman!" Lane darted for the mudroom. "Nice to meet you, Erin." The door slammed behind him.

Beulah Ann hung up the flyswatter. "I guess you've figured out he makes my knees weak."

That trait ran in the Cockburn family. Erin asked, "Where should I put Maeve?"

"I just mopped the floor. Here." Beulah Ann opened a cabinet and dragged out an old pot and a pie tin. Banging through a drawer, she found a deformed spatula, a wooden spoon and an egg beater. She piled them on the linoleum, and Erin sat the baby beside them.

"You can help cook, Maeve," said Beulah Ann. "Would you like that?"

Maeve crawled toward the egg beater.

Erin retrieved the vegetables from the pantry. On the floor, her daughter experimentally dipped the wooden spoon into the pot.

Chaley returned then. She eyed Maeve like a dog who wasn't allowed in the house. "Beulah Ann, if they pull up here in the truck, will you catch Abe and tell him I'm looking for him?''

''If I can.''

''Thanks. Oh, see you later,'' she added to Erin, and went outside.

Beulah Ann ended the silence. ''Chaley's nice. She's just in a mood. *Men.*'' She squinted at Erin. ''Guess it would be nosy to ask if you've got one in your life.''

''I don't.''

''Must be hard with a baby. How old is she?''

''She'll be one on Tuesday.''

''That's Lane's birthday.'' Beulah Ann repeated what Erin had learned from Abe. ''We should have a party. Lane's counting the hours. He'll be eighteen, and that boy would rather have his PRCA card than a million dollars. Wouldn't it be great to want something that uncomplicated?''

PRCA was the Professional Rodeo Cowboys Association. ''What do you want that's complicated?''

''A different past. And a fast metabolism.''

You couldn't ask a woman you'd just met what was wrong with her past. Or why she and Lane had exchanged those looks when Chaley asked about Abe. Erin helped herself to a cutting board. Outside the water-blotched window, Chaley ducked between the rails of the corral fence.

''Here's the knife you want,'' said Beulah Ann. ''Thanks for doing this, Erin. You sure don't have to.''

''Oh, I want to help out.''

''Well, visiting a working ranch, you probably didn't think you'd be stuck in the kitchen.''

Chaley caught an Appaloosa from the corral.

''I've ridden my whole life,'' said Beulah Ann, ''but she's way better with horses. Of course, she grew up on them.''

''Does she work here?''

"Oh, no. I mean, we all work. But she's Uncle Kip's daughter."

Erin's eyes saw the vegetables, but it was some time before she remembered what to do with them.

As KIP KAY PUT UP the harness in the tack room, he searched the barn for chores so he could postpone facing the ranch's new guest.

Erin O'Neill.

Kip rejected the creeping intuition. This was just life playing a trick, by making her eyes and face so like Jayne's at that age. He'd probably imagined it, and he had other things to worry him, so why stew about it?

Leaving the barn, he paused at Rowdy's stall. He'd planned on their guest riding the bay gelding, but the last time he was on Rowdy, the nine-year-old had spooked at a tractor. He'd have to lease gentler horses for the summer guests; in the meantime, he'd borrow one. For a thousand dollars, the woman deserved to ride, to participate in ranch life. Beulah Ann and Chaley could help with the baby.

He gave the horse a pat and went outside. The border collie and the blue heeler, named Gus and Call by Chaley and known by other handles to everyone else, watched him from near the shed. They were working dogs earning their keep and seldom asked so much as a scratch behind the ears.

Chaley was saddling Mouse under snow clouds.

"Where are you going?"

"Oh." His daughter wrapped the latigo through the cinch ring. Once. Twice. "For a ride."

Kip knew where. Down the road toward Gunnison, so as not to miss that old red pickup. "Why don't you come in for dinner, take your ride later?"

"I'm not hungry."

A woman who'd spent the morning driving the team through three feet of snow and lifting hay bales? But she had energy left to chase a bullfighter who didn't want to be caught. Kip sighed. "Suit yourself." *They'll work it out.* Once upon a time, he'd thought Jayne was right for him, the angel who would root him in these mountains so that his mind couldn't wander back to steaming jungles of mind-horror and death. But Jayne had flown, and it was Lorraine, Chaley's mother, who had saved him. Who had helped him save himself.

Chaley swung into the saddle, sitting a horse better than any woman in the state. *They'll work it out.*

"Chaley?"

"Yes, Dad?"

"If you catch him—" he winced a little at the word choice "—ask if we can have Noon for a week, for...our guest." Erin. That was a name he didn't want to say.

"Sure." She smiled, like the sun. And Kip recalled that Chaley had saved him, too. That Chaley, most of all, had saved him.

"DON'T STEP ON THE BABY!" Beulah Ann cautioned.

But Kip Kay was already crouching to speak to Maeve. "Well, aren't you the cat's meow?"

Erin had finished the salad and set the table. She noticed the rancher and her daughter, the only things in the room that mattered. *He likes babies. He likes Maeve.*

She stored the thought in a distant place.

He hung his coat and hat by the mudroom door. "Like your cabin?"

"Yes. Thanks. Everything's great." The span of the room felt like the emotional miles between them. This stranger had a daughter.

Chaley.

Abe's fiancée.

Stepping around Maeve, Kip glanced at Erin again. She thought he sighed. "Chaley's gone to see about getting you a horse to ride," he said. "We've never had a guest this time of year before."

His eyes challenged her, asking for the truth.

Erin felt her lips half-parted. He was the one with the truth.

"We'll try to make you feel a part of things," he concluded. Picking up the *Rocky Mountain News* from the table, he left the room.

Erin made it a point to feel nothing. But it was a nothing like the inside of an empty juice can, like the inside of a pencil holder that would never hold pencils.

THE FOOD—chicken-fried steak, mashed potatoes and fresh-baked bread—was almost ready when Lane came in, hauling a baby's high chair. "Thought we'd need this."

"Thank you," Erin said. It seemed a thoughtful gesture from an almost-eighteen-year-old.

"Look out for spiders," he warned. "It was in the shed."

Beulah Ann gave Erin a wet washcloth to wipe the chair. "I think we're ready." She went outside and rang the dinner bell.

Erin cleaned the high chair, then carried it and Maeve into the spotless formal dining room. She'd gotten to know the plates in the antique china cabinet and the silverware as she laid the table. Buckling Maeve in her chair, Erin heard more voices in the kitchen. Three ranch hands came in. The only name she remembered minutes later was Lucky. Anyone that young and cute, with round gold-rimmed glasses, ought to be lucky—if you didn't count the receding hairline.

When everyone had sat down, there were several chairs empty. Beulah Ann said, "Well, this is a crowd. Think we'll have enough?"

"Abe and Dad are probably eating at Stockman's. They don't want indigestion."

"Neither do I," growled Kip.

Afraid she herself couldn't eat, Erin spooned mashed potatoes to Maeve, but Maeve turned her head with a fussy noise.

No, thought Erin. *No, please be good.*

No one looked up but Lucky, who said kindly, "Kids are great."

Erin had poured some apple juice into a baby bottle. She gave it to Maeve, and Maeve hurled it to the floor and fretted, her volume rising.

"Wish I had one," said Lane.

"You probably do somewhere."

"Enough."

One word from the rancher silenced Beulah Ann and Lane.

Erin stood, her napkin falling to the floor. She unlatched the tray on the high chair and unfastened Maeve's harness. Crying now, the baby lifted her arms to be held.

"So Dad had a wreck." Lane made another attempt at conversation.

"So it seems."

"Excuse me." Erin took Maeve to the kitchen and sat down to nurse her. Minutes ticked by with Maeve whimpering and nursing, but it was peace. Her place in the world was with this child. They were extensions of each other, and Abe Cockburn was just a sperm donor, a careless cowboy, and Kip Kay was just the rancher king who kept the truth. The only person who knew...

It matters, Abe had said, about having a daughter.

Well, aren't you the cat's meow?

Footsteps paused in the door.

She started to move, but Kip said, "No, that's all right. You're fine." With a smile that avoided watching her but seemed to like women who nursed their babies, the rancher carried his plate to the sink, gathered his coat and his hat, and said, "Well...back to work."

Then he was gone, whistling as the door closed, leaving behind a mix of cold and warm air, along with something Erin had never had in her life before and didn't give a shit about, really didn't *care* about. So why should her eyes start watering? All she'd seen was part of the truth, and she wasn't that damned hungry for it, even if it was the approval of her father.

Her father, Kip Kay.

HOURS LATER and five miles down the road, Abe was stroking Guy Loren's newest foal, getting her used to him, when Chaley appeared outside the stall. She let herself in, squeezing cautiously around Maylights, the mare.

"Pretty foal. Guy named her yet?"

"No." Abe had to tell her. Immediately. Now that he'd seen Maeve and felt it sinking in minute by minute that she was his, now that he'd recognized himself in her tiny face, all he wanted was to be with her and renew his acquaintance with her mother. He had to tell Chaley.

A few things.

"Dad wants to know if we can borrow Noon for our lady dude."

Noon was the first horse Abe had ever owned, the first that wasn't his father's on paper. He and his mother had gone to the sale barn together and bought him. Noon had all the best qualities of a cow pony, and at twenty-four he was gentle, a good horse for Erin. "He needs shoes."

"Can you do it today?"

Abe hadn't slept for twenty-four hours, and on the trip back from Gunnison with Lloyd he'd learned the extent of their problems. Lloyd's insurance *had* lapsed, and he'd hit a fifty-thousand-dollar vehicle. How were they going to pay for the damage to the Range Rover?

When the clerk at the courthouse had set a date for Lloyd to meet with a police officer and arrange forty hours of community service, Abe had talked her out of it under the office noise. *Look, he's seventy-two years old; he just forgot to pay his insurance.* She was all ready to write off the community service when Lloyd had cut in. *What are you doing? I'll pay the penalty.*

Though the clerk put him off with a story about the police being too busy to schedule people for community service, she also said Lloyd had to take a driving test. And the fine was more than two hundred dollars.

Abe had paid it, and now he had six dollars to his name till payday.

Six dollars. And a baby.

"I'll bring Noon over tonight or in the morning," he told Chaley. Shoe the horse, get some sleep, see Erin again. At least Guy let him have unlimited gas for his truck. Abe gave the foal a few last strokes, then released her and let himself and Chaley out of the stall.

"Billings place must have sold," said Chaley. "New fence. White PVC."

The Billings family hadn't lived on the place for fifty years, but that was what everyone still called the ranch, which was north of Jack Draw's. Lately, new fences announced the sale of local property—barbed wire wasn't pretty enough for these owners. Abe had driven all over the West for rodeos, and he knew how fast the range was being bought up, sold out of the families who'd settled it. Soon celebrities and tycoons would be the only ranchers left.

Chaley's voice distracted him. "I got tickets for the Dwayne Redd concert in Gunnison."

Dwayne Redd was the latest name in real western music, out of the mainstream, like Ian Tyson, and Abe liked his songs, which were about cowboy life. "When is it?"

"April eleventh."

"Farmington."

Rodeo.

"*Abe.*"

"It's my job."

"It's not a job, it's a *hobby*." Down the row of stalls, the barn door creaked, but Chaley turned a deaf ear. "You ought to have a job sometime so you know what it is."

Abe *had* heard the barn door. Guy was coming to check on the foal.

"How is she?" The stock contractor ignored whatever he'd overheard.

"Doing good," Abe reported. Taking Chaley's arm, he guided her out of the barn. Snow fell, March snow that would not quit. "I have a job, Chaley, and it's here."

"You should be working for my dad."

His throat swelled. Time to confess what he'd done back down the road. Maeve's face, her soft reddish curls, the feel of her small warm body, reached into his mind. He pictured Erin, playing dress-up in her Stetson and duster. Erin's dark brown eyes and white skin. Erin didn't know about fences; she'd admired Jack Draw's.

Abe shut his eyes.

"What?" said Chaley.

He opened his eyes, saw her waiting with an expression that meant, *When are you going to grow up and be the man I want?*

"Chaley. I have a child."

"They're full of manure."

—Beulah Ann Ellis,
   when asked the truth about cowboys

CHAPTER FIVE

CHALEY'S THROAT vibrated with each steaming breath. "When did you discover this?"

"Today. She's staying at your place."

"That baby."

She sounded annoyed and disgusted. Hoping for the best—that she would promptly return his grandmother's engagement ring—Abe said, "She's mine."

Chaley studied Mouse, tied nearby. "Well, I'll have to get to know—her? It's a girl, right?"

Tension wrapped around him like baling wire. Abe recalled the night they'd become engaged, how it had happened. Mistakes Made While Drinking and Dancing.

He turned his coat collar up around his freezing ears.

"Abe? I'd love any baby of yours. Maybe that woman will let me baby-sit. She can go riding, help Dad and Lane check on the calves."

That woman. *I really like that woman, Chaley. I really wanted to see her again, but I broke my neck and couldn't. The next summer, I was dancing with you and dreaming of your dad's spread. Of making it my own. Now I see that woman, and it's just like before, like it's never been with you, Chaley.*

He met her eyes. "Let me go."

She spun away, stalking through the snow and mud to get Mouse. Abe caught the Appaloosa's reins as she mounted.

Chaley averted her face. "I love you. I've loved you my whole life."

He'd been afraid that was the case. Abe dropped his cold hand from the reins and stroked Mouse's neck, reassured by the feel of a warm horse.

Chaley clucked to Mouse, and Abe opened the gate for her.

It wasn't over.

CHALEY WAS SMOTHERING Maeve with a pillow, only it was Abe who couldn't breathe. He pushed the pillow off his face, and Lane grinned down at him in the early-evening light. "You called?"

Groaning, Abe rolled onto his stomach. He was in the fifth wheel at Guy Loren's place. Home. Recollecting why he'd phoned his brother, asked him over, he sat up. "I need you to do something."

Lane sank onto the edge of the bed.

Abe sniffed the air. "What is that?"

"It's your place—don't ask me."

"No, what are you wearing?"

Lane thrust the pillow into Abe's bare chest. "Alicia likes it. She likes to smell it *all over* my body."

The world fell on Abe, the magnitude of what he'd done after the Reno Rodeo.

"I want you to baby-sit."

"What?"

"Tomorrow morning. Six. For Maeve. The baby at the ranch."

Lane covered his face. "No. Say it's not true. It cried through two meals. It barfed on its mother. It did number two right there at the table, and then it smiled at everyone."

"She's your niece."

"Niece? Who had a baby? Oh, my— Oh, my— No, not mine. *Yours.*" Lane pitched to the floor and sprawled immobile. "I'm related to it."

Abe sprang out of bed, pinned his brother and ringed his hands around his throat. "She's the most beautiful child you ever saw."

"She drools. Oh, all right. Uncle. Oh, I'm an uncle. Let up, all right? Yeah, she's okay, for someone short and fat." He gasped and choked. "All right, I'll learn to like her."

Abe released him, and Lane sat up, rubbing his neck. "Jeez. Does Dad know?"

"No. And I want to be the one to tell him."

"The boss?"

Kip. "I doubt it."

Lane's eyes lit up. "Does *Chaley* know?"

"Yes." Abe dragged himself to his feet. He hunted for clothes in the cheap built-in drawers and as he dressed, said, "Tomorrow I want you to baby-sit so Erin and I can go riding." Saying her name now felt physical. Thoughts of her made his blood hum, and sorting right from wrong was easy. Making things right would be trickier.

His brother still gawked. "Hey, can Alicia baby-sit, too?"

Lane's latest girlfriend lived in Alta and would be forgotten the day Lane got his PRCA card. "No. This is bad enough for Chaley without Alicia spreading it all over Alta."

"Does Chaley know about this ride you two are taking?"

"I'll tell her."

"I bet that's why she didn't show up for supper. Hey, tell me about Dad's wreck. He's in a humor."

Abe related the Range Rover calamity, but Lane's attention jumped to the countdown till his birthday and from there to his first professional rodeo, in Laughlin, Nevada, the same rodeo Abe was scheduled to work the next weekend.

On the surface it looked like a great weekend to get out of town. But he'd held Maeve, and he'd heard Erin say, *I didn't come here to get you to marry me or anything like that.*

She talked like a woman used to letting men go.

AFTER LANE STOPPED BY to tell her about the ride and offer to baby-sit, Erin set the alarm in the cabin bedroom for five in the morning. She went to bed with Maeve, ignoring the crib, but she was too busy dreading the ride to make her nightly meeting with death.

Abe was in her mind. Before, her images of him were grainy rodeo news photos. It had been hard to remember details like the shape of his nose and the way his mouth moved when he spoke and his lazy nimbleness, a clown's mercurial grace in cowboy clothes.

Mothering was a good cure for wanting cowboys, but it was no cure for wanting Abe. He was engaged to Chaley, and the memory of making love with him made Erin imagine him with Chaley. He loved Chaley, and he'd never loved her, Erin.

Just like the first cowboy who had ever dumped Erin, a man who made a better cowboy when he was just a photo in a plastic gilt frame.

IN THE MORNING she bathed a cranky Maeve, dressed her in clean sleepers and put her down in the crib. Erin had picked out clothes for the ride the night before. Wool tights and sweater, her duster, hat and wool knit gloves with leather palms. She was ready except for her coat and hat when she heard feet on the porch, the low sound of male voices and a knock.

The dark shapes with cowboy hats and the landscape behind them were out of her dreams and made her want to be part of what they had and to know what they knew. They'd tied the saddled horses to Abe's two-horse trailer, under the firs. The morning was blue, and the blast from the door chilled Erin, but she didn't care. She hadn't ridden a horse in almost a decade, and when she saw the horses, that was all she could think about.

Abe closed the door. "Where's Maeve?" he asked, reminding her of what was permanent, what would still be there when Erin left this cowboy land.

"Sleeping."

They all trailed into the bedroom. Abe crouched beside the crib and reached between two rails to touch his daughter's small back. In response Maeve gave a small sleeping sigh. She slept on her stomach, with her legs tucked under her. Standing, Abe rearranged the pink baby blanket.

He likes her. He really likes her.

Some things were too black to think about, like tomorrow and the day after and all the years of her life that Abe would love Maeve and not her. She got down to business. "Lane, if she wakes up while we're gone, there's applesauce and some bottles of juice and soy milk in the fridge." Erin buttoned her duster, pulled on her gloves. "She likes bananas, too. Do you know how to change diapers?"

The teenager reddened. "I'll work it out."

"Thank you. If she starts shoving her fists in her mouth, it's because she's teething. I put some teething rings in the refrigerator."

"Dad used to give us whiskey," Lane suggested. "Knocked us right out."

Abe squeezed his brother's shoulder. "Thanks for watching her like she's your own."

"Yeah, yeah, I get it." They all returned to the spare rustic living room. "There's not even a TV in here."

"Don't leave her alone," said Abe. "If you go flirt with Beulah Ann, take Maeve."

"Beulah Ann! There's an idea. You know, I'm going to

come back and marry Beulah Ann someday, when I'm as rich and famous as Ty Murray and can afford to send her to a diet spa.''

"Beulah Ann is too good for you.''

By miles, thought Erin. Last night at supper, Beulah Ann had been like a flashlight in a blackout. Abe's father was immersed in cows and auto insurance, and her own father...well, he'd been preoccupied. He'd scarcely spoken to Erin or looked at the baby. But people didn't come better than Beulah Ann.

Abe held the door for Erin.

"Have fun, kids.'' Lane went back into the bedroom, and Erin heard him lie down on the bed she'd made.

Was she crazy to leave Maeve with him?

"They'll be fine. Come on.''

The cold was brutal, but it didn't matter.

"Ridden before?''

"Yes.'' Speaking seemed to crack her lips. The snow had a layer of ice on it, and the trailer was white with hoarfrost. "Not for years, though.''

He led her around a dark bay quarter horse and untied the reins. "This is Noon. Why don't you get up, and we'll see how the stirrups fit?''

Behind her, his body radiated heat and a security she could never have. Hating him for that, Erin grasped the saddle horn and the cantle and slipped her left boot through the stirrup. Abe's hands in worn leather work gloves reached around and put the reins in her left hand. He moved her right hand to the horn.

"Thanks.'' She swung herself up. The day before, Chaley had saddled that Appaloosa and ridden away so naturally. Erin practiced forgetting.

"Stirrups look good. How do they feel?''

"Fine.''

"You just lay the reins alongside his neck to turn him,

like this.'' Abe demonstrated, the worn sleeves of his coat brushing her legs.

The touch seduced her. She didn't answer.

Abe stroked Noon's neck, then left him to untie Buy Back. Mounting up, he turned the chestnut. They'd head past the cabin, away from the house. His phone conversation with Chaley last night had ended in a stalemate. She wanted him, the way she used to want a stable for her Breyer horses. And he was caught.

Noon walked beside Buy Back, hooves pressing into the snow.

''We'll go up this road a ways and cross the highway,'' said Abe. ''There's a back road leads down to Guy Loren's.''

''Is that where we're going?''

''Guess Lane didn't tell you. Thought we'd have breakfast together.''

''Oh.'' Erin wiggled her toes, trying to feel her feet. ''Is this okay with your fiancée?''

''She knows.''

Erin's dark eyes were on Noon's ears, and she gave him just enough rein. She looked cold.

Abe took off his earmuffs and passed them to her. ''Try these.''

''Thanks.'' The earmuffs still held the heat from his head, but they were just earmuffs. And he was Chaley's.

Up ahead in the morning dark, a man in a coat and hat cut a path through the snowy pasture. He waved to the riders as they neared, and Erin recognized Lloyd, Abe's father.

The border collie slunk under the barbed wire as Abe walked Buy Back to the fence.

''I need you,'' Lloyd said. ''Twins. Cow's got a foot back on the second one. Damn, she's leaving.''

"I see her." Abe opened the swing gate from horseback.

What was he seeing? Erin wondered. There were dozens of cows out there, and even with the dawn lighting one of the passes to the east, she couldn't make out details.

At his bidding, she rode Noon through the gate while Lloyd slogged toward a distant stand of piñon.

"What are we doing?"

"Helping my dad." Abe secured the gate. "You warm enough?"

"Yes." Noon's body helped. She wished she could ride forever.

They walked the horses over melted snow where the sleigh had dropped hay for the cattle.

Lloyd called, "You take the calf in. I'll get the cow."

"Can I help?" asked Erin.

"You can help bring that cow in. It's the Hereford over by the piñons."

"What do I do?"

"Try to make her go toward the gate. Keep the reins loose. When Noon figures out you want her, he'll do the rest."

Erin tapped Noon with her heels, and the bay zeroed in on the cow. She didn't mean to keep looking at Abe.

He's going to marry Chaley. There was no point in getting stupid over the sound of his voice or the way he looked on horseback or the sight of his back as he reached down from the saddle to take the wet calf his father lifted up to him.

The white-faced red cow went deeper into the trees, and Erin led Noon in a wider circle. Erin glimpsed the cow's vulva; it looked like a giant pink balloon, and a calf's hoof, still in the sac, hung out of it.

Noon did what Abe had promised. He went after the

cow, crowding right up to her, until she tried to get away, and then the border collie was there, too, herding. All Erin had to do was hang on. *Toward the gate. Come on.*

The cow went. Lloyd, from the back of a bay gelding, opened the gate, and the cow followed her calf, packed on Abe's saddle. The dog trotted behind.

Lloyd's horse tried to bite Noon. Swearing, Lloyd released the gate and it swung back to the fence.

"Close the gate, will you?" he said to Erin, bringing his horse under control. To Abe he grumbled, "I told Kip not to buy this animal."

Erin hesitated at the gate.

"Just get down," Lloyd called, before his horse shied.

Erin dismounted. Her legs wobbled under her, and the blood sped back to her feet, filling them with tingling hot-cold pain.

Gripping the reins, she staggered to the gate. She grasped it, and something rammed her so hard that the reins flew from her hand and the gate banged the fence. A black animal more monster than cow pressed on her legs, and Erin climbed up on the gate as a cow and her calf went through the opening.

Oh, shit. Oh, shit. How was she going to get to her horse? Noon had walked across the road.

The black Angus snorted steam and rolled her eyes at Erin.

Abe and Lloyd were already halfway to the barn. Only the border collie looked back. Erin jumped down in the snow, sliding on an icy patch as the Angus charged. She was sprinting for Noon when the cow hit her again, boosting her across the road. The horse sidestepped.

Hooves clattered softly on the hard snow and Erin heard reins snap and Abe's "Get out of there!"

She grabbed Noon's reins and scrambled into the saddle with a leg that would never be the same. While Abe and the dog chased the cows back into the pasture and shut the gate, Noon stood calmly, tolerating his trembling rider.

Turning Buy Back, Abe rode up beside Erin, facing her. "You okay?"

"Yes."

"Come with me, then. I've got to help my dad." With a slight laugh that could have meant anything, he clucked to Buy Back and led the way to the barn.

IT TOOK ERIN longer than Abe to tie her horse outside the barn, and the whole time she felt the two ranch dogs, now together, watching her from the shed. When she limped inside, the men already had a halter on the cow and were maneuvering her behind a gate, placing a chain across her rump to hold her there. Abe stroked the cow's head. "Just one more, sweetheart. You had that first baby just fine."

Erin approached warily, the pain in her leg dull and distant in the presence of the straining lowing cow, and a man who talked the same way to women in bed. Who'd talked to *her* that way. *You're all right. Shh.*

The new calf waited in a nearby pen, warm and dry. Mind-fogged, Erin stared at it while Abe and his father shed their coats and washed their arms in a white plastic bucket. In the animal smells of the barn, unfamiliar scents of new life and earth, she watched Lloyd reach into the cow's vulva while Abe pushed hard on the body. Both men were sweating, Lloyd's face grimacing as his arm disappeared in the cow. The cow bawled and dropped manure, and Erin's heart raced at this strange spectacle of midwifery.

She'd never seen men work so hard before. Time seemed to take the cow's pace, the unrushable pace of birth.

Abe grunted something to his father as Lloyd pulled a second hoof from the cow. Then the calf's head emerged, teeth and tongue showing, and blood and yellow fluid gushed over the men. Abe caught the slimy wet calf and lowered it onto the straw, where it breathed for the first time.

The veins stood out in his arms, and sweat darkened his shirt. Erin was in a black hole, like being in labor with Maeve. She tried to stop her feelings. She couldn't let herself care about the way he touched the calf, which was like the way he touched Maeve.

Jayne had seen Maeve first, emerging from Erin's body. *Oh, she's beautiful, Erin.*

Her eyes felt wet.

Oh, God, not here. She hadn't cried for seven months, and it wasn't going to happen in this barn with these two cowboys. Though she knew they'd let her be.

Abe caught her gaze as he carried the calf past her to a stall lined with fresh straw. There was blood on his clothes, and manure, and she'd never seen anyone she wanted more. Faces like Abe Cockburn's didn't show up in university lecture halls. It depressed Erin that one second of eye contact was intimacy for her and not for him, and she stood numb while Lloyd released the mother to follow the calf, to lick it dry and shaggy.

"HERE WE ARE." Abe swung down from Buy Back outside Loren's barn and watched Erin dismount, as well. Her legs vibrated like the foot on a sewing machine when she touched the ground, a sure sign of a dude, but he checked her face to see how she was feeling. Those moments in the barn had been intense. He'd wanted Lloyd to meet Maeve. He himself had missed Maeve's birth.

And Erin wasn't the same woman he'd slept with almost two years ago. She talked less. And didn't smile at all.

Abe tied the horses. "This way. I'll show you around after we eat." They walked in silence to the fifth wheel. "Hey, Martha. There you are."

The Australian shepherd emerged from under the rig wagging her tail. She sniffed them both, and Erin petted her while Abe opened the door and warmth rushed out. Inside, on the blue-green rug, he tugged off his boots. Erin sat on a love seat built into one wall and untied her ropers. Removing her hat, she shook out her hair and looked around.

The tiny woodstove had replaced a booth seat on one side of the kitchenette. While Martha flopped down in a threadbare spot by the stove, Abe hung his coat and hat on hooks by the door and took Erin's, too. "I'm going to clean up."

He disappeared up a step into the sleeping compartment. No door, so Erin turned her back as she heard him rummaging in drawers, heard water running.

He returned in a fresh canvas shirt and clean jeans. "Bacon and eggs?"

"That sounds great. Can I help?"

He nodded toward the table. "Come talk to me. You can tell me about Mr. O'Neill."

Erin squeezed past him to the remaining upholstered bench. She'd thought they'd already covered her assumed name. But now there would be questions she didn't want to answer.

"There's no Mr. O'Neill." She rushed out an explanation that wasn't. "I didn't know what to expect here. But now you know about Maeve, which is what I wanted. We'll be here till the end of the week—"

"Whoa whoa whoa."

"What?"

Abe dropped to the bench beside her. Cheap curtains in the windows darkened the interior, but Erin could still see the green in his eyes.

"Look, Erin…"

How could he finish? Briefly Abe felt concentrated hatred for Chaley.

He thought harder.

"You know," he said, "I've only been engaged since last June, and you've known about Maeve for much longer than that."

She'd heard that accusation the day before. "You didn't show up in Twin Falls. I sure didn't think you'd show up for your child's life." It was a bald truth that Abe couldn't understand, not the way she did. Erin simplified. "I didn't think you'd want her."

I'm not the only woman who's been Dumped by Cowboys. Cowboys had been leaving women since Theseus abandoned Ariadne; after she'd saved him from the bull-sired minotaur. *So this isn't about you, Abe.*

"I broke my neck. That's why I wasn't there."

"I know. I read about it the day Maeve was born."

Abe played with a newspaper on the table, *Prorodeo Sports News.* Sorry wasn't enough. For nine months—give or take a month—she'd believed he had stood her up. He slid out from the table. At the counter, he unwrapped the bacon, heated the skillet.

Erin slumped against the seat back. This changed nothing. Chaley was a cowboy's cowgirl, the kind who kept the men she caught.

"I need to understand you."

She started. He was looking at her again.

"I need to know," he said, "why you had Maeve. Why you kept her."

Some things a man shouldn't ask. "I love her."

"You didn't tell me."

She sat up. He was different from what she'd thought in Reno. She'd remembered him as more boy than man, more clown than cowboy. But he was a man—who cared enough about another woman to have promised his life to her. Now, he was angry like a man. Because Erin hadn't told him they had a child together.

His green-gray eyes demanded answers.

It took effort to push her hair back from her face. Her head felt like a bowling ball, and she breathed so her voice wouldn't shake. "We weren't careful enough with birth control. I knew it at the time, and I take responsibility for my actions. Anyhow, I wanted her."

He couldn't ask *why* about that. He faced the counter. "Tell me what your life is like in Reno."

The request sank into Erin.

Her life.

The museum, day care, coming home to check all the closets and under the beds and hear the latest report on her mother's estate and on the sale of the house. Losing her job. Nights with the lamp on the desk. "It's..."

Abe was throwing the cellophane from the bacon into the trash.

"I still live in the same house."

"With your mom?"

Erin shook her head.

He turned. "Erin?"

"She was murdered."

Fingers raked the inside of Abe's throat. He slid back into the booth.

She told the dingy fake-wood tabletop, "It was one of several...murders. The guy worked at the casino, and he found out when people were leaving with cash. My mother knew him. She'd gotten cash because she was going to an antique sale that weekend. He shot her in our house. They caught him in Montana, buying land."

There was nothing Abe could say. The way she sat refused touch, and he understood. It was like climbing out of the barrel and taking a bow with a broken neck.

Crying, she turned her head away and wiped her eyes with her hands. "I'm sorry. Do you have a tissue?"

Abe got up and raided the bathroom cubicle. He handed her some toilet paper.

Make breakfast, Abe.

There was a sound on the floor, four feet and metal tags. Martha jumped up, into the spot he'd vacated, breaking rules. She sat and watched Erin's face with concern.

Abe didn't order her to attack.

He said the most inadequate words in the world. "I'm sorry, Erin. I'm really sorry."

"The cowboy wants to be understood. Tragically, he speaks a foreign tongue."

—Erin Mackenzie,
"Cattle and Cowboys: The Ancient
Currency of a Modern Enigma"

CHAPTER SIX

SHE GAVE DETAILS during breakfast, between spells of tears. She had not cried, she said, till now.

Maeve was two months old at the time of the murder. Erin had been working at the museum in Reno, with the baby in day care. The killer left the door open, and a neighbor found Jayne Mackenzie's body.

Since then, the Museum of the American West had lost funding. Erin was laid off, waiting for response to job applications—museum work in other parts of the country. Were there any openings like that around Alta or Gunnison? Abe wondered. Incentive for her to move here?

His problems were like hay in September, and Chaley was stacking the bales.

"Want to see the stock?" he asked as they left the trailer. Guy Loren had some fine animals.

"Sure." Though early rays of sunlight danced in the yard, pretending at warmth, Erin shivered, freezing. Walking hurt.

"You had a wreck with that cow, didn't you?"

"I'm fine."

Martha padded after them in the icy snow. Beyond the

nearest barbed-wire fence, five bulls watched the humans. Abe told her their names. Two had performed at National Finals Rodeo. One had never been ridden.

"That brown-and-white one over there—that's a fighting bull."

"You don't compete in bullfighting."

"No."

Two bulls lay at the feet of the other three. "They look so...docile." *Fathers,* thought Erin. These were the fathers of calves. They wore their virility, their authority, their dignity.

"How did you know I don't compete?"

She started. "Oh. *Prorodeo Sports News.* Why don't you?"

Abe shrugged. He'd never put it into words.

She waited.

"It used to be that the clown's job was making people laugh, and the cowboys looked out for themselves. Then clowns became bullfighters, too. Now, there are lots of bullfighters and not many clowns."

"So you want to be a traditional clown?"

"Something like that." He couldn't explain. When the new bullfighters were introduced before a performance, the way they walked said, *You can depend on me. I'm a hero.* Like them, Abe drank in the applause, lived on it. But bullfighting wasn't cowboying; it wasn't getting calves to market. It was just another way to feed your cowboy pride when your business wasn't cows. When maybe you worked behind a desk five days a week.

"I want to save cowboys," he said at last, and meant that he wanted to save things the way they used to be. Abe tried to explain about fences. "It's like rich people buying ranches. They tear down the barbed wire and put up lodge pole. They hire some cowboys and buy some cows, and they show up at their places a few times a year and ride horses and have a barbecue. But it's not ranching.

"Now, somebody like my dad or Kip Kay relies on the land, gets his living from it. If the Kays mess up, they lose everything."

Erin hid her feelings. "Of course," she pointed out, "the Kays could sell their land for a lot of money. Millions of dollars."

"That would be the easy thing."

"I'd trade places with them." The envy came through. Hearing herself, Erin ran for the shelter of academics. "Ranchers can't scream poverty and make anyone hear, because the symbol of cattle as wealth is so deeply ingrained in the human unconscious. It's prehistoric, as old as the domestication of animals. Livestock growers are part of an archaic culture that goes back to the earliest Mediterranean societies, thousands of years before the time of Christ." Erin made herself draw a breath, slow down. "Someone from the city can't see that when you ask a man the size of his spread you're asking his income. Yet instinctively those same city dwellers see cattle ownership as a sign of affluence. They always will."

A tree creaked in a stir of cold wind.

"You've given this some thought," Abe said.

"It was the subject of my doctoral thesis."

She was serious, almost defensive.

Abe was bewitched. "What's your Ph.D. in?" *What.* He wanted to ask why. He remembered her fatal flaw.

"History of the American West," she said as though it didn't matter. Almost to herself she asked, "Who doesn't want land? Who doesn't want to live close to the earth?"

Her words revived an ache in him the way cold weather brings on rheumatism.

I'd trade places with them.

So would Abe.

Erin's skin was white under the brim of her hat, her dark eyes thoughtful. Even Loren's bulls seemed smitten with her.

"I take it you do. Want to live...close to the land."

Erin wiggled her fingers inside her gloves. It would probably be convenient for him if she settled nearby. Maeve could have visitation with him and Chaley. "I've always wanted to live on a ranch."

Abe wished he had one.

"Let's look at the broncs," he said.

He named Loren's horses with their long manes and tails, muscular athletes breathing out clouds. In the barn, he introduced her to a buckskin roping horse and showed her Maylights and the new foal. There were other roping horses, too, and a chestnut quarter horse named Wish. "Guy traded a bull for her. She's an NFR barrel-racing horse."

Erin touched the neck Wish stretched over the stall. Stroking the satin hair with its coarse ends, she was twelve again. "I used to want to be a barrel-racer."

"It's not too late."

"Just too expensive." Jayne's legacy, what was left after taxes, would be enough to relocate her and Maeve wherever Erin's new job took them. No extras.

"You don't need that much horse." Wish was worth $100,000.

"Any horse is too much horse." She repeated what her mother had always said. "You have to feed them and shoe them and pay vet bills."

Feed for his horses was one of the perks of working for Guy Loren. Abe could shoe anything with hooves. And he did a lot of doctoring himself. He'd never not had a horse to ride, since he'd been big enough to sit on one.

"When you have horses," he said, "you sacrifice other things."

In the shadows of the barn her eyes widened. "You just don't get it, do you? I'm a single mother."

And you're the father, asshole.

A direct hit. Abe was glad of the darkness.

He thought before he spoke again. "Would you feel differently," he asked softly, "if you were married? Say you couldn't have some things you were used to. Say you couldn't have nice clothes. Or a real house. Or medical insurance. But you'd have horses, live in the country. You'd have...the good life."

Erin's heart pounded. This man wasn't standing in a dark barn with her, all the animals breathing around them, talking hypothetical. He was talking about living in the promiseland, as though there was such a place, with room for her.

Here, where he had described the country of her dreams, she could be honest. As honest as she'd been at twelve, begging Jayne for a horse. "If I was married to a good man who loved me and loved Maeve, there's nothing I couldn't stand."

Abe didn't ask what a good man was and Erin didn't define it. They both knew he was one.

Too good to linger where talk could lead to touch, to finding an empty stall filled with clean hay and remembering what it was to kiss each other. And more.

"Let's get you back to the Kays'."

They left the barn.

Abe was checking Noon's girth when a man strode toward them from a double-wide trailer beyond the corral. The lenses of his metal-rimmed glasses winked in the early-morning light. In his sheepskin vest, he reminded Erin of a bear.

Abe stepped around the horse. "Guy, this is Erin. Erin— Guy Loren. Erin's staying at the Kays'."

Guy had a gift for minding his own business. The stock contractor said he'd need Abe that afternoon. They made arrangements to load some bulls to take down the road to be tipped; the tips of a rodeo bull's horns could be no smaller than a fifty-cent piece, so the sharp ends had to be sawed off.

Before leaving, Guy remarked, "Jack Draw's listed his place."

Abe's head shot up. "Really. That's news. What's he asking?"

"Five thousand an acre. About makes you sick. Let's hope they don't subdivide." He sighed. "We'll be seeing you."

Guy departed, and Abe thought about what he'd said. The television star was selling his ranch. Five thousand times fifteen thousand acres.

Seventy-five million dollars.

A second passed before he remembered Erin. He asked, "Want to ride Buy Back?"

Almost at the barn, Guy missed a step.

Erin's eyes swept the sleek chestnut horse, Abe's rodeo companion, then came back to him. "Are you sure?"

"Yeah."

Spots of pink stained her bloodless cheeks. "Thanks."

Abe turned to adjust Buy Back's stirrups. He crooned "Old Corrals and Sagebrush," and Martha came around and sat looking at him, thinking it was for her.

"WE DIDN'T COME this way before."

"Yes, we did. You were so cold you didn't notice." They were plodding through Jack Draw's ranch.

"Isn't this private property?"

"Public road. Forest-service access." Across the meadow to the north, cows—Highlands, Normandies, British White and Pinzgaus, talk about obscure—followed hay dropped from a horse-drawn sleigh. "How do you like that horse?"

She smiled, the first real smile he'd seen since she'd come here. "I love him. Thanks for letting me ride him. I think he's got more go than Noon."

"That's a fact, so keep after him. He'll try to run on the downhill."

The original homestead was a black skeleton in the southern field. Old chutes and sheds poked through the snow in front of an ancient cabin with the roof collapsed. The road eased upward, through aspen, and Abe stopped Noon. Quakies were notorious for falling, but these had stood since the last century.

Erin walked Buy Back past Noon and peered into the trees. Someone had carved an inscription on white bark:

THANK YOU, GOD. I LOVE THIS RANCH. C. COCKBURN, 1897.

The history grabbed at her, sucked at her irresistibly. She grabbed back, her mind dating Colorado statehood—1876. By that year, four million beef cattle roamed Western land, and by 1885 the grasslands were overgrazed. From ecological catastrophe came economic disaster. The large ranches that survived the depression gave way to smaller cattle operations relying on irrigation. In that time, C. Cockburn had found his spot of high country. "Who was he?"

"Great-grandpa."

"Was this your ranch?"

"My dad's. We lost it twelve years ago."

Lloyd. The magician who could reach inside a cow and pull out a calf had lived in another world, another time. He would have stories. Erin wanted them.

"We'd borrowed against the land, overextended. Interest rates went up, and that's all she wrote."

The new history of the American West.

And the history of Abe.

They rode on. As the trees fell away, wind bit Erin's face. A frozen creek divided a meadow crowned with mountains miles away. "So your dad started working for...the Kays?"

"Yes." Abe was ready to change the subject. If Jack

Draw sold to a developer, old Charlie's aspen might fall. He was glad he'd shown it to Erin, to the mother of his child.

It killed him that the tree might be gone when Maeve was old enough to read. Erin said cows were a symbol of wealth. But they *weren't* wealth. Not anymore. Here, real estate was wealth, and poor men held their land by gossamer strings.

Abe could never take back this ranch.

"So you lived here till twelve years ago?"

Abe nodded.

And the Kays had been their neighbors. "You and Chaley must have been childhood sweethearts." Erin envisioned them galloping across wildflower meadows, making out in a hayloft. Buy Back moved smoothly beneath her, and she told herself it meant something that Abe had let her ride him.

Abe focused on Buy Back, too. And on Erin, so he wouldn't think of land. "You had some lessons?"

"Six weeks every summer." She knew how her mother had saved for them. Kip Kay had never offered help.

Jayne had never asked.

He was the absent father of Erin's childhood, and she couldn't fix that now. She was seeking the truth about cowboys. It couldn't hurt her. Not now.

But Colorado seemed colder than ever, and the white of winter was a kind of death. And the breathing and footfalls of the horses were too honest for her lies.

THE PLAN WAS to leave Noon at the Kay Ranch for Erin to ride. When she and Abe reached the barn, Erin asked, "Can I take care of Noon? Put away the tack?"

"Sure. Then we'll go see how Lane got along."

Erin lugged the saddle and saddle blankets to the barn, and when she came out, Chaley was with Abe and the horses. Snow and mud darkened her scarred and faded boots. Her sheepskin coat was luxurious against her slender neck. Seeing Erin, she began to remove Noon's bridle, a gesture that said, *Run along. You'll just be in the way.*

Abe turned Buy Back loose in the corral. "I'll be over in a bit, Erin."

"Thanks for...everything."

Erin limped toward Mears Cabin. The back of her neck suddenly prickled, making her spin her head. Kip Kay stood on the porch of the big house with a cup of coffee. He nodded to her, then gazed toward the corral, at his daughter and Abe.

Erin knew herself for an interloper who had shown up with Abe's baby.

To spoil everything.

"ENJOY YOUR RIDE?" Chaley asked Abe.

She must have seen Erin on Buy Back but hadn't mentioned it. Abe knew she wouldn't. "Sure."

His mind was full of Maeve. He hadn't held her yet today. Hadn't smelled her skin.

This was Kip Kay's property, where his own father had worked for twelve years, where his brother had grown. The land enlarged the insult of his words. "Chaley, I can't marry you."

"I knew you were going to say that."

Like, *I knew you'd be going to a rodeo that weekend.*

"Good grief, Abe. Obviously she's gotten along fine for the past year. If she's not making out on her own, the baby can come live with us."

Her blue eyes were willful, seeing only what they wanted.

"Why are you making this so hard?"

"Because I know you." Chaley leaned against the corral fence, confident as the sun that had gone away. "You need space. You've always been that way. You're doing this rodeo thing because you're too noble to allow yourself to be part of this ranch. In twelve years you've never accepted money from my dad for work, and it's easy to see why. You feel like you need to have some birthright to the land before it's yours.''

Chaley, I don't love you. He itched to tell her. And avoid hearing her scary perceptions.

"In fact, you probably think you don't love me enough, Abe, but I know you, and I know why you think that way. It's because you love the land so much.''

"Chaley, I don't want your father's ranch.'' He wanted his own.

"Of course you do. We talked about it the night you proposed.''

The night *he* proposed?

She squirmed away from his gaze. "You can't raise a family just cowboying, Abe. You think *she's* going to put up with that?''

Abe was back in Guy Loren's barn, inches from Erin, who seemed so used to getting less than she wanted.

Chaley kept her profile to him, and the afternoon sun outlined her silhouette. Using her teeth, she tugged the glove off her left hand. She drew off his grandmother's engagement ring and gave it to him, and placing her hands on the corral fence, jumped over it and hurried toward the big house, her father's house.

Abe suppressed the feeling he was about to get told on.

He zipped the ring into an inside pocket of his coat to put away later. Freedom should have felt good, but Chaley's parting gesture had been to plant doubts. She'd done a good job.

HE GOT TO HOLD Maeve for only a few seconds when he stopped at Mears Cabin. Erin said Lane had been a great sitter, that he and Beulah Ann were playing with Maeve, trying to help her walk, when she came in.

Abe had to return to work, and it didn't seem like the

moment to tell Erin about Chaley. There definitely wasn't time to take Maeve out to his father in the pasture and introduce her.

So he went back to Loren's and helped Guy load the bulls. They rode to the sale barn in Gunnison, where each bull was held in a hydraulic iron compartment while a man used a circular saw to tip the horns. The animals bellowed. Abe saw the bloody horns and smelled the smoke and went outside into the cold to breathe.

The place was familiar. He had a memory of being at a livestock sale when eye level was Lloyd's thighs. He'd gotten separated, and there was just a sea of jeans and coveralls and boots, till a lean-faced cowboy had crouched down and said, "Well, you're Lloyd's boy." Abe must have been crying, but all he remembered was being lifted up to ride on the man's shoulders, and then he could see hats, and the man found Lloyd.

The cowboy was Kip Kay, and it was Abe's first memory of him.

And now if he closed his eyes, he could hear the background ruckus of the animals and the auctioneer's voice and see the old men in the back row soundlessly making their bids, their expressions unchanging. In a few years, Abe thought, he would bring Maeve here for a sale.

You can't raise a family just cowboying.

Guy paid him five hundred dollars a month, and he picked up extra money here and there shoeing horses for neighbors. The fifth wheel was too cramped for three, but he and Erin could scare up a larger trailer.

It wasn't enough. A man should give his family more.

That ancient symbol of wealth Erin recognized. Cattle and land.

Listening to the bulls inside, Abe shivered. Since they'd lost the ranch, he hadn't let himself imagine having his own spread. Success was just the fact that Lloyd had never arranged a tractor accident to trade his life for the ranch, like a neighbor of theirs had that year.

But he couldn't buy land on Guy Loren's pay. And he couldn't raise a herd without land. To become a cattleman would mean giving up cowboying, taking a job in town to earn enough money for a down payment.

Either that—or selling out. There were ranches that paid hands a living wage. Jack Draw's, for instance.

Strange to be thinking this way. Before his engagement to Chaley he'd stopped believing that his future held more than rodeo, more than a drifter's life. With the promise of marrying her, he *saw* what could be his, the Kay Ranch, and seeing was believing. Now, however, he needed a leap of faith.

He had to make it. What other work was there for a man with a family than to raise cows on his own land?

THAT AFTERNOON, while Maeve napped, Erin soaked in the cabin's oversize claw-foot bathtub until the pain leached from her muscles and her bruised right leg.

Everything, she told herself, was fine. It couldn't be helped that Chaley was Kip Kay's daughter and Chaley was engaged to Abe. Or that Erin was the mother of Abe's baby. She *wasn't* an interloper. She was a ranch guest minding her own business, which was the pursuit of truth.

It didn't quite play. If the week at the ranch wasn't so expensive—and nonrefundable—she would take a hotel room in Alta, explore the historic mining town with Maeve. Relax and forget about her quest. Call it failure and say that was part of life.

In fact, since her inheritance was coming, since the house was under contract, why not do it, anyway?

A vehicle pulled up outside, the engine went off and a door slammed.

Abe.

Erin yanked the plug from the bathtub. She was dragging

on jeans and an indigo blue long undershirt when he knocked. "Coming."

No time to comb her hair. Barefoot, she crossed the plank floor and opened the door. It was Abe, in his barn coat and hat. His green-gray eyes held feelings. There were cracks around his lips from the weather and a half-burned look to his skin.

She recalled he'd been moving bulls.

Abe was thinking about breasts and sex and nipples that showed under cotton T-shirts and the way her bed had creaked in Reno, how the headboard had banged the wall and he'd liked it. He'd bought a $3.99 City Market bouquet for her in Gunnison; while the cashier rang up the sale, he'd worked story problems: *If Abe has six dollars and he spends four on flowers, how many does he have left?*

He'd thrown the flowers in a field on the way to the Kays'. And he didn't know how to tell a Ph.D. in the subject that history meant Chaley Kay.

"Let me in," he said.

She did. "Maeve's asleep."

"I want to take her down the road, introduce her to my dad."

Erin used her fingers on her hair and chain mail on her heart. She couldn't afford to care how he looked on horseback with a new calf on his saddle or that he'd let her ride his favorite horse. Or that his dad had lost ten thousand times more than she'd ever had. "He's seen her."

"He'll see her better when I tell him she's mine." He went into the bedroom.

Erin pressed her spine to the doorjamb and watched him contemplate his sleeping daughter like a man in a church.

"I'm not going to marry Chaley," he said. "It's settled."

You couldn't tell much from a cowboy's face. Erin left him, walked to the kitchen. Taking the chair near the woodstove, a battered oak piece with fat cushions, she warmed her feet and worked out how to tell him that he didn't have to give up true love for some imagined duty to his child. This was a song with lots of verses, and she'd written it herself; she ought to be able to sing it for Abe.

When he joined her, she started in. "You don't have to break up with Chaley." Erin let her head fall back till she could see the beams in the ceiling. "I'm not one of those people who think biological parents have to be married to each other for the kids to grow up normal. You told me in Reno your folks are divorced."

"They were married most of the time I was growing up." It was Lane who'd been broadsided by their mother's leaving.

Erin turned to find his eyes alert, waiting for her. She would do fine Jayne's way, she thought, raising Maeve alone. After all, *she'd* turned out all right, if you discounted the business about cowboys. Pencil holders *were* trivial. "Abe, what I'm trying to say is, if you love Chaley, you should marry her."

The green eyes darkened. "I don't love Chaley."

"Then why were you engaged?"

An ember exploded in the woodstove.

"It made sense when she asked me."

When the crib creaked, Abe jumped up and hurried into the bedroom. Erin heard him say, "Hello, Queen Maeve. Hm. Soggy. And fragrant."

Erin went in. Maeve had decorated his Carhartt. The man who'd helped pull a cow that morning seemed paralyzed.

She set the disposables in front of him. "Cowboy up, Abe."

He met her eyes and grinned.

While Erin brought him a washcloth, Maeve lay patiently on her changing mat, trying to put her foot in her mouth, spreading the mess. As Abe faced his ordeal with memorable expressions, Erin couldn't help giggling, and Maeve joined in.

"Enough," he said. "Both of you."

Maeve giggled again.

Erin hunted clothes for her. She handed Abe some purple pile overalls and a white turtleneck. "Is this okay? My mom bought it for her."

"They're cute." Her mom. The trees outside made longer shadows. Her mom was murdered. "Hey, where are you going?" Abe caught Maeve as she began crawling across the bed in her diaper and plastic pants. When he sat the baby back down, she laughed.

"Daddy," he said.

"Da-dee."

"That also means doggy."

"I'll answer to it." He pulled the white turtleneck over Maeve's red curls, drew her hands through the sleeves. "God, Erin."

"What?"

He shook his head and gazed at Maeve's face and saw all the ways she was his.

LUCKY, KIP'S TRUST-FUND ranch hand from Alta, waved as Abe approached the pasture with the baby. Lloyd was checking an Angus heifer. When he finished, he led his horse through the melted snow and stopped on the other side of the barbed wire to stare at his son holding Maeve.

"Dad." Abe neared the fence, trying to keep both of Maeve's hands warm in one of his.

Lloyd stepped closer, almost scraping the wire.

"This is my little girl."

His father cocked an ear, as though to catch words blowing by. Then, in slow movements, he handed Bo's reins to Abe, over the barbed wire. Abe whispered, "Maeve, this is your grandpa," and gave her across the fence to his father, to hold.

> *"A working cowboy is no one.*
> *A clown is no one in public."*
>
> —Abe Cockburn

CHAPTER SEVEN

"ERIN, DOES YOUR FAMILY live in Reno?" Beulah Ann asked, serving mashed potatoes around the table that night.

Everyone was there—Kip, Chaley, Lloyd, Lane, Beulah Ann and the four ranch hands. Everyone but Abe, who wasn't part of the household. Who had headed for his truck at the sound of the dinner gong without saying when he'd be back.

"I don't have any family. Except Maeve." She added, "My mother died this year."

Silence.

A chair scraped back from the table. Leaving his plate, Kip Kay stood and walked out of the room.

Erin listened to the door open, then slam behind her father. The emptiness that followed had a still quality, like the inside of a temple, and everything was quiet inside her, too, because she was within a breath of the truth.

Kip Kay knew who she was. Knew who her mother was. And he cared that Jayne was dead.

MY MOTHER DIED this year.

Were his senses deceiving him? For two days Kip had listened to her voice, caught her mannerisms, found them like Jayne's. And her name was *Erin*, like Jayne's child.

Jayne's, never his.

His boots crunched in the half-frozen mud outside Mears Cabin. Shielded by moonless twilight, he jangled his keys in his pocket, wondering what law he was about to violate and what the penalty was. But she was a guest at his ranch.

Kip made the laws here.

With no backward glance, he mounted the porch steps. If she saw him, found him out, so be it. His instincts were shouting. He was right and only wanted confirmation.

He received it, through the wallet she'd left in the top drawer of her dresser. It was worn gray leather, old and dirty and taped in one place with duct tape.

That surprised him. Almost stopped him, because Kip had always associated thrift with decency. He began to shut the drawer, leaving the wallet undisturbed. But an icy draft from the door made him colder than cold. In his heightened state of sensitivity, irrelevant morals lost to imperative justice. He had to know. Swiftly he unfastened the billfold and found her driver's license to read her name. Her date of birth.

Closing it, replacing it in the drawer, he saw himself facing her, saying, *Get out. Leave, and don't come back.*

But nothing could be that easy. He didn't know why she'd come. He doubted it was to tell him callously at the table that his first wife was dead. She was a single woman with a baby. *God knows what she intends.*

What she meant to take from him.

But what could he do without confronting her? And confronting her meant speaking the truth. A truth she might then make known to Beulah Ann or to Lane.

Or to Chaley.

She might tell them, anyway, but Kip sensed she wouldn't. She might have come because of natural curiosity, to see her father. Guilt needled him. She didn't seem like a schemer.

Except that she'd lied about her name.

Kip decided. For five more days, the week she'd arranged to stay, he could tolerate her presence. Then she would leave, and that would be that.

He let himself out into winter, closed up the cabin as Erin had left it. When he turned, his daughter with her yellow braid and Stetson made a totem-pole shape at the foot of the porch steps. "What are you doing, Dad?"

In the night he could dissemble easily. "Checking the ashes in the stove." He came down the steps. Chaley was why he would not confront Erin. Chaley was why he could keep his distance from Jayne's daughter for five more days. Chaley was why he could let Erin Mackenzie walk through his life uninvited, unwelcome, and do nothing in response. He smiled at Chaley encouragingly, knowing the kind of hard day she'd had. Finally accepting that it was over with Abe. "Where are you headed, sweetheart?"

"Thought I'd look at the heifers." She didn't move. "Dad."

"Mm?"

The cutout portrait of her face watched the cabin.

Kip wanted to say something about Abe. There was nothing in the world Chaley wanted—and that he'd thought was good for her—that Kip hadn't found a way to give her. He liked Abe Cockburn far less this evening than he had in the morning.

You may as well know, Chaley had said bluntly, *Abe and I are no longer engaged.*

Ah.

There wasn't anything else to say.

Until Chaley admitted, "That baby inside is Abe's."

KIP WAS HALFWAY to Guy Loren's place when he realized he was ashamed that Chaley had told him. Ashamed *for* her, for telling on Abe, for telling something Abe might just have learned and be figuring out how to deal with himself.

He pulled his truck to the shoulder alongside his own south pasture, startling a coyote eating roadkill. Its shape loped across the highway and disappeared into the trees, ignoring the feast beyond the barbed wire, cows with new calves, tagged so the hands could keep each pair together. They were Kip's own cattle, but the coyote was a symbol that something was right in the world. He'd seen no more than scat for three years and a den on Alta Creek; he heard their song.

The last firearm he'd held was an M-16.

Oh, Chaley.

What would Lorraine say?

It was the question of his life, of every day since she'd died, giving out to a sudden liver ailment; he and Chaley had watched it kill her.

It was the question of their twenty-four-year marriage.

Kip had told his second wife that he'd been married before, told her the first ran out on him, that Jayne's desertion almost killed him. He'd told her that Jayne had reasons for leaving, that he drank too much, that there had been other women.

But his second wife was deeply moral—and not always just. He'd feared in those early days that she would never have him if she knew that Jayne Mackenzie left pregnant. When he'd known Lorraine better, when they'd been married longer, he was afraid she would never forgive the lie.

She'd died never knowing of his other child.

Erin's existence would be news to Chaley, too.

Headlights whipped by him on the road, outside his windshield smeared with dried water drops and dust. His truck idled warmly, puffing exhaust into the night.

Was that baby at the ranch really Abe's?

The baby was biologically his own grandchild, but Kip dismissed that. He did not love the woman Erin or her child. Was not interested in knowing them or loving them.

Only in keeping them away from Chaley before they could do more to hurt the daughter he did love.

A breath dragged through his lungs, and he contemplated whiskey and vices he'd abandoned twenty-four years ago, self-prescribed painkillers he'd traded for Lorraine's arms.

"Oh, Lorraine," he said to the glowing dash, "what would you think of me now?"

He didn't know why he'd been going to Guy Loren's place, what he'd planned to do when he found Abe. Throttle him, but why?

Native rages stewed with old horrors inside him, and Kip told himself his anger was on Chaley's behalf, because Abe had hurt her this way. Made another woman pregnant and couldn't marry Chaley, after all. Broke Chaley's heart.

But Lorraine's voice was a ghost in his ear, saying what she had in life. *You keep giving in to her, Kip, and it's not doing her any favors. It wouldn't hurt Chaley to know there's some things she just can't have, and that's part of life. If she has to wait till she's grown-up to find out, it'll be a rude awakening.*

"She's waking up now, Lorraine."

He checked traffic and spun the wheel, driving for his own gate. His cows were calving and would be throughout March. If he could do anything for Chaley now, it was build the ranch, make it stronger each year, so that someday she would have it for her children. There was nothing he could do about this other situation. One thing he couldn't give Chaley was Abe.

He'd sure as hell tried.

But Abe had a baby with Erin Mackenzie.

A coldness crept over Kip's heart, recollection of bleak days of abandonment, of desertion to the solitude he most feared. He wanted nothing so much as to get the reminder of that pain off his property and out of his sight.

HER MOTHER'S MURDER was with Erin that night. She'd said the words out loud at dinner, that Jayne had died, and now she couldn't put it out of her mind. When she turned in, Erin left the kitchen light burning.

She would keep it lit all night.

In her white flannel nightgown, she lay on the sheet beside her daughter. That awful night came back. She hadn't cried. Too numb.

And the tears never came, until this morning at Abe's.

Erin tried to think of something else, but thinking was an enemy when the truth was so near. His leaving supper like that, a message just for her, that he knew who she was. Other messages invited decoding, but Erin didn't want to read them yet. She tried other topics—the half sister who hated her, the cousin who didn't know they were cousins. A cowboy who couldn't be trusted. She could hear the wind in the stovepipe and the ice on the pine needles tapping the gutters.

She'd been at the Kay Ranch only two days.

It felt like a century.

Hooves clip-clopped outside. Someone was riding, and she considered pushing aside the curtain to see who. But the sound had come from the far side of the cabin, away from her window.

Erin heard the creak of saddle leather and soft whistling.

Abe?

It was ten-thirty.

Boots on the porch. Erin got out of bed. Orange glowed around the door of the woodstove. The dry heat crept through her nightgown to her bare skin as he knocked. "Who is it?"

"The clown in your life."

Erin opened the door. Snow clung to a misshapen black hat and his Carhartt and gloves. Oversize flakes fell in a backdrop behind him.

His face was painted, and he carried a battered tapestry satchel.

He'd come too late; death had arrived first for its nightly talk. She just stared at the clown.

"There's a rodeo this weekend," he said. "I have new tricks. I need you to tell me if I'm funny."

He wasn't, but his boots looked cute with his tights and baggies. She let him in.

"Thank you. Did I get you out of bed?"

She shut the door. "Yes."

The kitchen light was on, Abe noticed, had been on when he rode up. The kind of person who slept with lights on needed to be visited by a clown after dark. Feeling like a doctor arriving at the scene of an emergency, he shrugged out of his Carhartt and pulled off his boots, ready to work.

Chaley was wrong; it *was* a job.

There just wasn't any money in it. A fact to keep him awake, weighing what he would sacrifice for land and cows. And for Maeve.

Erin curled up in a corner of the couch and pulled a throw over her.

"Since you're not a rodeo announcer and may be unfamiliar with the finest selection of jokes, I've prepared some for you." Abe handed her a piece of notebook paper. On it was written in pencil: *I want to lick you.* "Oh, wait, that's not it. That's just a note my dog left me this morning." He handed her another sheet, yellow paper typed with recognizable rodeo jokes.

Erin wanted to suggest they skip the clowning and get down to the part where he licked her.

"You've been to rodeos, so you know how to fill in with patter, right?"

"I'll do my best." After a sigh he saw and didn't hear, she straightened in her seat and found an announcer voice. "Now, before I introduce this next cowboy... Abe. Abe. Where'd you get that watering can, Abe?"

Indeed, he'd produced a small watering can from the satchel.

"You found it *where?* No, wait, no. This is too stupid. No one will laugh at this, Abe."

What she'd said wasn't in the script—in fact, the joke *was* stupid—but Abe made a deal of starting to cry and letting his tears fall in the watering can, then watering the rag rug with them.

"Okay, okay. I'll read the joke."

It was hard to be a good rodeo announcer while imagining she was being licked by Abe, but Erin gave it her best shot.

At last Abe collapsed beside her on the couch.

"What?" Erin asked.

"You don't smile much."

"I'm grieving." She was also in heat. When he touched the hem of her nightgown, she thought they were getting somewhere.

"Want to go to the Laughlin rodeo?" he asked. "I leave Thursday. I thought you and Maeve could come."

Erin considered. She'd been toying with the idea of talking to her father. Saying in front of him what he must know, that she was his daughter. She could ask why he got up from the table so fast, and then maybe the truth would come, and it would be what she hoped. Not that he hadn't cared about Jayne's leaving him, but that he'd cared too much.

"I said I'd stay here for a week," she told Abe.

"They won't be heartbroken if you leave early." When she flinched, he said, "They're calving." *And there's the matter of Chaley, of Kip Kay's daughter, hating you for having my baby.* "If you come, you'll get to see my act with Marauder."

Erin tucked the throw around her legs. Abe didn't know she was related to the Kays. How would he react if she told him? She kept her secrets. "Who's Marauder?"

"A bull." Marauder had been retired from the arena for refusing to buck and was headed for hamburger. Only Abe could save him, by making him a vital part of his act, so vital that Loren would keep him around.

But Abe's rodeo career was on death row, too.

The years ahead stretched in front of him. In some versions he worked construction; in others he was a farrier; in others he signed on with Jack Draw or someone like him. He could barely see ahead to rewards—his own spread, somewhere land was cheap, somewhere colder than Alta or hotter than hell.

But one reward was close.

"What are you doing?" asked Erin.

He'd gathered her up, her nightgown against his patchwork shirt and suspenders. She was bare beneath it, Abe knew, and he wanted to lift up the hem and get his face under there. But he wouldn't for the same reason he'd thrown out the flowers.

He carried Erin to the bedroom, imagining her hand wrapped around him. There was sure something for her to hang on to, which he hoped she wouldn't notice and hoped she would. He hoped she would insist on having him, which didn't seem likely but was possible. "I'm tucking you in. Sleeping with the lights on is easier if a clown tucks you in."

Maeve slept on the bed, with the spread turned back. Abe remembered sleeping with his parents, too. He put Erin down beside Maeve and turned the covers over her.

Erin gazed up at him. The room was dark, and he was there, the masquerade man who'd haunted her bed in one form or another since he'd shared it. She loved his eyes. He was smart. And funny.

He was Maeve's father, though "father" was a word she didn't want to think tonight. She wanted Abe, for himself, but there was something she had to know first. "Why," she asked again, "were you engaged to Chaley?"

The ragged clown was a solemn statue and a cowboy. And a man. The wanting, Erin knew, went two ways.

"Guess."

At first Erin thought she'd heard wrong. But he'd given her the clues that morning on their ride.

"And what I said before was true," he added.

That it had seemed like a good idea when Chaley asked him.

To marry her for her father's land.

His eyes were deep as he stood over the bed. They didn't expect love or acceptance. "Good night." He reached across her to touch Maeve's back, but didn't touch Erin at all, just left—conspicuously free or not worth catching, she didn't know which.

Fabric rustled as he gathered his things. A boot thumped on the floor. She heard him zip his coat, singing a verse of "The Old Chisholm Trail."

With my foot in the stirrup and my hand on the horn,
I'm the best damn cowboy ever was born.
Come a ti yi youpy, yippy-yay, yippy-yay,
Come a ti yi youpy, yippy-yay....

His song lingered after the door had shut behind him and the sound of his horse's hooves had faded away. And Erin bunched the sheets under her, remembering how badly she could want a man.

TUESDAY AFTERNOON, while waiting in the Gunnison Department of Motor Vehicles office for Lloyd to complete his driving test, Abe reviewed Colorado traffic rules and regulations. He was testing himself when Lloyd walked through the glass door, followed by the testing officer. Abe dropped the manual and got to his feet.

"Let's go," growled Lloyd.

Chewing on his lip, the officer meandered behind the desk with his clipboard. Abe silently posed a question.

The officer shook his head.

Damn.

Outside, sunshine slanted on the Gunnison storefronts. Abe's front truck tire kissed the curb over a patch of blackened snow, while the back wheel sat a foot from the concrete. *Looks all right to me, Dad.* Wondering where his father had failed the test, Abe took the wheel. It was awkward to turn to Lloyd. "I need the keys."

"Oh. Here."

How could his father be foreman for Kip Kay if he couldn't drive? Tractors, trailers, trucks...

Abe started the engine. This had put a kink in his own plans, too. He'd counted on Lloyd being in a good mood after his driving test. *Well, to hell with it.* He had to ask, anyway.

And while he was at it, he might as well broach another difficult subject. A logging truck rolled past, and Abe pulled into traffic. "So, what's the story with the Range Rover? What's the damage?"

"I have no idea. His insurance is going to pick it up, if you can believe that. Seven hundred dollars a month he pays on one vehicle."

"How did you find that out?"

"Bought me a cup of coffee at Stockman's while I waited for you that day."

Abe was touched by the kindness.

At the traffic light Lloyd stretched in his seat, readjusting the shoulder strap. "Lots of questions about horses. Nice enough fellow. But too much money and not enough sense."

Abe pictured the young driver of the Range Rover huddled over Stockman's thick brew with Lloyd, soaking up information about horses. He'd asked the right man.

Abe parallel parked in front of the coffeehouse and killed the engine.

"What are you doing?" said Lloyd.

"I need some money. I paid your fine, and I'm broke."

His father blinked. "What do you need money for?" When Abe didn't answer, Lloyd dug for his wallet, opened it with sun-spotted, knuckle-swollen hands and selected a twenty. "That enough?"

For Abe it was fair time again. Nights Lloyd had given him and Lane money for the Zipper and the shooting gallery. Even when they had the ranch, there'd never been much spare cash. But when the county fair rolled around, Lloyd had given what there was. And when they got bored at the sale barn, he'd dished out money for ice cream, and Abe and Lane had walked down the street and gone into the store. And he remembered how they'd looked through the glass at the flavors and seen their hats reflected there. *Yes, please, ma'am. Thank you.* Sugar cones dipped in chocolate making puddles on the concrete and in the dust back at the barn.

Now the silver-haired man, the generous father, seemed uncertain about the amount of his fine. What fine?

Abe couldn't bring himself to clear things up. Friday was payday. "That's plenty. Thanks, Dad." He took the twenty, and feeling like he was soaking the old man, got out of the truck.

Lloyd didn't move from the passenger seat.

Heading for a toy store two doors down, Abe tried not to hear the gong inside him. Its toll announced his father's old age; it warned of hard decisions to come. What would Kip Kay do when he learned Lloyd had failed his driving test?

And what would happen to Lloyd?

ABE PLANNED to park at Mears Cabin when he dropped his father at the Kay Ranch. It was Maeve's birthday. Lane's, too.

But Lloyd wanted out at the corral. "Stop," he ordered.

Beulah Ann was hustling down from the deck. As Lloyd got out, Abe lowered his window.

"Birthday party tonight!" she said. "It'll be for Lane and Maeve both. Chaley's gone to Fort Collins to see friends."

That was supposed to ease his mind. It failed. Chaley might be gone, but her father wasn't. "Did you mention this to Kip?"

"He said it's all right with him, but I thought we'd have it in the trailer."

Tactful, Beulah Ann.

"Oh, come on, Abe! It'll be you and me and Maeve and Erin and Lane, and the hands said they'd pop in for cake. It's a farewell party for Lane, too. He's going to that rodeo with you Thursday." It seemed like she had more to say, but she stopped there.

She was right. Lane had signed on for the Mountain States Prorodeo Circuit—Colorado and Wyoming—but he'd try to hit performances all over the country. Lane would not be returning to the Kay Ranch. Though he'd spent most of his life there, he'd never really considered it home.

Same as Abe.

"It's your daughter's birthday," said Beulah Ann.

Abe stared, and Beulah Ann looked so guilty he knew she wasn't covering for Erin. Lane was the culprit.

So, now it's out. Did Kip know?

"Where's Erin?"

"Inside, making icing for the cake."

A glare fired up the kitchen window; he couldn't see past it. Why hadn't she come out? But why would she after what he'd admitted about his engagement? About his love of land? She'd never even said she'd go to the rodeo.

He wanted to ask Beulah Ann if Erin knew he'd be at the party. But of course she knew. Funny how comfortable she seemed here, how cozy with Beulah Ann, how at home on the ranch. She was just a dude, a guest, but now Abe felt like the stranger, the disconnected one.

He'd earned that role.

He asked Beulah Ann, "What time?"

"Seven."

"Okay." He put the truck in gear. Kip was riding down the road in his winter overalls.

"Sorry." Beulah Ann scooted back from the cab.

"I'm not avoiding anybody."

She made for the house, and Abe edged the truck forward, but Kip dismounted and waited on the road.

When Abe pulled up beside him, the rancher asked, "Did he pass?"

Lloyd's test. Abe had forgotten. He shook his head.

Kip gazed south at the equipment shed, nestled among the pines. The forest rose to the west, and on every horizon mountains jutted skyward.

Country worth having. A man's pride.

Never looking back at Abe, the rancher gave a nod and walked on.

Chaley. Abe's gut twisted. Things weren't going to be the same between him and Kip Kay ever again. And the birthday party already looked like a mistake.

"The truth will set you free."

—the Bible, John 8:32

CHAPTER EIGHT

ABE ARRIVED at his dad's at six-thirty and parked beside the trailer, wishing Kip Kay didn't have to look at his truck all night. A horse would have been just as conspicuous. No help for it. It was his brother's eighteenth birthday.

And Maeve's first. Yes, Kip must know by now that the most beautiful red-haired baby anyone ever saw was Abe's daughter.

Lane was watching bull riding on ESPN when Abe carried in the canvas duffel bag that contained his clowning gear. Martha squeezed in after him, making a beeline for Lane's feet, a banquet of scent.

"Hi, Martha, ol' girl. My brother treating you right?"

Using his left hand, which held a bottle in a paper bag, Abe shut the door. "Where's Dad?"

"Calving." Lane slammed his feet to the floor and sent Martha leaping back. Leaning toward the TV set, he slapped his hand hard on his knee. "Did you see that?"

On the screen a bull rider was trying to get up after being trampled. Abe handed his brother the paper bag. "Happy birthday. Use some sense."

His attention captured, Lane eased the bottle of Jim Beam Rye from the sack. Eyes slowly lighting, he built his voice to a rising, "*Yeee*-hah! Get a glass, brother. No, wait, who needs a glass?"

Ten minutes later, in his father's room, Abe sat before a lighted makeup mirror he'd bought at a garage sale, while Garth Brooks rattled the walls of the trailer. Beulah Ann had arrived, looking special in a fringed shirt and black jeans, and now she and Lane were drinking Jim Beam, cranking the music and still watching rodeo.

Abe had a glass beside him, but he wasn't enjoying it as he applied white greasepaint to his face. Kip hadn't said anything about Lloyd, but it wasn't hard to read his mind. You couldn't have a foreman who couldn't drive. Added to that, the foreman should have the best lodgings on the place, next to the owner.

Lloyd might be out of a home, too. This trailer.

Abe had tried to talk to Lane about it, but his brother had just shrugged, never taking his eyes from the screen. *So he moves to the bunkhouse. You and I both know Kip's not going to fire him. He'll still let him cowboy.*

When your brother thought that way, you had to point out, *It's a demotion.*

He's a tough old man. I'm not going to worry about it. I'm outta here.

Like their mother, a long time ago. She'd had an excuse, if there was such a thing. Lane was just Lane.

Martha rested her head on Abe's knee as he painted a black patch around one eye, a black circle around the other, a dog's black nose and mouth, and the brown and black and gray spots on his cheeks. "I'll never be as pretty as you, Martha." When he'd finished with his face, he fished a dog biscuit from his bag and tossed it to her.

Behind him, the phone gave a staccato rattle that was someone's idea of ringing. They'd gotten the phone with the trailer.

Abe waited for his brother to answer it, but Lane and Beulah Ann were backing up Garth on "American Honky-Tonk Bar Association."

"Erin," Abe muttered as he made his way around the

bed to get the phone, "I hope you'll still tolerate me after you see how my nearest and dearest relative behaves tonight."

The phone buzzed again and he lifted the receiver. "Cockburns'."

"Abe?"

The voice was Kentucky sweet, always familiar. Abe's stomach dropped a mile. "Mom. Mom. Hi, Mom."

"Hi, honey. How are you? Are you there for Lane's birthday?"

"Yes. Yes." He met his dog's eyes. "Martha. Shut the door."

With her head and one front paw, the Australian shepherd pushed shut the flimsy door separating the master bedroom from the rest of the trailer. The music volume hardly lessened.

"Good girl. Yes, you're a good girl." When she came to his side, Abe petted the dog, then stretched the phone cord across the bed as he reached for the glass on the dresser. "How are you, Mom?" The phone crashed to the floor. "Sorry. That was just the phone. It's all right, Martha."

His fingers found the glass. The glass found his lips. He drank deep, swallowed hard, and the whiskey's fire braced him. *Cowboy up, Abe.*

"I'm fine," said his mother, bringing to his mind a picture of her smooth shoulder-length light brown hair. Abe had seen her just a few months before, back in November, during the Louisville rodeo. He'd gone to her place, to the stable she co-owned. Annabelle did not attend rodeos, especially when her son was bullfighting. *If I wanted to see you get killed, I would never have left Colorado.* One of those things that probably shouldn't have been said; he'd had to leave pretty quick afterward, once he'd comforted his mother through her tears of regret. Now, the incident in the past, she told him, "We've got the prettiest new foal.

And we just signed on the owners of Total Eclipse, who won the Triple Crown?'' Abe's mother and her sister and brother-in-law trained racehorses.

"Mom. I have a baby." There. He'd said it. "I just found out. She was, um…" He'd learned this word a few months ago—the name of a barrel-racing horse. Time to impress his mother. "…Serendipity." *Which, rodeo fans, means "a happy accident." And Serendipity sure has been a happy accident for this cowgirl….* "Her name is Maeve. Today's her birthday, too. Her first birthday."

Annabelle was a lady to her core. After just long enough to blink three times, she said, "Why, honey, that's wonderful! When can I see her?"

Abe contemplated the empty bottom of his glass, set it down and stroked Martha. "Well…I won't be back out your way for a while. You could come here, though." Annabelle hadn't been west of the Mississippi in thirteen years.

"Well, surely you'll be coming somewhere close."

He imagined traveling to the South with Maeve for a rodeo. He wondered how best to acquire cows and land. He mourned the dry glass and the fact that his rodeo days and maybe his cowboying days were numbered. "I'll let you know."

"I want to see her, Abe. If you can't come here, you tell me, and…well, I'll go there."

Annabelle—in Colorado again? His heart pounded. "That's great. That's really great." Complications suggested themselves. That he'd known Maeve himself for just four days. That only two had passed since he'd broken up with Chaley. That nothing with Erin was *settled.* But he wasn't going to say anything to discourage his mother from visiting her only grandchild.

"Will you send me a picture right away?"

"Yes. Yes." He was afraid she'd back out, so he said, "Did you want to talk to Lane?"

There was a whisper of quiet before she said smoothly, "Yes. That's why I called. I love you, darling."

"I love you, Mom." He laid the phone on the old Navajo blanket that covered his father's bed and went out into the musical din to get Lane. The boom box balanced on the edge of the kitchen counter, and Abe turned down the volume before he addressed his brother, who was glued to the tube with Beulah Ann beside him. "It's Mom. On the phone."

Lane's mouth twisted down, and his eyes remained fixed on the set for another three seconds, until the end of the televised ride. Then he slowly stood and stretched and started to make his way past Abe. He looked surly.

"Be nice," said Abe. "She's your mom."

"And such a good one, always."

The sarcasm was black smoke spewing after him as he headed down the hallway. On the couch Beulah Ann somberly directed her eyes to the television screen. "Someone knocked."

It came louder and Abe opened the door. Erin stood on the wooden landing that served as a porch, pretty as a barrel racer who'd just won a buckle.

Maeve, in her arms, took one look at Abe and began to cry.

IT WAS FIFTEEN MINUTES before he made her laugh. The followed-by-shoes trick did it. Pieces of string ran from the toes of some oversize black shoes to Abe's running shoes—no cleats in the house. Whenever he walked, the shoes followed him, and he kept checking over his shoulder to see who was there. Sitting on the floor with the small stuffed rabbit he'd given her, a birthday present that had helped win her trust again, Maeve watched his antics and giggled.

After a while he sat down on the rug, blew up a long

balloon and twisted it into a poodle for her. Maeve giggled again. "Da-dee!"

She meant him of course. That balloon didn't really look like a dog.

As Abe picked her up and hugged her, Erin watched from the nearest chair, a tattered recliner that no longer reclined. Willie Nelson was cautioning mamas not to let their babies grow up to be cowboys, and Erin wondered if there was a song about not letting your daughter grow up to be dumped by cowboys. Well, she'd saved Maeve, maybe, by coming to Colorado. She'd *always* admitted that her own problem in that direction probably came from being ignored by her cowboy dad.

And Maeve had won her own dad's heart. On the floor Abe was letting her sit on his chest and try to eat one of the sunflowers off his suspenders.

I should feel some satisfaction in this.

Instead, she felt nothing. Last night he'd left. After admitting he would have married Chaley for the Kay Ranch.

And I still think he's sexy.

The bull riding ended and Lane switched off the television.

"Birthday-cake time," said Beulah Ann. "I'm going out to ring the bell so we can get the hands in for a piece."

Lane rearranged magazines on the coffee table, swept up his and Beulah Ann's glasses and set the whiskey bottle on the counter. Leaving Abe, Maeve grabbed on to the leg of a chair and pulled herself to her feet. She tried to walk, holding on to the chair, then the television, then the coffee table.

Beulah came back in, and Erin heard voices outside asking, "Where are they? In the trailer?"

Soon the living room was full of ranch hands.

"Where's Dad?" Abe asked Lucky, careful to sound unconcerned.

"He and Kip are working on a cow. They said they'd have some later. Hey, cool duds you got there."

After two renditions of "Happy Birthday," addressed both to Maeve and to Lane, everyone had some cake and whiskey or lemonade, and the four hands drifted out to the bunkhouse or the pastures.

Abe's mind was still on his father. When Maeve got sleepy, he'd walk Erin back to the cabin, then go find Lloyd.

But for now...

Lane, modeling a new pair of turquoise chaps sprouting fringe from every edge, danced lewdly on the sturdy pine coffee table. He sang along with Alan Jackson into an invisible microphone, encouraging Beulah Ann and Erin to join in.

The door of the trailer opened and Lloyd stood on the threshold.

Peering from the bull-riding pop star on the coffee table to the clown lounging against the kitchen table—his progeny—he muttered an oath and entered his home.

"Hi, Dad." Lane leaped down from the table. "Now, don't drink all that whiskey. It's mine."

"It's just what you need to go with that hole in your head. Where's this cake I keep hearing about?"

"I'll get you a piece." Erin rose, holding Maeve.

"Hello, Tumbleweed," Lloyd greeted the baby. "I'll take her off your hands, Erin."

As Erin handed Maeve to her grandfather, Abe breathed easier. If Kip had demoted Lloyd, he was taking it well. While Beulah Ann danced through the living room, Lloyd sampled the cake. "You make this?" he asked Erin.

"Beulah Ann and I did."

"You'll do." He slanted a look at Beulah Ann, twirling under Lane's arm. "Not so sure about them."

Lloyd's praise reminded Erin of the single time she'd felt her father's approval. It made her wonder, again, if the way to get at the truth was to tell Kip she was his daughter, so that they'd have to look each other in the eye and admit it. *Look. I have your nose.*

She didn't want to wreck the night thinking about it.

The foreman's boots were cracked with dried dirt, his insulated coveralls made for warmth at work rather than fashion. As he exchanged grins with his grandchild, he said, "How do you like March in Colorado?"

"It's cold."

"That's so." Lloyd was admiring Maeve's incoming front teeth, but he said, "We used to have woodstoves and firewood in the school buses."

History. Erin held on to it like a tick on a dog, and only a small part of her mind kept worrying at her own missing history. "You're kidding."

"No, I'm not. One winter I'll never forget. My daddy used to keep the cattle in a corral near the barn at night, and in the morning, we'd let 'em out to roam. Well, one morning he looked at the sky and said he thought he'd just keep 'em in, and in the afternoon he brought 'em into the barn." He smiled at Maeve, swung her feet with his free hand, then met Erin's eyes to give impact to his next words.

"That night came a blizzard so fierce we had to tie a rope from the house to the barn. Horses we didn't know came and stood on the leeward side of our barn, rubbing against the building to keep warm. When the storm was over, that side of the barn was thick with hair."

Erin was riveted now, the other rancher almost gone from her thoughts.

"Every cow in the county died, except my daddy's."

Clouds traveled fast in the West. What kind of person could look into the morning's sky and see an evening's blizzard?

"You like history," said Lloyd, "you should visit the Alta museum."

"They have an historical museum?"

He only had time to nod before Abe interrupted. "You don't mind, do you, Dad?" While Lloyd shook his head and grinned at the baby, the clown caught Erin's hand and led her into the living room to dance. He wasn't to be outdone by his little brother.

Erin wondered if he noticed, like she did, that it was their first real touch since the night they'd made Maeve. Holding his hand.

In order to become a member of the Dumped by Cowboys Hall of Fame, one had to have been whirled around the floor by a few cowboys, and Erin had known her share. Abe was the best. As he spun her close to him and away, skillfully giving Beulah and Lane their space, Erin found herself laughing, the way dancing could make you laugh.

Abe grinned back from his clown face. The God-you're-pretty-I-could-love-you look in his eyes made her half-giddy. Across the room his father held their child, rocking her to the music and smiling at his sons. The idea that she had any claim on these people—or even this moment—was illusion, Erin realized, the kind a person sought when she visited a working ranch. The illusion that there was a place in this West where she could belong. And so what if Lorrie Morgan's "Heart over Mind" was the anthem of Dumped by Cowboys Anonymous?

The song ended the tape, and as the dancers separated, Lloyd hummed a few bars of an old cowboy tune. "Abe, how about some 'Red River Valley'?"

"Sure, Dad." He beckoned Erin to follow him. The glossy cherry-wood stereo cabinet had been made in the late 1950s. It had been his parents' wedding gift from his father's parents.

Erin knelt on the rug beside it as Abe popped open a door and flipped through some albums. He chose a tattered jacket with a Remington print on the front, *Music of the West,* and reverently removed the album from its sleeve.

"I love records," said Erin. "They sound warmer than CDs."

"Well, this is real cowboy music. And that's what we like." He placed the record on the turntable, and Erin glanced up to see Lane gallantly offer Beulah Ann his arms in a gesture of friendship. Abe was taking her own arm, guiding her to her feet.

Across the room, Lloyd whistled along as a cowboy singer began crooning "Red River Valley." He turned in a graceful circle with Maeve, resting the baby against his broad comfortable shoulder.

But Abe took Erin's attention, catching her left hand in his right. His heart beat strong against her breast as his arm drew her closer, and he taught her a gentle dance of the Old West.

Come and sit by my side if you love me.
Do not hasten to bid me adieu...

A blast of cold whisked into the room, carrying whorls of fresh snow. Abe lifted his eyes and met those of the man whose daughter's heart he'd just broken.

The dance fell apart. Erin saw him, too. Her father with snow on his hat and his coat. Shunning her eyes and Abe's, he cocked his eyebrows toward Beulah Ann and Lane. "Where's the cake?"

Erin shot out of Abe's arms so fast his head spun. He stared after her. Why was she so keen to wait on Kip?

Shutting the door, Kip wondered how he'd be able to choke down a piece of cake. Twylla, Chaley's cow, lay dead in the yard with the bodies of the calves they'd lost. Chaley had fled to Fort Collins so she wouldn't have to see what she was facing now, Abe falling in love with another woman. Lloyd's revoked license and Jayne's daughter cutting the birthday cake... Well, it was plenty.

Lloyd knew about the cow, had helped him try to save

her. He shook his head at Kip in shared regret. For the cow. Maybe for a son who'd fathered a child on the rodeo road.

It's me who's sorry, old friend, Kip thought. He'd decided to hold off mentioning the driving test. Lloyd was losing one of his kids tonight, and Kip knew how that felt— like Chaley going off to college. He wasn't going to kick a man when he was down. Though Lloyd didn't seem down with that baby sleeping in his arms. Singing:

But remember the Red River Valley
and the cowboy who loves you so true....

Abe eased around the counter behind Erin, glad she couldn't see his eyes. He wasn't jealous—just bothered. Like there was something he was missing that he ought to be able to see. "I'll take another piece of cake, Erin."

You never talked to Chaley like that, thought Kip. *With love in your voice.* Royally angry—at Chaley's stubbornness as much as Abe's taste—Kip accepted the cake plate from Erin's shaking hand. The hand made him look at the eyes.

Jayne's face stared back, and with a tight sigh he turned away.

MAEVE FELL ASLEEP on Lloyd's shoulder. She lolled against her grandfather with her head tipped back and one hand on the cowboy's creased red-brown neck. Knowing it was time to go, Erin collected the gifts. Beulah Ann's plastic dog with wheels and blinking eyes and a tongue that stuck out. The bunny from Abe.

Abe took Maeve from his father and carefully rested her against his own shoulder. She sighed in her sleep.

Erin kept her sighs to herself. Kip had eaten his cake and teased his niece and Lane, then departed. That showed grace, considering the circumstances of Abe's breakup with Chaley. Considering Maeve, having her first birthday on

Kip Kay's property. The minutes he spent in the trailer had twisted Erin's mood. She'd been ignored. But Maeve earned his smiles, the warmth of his eyes. He wasn't, Erin thought, a cold man.

With distance, she counted the ironies. Kip must feel Abe had wronged Chaley. But if he knew Erin's identity, the rancher showed no fatherly concern for the daughter who had borne Abe's child. Maybe he believed Abe intended to marry her; Erin half believed it herself.

Or maybe it was just more evidence that, in Kip Kay's eyes, she wasn't his. *The truth about cowboys,* she told herself. *That's all I want.*

The wooden steps outside the trailer were slippery. Erin's boots made wet-wood prints as she descended to the snow-blanketed yard. Flakes dampened her eyelashes and settled on Abe's hat as they rounded the corral, Abe carrying Maeve.

"That was fun," said Erin. "Thanks for being a clown."

"Can't help it."

But he was staring ahead and he wasn't with her.

He'd lent her his denim jacket for the walk to the cabin, and Erin turned up the sheepskin collar against the frosty night. Snowflakes wet her nose. "What's on your mind, Abe?"

He stopped walking for a second. *Why not?* The barn was dark, no hands near. "Oh, my dad." Briefly he told her about Lloyd's test and that a man without a license couldn't be a ranch foreman. But before she could answer, his eyes caught something in the hump of dark shapes behind the barn. The mound had collected snow, too, and was indistinct beyond the veil of falling crystals. Abe walked toward it.

Erin knew that was where the carcasses were, the bodies of cows and calves who had died, and she didn't go close. In an instant of paranoia, it had even occurred to her that Kip had told the hands to put them there, just so she'd have to walk past them every day and smell the death. "What is it?"

Abe came back. "Oh, it's Twylla. Chaley's dad gave her a cow when she was nine to start her own herd, to put herself through school. My dad did the same thing with me, would have with Lane, too, if he'd still had the ranch when Lane turned nine. Twylla was Chaley's first cow."

Poor Chaley. But her sympathy felt shallow.

Some things you tried not to think about. Like the way rancher fathers raised the daughters they raised. "What happened to your herd?"

"Lost with my dad's." If he was bitter, he didn't say.

"You never went to college, then?"

"No."

His battered clown hat shut any light from his face.

As their shoes broke up the snow, Erin began singing "My Heroes Have Always Been Cowboys," and Abe sang with her.

On the porch of Mears Cabin, he paused. "Why is that?"

"Why is what?"

"For a city woman, you take a strong interest in cows."

She hedged. "Reno's really just a cow town with casinos."

"Yeah, I know." He repositioned Maeve, took Erin's key and unlocked her door. Fingers of heat reached out to them. In the open doorway he said, "But you're not a cowgirl."

The clown was too savvy. A trickster.

"People like...what they like." Erin glided into the cabin, unaware that she'd tossed her hair, lifted her chin. And made him wonder what lie she'd told.

Abe flicked on the wall switch, and a lamp beside the couch sent out a soft glow. The edges of the room hid in shadow. Abe took Maeve into the bedroom and laid her on the cowboy-print spread to take off her coat. He settled her in the crib, then returned to Erin, who was arranging an aspen log in the stove.

He got her out of the way and stoked the fire himself, building it warm. When he turned, Erin sat on the rug behind him, resting on her hand.

"Don't want to tell me why you like cows," he said.

Erin heard, *You don't want to tell me the truth.* Abe had known Kip Kay his whole life. Erin hadn't. And she hadn't known Abe that long, either.

She shook her head.

It made Abe think of Lane, coming home from grade school after someone had said Annabelle ran off with a man—which was a lie—or after someone had described what happened to dead bodies, what Busy would be like decomposed. Erin reminded him of Lane. Shaking her head, not telling.

He wasn't satisfied. "Come to the rodeo with me Thursday."

An overnight trip. Would they sleep together? "Keep talking."

He lifted one shoulder. "We could get a room with a couple of beds."

Which meant they'd sleep together. Erin had changed since he'd stood her up in Twin Falls, when she was pregnant with Maeve. Not resisting cowboys was unacceptable now.

But this is different, she thought. "Okay."

He kissed her the way you kiss someone if you're wearing greasepaint. Erin heard the log in the stove split.

"I want you to tell me now," he said.

"I'll tell you sometime."

"You trusted me more in Reno."

"You're mistaken."

When he stood, she saw his running shoes and thought, *Cowboys don't always wear boots.* She didn't move as he left, and afterward she sat there in front of the stove knowing she hadn't changed, after all. She still couldn't say no to cowboys.

It took effort to go to bed.

Moonlight coming through the limbs of a pine tree cast spotted shadows on the bed where Maeve slept. Erin had never seen that sight in Reno, pine-tree shadows. Reno had its own beauty, and the high desert and the lights of the casino were tied up with the vivid painted beauty, the world-weary humor, of Jayne.

This, Erin thought, *is my other side.* The mountains were the other half of her roots.

When half your roots never grew right, you did lopsided things. When your father was a cowboy and didn't...didn't have a part in your life, you looked for other cowboys to fill the gaps.

I need the truth. She thought it in the dark, and she thought it in the language that was comfortable. *I need to know the truth about cowboys.* Until she did, she'd never be able to say no to cowboys, to the restless search that always left her alone, abandoned like a kid in a casino parking lot.

There was only one way to the truth, and that was to face her cowboy father and say, "I am your daughter."

Tomorrow she would.

A HELICOPTER FLEW over the ranch three times the next day. Erin didn't pay much attention to it—she was thinking about telling Kip Kay she was his daughter—but at lunch her father stood up from the table and said, "I've had enough." He meant he'd had enough of the chopper, and he went outside, as though he intended to do something about it.

Erin thought she understood. That helicopters must affect him; so would a heavy downpour. There must be lots of things like that. She'd read that an ice maker could mimic an AK-47. She wondered what ghost sounds there were on a ranch.

While she and Beulah Ann washed lunch dishes, the helicopter hovered against the distant range, and Beulah Ann stopped singing "Someday Soon" long enough to say, "It's developers, looking at Jack Draw's place."

This pulled Erin's thoughts from her father. "Really?"

"Yes. There's no conservation easement, so whoever buys it will probably subdivide."

Erin winced. Abe would hate that. *She* hated the idea, and Jack Draw's ranch had never been her home. It surprised her that the actor hadn't put a conservation easement on the property; deciding the land couldn't be subdivided would have reduced its resale value and, therefore, his taxes.

But here he was reselling; maybe it was what he'd planned all along.

Two small feet showed just outside the mudroom as Maeve crawled toward the back door. While Erin retrieved her and set her near her toys in the kitchen, Beulah Ann resumed singing. She was in an awfully good mood, considering that the person who made her knees weak was leaving forever on Thursday morning.

Before Erin could ask if she'd come to her senses regarding Lane, Beulah Ann stopped her song and said, "But you know, if that happens, maybe he'll sell the brand."

"Who? What brand?"

"Jack Draw. The Cockburns' brand. It's one of those real old brands—they were the first ones to have it. Abe's tried to buy it before, but Jack Draw wouldn't sell. Wouldn't even talk to him in person."

"You can buy a brand?" Everything Erin knew about brands was historical. Branding and earmarking of cattle were used in the British Isles and in Iberia before the seventeenth century, and British colonists in the New World used both techniques, as well.

"If it's not being used, you can," Beulah Ann explained.

"An old brand like the Cockburns'—you see them for sale sometimes for three, four thousand dollars. Lane says it's a real family symbol. A symbol of when they were all together before Busy died."

Erin knew she'd missed something.

Holding a chair at the kitchen table, Maeve pulled herself up to stand. She gazed up at her mother, waiting for approval. "Look at you," said Erin, her mind still on Busy. "You're standing!"

"She's going to walk any day," predicted Beulah Ann, drying a serving bowl that didn't fit in the dishwasher.

"Who's Busy?" Erin asked.

WHEN ABE WAS FOURTEEN, his ten-year-old sister had fallen between the wheels of a tractor and been killed. Beulah Ann thought it was somehow related to the Cockburn parents' divorce, but she didn't know the whole story. And when she got that far, she seemed to feel like she was gossiping and stopped altogether.

"Horse," said Maeve as Erin carried her past the corral. She was pointing at Noon.

"Yes, that's Noon. He's a horse."

The helicopter came over, a shadow sweeping the road and disappearing beyond the near ridge. Slowly, its chatter left silence.

"Da-dee?" Maeve was still looking at the horse.

Erin wasn't sure what she meant, but she gave it her best shot. "He'll come get us tomorrow. We're all going to a rodeo."

And she had to tell her father they were leaving early.

She was going to tell him more.

Kip's pickup truck was dead ahead, a quarter mile up the road, parked beside the north pasture. Erin walked toward it with her daughter in her arms, trying to step in the snow, instead of the mud where the snow had melted. She passed the barn. She passed the carcasses, some of them skinned and raw and rotting beside the shed. She passed Mears Cabin.

Erin rehearsed as she walked. The cold air on her face helped her nerve. It was honest, like the dead grass and the snow and the Rockies. She would be like that, too, and the truth couldn't hurt her.

He was alone in the pasture. Glancing up, he saw her coming and stood still. Erin kept moving her legs, kept marching toward him in the withering sunlight. Eventually he slogged through the snow and mud and old yellow grass, and they faced each other across the barbed-wire fence in the sunlight of a March afternoon.

"What can I do for you?" He was weary and matter-of-fact—slightly tense and plainly ambivalent. "Everything all right in the cabin?"

"Everything's been perfect. I've actually decided to leave early."

He lifted his eyebrows.

A breeze gusted through her like the truth.

"Before I go," said Erin, "I want you to know…"

His expression hardened almost imperceptibly, but she ignored the cue. She was a wind that couldn't be stopped, and she said, "I'm your daughter."

Then, as though the wind had died, came the wait. A calf bawled somewhere behind him, and Erin watched his face. But his features didn't shift, and the silence became ghastly, eternal. His eyes were pale blue, like Chaley's. Impassive.

"I have just one daughter, Erin."

Another soft breeze made sounds she didn't register. Things blowing.

His words went through her, and it wasn't a shock, though she flashed on an imagined scene of her mother facing a man with a gun, a man she knew, and realizing he was going to kill her.

Maeve sat quietly in Erin's arms, a leg dangling on each

side of her mother's hip, watching cows. Pointing to a calf, she said, "Da-dee."

Dogie. Erin suppressed a wild impulse to laugh.

Keep it together. Keep it together. Be a cowboy, Erin.

Her voice shook some as she said, "Then I guess we just need to settle for my week here. I'll pay for the entire week, since I know you don't have a by-the-day rate."

"That's fine. You can give the check to Beulah Ann."

"I have cash. It's right here." Erin dipped into the pocket of her duster. Watching her fingers and the paper, she counted out hundred-dollar bills, the balance of what she owed. She passed the money over the barbed wire to her father, and as he took it with his work glove and pocketed it in his barn coat, Erin tried to think of the truth about cowboys.

His lie didn't change the truth. And she told herself that, told herself she was still as strong and honest as the dead grass. It did not hurt to be the grass. It did not hurt.

"Well, I'd say we're better than the next man."

—Lane Cockburn,
    discussing the truth about cowboys

CHAPTER NINE

THE LIGHT on Abe's answering machine was blinking when he came in that afternoon. He'd earned two hundred dollars in Gunnison shoeing horses and he'd just returned to shoe Loren's, as well, for the rodeo.

As Martha danced around his feet, he pressed the button on the answering machine.

"Abe, this is Erin. I decided to check out of the ranch. I'm in Alta, at the Victorian Hotel, room 213. It's nice here. I just didn't want you to think I disappeared. So...I guess I'll see you here Thursday morning? Thanks. Bye."

The machine beeped, concluding the message.

She sounded nervous. But then, she'd never called him before.

Abe replayed the message and scrawled down her room number. Why had she left the ranch?

Probably the tension was too much for her. He couldn't fault her decision. It was good for him, at any rate. His father still lived and worked at the Kays', but after he picked up Noon, Abe could keep his distance. He'd hoped for a chance to talk to Kip about his dad, but maybe it was best left alone. The two men had known each other for decades. And Abe would be there for Lloyd when it was over.

Provided that *over* didn't happen this weekend, which it might. Abe had no solution to that. He'd made a commitment to Guy and another, unspoken, to Lane. Abe needed to see his brother's first professional bull ride. Because neither Lloyd nor Annabelle would.

Why had Erin left the ranch? Something was off, the way there'd been something off with her coming to stay at the Kays' in March. Her wanting to tell him about Maeve explained that, but still...

Something had happened.

He dragged out the phone directory, looked up the number of the Victorian Hotel and phoned Erin. The desk clerk put him through, and Erin answered on the first ring.

"Hello?"

"Hi. It's me. I got your message."

In the hotel room, Maeve was playing with a football-size plastic car on the four-poster bed. Erin watched her without seeing and clung to the voice on the phone. For the past two hours, ever since she'd checked in, she'd wanted to call Jayne, to tell her mother, *You were right. You were right about him.* About Kip Kay, father no more.

It wasn't any fun to want to call someone who was dead.

Abe said, "What happened?"

"I left." She was honest. She had become honest that afternoon, and she didn't need to know the truth about cowboys now that she had said the words she'd said.

It does not hurt.

"You could have come here."

To his trailer at Guy Loren's. Not a chance. She wasn't going to cry on anyone's shoulder about this. Why cry, when she'd been courageous, when she'd confronted her greatest bugaboo?

"Erin?"

"I didn't want to show up at your place without being invited."

"You're invited now."

"Well, I paid for tonight. And tomorrow we're leaving for the rodeo, right?"

"Have you had dinner?"

He sounded almost stern, like he knew something was wrong and suspected she wasn't taking care of herself. Till now, no man had ever talked to her that way.

"No," said Erin. "We haven't eaten." When had his voice become a friend? When had *he* become one?

"I'll be up there in a half hour," said Abe. "After I have a shower. We'll go to the North Forty. Good steaks."

No cowboys, Erin thought. "Okay," she said. *Hurry, Abe.*

ERIN ANSWERED the door in a purple shirt and matching jeans. She looked like nothing was wrong.

But she'd left the ranch. For some reason she had left.

The hotel room was furnished with Tiffany lamps and antique nightstands. The wallpaper was tiny flowers, like the flowers on Maeve's corduroy overalls, and his boots looked messy on the gray plush carpet.

On the bed, Maeve smiled. "Da-dee."

Abe lifted her to his side, met her eyes. "Hi, Maeve. How's my girl? Round up any cattle for me?"

Erin stood at the window chewing her nails. She didn't watch Abe and Maeve. She didn't want to think about Abe or rely on him. He was just someone to be near. Dinner would help. You didn't need anyone when you knew yourself—and knew you were honest. She really was perfectly fine.

"You look pretty."

"Oh, thanks." He hadn't taken off his denim jacket, so he must be hungry for dinner. "Let me get my things."

The tote bag was ready. She shrugged into her duster and picked up Maeve's parka. While Abe guided the baby's arms into the sleeves, fishing in the cuffs to pull her little hands through, Erin stared across dusky rooftops to the gray-white mountains. No stars, no moon. She couldn't see the lights of the ski village from here, but the hotel was full of skiers; it must be spring break.

"Why did you leave?"

She snapped her head around. "What?"

Maeve was stuffing the collar of his shirt into her mouth. Abe set her on her feet on the floor, and the baby clung to the bed and tried walking. "Why did you leave the Kays'?"

Why.

Of course he would ask.

"Did something happen?"

Erin remembered the mud on the road where she'd stood. The mountains that were what they appeared and nothing more and nothing less. Hadn't she promised to tell him sometime why her heroes had always been cowboys? She'd said the truth once today.

You're my friend, she thought. *You let me ride Buy Back.* The striped sateen chair by the window was ready support. Erin folded herself into it, gripping the arms like an old woman beginning the story of her life. "Kip Kay is my father," she said, and time creaked by with the rhythm of a rocker till her next words. They poured out slowly. "My mother was his first wife. They were married fresh out of high school, and he was drafted. While he was in Vietnam, his father died, and when he came home on compassionate leave, he and my mother conceived me. He was home again, for good, three months later, but my mother said he was different from the man she'd married. She said he was unfaithful and an alcoholic and…scary. So she left."

The rhythm of the words carried her on. Talking loosened rocks and debris inside her, old junk, but it scattered free in a steady flow, no avalanche. There was no rush to tell Abe; a man who waited for cows to calve didn't know hurry. So she took her time.

"I'd never seen him in my life," said Erin. "He'd never tried to see me. But…when my mother died, it became important to see him. Like I needed to find you, for Maeve.

"I never thought I'd tell him who I was. That wasn't the point. I thought I'd just see him, see who he was. But—" She stopped, not wanting to say why knowing the truth was so important. She didn't want Abe to know how many cowboys had dumped her. "Since I had to tell him I was leaving Thursday for the rodeo, I decided to tell him I was his daughter, too. So I went out to the pasture to see him. I told him I was his d-daughter. He said…" Erin told it. Repeated her father's words. When she felt the tears on her lashes and cheeks, she thought, *The grass cries, too, in the morning, when there's dew on it.*

It did not hurt.

Maeve's sudden tears brought her out of her trance. Erin came up from underwater, and Maeve was staring at her face and crying.

"It's all right, Maeve." Damn, her breasts were going to leak. Erin wiped her eyes with the back of her hand.

"Mama." Crying, Maeve let go of the bed and toddled four steps to her.

"Maeve! You walked!" Erin scooped her up. Maeve was so sensitive, so connected to her. "I love you," she whispered. Abe handed her a bandanna, and Erin wiped her eyes, comforted by a piece of cloth and by Maeve's bottom on her lap. "Mommy's okay, Maeve. You took your first steps. Aren't you proud of yourself?"

After a moment Maeve reached for her bunny, and Erin got up to set her on the spread. She dabbed at her eyes again and didn't give back the bandanna and didn't plan to. "Let's go to dinner, Abe. I'm really okay."

When she turned, she bumped into him. He caught her arm, and Erin studied his hand. His shirt cuffs weren't frayed, but new. He'd dressed up for her. The shirt had an Aztec design and black buttons, and where it was open, she could see his throat. His mouth and eyes held her for a long time.

"I want to sleep over." The rodeo belt buckle almost touching her was a force field.

"Why?"

Abe released her to hold the collar of her coat, to turn it up because it was cold outside, because it was going to snow again. "Because I think about you too much." *I see your eyes when other things are in front of me.* "I like you better than Martha."

She crossed her arms and Abe tightened his grip on her coat. His voice would only stay low. "And I want you how I wanted Buy Back after I sold him."

He held her by her coat and stifled the words he couldn't say about a man he'd known all his life. *And he hurt you! Dammit, how could he hurt you like that?*

THE NORTH FORTY was gone, the windows empty and painted with the words COMING NEXT WEEK: RUNNING DEER GALLERY.

His favorite restaurant was gone.

Embarrassed that he hadn't known, Abe said, "Well, let's go…" He cast his eyes across the snowy street, over the ski racks on the roofs of parked Jeep Cherokees and Saabs. While people his age rode past on mountain bikes, he strained through the dark to read the shingles swaying over the sidewalk.

Alta had plenty of restaurants. Italian, vegetarian. Holding Maeve, Abe drew Erin back under the old North Forty's awning as a man and woman in matching leather coats and hats walked past.

When he was a kid, this was *town.* Now, he always went to Gunnison for supplies; no one could afford Alta's prices. Abe felt out of place, a century removed from the mountain bikers and snowboarders. Because he had to suggest a restaurant quickly, had to get Erin and Maeve out of the weather, he chose the only one he could think of that he'd been told served steaks. "I guess we'll go to the Okay Corral."

The route took them past a three-story stone building with a historical marker in front. A four-inch layer of snow was heaped on top of the sign, and Erin had to brush more snow away from the front to read the history of the old hospital. Now it housed the Alta museum.

Abe tugged Maeve's floppy-brimmed pile hat down around her ears, keeping her warm. "Think you could get a job here?"

Shivering, Erin eyed the closed door. "It's probably run by volunteers. These small local museums are usually run on a shoestring. But I'd love to go in when it's open."

"I'll take you sometime."

They walked on through the fluffy flakes.

The restaurant sat on the outskirts of Alta on a wide lot with plenty of parking. It was a grand cedar-sided barn, and signs at the entrance read, LINE DANCING EVERY NIGHT.

"Pretty building," Erin said as Abe held the door. He'd put Maeve down, and the baby practiced her new skills, teetering into the restaurant on her own two feet.

A blond woman with a fringed leather jacket and matching miniskirt beamed at them on her way to the waitress station. "Be right with you." She noticed Maeve's wobbly walk and said, "Well, look at you!"

Maeve laughed up at her, then fell over sideways like a drunk stumbling off a curb. Abe crouched near the baby, and a smile lit Maeve's face again. "Da-dee."

"Maevey."

A lantern made from a tin can punched with holes lit their booth—a thick pine table and good vinyl-covered seat edged with brass tacks. The waitress brought Maeve a maple high chair, and the baby gazed, mesmerized, at the flame in the can.

"This is nice, Abe."

He thought so, too, though he wouldn't have said it where anyone could hear. The I'm Okay, You're Okay Corral was owned by one of the most rabid developers in the Alta area, who made his fortune converting family-owned ranches to subdivisions with houses every half acre.

Erin sensed what he didn't say, that this was the lair of the new cowboys. "Beulah Ann said that if Jack Draw sells, you might want to buy his brand?"

"Our brand."

Smiling, Erin wriggled her hand into the stuffed tote bag and drew out the plastic dog Beulah Ann had given Maeve for her birthday. Maeve reached for it with both hands, but Erin cleared a path on the table, instead. Setting the dog so it faced Maeve, she pressed a knob on its head. It shut its eyes and lifted one ear, then the other. Its eyes shot open, its tongue popped out, and it rolled slowly toward Maeve, who watched studiously.

Abe studied Erin in the candlelight, trying to see a resemblance to Kip. And to Chaley.

He saw some. Her nose and chin were just like her dad's. You thought you knew a man. Kip must be worried now; Chaley sure didn't know about Erin, and Erin held the cards. But Abe couldn't picture Erin making a scene.

She hadn't wanted him to see her cry.

Insight came like a pile driver out of the chute. Wranglers. Riding lessons. Rodeos. A doctorate in Cows.

Her heroes had always been cowboys, and he knew why. She loved cowboys. Because she loved her dad. Without even knowing him. She'd come here to Alta...

To Alta.

Keep your head, Abe.

He kept his thoughts, too. Kept them quiet.

The waitress came around and they ordered. Then Maeve began to fuss, refusing to drink from the bottle of juice Erin had brought. Erin took a receiving blanket from the

tote bag, got Maeve out of her high chair and turned toward
the wall to nurse. As Maeve latched onto her and the milk
let down, Erin relived the first day she'd come to the Kay
Ranch, nursing in the kitchen. The approval she thought
she'd received from her father.

It doesn't hurt. You never cared, Erin.

Maeve jerked away, not really wanting to nurse, something that happened often lately. It was time to wean her.
She began to cry, and Erin unfastened a teething ring from
the tote bag.

Abe was thinking about Alta, about being a bullfighter
clown from Alta. He stood and reached for Maeve. "I'll
take her for a walk."

He lifted the baby and settled her against his shoulder,
where Maeve laid her head sleepily, still sniffling. His jeans
passed Erin's eyes as he carried their child toward the dark
and deserted dance floor.

Good father.

I have just one daughter, Erin.

On the dance floor, Abe turned about with Maeve in his
arms, singing to her. Erin craved a pint of Jack Daniel's.

She'd said she was his daughter. She should be cured of
cowboys now. But Abe had asked to spend the night, and
she'd agreed. Liking her more than his dog and wanting
her more than Buy Back were lines she couldn't resist.

They're not lines.

Yes, they are.

She still couldn't say no to cowboys.

She couldn't say no to Abe. Abe, revolving on the dance
floor with Maeve, who was Daddy's girl and the light in
his eyes.

So I can't say no to him. So what?

So, it would kill her if he dumped her. *Again.*

He never dumped you; he dumped Chaley.

That didn't comfort her. And *no cowboys* wasn't going
to help, not now.

It never had.

Erin tipped back her head, eyeing the chandeliers made from wagon wheels. *No cowboys* wouldn't work. She needed something else.

When she righted her head, she peered through the darkness at the silhouette scene played against a backdrop of red velvet curtains. Cowboy hat and floppy baby's hat, Wrangler legs and boot heels. Maeve's baby hand reached up to touch the square jaw of a descendant of the people who'd settled the West.

Erin forged a tenacity that would put her half sister to shame.

"Cowboy," she said, "you're mine."

She made a vow, and she swore it on the barbed-wire fence where her father had totally and completely rejected her. Erin Mackenzie had been Dumped by Cowboys for the last time.

BEFORE THEY LEFT for dinner, Abe had asked for a crib to be brought up to the hotel room. When they returned, it was there, and Maeve was so sleepy she drifted off while Erin changed her for bed.

Erin wasn't grateful. Because it was down to the matter of sleeping with Abe again and not getting hurt. Not getting left.

Jayne would have suggested—in fact, on occasion *had* suggested—that a little hard-to-get wouldn't hurt.

Too late. There was a cowboy on the bed, with his boots and his hat off. She'd had his baby and he was spending the night.

Erin sat in the wing chair and bent over to untie the laces on her boots. "Your dad's amazing," she said so it wouldn't be quiet in the room. "He told me about your grandfather knowing the blizzard was coming."

"And the hair on the barn."

"Yes." No wonder Abe wanted their brand back. Erin

wished he could get it. But the West had already been won, and from now on it could only be bought and sold. Not the hardy or the brave, but the highest bidder would win.

The bed creaked. Abe phoned for a wake-up call, then stood and stretched. Erin dared to meet his eyes.

When he sat down on the edge of the mattress, near her, Erin asked the knees of his jeans, "Does your dog really write you notes?"

She wouldn't look up, so Abe read her question, turned it over and looked at the other side. She was in the game but bidding low; they could joke about "licking." Abe sat motionless, stuck in his own hand. He knew how to bluff and win, but he'd never told a woman he cared.

If he did, it would have to be without words. He didn't know the right ones. What came out was, "I want to kill your father."

Erin laughed, flushing.

Somehow, he *had* said the right thing.

Her eyes were with him then. He could see twin reflections of the Tiffany lamp in her irises. Her graduate-student skin, so much paler and finer than a cowgirl's, got to him. So did her mouth and thinking about the glimpse he'd had of one erect enlarged nipple while Maeve was messing around, not nursing.

You're in trouble, Abe. You're over your head.

He said, "You used me."

Erin jerked her head up, and he was waiting, eyes unblinking. This was the part where she got dumped, and she didn't know why. She tossed her head, used a hand to hold her bangs out of her eyes. "No."

The clock whirred on the nightstand. "What do you mean?" She felt her lips shaking, as though she were lying.

"Alta."

Nobody had ever talked to her like this. So straight that she knew what a single word meant. "I showed up in Twin

Falls." When his eyes didn't change, she said, "I had your child. Let's not talk about 'used.'"

His eyes kept watching, and she watched back until it became a different kind of looking. Time moved in the slow beats of a Patsy Cline song. "You're Stronger than Me."

He was leaning toward her, and Erin's lips met his, and her eyes watered. His hands took her face.

In bed with her just a little while later, Abe still felt the stuck words, the hand he couldn't play. He kissed them into her mouth, not knowing what they were. This was not Reno. This was not sex as he'd known it.

The insides of her thighs were soft in his hands. He held her and opened her and kissed her.

Erin heard her own moans. "Abe..." The blackness she'd known earlier that day was just outside the circle of pleasure. She could almost not see it. His fingers opened her, slipped inside her and he stroked her with his tongue. "Abe." *I don't want you to know me.*

But this was different from Reno. Different from ever.

He was careful with the condom this time, but it took too long. Long enough for her to forget the way he'd looked at her. His entering her was a return to the graveyard where she'd buried all her hopes and dreams.

Seeing her face, her closed eyes, he knew where she was. The place where fathers rejected you and someone shot your mother. And cowboys didn't show up in Twin Falls.

"Erin."

Her beautiful dark eyes opened.

"Be with me."

The eyes cried.

"It's okay." He laid his body against hers and felt the breasts that nourished his child leak milk against him.

"It doesn't hurt, Abe. It didn't hurt at all."

Bull riders always said the same thing. "I know."

But her eyes still cried and her tears said, *I'll call.* They said, *Show your hand. Like my daddy showed his.*

She was too damned used to letting men go.

He's a son of a bitch, Erin. His arms tried to hold all of her, her breasts and arms and tears and the head that knew all about cowboys. That knew too much.

Erin couldn't stop crying, but it was okay. This friend was with her, and he was such a good friend she could ask him for the truth about cowboys. She could ask him what she couldn't ask a man with two daughters who said he had just one. She could ask him what she'd known never to ask Jayne.

And she was crying so hard it didn't matter, it didn't matter if she said it out loud, if she wept it to Abe and the words were incoherent. *"Why doesn't he want me?"*

"And my gal has gone away,
Left my shack and traveled away
With a son of a gun from Io-way
And left me a lone man, a lone man today."

—"Ten Thousand Cattle,"
Nineteenth-century cowboy song

CHAPTER TEN

"I MADE HIM a pencil holder in day camp for Father's Day.
I didn't want to. I wanted to make something for my mom
and pretend I had a dad to give it to. The counselor kept
asking me what my father liked, so I said cows, and then
I was cutting out pictures of cows. I pasted them on this
orange-juice can. Then, the day we took it home, I threw
it in the outside trash can where my mom wouldn't see it."
The clock whirred in darkness. "I've never told anyone
that."

And she told him about the older kids making juice-can
pencil holders at Maeve's day care. And about his being
on the cover of *Prorodeo Sports News* the same day. She
told him about the manila envelope, and then she was
naked.

Sometime after midnight he said, "I want you to move
in with me. I want to drive to Reno after the rodeo and get
your stuff."

His hands and body had heated her skin for hours. There
was no pain anymore. Just a bliss so complete that Kip Kay

was irrelevant. What Abe said wasn't, and she imagined packing up everything in her mother's house.

It had to happen, anyhow; the sale would close soon, and where would she go? Earlier that day, she'd checked her answering machine long-distance. No one calling to request an interview. "I don't have a job here."

"That's okay."

I'll have some money from the sale of the house. His engagement with Chaley, the fact that he might have married for land, nagged at her for one second, then went away.

"Okay," she said.

Abe didn't answer. Her head was against his chest, and she raised it to see if he'd fallen asleep. His mouth was a bleak line that changed only when he saw her notice. "Great. Thanks."

"What's wrong?"

"Nothing." Abe hugged her. Nothing was wrong, except that soon he'd be out of a job, too. Looking for a new one, to carry him high and fast to his goals.

He would reach them, whatever it took, and someday he'd have a ranch of his own, a ranch for Erin and Maeve. But when he imagined that time, he thought of the best cowboy he knew, who wouldn't drive a tractor or pull a horse trailer again. He saw Jack Draw's lodge-pole fence and developers coming and going in helicopters.

He saw a world that had become hostile to his dreams.

THEY ARRIVED at Guy Loren's place at five the next morning. While Erin went back to sleep with Maeve in the fifth wheel, Abe helped him load broncs and bulls into semi trucks for the drive to Nevada. Buy Back would travel with the other horses so that Abe could go to Reno with Erin to help her move. Martha would ride in the truck bed, under the camper shell.

"So you've got a family now," remarked the stock contractor, who never asked what had become of Chaley. "Yes."

Loren must have seen the future in the clouds. "There's room here for a bigger trailer than that fifth wheel. Feel free to bring one in."

"Thanks." He needed more than a bigger home. Abe worked twelve-hour days for Loren, feeding the stock, helping with calving and foaling, mending fences, shoeing horses, trimming the bulls' hooves. "But I can't support a family on four hundred a month."

Steam from the trucks billowed around the stock contractor while he considered. "Five do you?"

Loren gave him gas, food for the horses, the fifth wheel and utilities. *We could get by,* thought Abe.

But he wanted more than that for Maeve.

And he wanted to give Erin what Kip Kay never would. *I've wanted to live on a ranch my whole life.*

"Well, you think on it," said Loren. "Let's put Buy Back in the big trailer with the ropers."

At six Lane showed up in his quarter-ton pickup, fired with energy, like a gun ready to go off.

When he could get in a word around Lane's running commentary on the bulls, Abe asked, "Kip or Dad hasn't said anything about the driver's license?" The rancher's name was a bad taste in his mouth.

"Nah. Dad was saddling Bo when I left."

"Did you remember to say goodbye?"

"I did. He said, 'Don't break your neck like your brother.'"

When they returned from Reno, Abe decided, he would go see his dad, even if it meant running into Kip Kay. He didn't believe the rancher would let Lloyd stay on as foreman with no license. And if he didn't...

Maybe we can all leave together. Get out of Colorado and try Wyoming or Montana. He didn't think about real-estate prices climbing in those states, too. About land values climbing all over the West. He'd find a way.

Because he never wanted Erin to have to see her father again. He never wanted Maeve to have to know him.

And it would kill Lloyd Cockburn to learn he was working for a man who wouldn't acknowledge their mutual grandchild.

ABE'S AND LANE'S PICKUPS led the semis down the road and soon lost them. Clear skies and dry pavement started the day, and when the sun came up, as they neared Delta, Colorado, the snow had disappeared.

He and Erin listened to music and talked. Abe asked about Maeve's birth and learned Jayne Mackenzie was there and that Maeve had been pink and pretty from the start. He learned Jayne had been shot in the chest with a .38. He learned Erin had had the living room repainted and the carpet replaced. She couldn't sell the house the way it was.

He learned it was hard to travel to a rodeo with a one-year-old baby.

All the way they startled magpies and ravens in the road, eating the unlucky. Raptors circled high over Utah's San Rafael Swell, so many that Abe wondered what was dead or dying there.

Heading south on I-15, Erin suddenly turned down the stereo. "Abe, Beulah Ann said you had a sister."

"Yeah. Busy. She fell between the wheels of the tractor while my dad was baling hay. She liked to ride with him."

"When did your folks get divorced?"

"Oh, you want the *whole* story." He told her about the days after Busy died, about his mother's leaving. "My dad said that Mom didn't know where she'd be going, that she'd be looking for a job, that she couldn't take care of us for a while. I was a teenager and wanted to stay where I was. I loved the ranch. But Lane loved Mom. He used to ask me every day when she was coming to get us." His voice quit him then. Lane was two vehicles ahead in his silver-blue pickup. The eighteen-year-old Lane. At six he'd been sweet. He'd turned from hopeful to heartbroken to bitter to thoughtless.

Did Erin need to know more? The phone call on Lane's birthday was worth a mention. "She hasn't been to Colorado since she left us. It sounded like she really wanted to see Maeve. But I'm not going to hold my breath." A prairie dog ran between his wheels and lived.

"It's interesting," Erin said, "that your mother and my mother both left their husbands."

"And for about the same reasons, sounds like."

"What's that?" As best Erin could make out, Abe's mother had left because she couldn't stand the pain of living on the place where her child had died. Jayne had left Kip because—

"Fear."

Passing a truck, Abe caught sight of Lane's bumper stickers. I'M A LOVER, FIGHTER AND WILD BULL RIDER. COWBOYS DO IT ALL. The seal of the National Rifle Association stained his rear windshield.

Lane was pulling off at a diner and Abe flipped his turn signal. As he shut off the engine outside the restaurant, he saw Erin twisting gingerly to unbuckle Maeve. "What's wrong?"

"Oh. I'm engorged. I'm weaning her."

He winced. Cows were never happy in that state of affairs; he doubted women liked it, either. "Is there anything you can do?"

She shrugged. "It should just last a few days. But she flinched again as she started to lift the waking Maeve from her seat.

"I've got her." But Abe leaned toward Erin first, knocking her brow with the brim of his hat before he managed to kiss her.

"WHAT ARE YOU telling me, Abe?" asked the announcer.

Erin shifted a restless Maeve in her lap. In the center of the Laughlin arena, Abe raised one hand and bounced, as though he was on the back of a bull.

"You want to be a *bull rider?*"

Nodding. Swagger. Abe rooted through his satchel and pulled out a pair of pink chaps with green fringe. They looked like they'd been made from a tablecloth.

"And you even have some new chaps."

"That's Daddy," Erin told Maeve. "Do you see Daddy?"

"Da-dee?" asked Maeve, not finding him nearby. "Da-dee?"

Oh, God, we're a family. It was relief and bliss at once. After letting Abe really see her last night and finding she was loved, anyhow, Erin had started on a full-speed gallop, and she was still riding, and she'd already forgotten what it was like to be thrown.

"Abe," the announcer was saying, "if you want to ride a bull, you need to go to the chutes. Go to the chutes, and they'll let you ride a bull. They said so. Why, Marauder is all ready for you."

But the clown argued, shaking his head.

Erin wanted to see better. She picked up her tote bag. "Let's go down to the fence, Maeve."

"All right, Abe, we'll let you do this your way. Now, we're going to let Marauder into the ring. Are you ready to ride him?"

Abe was cool. Abe was ready to ride. Abe was making hundreds of people laugh. Their laughter exploded around Erin as she negotiated the wooden steps, picking her way over half-eaten hot dogs and strewn buns and mustard.

A gate opened and a gray bull with a Brahma-type hump trotted into the arena, spotted Abe and stopped. Abe tiptoed toward it and the bull trotted away.

"Abe, how do you expect to get on that bull when it won't hold still?"

Finding an empty seat in the front row, Erin set Maeve on her feet. The baby squatted in the dust and slowly lifted her plastic dog out of the tote bag. Erin marveled at Abe. Mixing athletic skill with a clown's clumsiness, he ran toward the bull in the most ridiculous way imaginable and sprang onto its back.

The crowd's breath was a drumbeat through the arena.

Marauder came to a dead stop.

"Abe, that bull's not bucking too good. Why don't you spur him some?"

Abe spurred.

The bull would not move. Laughter rolled over the stands.

Abe slid off the bull, then came around in front of it, drawing out a bandanna to use as a matador's cape.

Marauder's head shifted from side to side. Then lowered. As he charged, Abe vaulted over his head and landed on his back, facing the tail.

Surely, Erin thought, it wasn't supposed to happen this way. It was all going too fast, with Abe being bucked through the air off the back of that bull, tumbling onto the ground. Scrambling to his feet, he ran, with the bull chasing, and Erin tried to revive the feelings of the first night she'd watched him clown and bullfight. When it didn't matter if he tripped and fell.

Abe hit the fence and flipped over it, and only then did Erin notice that her jaw hurt, that she'd been clenching it.

"Well, Abe, you didn't make eight seconds, but what do you say, folks? Let's give this cowboy a hand." Even the announcer was chuckling.

Cowboys would be cowboys, from Theseus to Abe. Erin asked Maeve, "Isn't Daddy silly?"

Maeve raised her head, hunting for him. "Da-dee?"

"Now, let's introduce you to our next bull rider. This

cowboy is from Alta, Colorado, and he's the brother of our bullfighter clown, Abe. Lane Cockburn is a rookie who went to the high-school national finals, and this is his first professional rodeo. Let's see if this cowboy can bring home some money on Lightning Rod.''

Abe and another bullfighter waited near the chutes. When number three opened, a black-Angus cross sprang out, bucking and spinning. Abe danced near the bull, turning him, helping his brother's score. Lane's arm sailed high, his body hung loose, and his turquoise chaps flapped and shimmered with each movement of the bull. When the bell rang, he dismounted with a well-timed leap to the ground and landed on his feet.

Erin jumped up, cheering at the top of her lungs till Maeve lifted her eyes, bewildered.

Even the announcer raised his voice to be heard over the roar from the stands. ''Ladies and gentlemen, that is how the cowboys do it! You have just seen some *buulll* riding!''

''*Yes,* Lane,'' whispered Erin as he hurled his hat in the air. Because superimposed on the eighteen-year-old athlete, she saw a six-year-old boy asking when his mother was coming to get him.

Lane's score was seventy-eight, and Erin was so excited for him that she scarcely listened to the next rider's introduction. A Brahma bull leaped out of a chute, losing his rider on the second buck. The cowboy fell directly under the bull's head, and its horns tossed him like laundry in the dryer while a figure in a patchwork shirt and Wranglers pushed on the animal's head, shoving against him.

Abe.

''Mama. Da-dee.'' Maeve pointed at a puppy going past on a leash.

The bull knocked Abe over, and its weight-bearing back hooves came down on his shoulder. Erin understood about seeing things in slow motion. Seeing him scramble away.

Seeing him run, holding his shoulder, to the edge of the arena.

Erin stuffed everything in the tote bag and scooped up Maeve. Her engorged breasts felt like hardwood, ready to break off if they were bumped. The announcer was talking about the brave bullfighters, assuring the audience that Abe was all right but was going to visit the paramedics. He thanked Justin Boots for their mobile sports-medicine program, which made emergency medical care available at professional rodeos.

Abe was sitting in the back of the ambulance, getting his shoulder wrapped, when Erin found him. Lane and Martha were with him, Lane still flying high after his ride. As Erin joined them, Abe winked at her and told Lane, "You'll have to beat seventy-eight if you want to impress Beulah Ann."

Maeve made a sound asking to get down, and when Erin let her stand in the dirt, she toddled toward Martha. "Da-dee."

"Beulah Ann's impressed," Lane said knowingly.

And Erin saw Beulah Ann drying dishes and singing "Someday Soon," and she knew the reason for the song.

Abe grew interested in watching the paramedic finish binding his shoulder. "Thanks."

As a mutt trotted past, Maeve earned Lane's disinterested glance by waddling after it. He was closest to her and didn't move. Erin took two steps to pick her up, but Martha beat her to the scene. The Australian shepherd froze in front of the baby, held her ground and herded her back to Abe and Erin. Maeve put her hands up to Martha's head and giggled at a tongue licking her face. Then she turned and toddled to Abe.

"Good dog," he told Martha, and asked the paramedic, "Isn't that the smartest dog you ever saw?"

"Just about."

Erin helped him with his shirt and his suspenders. Her

fingers liked even the sweat-soaked cloth of his shirt. He was warm—and hers. "Think they'll give you a reride on Marauder?"

Nearby Lane sang Chris LeDoux's "Reride" and threw his hat in the air again. Abe didn't smile at what she'd said, and Erin wondered if he, too, was thinking about Lane and Beulah Ann.

IN ABE'S OPINION, nothing short of a bone sticking through his skin deserved an X ray. And nothing less than a broken neck could have kept him from bullfighting and clowning over the next days. Filing this information under the truth about cowboys, Erin enjoyed the rodeo. Abe looked after Maeve so Erin could ride Buy Back before the performances. He introduced her to the other bullfighters, who treated her like a lady and flirted with the baby. And Lane kept the lead four days running and finished out the rodeo with eight thousand dollars in cash.

Erin learned more about Abe.

That he'd always loved clowns and that he'd only been a bulldogger two weeks before he decided he'd rather be a bull*fighter*. That, like every rodeo cowboy she'd ever met, he really wanted to raise cows—his own. That the loss of his father's ranch had colored his horizons the shade of futility. And that she might find a rose on her pillow from time to time.

If she'd had seventy-five million dollars, she would have given him back the ranch. Short of that, she created other dreams.

Sunday night, after the last performance, Erin and Abe drove to Reno, an eight-hour trek. They arrived at Erin's mother's house, the scene of Jayne's murder, at five in the morning. In Erin's room they set up Erin's old crib for Maeve, and when the baby was asleep, they made love in the bed where they'd conceived her.

In the morning Erin phoned her attorney, told him she

was moving, and made arrangements to come by and give him power of attorney so that he could close on the house and finish settling her mother's estate. As Abe helped Maeve with her breakfast dish of applesauce at the kitchen table, Erin said, "We've got to pick up Taffy, too."

"Who's Taffy?"

"My mother's cocker spaniel."

Abe remembered Taffy. She would never make a decent cow dog. In fact, she was the kind of creature that gave dogs a bad name. "I'll get her when I pick up the U-Haul."

"Thank you."

"Want to come with me, Maeve? We can have a good time in Reno."

He spent the next few hours helping Erin pack boxes, but at eleven she caught him loafing in the bedroom with Maeve. The baby was pulling tissues out of a box one by one. Abe was reading her doctoral thesis.

Erin left them there, and Abe didn't say anything about it when he came downstairs with Maeve. The two of them headed out to drop off some boxes and furniture they didn't want at the Salvation Army, rent the trailer and pick up the dog.

Even after he'd gone, the house felt safe. But Erin was glad to be leaving it.

She'd already sorted through her mother's closet, saving a few clothes and some jewelry, boxing the rest to give away. She planned to keep the cedar chest Jayne had kept at the end of her bed, but she should also go through the contents.

On the top layer inside was a patchwork quilt Erin had asked years before if she could have. *No, it was my grandmother's.* Jayne's family was all gone.

I could have had family from the Kays' side, thought Erin. Beulah. Chaley.

It wasn't worth contemplating.

The box beneath the quilt contained her mother's

wedding dress, which Jayne had let her try on when she was in high school. Erin set it on the bed, then lifted the lids on the shoe and hat boxes beneath. Costume jewelry. Photos.

Letters from Vietnam.

Erin snatched up the shoe box, tearing one side of the flimsy cardboard. Hurrying, shaking, she made a place for herself on the bed. She'd found her mother's letters from her father.

And she was going to read them.

The paper crackled as she opened the first airmail envelope with its military address and foreign stamps. Vietnam had happened before she was born and had taught Erin that war was a call for peace. Movies showed gore and evil and brutality. The writings of veterans told more, and Erin had read them until she thought she grasped the war and its aftermath as well as she could any history she hadn't lived.

But Kip Kay had been there.

And he wasn't what she'd expected at all. He wasn't like her history professor, or the man who ran the dry cleaner she and her mother had used, or their mail carrier, or Dan in the wheelchair at the university library, or any of the other Vietnam vets Erin knew, slightly or otherwise. Those men wore their sensitivity in their eyes and their smiles. Even their joy, friendliness at seeing her, had an aching quality, as though they had become helpless channels for emotion. She thought their pain must fill their whole insides, pack every pore.

She found them beautiful.

But she could only see Kip Kay through the eyes of the daughter he did not want.

Erin unfolded a letter.

"ERIN?"

Taffy raced ahead of Abe into the house, sniffing corners,

madly wagging her tail. While Martha demonstrated more reserve, Abe set down Maeve, who wanted to walk. She made straight for the nearest dog, who was Martha.

"Erin?" he repeated.

Then he saw her, outside in a chaise longue, her face pointed to the sun, dark glasses over her eyes. Abe crossed the room, slid open the door and went out. "Hi." He kept an eye on Maéve and grinned as Martha herded her toward him.

Erin's eyes shifted from his boots and jeans to Maeve, who paused before testing out the step at the door. She couldn't decide whether to ask Abe to read her father's letters or to keep them to herself. The earlier letters were a man's attempt to conceal ugliness from his loved ones. In later epistles he'd told things.

It was hard to be a cowboy in Quang Ngai Province in 1969. It was hard to be at all.

"You okay?" Abe crouched beside her chair. He wished he hadn't left her alone in the house where her mother was murdered. Alone with her memories.

"Yes. Hello, Maeve."

"Mama."

Erin lifted the baby into the chair. The sun felt too intense on her skin; she burned easily, and she knew they should go inside. "I found my father's letters to my mother. From when he was in Vietnam."

Abe backed up and sat in the other folding chair. His hat cast a shadow across Maeve's body.

"She shouldn't have left him, Abe. She said he was scary. But I bet he was just afraid. Intense. He needed her."

Abe didn't know what to say. Except, "That doesn't make up for what he did to you."

"It does." She lowered Maeve to the ground, got up and went inside. She'd packed the letters in her duffel bag in the living room. Now she brought one out to him. "Read that."

Not sure he wanted to, Abe opened the envelope and unfolded the sheet inside. He read the whole letter, then folded it and replaced it in the envelope. He handed it to Erin. "Nice thing to do to your mother."

"Don't be such a cowboy," she snapped, surprising them both.

"What is *that* supposed to mean?"

"He couldn't stand it anymore! Terrible things happened to him." Erin's voice was too high, too insistent, almost hysterical. "It was my mother's fault, too. She should have gotten help for him, and she just left."

"Yeah, it's pretty easy to help a six-foot cowboy getting drunk and going bonkers on a ranch too faraway for the neighbors to hear you scream." "Scary" sounded definite to Abe—definitely not a good place for a baby. Baby Erin.

Kip Kay was an asshole.

"I don't care." Erin seemed to be gazing at the board-and-batten fence. The sunglasses hid her eyes. "Maybe she should've left, maybe not. But now I understand him. He *is* my father. And he's still my hero." Her lips trembled like they had when she'd told him her father said she wasn't his. "Just for walking around today, being sane. Just for raising Chaley to a functional adult. Just for raising cows. Just for waking up in the morning. He's my hero."

Abe had never heard anyone's voice shake like that. If he'd believed in premonition, he would have acknowledged the goose walking over his grave. Would have acknowledged that Erin's declaration meant something, some unfocused determination in her.

He didn't listen. Erin's sweet loyalty made him want to get his hands on Kip Kay's throat. So did the sight of his own daughter, with her soft red curls, lifting up her arms to him. "Da-dee."

WHEN THEY REACHED Guy Loren's place Tuesday afternoon with Abe driving the U-Haul and Erin following in her mother's car, Kip Kay's truck blocked the steps to the stock contractor's trailer. The rancher leaned against the cab while Guy Loren rested at the edge of his porch with his arms across his chest. In the truck bed, the border collie and blue heeler stood alert, watching the vehicles drive in, barking as they spotted Martha in the window of Abe's pickup. Taffy was crated in the Mustang.

Abe turned past the corral and barn. What was Kip doing here?

It took only a heartbeat to figure it out.

Kip had come to see *him,* to talk about Lloyd. About Lloyd's not being foreman anymore.

Little as Abe wanted to breathe the same air as Kip Kay, he had to face him on this. He had to find out about Lloyd so he could be there for his dad when the blow came. If it hadn't come already.

He shut off the engine, and the Mustang parked beside him. Martha was whimpering, and he let her out to go have a reunion with the Kay Ranch dogs. Erin was unbuckling Maeve. When she put the baby down on the gravel, Abe asked, "Why don't you two go on inside? Don't unload anything. I need to talk to Kip. I think he's here about my dad."

Erin's face was startlingly white, her eyes strange.

"His job," Abe explained. "His license."

"Oh."

"Hold on to Taffy. That blue dog will eat her."

He left his family and walked back toward Guy's double-wide. The snow on the road had partially melted, and mud grabbed at his boots. The dogs were out of the truck bed, making rounds with Martha. The men watched him and then Kip straightened up and came to meet him, his hat low over his eyes.

Abe felt dizzy and, when the cattleman neared him, told himself it was just the usual uneasiness that never came to anything. Kip Kay's blue eyes were sober and steady.

"Abe."

"Kip." *I hate your guts. I hate you for hurting Erin, but I'll talk to you for my daddy's sake.* "What's going on?"

"Abe, your daddy had a stroke last night. He died."

There was some kind of scream inside him. He was going to cry. Lloyd couldn't be dead.

Kip kept his eyes on him, looking like a man who had seen other men break down and knew what to do. His eyes radiated—reached out—with a compassion Abe couldn't take. He turned his back, ducked his head to keep his face in the shadow of his hat. To block the force of the afternoon sun, the spring day his father was dead.

Kip was still there, his shadow stretching beside Abe's.

Abe started to walk away, to escape the gray shape on the ground, the man who had cast it, but Kip said, "Beulah Ann took off to tell your brother. She felt, since you were on the road, that waiting till you got home would increase the chances of Lane learning it from someone else."

Half-turned, listening, Abe nodded. Lane would be coming home. He wished he could have been the one to tell him. But Lane had taken this risk in chasing rodeo.

Abe had taken it.

That his dad would be dead someday when he came back.

"In a while," said Kip, "when you're up to it, I have some business I'd like to talk with you."

"You can talk now."

The cattleman's eyes were calm. Their calm muted the impact of Abe's quick wrath. "Let's wait till your daddy's in the ground."

"You and I don't have any business we can do together when you say something to Erin like 'I have only one daughter.' Do you have grandchildren, Kip? Do you? Because I have a beautiful red-haired daughter, and I had her with your beautiful red-haired daughter. I think that makes you a grandfather, don't you?"

A gust of wind shivered through the cottonwoods. High overhead, the branches creaked. "Your daddy had wages coming." Kip unfastened a pocket of his barn coat and drew out a folded bundle of hundred-dollar bills. "One month's foreman's pay."

Money to bury Lloyd. *He knows I can't do it.* Abe watched his own hand take the bills.

"I loved your daddy." Kip's eyes were square on Abe's. "I'd like you to have his job."

He wanted to say *no.* And *I'd like you to acknowledge your daughter.*

But he had no leverage with Kip Kay. He was a good hand, but he was young, without experience in running a ranch. Only the experience of watching his own father. No one else would offer him the position of ranch foreman.

And after he'd hurt Chaley...

There wasn't anything to say. He couldn't think or fight or hate anymore. So he walked away without looking back. He walked to the corral to rest his arms on the fence and stare at Buy Back till his horse came to him, the light glinting on his shifting muscles, moving the shadows on his coat, his red mane blowing.

With Kip behind him, out of sight and mind, there was only one thought left, only one reality under the dreadful afternoon sun.

He wouldn't see Lloyd again. Not alive.

The last of the great cowboys was dead, and Abe hadn't been there to save him.

*"Those who work the land control the food.
Nature prevents their being tyrants."*

—Erin Mackenzie,
   "Cattle and Cowboys: The Ancient
   Currency of a Modern Enigma"

CHAPTER ELEVEN

WHEN HE ENTERED the trailer, Maeve's toys made an obstacle course on the floor, and the dogs ran it to get to him. Erin was on the love-seat bench, and Abe said it out loud to her eyes, trying to make it real. "My daddy had a stroke. He's dead."

Erin got up and held him. She pictured an old cowboy gracefully spinning in place, dancing with a baby in the kitchen of his trailer, heard him singing "Red River Valley." Now she would hear no more stories from the man who had ridden to school in a bus equipped with a woodstove. Whose father had predicted an afternoon blizzard by looking at a morning sky.

And Jayne was newly dead. Parents left like this, one by one. Or they left their children by choice, and death's pain came twice. Or they never arrived, like her father.

Maeve stood up, wobbled and tried walking toward Martha. "Da-gee."

"Does she know the stove is hot, Erin?"

His voice was different. Slower, like his voice was trying to go somewhere and death had caught it.

"I watch her."

Abe picked up the baby, set her near the stove and put her tiny hand against it.

"Abe!"

Maeve began to cry and pulled her hand away. She wailed, gazing up at Abe with a look that said he'd betrayed her.

Meeting her eyes, he said, "Hot." He carried her to the sink to put her hand under the cold water.

Erin had risen. "I can't believe you did that."

Maeve was still crying as Abe shut off the water.

"There's a woodstove in half the buildings in Alta. Now she knows the stove is hot. This way, she didn't get hurt."

There were names to call him. Old-fashioned, pigheaded, stupid, ignorant cowboy whose father had just died. Spreading his pain around.

Maeve cried, "Bah-bah!"

Erin took a bottle from the refrigerator and Abe reached for it. He sat down with the baby in his lap, and Maeve held the bottle and drank greedily, sniffing only occasionally. Then she threw down the bottle and cried again. Erin picked it up.

"Don't give it back," said Abe. "She can start learning not to do that right now." He let Maeve down to the floor.

Beneath the table, the baby gave the stove a look that said it, too, had betrayed her. Then she made tracks for Martha. "Da-gee."

Abe dropped the bills Kip had given him on the table. Lloyd's last pay. *Lloyd. Oh, God, Lloyd, he must be wrong.*

When would Lane hear the words that their father was dead? And Abe had to call Annabelle, had to call her right away…. His eyes were wet, stinging, as Erin slid into the booth beside him. Family had changed, and he and Erin were the head of it, and he was a child no more. He was the father. He held Erin, the mother, needing her. Her mother had been murdered, and she'd shown him how strong he could be.

When he released her, Erin saw the hundreds on the table. On the outermost bill, someone had drawn a peace sign in ballpoint pen.

They were the bills she'd given her father for her week at the ranch.

"What's that from?"

"My dad's last wages. Kip offered me his job."

The foreman's job? The foreman's job came with the foreman's trailer, on the Kay Ranch. She refused to analyze this. She had turned her back on the truth about cowboys. Or maybe she'd read it in her father's letters. He'd played dead and survived. He said the wounded cried for their mothers.

"I won't take it," said Abe. Maeve had returned to him and was holding on to his knee. "Not while he won't acknowledge his granddaughter." Lloyd's granddaughter. *Lloyd… Oh, Daddy.*

"Maybe this is his way of giving her what he can. Of giving both of us…all of us…what he can."

Abe stared. He'd held a weeping child in his arms Wednesday night. *All I wanted was the truth about cowboys.* Her words had made no sense, but she'd made plenty. He hadn't been able to tell her why her daddy didn't want her. And she'd found love letters and war letters, and on the patio of her murdered mother's house she'd said, *He's my hero.*

There were answers to that, and he could say them now, when she defiled Lloyd by pretending Kip was generous. "He's not a hero and this isn't giving. He's sick, and we'll all be better off where we can't catch it."

She was white, and her lips shook, and then she wouldn't look at him.

LANE WAS HOME the next morning, and in the afternoon Abe drove to the Kay Ranch to pick him up so they could go to the funeral home in Alta and see Lloyd.

Chaley's truck was parked by the big house. She must be back from Fort Collins, but Abe didn't see her and was glad.

Lane was waiting outside the trailer like he couldn't stand to be inside. To get in the cab, he had to scoot Martha and Taffy out of the way. "What's that?" he said of the cocker spaniel.

"Taffy." Abe opened the door to put both dogs in the back, and Taffy took off down the road, chasing a bird. "Taffy!"

She stopped, looked back and sprinted away. The blue heeler sleeping in the sun by the shed opened his eyes and lifted his head. He sat up.

"Leave her," said Lane. "Maybe something will eat her, or she'll wander in with the cows and they'll step on her."

Abe went after the cocker spaniel and found her behind the barn where George, one of the hands, had caught her. The blue heeler was wagging his tail and all but French-kissing her. The cowboy smirked as he handed over the dog.

"I didn't pick her out," Abe told him. You spent five years raising the smartest dog in the world, and God gave you this to keep her company.

George said, "Sorry about your daddy."

"Me, too."

When Abe had put both dogs in the bed of the pickup under the camper shell and joined his brother in the cab, Lane passed him a pint of Jack Daniel's. Abe took a swig, gave it back and started the truck. Nothing was going to ease this pain. He'd called Annabelle yesterday, and she had cried, too, and asked if there was anything she could do and where to send flowers.

To the same place they'd sent them for Busy. But Abe didn't say that. Only the name of the funeral home.

Annabelle did not mention coming to Colorado.

At the highway Lane got the gate. Back in the truck afterward he asked, "You ever seen a dead person?"

"Busy."

"No one offered to let me see her." He swallowed more whiskey.

It wasn't the kind of thing you showed a six-year-old. Abe wished he could make the world right for Lane. His brother's meanness was like an unripe patch on a peach. A lot of the fruit was fine, and the bitter part could be, too.

If Lane could forgive what their mother had done.

Abe had forgiven her long ago. But part of him doubted his brother ever would. And he didn't know the words to tell Lane that the resentment, if he kept it, would eat away and make him rotten inside, all the way through.

THE FUNERAL DIRECTOR, who was in shirtsleeves and jeans and boots, said, "Sure you don't want to wait till I fix him up?"

Abe shook his head without consulting Lane. He'd seen Busy before and after this same man worked on her. Dead people were dead. With makeup or without.

"Well, let me wheel him out of the lab at least."

The funeral director left them in the foyer. The whole place had a smell Abe couldn't name but remembered from Busy's death thirteen years ago. He and Lane passed the pint in silence before the mortician returned and opened the doors to the chapel.

Abe removed his hat and Lane snatched off his, too, and they went in. Their boots on the oak floorboards made church echoes. While the funeral director hung back, Abe led his brother toward the gurney where their father lay, covered with a sheet. Then it was real. He saw Lloyd's face, so different with his mouth sealed shut over his overbite and something like Vaseline on his eyelids. His bare shoulder with its freckles and moles showed above the sheet, and Abe touched it. The body was hard and cool. Room temperature. Totally unmoving.

Dead.

His hair was combed right, because the funeral director knew Lloyd.

Lane's sob choked into the dark chamber. "Daddy."

Abe gazed at his father's face that would not awaken.

I miss you. I'm going to miss you.

After a bit he sat on an oak bench in the front row, three yards from the body, to get to know his father in death. Lane followed, sticking beside him, the way he had when he was a kid. The pint was stowed. Lane leaned forward, his hands toying with his hat.

The shadowed profile of their father's death mask, the body under the sheets, was not obscene. It was just death, and Lloyd's spirit was there with his boys. Abe's lips moved, and he sang softly:

"From this valley they say you are going.
I will miss your bright eyes and sweet smile.
They say you are taking the sunshine
That has brightened our pathway a while."

Lane chimed in, low at first, then strong. They harmonized as they had around mountain campfires, summer nights. Each note fell true and on key. Every word, every verse, every beat honored the waltz that was Lloyd, and the serenade swelled to its end with a sweetness born of deepest loyalty and love.

"But remember the Red River Valley
and the cowboy who loves you so true."

"HE HAS A PLOT," the funeral director revealed later across the desk where business was conducted, "with his parents and his sister. And with Busy."

"Fine."

"You'll need to choose a casket."

Abe and Lane descended to the basement, where the satin-lined caskets were all opened. The funeral director told them the prices, and they were all too much. Abe and Lane exchanged looks. Lloyd would have a fit if he knew they paid so much for a box to bury him in. Abe said, "We'll make one."

"You know, arrangements can—"

"No. We'll build it." Oak. Lloyd would look fine in his black suit and bolo tie.

Upstairs the funeral director gave him the figures and discussed payment plans. The brothers' eyes met again. As one they said, "We'll pay cash up front."

Abe brought out the bills Kip had given him and money from his own paycheck. Lane produced his wallet, stuffed with Laughlin rodeo winnings, to make up the difference.

They paid for these rites of death and left to go to the lumberyard to buy wood for another.

"I'M NOT STAYING for the funeral," Lane said.

They'd almost reached the Kay Ranch. Abe nearly swerved.

"I'm leaving for Texas in the morning. Corpus Christi."

Thirty-thousand dollars. Rodeo.

Abe flicked on the turn signal.

"I've seen him. We said goodbye. It couldn't mean more than that. More than 'Red River Valley.' I'm at peace."

Abe supposed he shouldn't blame his brother for thinking the world spun on the axis of his own existence. He sure hadn't thought of Lane when he'd signed on with Guy Loren at eighteen, when he'd hit the rodeo road.

What goes around comes around.

"You know, that was Dad's favorite song," said Lane, "and it's all about a sweetheart leaving. Does that make sense to you?"

"Maybe." Lloyd forgave. Lloyd had forgiven a president and an economy that cost him his ranch. And Lloyd had forgiven his wife, his sweetheart, who couldn't stay where her child had died.

From this valley they say you are going...

When Abe pulled up beside his father's old trailer, Kip was in the corral inspecting the shoes on his horses. He patted the horse he'd just been checking and let himself out the gate.

"Want me to help you clean out the trailer?" Lane asked.

"Just get whatever you want." *And go rodeo.*

As Kip Kay made his way toward the truck, Lane fiddled with a thread on his jeans.

"I'll help you build the coffin."

"I'll do it."

Biting his lip, Lane climbed out of the truck to go inside.

Kip Kay stopped six feet from the front bumper, and Abe got out, went to lean against the hood. It was almost warm, a balmy spring day. A day when calves were born and a cowboy was tempted to buy a new hat.

Lloyd...

"Given it some thought?" asked the rancher.

The heat in Abe's chest was painful. It hurt to be calm, to be level, the way you knew Kip Kay expected you to be. Kip Kay had been a soldier and had written things to his wife that had kept Abe, a man, awake nights. "I don't," Abe answered slowly, "understand you." He measured his words, shaped them. "You know I'm going to marry Erin. You know she's the mother of my child. And you won't say she's your daughter."

"She knows better than to expect to have part of this ranch. But if you take this job, you can give her a chance to know the life."

"She doesn't want your ranch. She wants you. My

father's *dead*. You'll live another twenty years. She just wants to be your daughter."

"Well, that's not going to happen. You get older, you'll see that you invest your life in certain quarters, and you protect those interests when they're threatened."

Abe couldn't see Kip's face well because of the sun. "Chaley?"

"Erin's got you, the one thing my daughter wanted more than anything. The only compensation I can give her is this land. And during my lifetime, you and Erin can earn your living from it, too. She won't be salaried, but I'll give you a living wage."

Abe had counted the bills Kip gave him the day before. Counted them out to the funeral director. Eight hundred dollars a month. That and the trailer and unlimited gasoline were the foreman's pay.

He wasn't going to do better—unless he went up the road to ask a movie-star rancher for a job. And maybe not then. The dream of his own spread came and went. "What makes you so sure Erin isn't going to tell Chaley the truth, tell her she's her sister?"

"That would be her right."

He knows Erin wouldn't do that.

Erin had come to Colorado to know her father. And so that Maeve would know Abe. *I've wanted to live on a ranch my whole life.*

Now she had the chance to live on this ranch, her family's ranch, and his honor, the price of living a lie, was the only cost.

Not sure that he wouldn't pay it, for her, Abe said, "I'm still thinking." And got back into his truck before he could give Maeve's grandpa the medicine he needed.

HE WORKED on the casket in Guy Loren's shop. It took him till nine at night to design it and to measure and cut the pieces, to join the sections for the bottom and top. Then, after kissing Erin and Maeve good-night in the too-small fifth wheel, where they would all share the bed, he headed back to the Kays' to see Lane.

His brother was gone.

Abe hunted the cabinets until he found half a bottle of Jack Daniel's in his father's nightstand, squirreled away from Lane.

He drank freely from the bottle. He looked in his father's closet and found his grandfather's bearskin chaps. His grandfather had shot the bear whose hide had made those woollies. Abe tried them on.

Have to clean out the trailer. Have to find a place for all this stuff.

The chaps were for subzero days, and he left them on the bed and went out to the front room. Even looking at the stereo cabinet was painful, so he just lay on the couch with the bottle, drinking till he passed out.

He had a dream involving Beulah Ann being kind to him, like an angel. When he awoke, a light burned in the kitchen, Taffy was sleeping against his arm, and Erin was on her hands and knees scrubbing the kitchen floor. Abe shut his eyes and let the world go away.

ERIN CLEANED the trailer till midnight, tackling Lloyd's room, as well. She found the woollies Abe had left on the bed and laid them on the dresser after she dusted it. She studied the framed photos of Abe's grandparents and maybe great-grandparents. In Lane's room, she found things that had obviously belonged to Abe, including photos of him and a girl at a high-school prom years before. His date was not Chaley.

She had put Maeve down for the night on the bed that must once have been Abe's, and when Erin felt her own edginess giving way to fatigue, she lay down with her daughter. Hours later she opened her eyes to Abe sitting on the side of the bed. He was shirtless and smelled of whiskey.

"How did you get here?" he asked.

"Beulah Ann called to say you were passed out drunk and she was worried about you. I drove the Mustang over."

"Oh." Abe held his head, thinking about Kip Kay's offer and his grandfather's woollies, about family tradition and about Lloyd being gone. Erin was Kip's oldest daughter, Maeve his grandchild. Someday this ranch should belong to Maeve.

People murdered for less.

Abe didn't want to work for a man he wanted to kill. Didn't want to remain on his land. "Let's go home."

"It's the middle of the night."

"Doesn't it bother you?"

"What?"

"Your father."

"No."

He saw that she'd take whatever crumbs Kip tossed her way. "Well, I've got pride."

And I don't? "If my pride threatened to kill me, I'd get rid of some of it."

The silhouette of his back and its muscles and ridges did not shift. Sometimes you could know a man was angry by the way the silence felt.

"It's my inheritance," he said. "I'll keep it, thanks."

The bed creaked and was light and empty where he'd been.

Abe went into the front room to find Martha. The cocker spaniel wanted his attention, too, and he told her, "Taffy, you make an awfully silly cow dog."

A few minutes later Erin came out, dressed, accepting that they would leave. It was four in the morning.

My pride's killing her, too.

His family would be comfortable on Kip's pay. Any

extra money he made shoeing horses would go to savings.
To their future. "Okay," he said. "We stay."

"We don't have to."

"Damned right."

Her jaw tensed. "Want some breakfast?"

She made him bacon and eggs from the stores in Lloyd's
refrigerator, and he ate, then showered and brushed his
teeth with the toothbrush Erin had brought.

At five-thirty, he went out into the mountain cold and
walked toward the lights of the big house. Stopping
halfway, he stood by the corral fence, remembering the
night Kip had told Erin he had just one daughter. *She cried
while I was inside her.*

Chaley's Appaloosa, Mouse, came over to the fence,
begging for a stroke, and Abe rubbed her warm neck with
gloved hands.

A ranch couldn't survive without loyalty. Lloyd had lost
his ranch and gone on to work another man's spread, tend
another man's cows. At seventeen Abe had asked him how
he could stand it.

Easy, Lloyd had said. *You wake up in the morning. You
go out to the calves. They're warm and wet when they're
born, and you figure out it doesn't matter whose they are.*

The man whose cows they were came outside to start his
day. The door shut behind him, a morning sound. He
stopped when he saw Abe.

Abe nodded, and Kip continued across the deck and
down the steps. He had coffee with him in a big plastic
travel mug, and when he reached Abe he lifted the cup.
"There's more where this came from."

"Thanks."

"Throwing in with us?"

"My daughter is your granddaughter. How would you
feel?"

The black shadow sipped his coffee. "I guess, like your
daddy, I'd just be glad for the chance to cowboy."

"If he were me right now, he'd have you on the ground."

The man's brittle smile was darker than the blue morning. "That's not so easy to do, Abe."

This is about Chaley. She had cried, too, and Kip Kay was righting the scales, pretending love was worth land and land worth love. Abe could have told him that neither could replace the other.

But Chaley wouldn't like his being foreman, and Kip must know that.

This hadn't been a whim.

Abe prodded the sore tooth that was Jack Draw's land. Might-have-beens and couldn't-be's weren't worth reckoning. Just can-be and can-do. "I'll be your foreman," he said. "For my daughter. And yours."

Kip's face held no shame. "Fine. Settle with Loren and start when you can. I imagine you'll want to move into the trailer right away."

Abe's next rodeo wasn't for two weeks. Guy would have no trouble finding a replacement. The foreman of a ranch couldn't rodeo on weekends. He was needed on-site every single day. *No more clowning around, Abe.*

His last performance was over.

Kip shifted his coffee cup to his left hand and offered his right to Abe, meeting his eyes.

Reaching out, Abe shook on the betrayal of his family, his father and everything he believed in. But as he clasped Kip Kay's evil and mug-warmed hand, he heard Lloyd talking in his stern-gentle way. *If you work for the man, ride for the brand.*

Kip Kay had shown an incredible and stupid trust.

And Abe would honor it.

It was what he'd been taught.

"Yes, your father is a real cowboy."

—Jayne Mackenzie on her daughter's
        sixth birthday

CHAPTER TWELVE

THE DAY WAS PACKED. Abe drove to Guy Loren's first off,
to tell the stock contractor the news. Loren said there was
no need for two weeks' notice; with Lloyd's death, he'd
anticipated Abe wouldn't be working much, anyway.

Abe used the rest of the day completing the casket—he
finished it by ten in the morning—and moving boxes and
furniture from Loren's place to the trailer. It was soon to
be dealing with Lloyd's effects, but Abe saw no good
reason to delay. The sooner he started work for the Kay
Ranch the better, and maybe this way he could get all the
pain over with at once.

But after moving the bed—loading the mattresses to take
to the dump—he left his father's room for Erin; she'd said
she would clean it when she was done sewing. She and
Beulah Ann had made a trip to Gunnison and bought yards
of silver-blue satin. Erin stitched up the lining on her
mother's sewing machine, and the box was ready for
Lloyd's viewing that night. As Lloyd's room was ready for
them to sleep in.

The trailer was theirs.

Lane had left for his next rodeo.

Evening came. Abe stood tall near the door of the chapel
trying to be as Lloyd had taught him. Talking to people,

saying the right things, while his dear father lay dead across the room. Everyone asked after Lane, and Abe said, "He's seen him." He didn't know what he'd say tomorrow at the funeral. *Lane had a rodeo. It's his way of closing with Dad.*

Erin and Maeve wore purple dresses. He called them his family and stared down the looks that meant something about Chaley. *What goes around comes around, Kip.* Though when Chaley and Kip showed up, he nodded to them both. Shook hands and met their eyes. Tried to be the cowboy Lloyd had been.

And when it was over and everyone was gone, his father lay in the casket Abe had made. And Lloyd was dead.

Abe went to look at his face a last time and tried not to cry, tried to believe everything was going to be all right.

Afterward, he found Erin in the back of the chapel, holding Maeve and reading the cards on the flowers. Maeve wore a floppy-brimmed purple hat with a silk flower on the band. She swung her feet in tiny black Mary Janes, kicking a steady rhythm, tired and trying to stay awake.

"Ready?"

"Yes."

They rode home in silence, in an icy snowfall, to the Kays' ranch. The taillights of the truck ahead of them made watery Christmas ribbons on the road, while Merle Haggard sang "Silver Wings" on the Gunnison station that was trying to reach them through the mountains. When all was said and done, people left in coffins, not on wings of any kind. Abe punched buttons, and the Mavericks said, "What a Crying Shame," and Mary Chapin Carpenter felt lucky, and Abe shut it off. "My daddy said Patsy Cline was the only good thing to come out of Nashville."

Erin thought it wasn't a good time to say Lloyd had been wrong.

At the trailer Abe took a sleeping Maeve out of her car seat, and she didn't wake as he and Erin trekked through the snow to the door.

Erin called the place home and paid no court to the owner, to the king of this land. There was room for a garden behind the trailer, between the trailer and the pasture bordered by the highway. Bulls were penned there now. In July and August, Abe said, they would be put in with the cows.

She opened the door and took the baby from Abe. "I'll put her down."

A small fluorescent bulb illuminated the kitchen, the same light Lloyd had always left on. Abe felt his father's absence, from the trailer and from his life, as Erin hurried away to put Maeve to bed.

He didn't notice time passing till Erin came back. Her dress was loose and soft, the color of an eggplant, and Abe grabbed for her as she neared the couch. The blackness was made tolerable by her heat, by her life touching him. She had laughed with Beulah Ann while they sewed the satin lining for the casket. Abe had heard their voices as he and Lucky moved furniture in and out of the trailer.

"Erin." He couldn't remember what it was like to kiss anyone else. His erection pressed against her, and Erin squeezed her body to his on the narrow couch, kissing him back. She was trying to help the way he'd wanted to when she'd told him about Jayne's murder.

He dragged up her dress as Erin lay over him, and she unfastened his belt buckle, opened the fly of the dress slacks he hadn't worn for years.

"Abe?" Her dark eyes above him talked sense.

Abe wanted to make up for Lloyd with Erin's children, and he met her eyes and entered her naked, and she pressed harder against him.

KIP KAY WAS CHECKING cows at midnight when Chaley parked her 4x4 outside the fence, spread the barbed wire to step through and braved the flying snowfall to join him.

She'd been away most of the day in Alta and had ridden to the viewing with Beulah Ann.

Kip figured she'd come out in a snowstorm for a conversation he'd been waiting for since six this morning.

Now she had to compete with the wind. "So Abe's the new foreman."

He'd guessed right. Chaley couldn't like it. But he was a fair man, and he was doing what was fair for his foreman's son. Moreover, he was doing what was right for the ranch, and *that* was best for Chaley, whether she could see it today or not.

More words blew toward him. "They're going to live here."

"When has the foreman of this ranch not lived here?"

She wouldn't stomp her foot and cry. That wasn't Chaley's way. A gray shape with her hat collecting snow, she huddled in her sheepskin coat, her back to the wind.

Continuing work, Kip trod on through the pasture and shone his flashlight on the cows. The beam reflected the glassy particles of snow, the same snow freezing his nose and cheeks.

Abe, I'm glad you said yes. Abe was smart, a hard worker and a good one. You could tell the kind of man he was by how he cared for his gear; he was Lloyd's son, all right. He'd figure out how to earn the respect of the hands—and if he didn't, he'd know to fire them and start with a new crew—and that was fine with Kip. Youth didn't have to be a disadvantage. On this cold night Kip wished he had it, too.

"I'm going to look for a job in town," said Chaley in the slurred voice of someone too cold. "Or maybe somewhere else."

Going for the jugular; Chaley's way of getting what she wanted. *If you keep them, you'll lose me.*

He didn't bother answering. He'd given Abe his word. Chaley knew that. What was she hoping to accomplish?

"Is my ex-fiancé the *only* cowboy you could find for this job?"

"Don't get sassy. He's Lloyd's son." Directing the beam on a black baldy, a Hereford-Angus cross, Kip ignored any other reasons he'd offered Abe the job. They had to do with justice, too. He didn't know if Erin and Abe were in love, but they were sweet with each other. If they were trying to make it work for the sake of their baby, well, Kip could respect that.

It sure wasn't what Jayne had done.

It was still early for Erin and Abe. The first year of marriage was hell, and these two weren't married yet. But more and more, he found himself rooting for them, instead of waiting for Erin to disappoint him.

"I just thought you'd consider my feelings."

His tall beautiful angel was small and shivering now.

"Chaley." Kip stood near enough to make sure she saw his eyes through the slanting silver snow. "I always consider your feelings."

She lowered her head, cutting the exposed space between her hat brim and her coat collar. Her lips trembled. "Then I should look for a job in town."

"Or stay here and grin and bear it and keep your pride." It might have been different if he'd even once come upon Chaley and Abe lying in a field or in his truck bed together. It might have been different if he really believed Abe had ever laid a lovemaking hand on his daughter.

This daughter… He wouldn't hear it.

Abe was doing as he ought.

"My pride will do much better somewhere he isn't," said Chaley.

"Fine."

Her father trudged on, and Chaley trailed him through the snow, pointing at a Hereford. "There's one."

The cow was lying down, pushing out her calf. Kip and Chaley watched and waited, stomping their feet. The calf would need to be taken in, warmed up. Kip had some battery socks to keep his feet warm—Chaley had given them to him for Christmas—but the batteries were dead. He'd make do till someone went to town.

"Can I borrow some money to get an apartment?"

Someday she would have to face living on this ranch with Erin and Abe, seeing the two of them together with their child. But for now, should he give her money for an apartment, for a place to heal?

"You see what you can find sharing a place with someone and let me know. Then we'll talk."

They grew cold as the cow strained, pushing. Two front hooves.

"There you go, Mama," Kip encouraged.

Chaley said, "Thank you."

Sweet Chaley. She was going to make it. Kip's snow-crusted lashes cracked as he smiled. "You're still my best girl."

Minutes later the calf was born into the storm with a hot gush of fluids, and its mother turned to lick the sac away.

"Want to use my truck to take her in, Dad?"

"Thanks, Chaley." *I'm going to miss you.*

But his heart knew that what was happening was right. And that it would come to good.

IN THE TRAILER Abe added more logs to the woodstove. He wasn't ready to enter his father's room. To make it his and Erin's.

She had put on a long-sleeved PRCA T-shirt that hung around her thighs, and she was looking through a cookbook in the kitchen and making notes. The funeral would be in the morning, with a wake afterward in the big house. Neighbors had brought food, and Beulah Ann and Erin planned to get up at five and prepare all kinds of extra dishes.

One more day. Then he could stop talking to people about it. Stop answering for Lane.

He arranged another log in the stove, shut the door and adjusted the damper.

Of course, that other recurring incident had been just as awkward as Lane's absence. *And this is Maeve's mother.* Everyone must have wondered what exactly she was to *him.*

She might wonder.

She'd been getting left since before she was born.

On his way past the kitchen, Abe stopped to kiss her temple from over her shoulder. She squeezed his hand before he moved on, heading for the master bedroom. Lloyd's room.

Curious, Martha followed.

The room wasn't so bad. With Erin's discount-house bed it seemed completely changed, even in the dark. Especially with the guilty sound of Taffy's tags. "Get down from there," Abe said.

The cocker spaniel jumped to the floor.

Without turning on a light he opened the sticky sliding doors of Lloyd's closet and dragged the black bag off the top shelf, the bag that held the person he used to be. He carried it to the bathroom, where he did use the light and let Martha slip inside with him before he shut the door.

Dropping his dress pants to the floor, he sang Martha's favorite song, which was "Stand by Your Man." He buttoned the patchwork shirt, stepped into the baggies, pulled up suspenders and athletic socks, and before the mirror he painted his face, ignoring the quivering in his heart that he wasn't a bullfighter anymore. Couldn't be.

"You probably wonder why I'm doing this, Martha," said Abe. "You *know* this won't change my feelings for you, don't you?" He sat down on the toilet-seat lid and stroked Martha's ears while she made eyes at him. "She even remembered your name after all that time...."

"WHAT ARE YOU DOING?" asked Erin.

In his athletic socks, Abe trooped to the stereo. While he knelt on the rug and selected an album, Erin shut off the kitchen light. The sight of Abe at the stereo, dressed as a clown, brought back the birthday party. But he didn't choose the album of cowboy songs this time.

Instead, it was an old Willie Nelson record. Erin crouched beside Abe to look at the faded jacket. The owner had scrawled his name in the upper left-hand corner. Kip Kay. "It's my father's."

"Was. He gave me a bunch of albums when we first moved here." *And this was his, so I'm playing it for you, Erin. I'll hope for you that he sees how special you are.* Abe eased the record over the spindle, guided it to the turntable. As the disc spun, he set the needle on the groove beside the most worn section of vinyl.

He drew her to her feet as the crackle of much-played vinyl came from the speakers. "Remember the night we met?" When she'd still had dreams, he thought, of knowing her father and having his love. She pretended it didn't hurt when a cowboy crushed her dreams; she told lies in riddles and poetry. It was better, he thought, that her heroes should always be cowboys. He'd try to keep things that way.

They slow-danced, hands clasped, clumsily kissing. With one arm holding her waist, Abe freed his right hand and fished in his shirt pocket. The invisible shape he pulled out was a box.

One-handed, he popped the lid and showed the treasure inside.

Erin's eyes watered. *This is it. This is the truth. This is what it's like when someone wants you.*

She savored it. "Oh, it's beautiful, Abe." Joyfully she held out her left hand. "Put it on me."

Abe took the imaginary ring from its box, then fumbled, almost dropping it out of nervousness. He slid it onto Erin's slender white ring finger, and she used her right hand to spin the ring, to test the fit. She stretched out her fingers, admiring the stone.

"Will you marry me?" he asked.

"Oh, yes." She was crying.

He had healed the lies of her father. The truth about cowboys was beautiful. And they danced in the faded night.

MUSIC FLOATED from the trailer as Kip left the barn. George and Lucky had come out to take the next watch on the cows. The world should have been asleep, but Ian and Sylvia were come back from the war years, singing folk songs from the trailer, casting Kip back in time.

Nowadays Ian Tyson was the favorite singer-songwriter of working cowboys across the continent. But Kip remembered when the singer was half of Ian and Sylvia, and he knew the cowboy folk song playing from the trailer, about a cowboy who loved rodeo as much as he loved his sweetheart. And the sweetheart's disapproving father, who'd known his own wild days. And banking on someday soon, when everything would be all right.

Behind the trailer curtains, a lamp lit two players, a man in a lumpy-looking hat and a woman. Good grief, Abe was clowning around in there, wearing his baggies.

No, not clowning. Slow-dancing with Erin, as Kip and Jayne had danced to the same song.

Somewhere inside, a red-haired baby slept.

Kip recalled a night of shattered glass, of pouring sweat. Tears and fear. Jayne huddled under the corner cabinets in the kitchen. She'd hidden under the table once, too. From him. With him. He'd clung to her, crying, he'd been so afraid she would leave.

Resting his arms on the top railing of the corral, Kip watched the black shadow-dancers holding each other gently. Kissing.

I couldn't be like that for your mother, Erin.

And the red-haired baby couldn't have slept peacefully in the night.

His heart pounded with the soft strains of the melody, and peace came, a peace the war had never bought. He couldn't have put it into words. But it eased him, made the world sweeter and better, that there was a cowboy and a pretty redhead with dark brown eyes, with her mother's face, slow-dancing in the trailer. With their child sleeping in the next room.

BEFORE THEY WENT to sleep, Abe stowed his clown costume and makeup and props in the black bag. "I wonder what to do with this stuff."

Erin heard no regret in his voice, but a cowboy wouldn't let it show. Abe had been a rodeo clown for ten years.

"Well, we've got to save it. It's tradition. Put it in the closet with the woollies." Erin couldn't see the old bearskin chaps without remembering about "our brand." In his grief over his father's death, Abe probably didn't even remember that Jack Draw's land was for sale.

She was wrong.

Certain facts became a property of the blood. Abe remembered, but seventy-five-million-dollar problems he could not fix. Quitting bullfighting he couldn't fix. Kip Kay he couldn't fix; he'd never met a human that broken. But he would fix what he could.

He was going to save cowboys in the way that really mattered. He was going to ride for the brand, like Lloyd. Like the greatest cowboy he'd ever known.

And someday, someday soon, he would win his own dreams.

He told Erin, "I'm going to wear those woollies if this weather holds. They're not history yet."

Yes, they are, thought Erin. Living history. She'd see it kept living. "Speaking of history, there's something I want to do."

Abe listened to her plan and believed in it. History was her passion. And he'd read her thesis; she could write.

"I just need to find out if there are adequate records."

"We have lots of stuff, Erin. The photo albums out in the living room, and there's boxes of stuff in the shed. Plus, Dad's given a ton of paper to the museum. Letters, that kind of thing. My mom could help you, too."

Erin grew drunk on her dreams and spun one she knew was grandiose. A dream of firmly reuniting Annabelle Cockburn with her sons. She focused on more manageable plans. "Well, I ought to be able to get access to the museum collections. I met one of the people tonight." At Lloyd's viewing. "The local DAR runs it."

"You should join."

"Can't. You have to have to be descended from someone who actively participated in the American Revolution."

"You are." Cold eyes belied his smile. "Chaley belongs. Your grandmother helped form the local chapter."

Erin's chest tightened. She already knew the truth; she'd read it in her father's letters, and she'd learned it from Abe tonight, and that was what the truth had to be. No need to look anymore. "Sounds like a good reason not to join. I don't have to belong to volunteer at the museum."

"You don't have to accept his terms, Erin."

"I do."

She was shaking, but he didn't touch her. He didn't want her to know that he'd noticed her emotion. Fear had never stopped the strong. "Why?"

The breath singed the insides of her nostrils, already made dry by the wood heat in the trailer. "His name is not on my birth certificate."

The spell of the night died, and Abe tried to forgive her mother, the mother someone had shot.

Beside him, his betrothed straightened her spine, stretched it, yawned. Shook off the tension and started clowning. *She* was a lover and a fighter.

"What are you doing?"

Erin was holding out her left hand, smiling at the backs of her spread fingers. "Admiring my ring."

Abe tossed the rodeo bag onto the floor.

To make room for him and Erin on the bed.

There, he told her about his grandmother's engagement ring, that Chaley had worn it.

If it wasn't for Chaley's feelings, Erin wouldn't have minded a used engagement ring. Because it was an heirloom—and because of the nature of Abe's first engagement. Abe had told her how it was and she believed him. Supposing she and Chaley were friends, as close as sisters could be—supposing Chaley was over Abe—the ring might even seem a link between them. That first day in the big house, Chaley had booted Lane in the butt for teasing Beulah Ann; he'd deserved it. If things were different...

"It wouldn't bother me," said Erin, "if it didn't bother her."

Abe said, "It would bother her."

"In that case, can I just keep the ring I have?"

He clasped her warmth in the deep sheets and blankets on that snowy night. "If you're sure it fits."

And after they'd made love again, Abe lay with his head against her breast, his mouth to her skin, and gave himself to her father's ranch.

*"Whoopee ti yi yo, git along little dogies,
It's your misfortune and none of my own."*

—"Git Along, Little Dogies,"
A trail song whose English antecedent,
"The Song," was first published
in 1661

CHAPTER THIRTEEN

SHE WAS DEEP in Cockburn family history before Jack Draw's ranch sold to a developer.

There were photos to keep her busy for months. The albums in the trailer held baby pictures of Lane and Abe, shots of their grandparents, pictures of the ranch and black-and-white images from the turn of the century—even a wedding photo of Maeve's great-great-grandfather, Charlie Cockburn, with his handlebar mustache, and his wife, Elizabeth.

Erin asked Abe for the stories Lloyd had told. Abe told them and sometimes cried for thinking of Lloyd. But a calf that didn't make it, a calf he couldn't save, made his eyes wet, too, and no one thought him less a man. He was mourning that he hadn't saved Lloyd.

He rose every day at four-thirty and went to bed at midnight. Erin made a habit of taking him his supper and sitting with him in the truck, listening to Ian Tyson while he ate. And in the evenings, when the weather was bad, she took Maeve's playpen out to the barn and warmed calves as the men brought them in.

Whenever she saw Kip, they both pretended they'd never spoken over the barbed wire that day. *But I have read your letters.* She knew him now.

Two weeks after Lloyd's funeral, she drove the Mustang up to Alta and visited the historical museum with Maeve. Using volunteer labor and local funding, the Daughters of the American Revolution had turned the upstairs rooms into a nineteenth-century hospital room, doctor's office, law office and general store. Downstairs honored Alta's mining history and earliest settlers.

But Erin imagined the addition of a children's room where kids could dress up in period costumes. Saturday workshops where they could try doing chores—washing clothes, cooking meals—the way Grandma had.

When she and Maeve had seen the whole museum, Erin asked the volunteer in charge about collections that weren't displayed.

"The documents are old and fragile, dear. They're not open to the public."

"I have a doctorate in history from the University of Nevada, and I'm planning a book on some of the history of the area."

"I can't help you," said the bulldog.

Making up her mind to call Ella Kelsey, a woman she'd met at Lloyd's viewing, and also to query some university presses, Erin stuffed a twenty-dollar bill in the donation box and left.

A week later Jack Draw's land sold.

"I WONDER WHERE Lane is."

Beulah Ann and Erin were using old windows and scrap lumber to throw together a cold frame for starting seedlings. The mid-April sun had melted much of the snow, and Maeve played nearby, trying to dig in the dirt with a hand-spade. Erin had been about to drive an extra nail into the box when Beulah Ann spoke. The remark made her lower the hammer and nail.

Tucking a blond lock back into her ponytail, Beulah Ann gazed down the road that led to the highway as though expecting to see Lane's pickup coming toward her.

But the only people expected were guests, three couples, college friends making a twenty-year reunion. Erin had helped Beulah Ann clean the cabins. Chaley used to do it, Beulah Ann had explained. Now Chaley answered the phone at a veterinarian's office in Gunnison.

"Farmington," said Erin. "He's in Farmington." Abe would have been working the same rodeo if he was still bullfighting.

As Erin prepared to bang on the cold frame some more, Beulah Ann asked, "Does Abe get *Prorodeo Sports News?*"

"Beulah Ann, maybe you and I need a ladies' night out." *So you can meet someone else and stop thinking about Lane!*

She wished she could tell Beulah Ann they were cousins. Beulah Ann's mother was Kip's sister, Beth, and Beulah Ann had three younger brothers and a little sister. Which meant one aunt and four more cousins to Erin.

Beulah Ann was frowning. "Have you and Abe set a date?"

"June twenty-first." The summer solstice. Branding would be done, and the snow should be gone from the high meadows.

"I know this is a personal question," Beulah Ann said, "so you don't have to answer. But do you think you'll have more kids?"

"Might. Maeve, what have you got there, sweetheart?"

It was a stick. In Maeve's opinion, good for eating.

Erin picked her up. Maeve needed a bath, and the cold frame was pretty well finished.

At a sound from the road, the baby broke into a smile. "Da-dee!"

Abe was riding Bo, his father's horse, down the road, helping Lucky drive heifers to the corral near the barn. The dogs were with them, helping or, in Taffy's case, getting in the way.

"That is one handsome man," said Beulah Ann.

"I'll keep him. Thanks for doing this with me, Beulah Ann. Tomorrow let's plant the seedlings." They'd bought potting soil in town the day before, after filling four grocery carts at City Market. Ranch shopping.

Erin helped Beulah Ann clean up, then took Maeve to the barn, where Abe was unsaddling Bo.

"Hi," he said, carrying the saddle inside. "I need to go shoe some horses for a man. Called and left a message with Kip. Want to come?"

She had ten minutes to bathe Maeve, and then they were off.

The horses were at the old Billings place, down a ranch road beside Jack Draw's land. White PVC fencing glowed against the landscape, degrading a beautiful turn-of-the-century Victorian farmhouse. Abe sang, "Home, home on the range…"

"It looks all right. Don't be such an elitist."

"Such a *what?*"

"An elitist. You are. You and your grandpa's woollies. You have something these people couldn't buy with all the money in the world."

She must mean family history. Erin thought history made up for everything. Even the inheritance she and their daughter would never get—the land that owned his sweat and whose fences cut wounds in his hands.

"I'll take the money, thanks," said Abe.

"They sent flowers to your dad's funeral."

Abe drove under a massive white sign: TANNER'S

PAINT HORSES. No one he knew. "Couldn't have. My dad never met these people."

Up ahead a man strolled out onto the gravel drive.

"He met him." Erin had seen the duster and the snakeskin boots through the snowy windshield of Abe's truck when their owner stood in Gunnison's main intersection. "That's the man whose car he hit."

Abe saw. This man had bought Lloyd a cup of coffee at Stockman's and asked him about horses.

They all got out, and Erin set Maeve on the ground, let her try to keep up with Abe on the slushy snow and mud and gravel till he stopped and picked her up.

The owner stuck out his hand. "Josh Tanner." Shaking hands, he squinted at Abe. "Have we met?"

"My dad hit your truck."

"Oh. Hey, I'm sorry."

"Thanks for the flowers."

"I liked him very much. He gave me some good advice about foaling."

With Maeve in his arms, Abe scanned the pasture. Tanner's Paints were brown and white, with black and flaxen manes and tails. Showy horses, with good American quarter-horse conformation. Abe didn't know anyone who rode a Paint, but Lloyd had sung the cowboy songs about them.

Maeve swung her legs against him as he followed Tanner to his barn to find a good place to set up. There was a large open area where the stalls ended. "This'll do."

Erin took Maeve, and while he backed the truck to the door and opened the tailgate to get his tools, Josh Tanner started catching his horses and leading them in. While Abe trimmed hooves, the owner asked most of what there was to ask about horses' feet. Nearby with Maeve, Erin watched Abe's hands and heard his answers.

Maeve wanted to walk, so Erin followed her toddling steps into the barn, where the baby squatted down and heeded the call of nature. When Erin returned from changing her in the truck, Abe was saying, "You need to call the vet."

"What?"

"It's probably laminitis. See this swelling?"

Holding the horse's hoof, Abe moved his hand to an area above the bulbs of the heel, gently probing something. With a look that said he was certain of what he'd found, he set the hoof down, stroked the horse's fetlock and straightened up. "You have a vet?"

"I have a card someone gave me."

"Dave Roe's good. Call him, and I'll do what I can here." Abe rubbed the Paint's shoulder.

They were at Josh Tanner's place for two hours, and while Abe tended the lame horse, the owner spoke with Erin. Josh, who hadn't seen forty, had just retired as CEO of a computer-software company.

"What do you do?" he asked Erin.

She told him her background in history.

"Boy, there's history in this area."

"If you're looking for a cause," Erin told him, "the museum in Alta is a good one."

"I'll keep that in mind. You wish you could do something, you know." He nodded stiffly toward the south. "About that place, for instance."

Jack Draw's place. The old Cockburn ranch.

"What do you mean?"

"Subdivision going in. Skyline Ranches. Martin Pickett got approval last night."

It was like being kicked by a horse. That beautiful country where she and Abe had ridden the morning she'd cried about Jayne's murder. The aspen tree. "I didn't know it was sold."

"Happened fast."

While they were burying Lloyd.

"First thing I did with this place," said Josh, "was put a conservation easement on it...."

Erin and Maeve waited in the truck while Abe presented the bill. The owner settled right then, and when Abe slid behind the wheel, he was whistling.

It would kill him, Erin thought. Josh Tanner had said, *Groundbreaking's set for July.*

"Abe. They're going to subdivide Jack Draw's ranch."

He stared. "Where'd you hear that? It hasn't sold."

"Josh Tanner just told me. He said it *is* sold. It all sounded true. The subdivision will be called Skyline Ranches."

Abe hadn't seen a paper that day. He tried thinking of other things. What came to mind was Josh Tanner having a cup of coffee with Lloyd at Stockman's. Friend and foe became one thing, a thing called New People.

Erin thought of the money in Abe's wallet and the check she was expecting from her attorney—the balance of her mother's estate. It couldn't outbid any developer. *But I can help save cowboys, too.* "Abe, do you think Kip would let us buy some cows of our own and raise them on his land?"

Abe glanced at Jack Draw's lodge-pole fence bordering the road to the left. He answered Erin's innocence. "That's the difference between being Kip Kay's daughter and the wife of his foreman. As far as he's concerned, you're one of those things and not the other."

Stopping at the highway, he could see only the back of her head. Abe wished he'd phrased it differently.

"Erin." He reached across the cab to touch her cheek.

She faced him, dry-eyed, her smile trying to hide that her lips were trembling.

Abe lost his words. There was nothing to say.

Chaley had a herd of her own on the Kay Ranch. Erin never would.

And Abe was glad Lloyd Cockburn hadn't lived to see the land he'd loved become Skyline Ranches.

SINCE LLOYD'S DEATH, Erin had not missed a sunrise. When the alarm beeped at four-thirty each morning, she and Abe both got up. She showered and headed over to the big house to help Beulah Ann with breakfast. Abe got Maeve up and dressed, took her with him in the pickup when he drove out to see the cows and brought her back to the house for breakfast.

On the morning after Abe shod Josh Tanner's horses, Erin left the trailer in the frosty dark. No lights burned in the kitchen of the big house. Beulah Ann must have been late getting out of bed.

Inside the ranch house, she flicked on the kitchen light and heard water running through the pipes upstairs.

There she is. Just getting a late start. I'll get breakfast going.

That meant checking the day's menu, which Beulah Ann wrote out every night on a spiral steno notepad and left on the counter.

An envelope lay on top of the pad, with Erin's name on it in Beulah Ann's curly writing, and Erin knew how Abe's grandpa had scented a blizzard coming. She felt a storm ahead as she opened the envelope.

It was the kind of floral greeting card the Boy Scouts sold, with the inscription "Friends Forever" inside.

Dear Erin,
Don't worry. I didn't leave you to explain this to Uncle Kip and everyone. He has his own letter stuck under his door. I'm pregnant, and I'm going back to Louisiana to have this baby, because you don't know how stupid I feel, and I can't bare to face everyone there, especially Uncle Kip. He's done so much for me.

What I'm asking you is this. I'm going to have my baby, and then I want you and Abe to take it and raise it like your own. I know what your thinking. That I'm

good with babys and all. But I can't be a mother. So
would you please take my baby? You can write to me
in Louisiana and tell me.

Love,
Beulah Ann Ellis

"Well." Kip Kay sighed in the door to the hallway.
"Need a hand with breakfast, Erin?"

Erin jumped. His eyes knew everything, and he hated
wasted words like any other kind of waste.

"No. No, I can handle it. Let me just..." She stuffed the
card in the envelope and thrust it into the pocket of the coat
she'd hung by the door, then rushed into the pantry to drag
a bag of potatoes off the shelf.

Kip put on the coffee himself, silently, then grabbed his
coat and went outside. When Erin turned on the radio to
keep her company, Garth Brooks was "Callin' Baton
Rouge."

Abe came in a half hour later with Maeve, and Erin,
spinning away from the hot skillet, snatched Beulah's card
from her coat pocket and handed it to him.

Holding his daughter, Abe read the card. Lucky came in
before he could say anything, so Abe returned the envelope
to Erin's coat pocket.

"Ring the bell for me, Abe, will you?" she asked.

He did, with Maeve's help, clasping her hand in his
around the cord. Her eyes widened at the sound of the bell,
and she grinned. Back inside, while Erin hustled about the
kitchen, carrying hot plates of bacon and eggs to the table,
Abe read the top story in the *Alta Independent*. Subdivision
approved. Below was an AP feature, "Can Earth feed the
world?" and the words "overpopulation" and "food-
growing" leaped out at him, and he knew that cattle took
half the water in the West. The world was getting crowded,
till it wasn't safe for cowboys.

And another baby was on the way.

George and Kip came in the door with Pete, a hand Abe had hired from Pueblo just two days before. They'd met through rodeo, and Pete played a harmonica to the cows and was teaching Abe how. The guests trailed in next, to eat before riding fence with Lucky.

Soon everyone was eating. Erin's mind was half on keeping the juice pitcher and coffeepot full, half on Beulah Ann.

When Abe had finished breakfast, he got up to hug Maeve, who was playing patty-cake with George. Erin cornered him in the mudroom. "What do you think?"

"Do you know who the father is?"

"I have a guess."

"Me, too."

"What do you think?" Erin asked again. There was no greater compliment than someone thinking you were the person to raise her child. But so far it was just talk. Once a child had grown inside you, everything was different. And if Lane was the father, Lane who made Beulah Ann's knees weak and apparently her head, as well… "What should we do?"

"I want to know why Beulah Ann thinks she can't be a mother."

"She's just eighteen."

Abe didn't think much of that. His mom had married at eighteen. So had Erin's.

"What are you two hiding in the mudroom for?" In the kitchen, Kip clapped his hat on his head and zipped his coat over his winter coveralls.

"Your niece wants us to raise her child for her."

He lifted his eyebrows. "You look like people who could do that."

Abe's brows pulled together. "You don't think she should keep the baby?"

"I imagine," Kip said, "that Beulah Ann doesn't think so." He addressed Erin. "That was a good job you did this

morning, everything on the table, everything hot. Would
you like to do that three times a day for a salary?''

How easily Kip had accepted Beulah Ann's departure.
But Erin guessed he needed to be businesslike. He had a
crew to feed. She looked at Abe.

"Fine by me.''

"All right.'' She asked Kip, "Can I vary the menu?''

"Erin,'' her father said, slipping past them to the door,
"on a ranch, no one criticizes the cook.''

She couldn't help the rush in her heart, couldn't help
feeling. But she'd gotten used to feeling in Abe's arms, and
it was honest. Like the land. As the door shut behind Kip
she lifted her eyes to her lover's.

His were grave.

He kissed her and left, and later, when Erin was cleaning
up and saw the newspaper, she thought she knew what had
made him sad. But she was wrong.

IT SNOWED AGAIN that night, and a prolapsed heifer died
before Abe's eyes, before he and Kip could do anything.
They cut the calf out, and it was alive. Abe packed it onto
Noon and rode back into the barn. In the barn waited the
mother of a calf who had died hours earlier. Abe warmed
the calf, left it and went out to retrieve the body of the dead
calf. He was in the shed beside the pile of carcasses,
skinning this one, when Erin's shape blocked out the snow-
fogged moonlight. Carrying Maeve, she slipped inside.

"Hi,'' said Abe.

Erin watched. "If you show me how, I could do that.''

Blood stuck his fingers together, stuck them to the knife,
made them slippery and sticky at once. Abe recalled the
first time Erin had witnessed this particular trick. She'd
blanched, then made herself look again. He'd told her the
whys and wherefores, and together they'd watched it work.

Abe didn't believe that skinning a calf was a skill she
really wanted. She wanted something she'd never admit to,

and he wasn't going to let her skin a calf to prove herself to Kip.

"No. You can keep me company, though."

It took him just seconds to finish the job. He took the calf's body outside and carried the bloody skin to the barn, with his family following.

In the barn, he tied the skin onto the orphaned calf, over the shoulders and under the belly, making sure the tail and hindquarters were covered, because that was where the mother would sniff. Then Abe led the calf to the stall where the cow waited. She sniffed the skin and recognized the scent of her own calf. Soon the orphan was suckling.

Erin heard Abe's deep sigh.

"What is it?" she asked.

"What do you mean?"

"You sighed."

"Tired." That was true. To win the respect of the hands, he made it a point to work harder, longer and better than any of them. Now, no one questioned him. George didn't even snicker at Taffy but stopped to pet her when he wasn't on horseback. And Abe had money in the bank, from the work he'd done for Josh Tanner.

Just keep thinking of that. And work like an animal. Try to forget Kip Kay and don't let this land catch your eye the way Erin did. He thought of his father's ranch. "How's your research coming?"

"Ella Kelsey said I should come to the museum when she's there and she'll help me find what I need. Abe, what is it really? Is it my father?"

For a fact. "Why do you play his game?"

"Because I know the truth about cowboys. It's you."

He knew she would never mention that birth certificate again.

But Kip held everything she wanted and what she didn't dare to want, because she'd grown up in a brown house in a field of brown houses just like it as far as the eye could see. *Someday,* Abe promised, *you'll have your own place, Erin, to make up for this mountain land that should be yours. And Maeve's.*

Forgetting his hand was bloody until he touched her face, he looked hard into her eyes. And didn't say a word.

KIP KAY PAUSED just inside the barn and prepared to duck back out into the snow, leave them to themselves. But before he could move, Abe came around the corner of a stall and saw him.

The foreman stopped, then passed on, ignoring Kip.

Kip ventured deeper into the barn, to where Erin still stood, looking at the cow and her adopted calf.

Is it my father? she had asked.

My father. So she and Abe called him that to each other. *What did you think would happen, asking them here?*

The rancher recalled the night he'd used his key to get into Mears Cabin, the night he'd seen Erin's driver's license.

Her calling him "my father" opened a door he didn't realize he'd shut. It wasn't a door to acknowledging her; that wouldn't happen. But he was curious.

"How did Jayne die?"

Erin started. Backing away from him, she gauged his blue eyes. No anger there. No warmth, either. Not exactly.

But his interest was sober and true.

Which left the question. Sometimes she actually managed to forget about her mother's death for hours at a time, sometimes for a whole day. Not now. Now it was hard and real and present.

"She was murdered. By a man from work."

Kip's breath caught. Like he'd walked into the muzzle of an AK-47.

She kept talking, telling him the rest. In Erin's arms Maeve rubbed her eyes, made a fussy sound.

Kip reached for the baby, and Erin, quavering, gave her.

Through his shock over Jayne, Kip knew quiet contentment as he held the child against his shoulder, patted her back. Like holding Chaley when she was small. Sometimes babies liked to be held by a man. Easier to fall asleep on a big shoulder.

Twisting slowly back and forth, rocking Erin's child, deliberately forming no attachment to the creature, Kip asked, "Where is this man now?"

"In prison, serving several consecutive life terms." She averted her eyes from Kip and Maeve.

His eyes were cloudy, but his cheek rested against Maeve's small soft body. "When did it happen?"

"Maeve was two months old."

Kip felt the baby relax against his shoulder. She'd drifted off. Putting away what Erin had told him, he slowly moved the sleeping baby, handed her back to her mother, who trembled again.

It was like fear in a prisoner, and you ignored it.

As kindly as he could, Kip said, "You best get some sleep. We'll want breakfast in the morning."

Erin's disappointment was blinding, like headlights on a highway. She wondered what she'd wanted. The sadness scarcely eased when Kip's eyes smiled at her and her daughter. "She's a good little thing."

THE STORY OF Jayne's murder did not leave Kip that night. As he drove back out to the cows, he could think of nothing else.

He was changing. Hearing Jayne was dead had started the change. Seeing Erin's face when he told her he had just one daughter had changed him more.

Bitterness was idiocy. He had spent twenty-five years hating Jayne, and now a man had shot her. She had shown Erin some kind of love, and Erin's voice had wavered when she told the story of the murder.

Like her body had shaken when their hands exchanged her daughter.

As he parked and got out of the truck, blowing snow burned his face.

He'd made every concession to her and Abe and their child. Even let Chaley, in her dissatisfaction, leave the ranch.

He had given. He had paid.

It was enough.

Though nothing could be enough to assuage the unexpected anger inside him that someone had murdered Jayne, had murdered Erin's mother.

LATE THAT NIGHT, while Erin slept beside him, Abe's thoughts kept going although his body resisted movement. Kip Kay wasn't the only thing that kept sleep away. It was all the parallels.

It was Beulah Ann.

No.

It was Lane.

Surely, *surely,* his brother had not done what he had, tripped and fallen into fatherhood. That was part of why he'd asked Lane to baby-sit Maeve, so that he would see the reality of a baby.

He had to talk to Lane. But how could he get hold of him? As foreman, he couldn't leave the ranch to track down his brother at a rodeo in another state.

It's not your place to tell him, anyhow. It's up to Beulah Ann.

And if Beulah Ann chose to keep it to herself? It was no light thing to miss the first months of your child's life.

It was something you would always wish you'd known.

Abe wondered if it ever bothered Kip Kay that he'd missed a quarter century of Erin's life.

His mind played a midnight movie of bulldozers turning up soil and mountain meadows erased by homes. He pictured his daughter sitting at a table with the man she couldn't call Grandpa. On a ranch that should someday be hers.

The sheets seemed tangled around him and wouldn't let him loose, wouldn't let his muscles go slack and drowsy. He sat up and held his head in the dark, missing Lloyd, for one cowboy's death had so diminished the honor of his world.

"I went to the boss to have a little chat,
I slapped him in the face with my big slouch hat...."

—"The Old Chisholm Trail,"
undated cowboy ballad

CHAPTER FOURTEEN

NO ONE COMPLAINED about Erin's cooking—the oriental
stir-fry with chicken or Greek turnovers stuffed with
spinach and feta—as long as there was meat on the table
every night and enough food to fill everyone. Kip gave her
a cooking budget, and every week she went to Gunnison
and loaded three carts at City Market and pushed them
through the checkout like a train, with Maeve in the
caboose. She repaired the ranch chicken coop and bought
baby chicks and feed. And she guided Maeve's baby hands
over the fuzzy chicks and over the fur of baby rabbits they
didn't buy. It was spring, and Abe had her burning weeds
and helping clear ditches. While Maeve napped, she read
books about the history of the area and organized her
material on the Cockburn ranch. And each afternoon she
and Maeve walked a mile down the road to the mailbox.

Four letters arrived for her the last day of April. She
opened them all at the box while a neighbor's tractor
crawled past on the highway. Carrying Maeve to keep her
from wandering in with the cows or the bulls, Erin read
Beulah Ann's loopy writing on the way back to the house.

Dear Erin,
Your so nice, all the things you said in your letter.
You are so sweet to ask me to be your maid of honor
and pay my way back out there and everything, but
it's just not possible.

To answer your question about why I can't be a
mother, I don't tell everyone this, but I was just out
of prison when Uncle Kip let me come to the ranch.
It was part of a probation thing, and now I've screwed
up that, too. I just keep making mistakes, and I can't
keep this baby.

You asked who the father is and if he knows. Well,
you can probably figure it out when I say the baby
might even bare some family resemblance to Abe. I
tracked him down right where you said to find him
and told him about the baby and what I'd asked you,
and he thought that was fine. So please consider it. I
know you probably never thought of adopting, but I'd
feel so much better if you would.

Love,
Beulah Ann

Abe was in the corral when Erin returned from the
mailbox. She showed him the check from her mother's
estate, which her attorney had sent.

"What shall we do? Buy land? Buy cows? Build a
house?"

Thinking that forty-three thousand dollars made his
savings look pretty paltry, Abe hopped the fence to join
her. "That's your money, Erin. You could buy yourself a
good saddle. You could even buy yourself a horse, if you're
not happy with Noon."

But he saw from her face that she wouldn't, though she'd
given him a new Navajo saddle blanket for his birthday last
week; she still thought a horse of her own was an ex-
travagance.

When Taffy came sniffing around his feet, Abe picked her up. "Whoever said you were a dog, anyway?"

"I heard from some publishers, too."

"Yeah?"

"They said there's not enough there—that the history of one ranch from settlement to subdivision isn't enough."

Erin found herself and Maeve crushed against him, smelling his skin, smelling horses on his canvas work shirt. *He thinks I'm disappointed about the rejection.* Or maybe he was disappointed himself, that his family's history wouldn't be immortalized. That soon there would be houses on the hill.

When he let go, she said, "I'm going to continue the research, anyhow. Maybe I'll make a scrapbook. Or go to a subsidy publisher."

There was nothing else to say, so she gave him Beulah Ann's letter.

He read, his skin darkening, his jaw aging before her eyes. Finally, almost blindly, he thrust the letter toward Erin and touched Maeve's little hand briefly. "I have to go see that Paint at Tanner's."

He got in his truck, and Erin watched through the dusty windows as he put his head in his arms on the steering wheel in a posture of defeat.

ABE SANG "Jack o' Diamonds" while he reset the Paint's heart-bar shoes.

> "Whiskey, you villain,
> You've been my downfall,
> You've kicked me, you've cuffed me,
> But I love you for all."

When he'd finished with the horse, Josh Tanner said, "You know, this is going to add up by the time we're through. I don't suppose I could interest you in a trade?"

"For what?" *I have a brother...*

"A horse."

A week earlier Abe would have refused, wanting the cash to buy his own spread. Erin's check changed things the way Lane had. Pride was manure, and registered Paints weren't running cheap. "Keep talking."

"Well, I've got a ten-year-old gelding that was sold back to me. You trimmed his hooves the first time you came. Rado? His owner's moved to the city. He's been ridden some, but has some bad habits. Say you continue to treat Naomi for laminitis as long as she needs it, do those heart-bar resets. I'd trade you the horse."

"Papers?"

"Included."

Abe rested his hip against the pickup's wheel well. The horse was probably worth more than the cash he'd be paid—if it was a good horse. Not likely he could work cattle, but the gelding might make a good pleasure horse for Erin. And that was one thing she'd never buy for herself. "I'll look at him."

"Like to ride him?"

"That, too."

Before he left Tanner's, Abe agreed to the trade. He would work up a certificate for one year's worth of farrier service for the horse with laminitis. Tanner would get the papers in order, and Abe could pick up the horse the following week. The gelding had some bad habits, as Josh had said, but he also had some go and mostly needed to be ridden.

Abe drove from the Billings place to the Dry Gulch liquor and antique store on the highway, intending to purchase a bottle of rye like he had on Lane's birthday. But the ranch, the Kay Ranch, sang to him, the sounds of bawling dogies and water in the ditches, which were the sounds of spring. He never went into the store, after all—just home to the ranch.

That night, he found reasons to stay outside. Hunting the mother of a calf lost in a gulch. Stitching up a prolapsed cow. Pulling a calf. He rode Buy Back under the stars, drinking coffee from a thermos Erin had filled for him. As he practiced what Pete had taught him on the harmonica he'd found in Lloyd's junk, he thought in unconnected waves.

What had Beulah Ann done to go to prison?

"Amazing Grace." It was sounding pretty. At least, Buy Back was putting up with it.

Lane thought it would be fine if Abe and Erin raised his child. That was what Beulah Ann's letter had said. *Just the way Kip thought it was fine to leave Erin's upbringing to her mother.*

Be nice to play "Home on the Range." Lloyd had always liked it.

How could he tell Lane to own up to his responsibility when he, Abe, was working for a man who'd never met his? When Lane had grown up on that man's ranch? Of course, Lane didn't know that Kip was Erin's father.

But Abe knew.

Buy Back picked his way over the trail the team and flatbed had used that morning to feed the cows. In the saddle Abe asked himself if he should go find his brother, try to straighten him out.

I can't go after him. I'm needed here.

So was Erin.

And Kip would not acknowledge his daughter and grandchild.

In that instant Abe made up his mind and thanked Lane's selfishness for helping him do it. He rode for home.

"WE'RE LEAVING."

"What?" Erin was still up. Unable to sleep, she'd begun sewing new curtains for the trailer, from sale fabric she'd bought in Gunnison.

The sewing machine was on the kitchen table, and Hank Williams, Sr., was moanin' the blues on the stereo. One of Kip's records, which he'd given Abe.

Abe pulled out a chair near Erin's. "I thought I could stand what your father's doing. Well, I can't. Now my brother's denying his baby."

"It didn't sound like he *denied* it."

If he answered that, he'd say too much. "I'll stay on till he finds a new foreman. That's it."

He couldn't be serious, Erin thought. This was her *home*. The trailer, the garden, her job. Researching the history of the Cockburn ranch—preserving it before the ground was altered forever. She'd already talked to Ella Kelsey about volunteering at the museum a few hours a week; she could even bring Maeve along.

"There's not a single day this has felt right, Erin. Every morning I get up and see that man's face and know…"

"Know what?"

"That I'm *taking* it. He twists my balls. He *knows* you're his daughter and Maeve is his grandchild. When he dies, this ranch should be yours. *Yours*. And I'm supposed to pretend I don't care, that I've forgotten about it. I don't forget. I remember. Every hour of every day. I could live with that before. But not when my brother…" He shut down.

Yours. Yours. The ranch should be hers. That he had those thoughts distracted her, and her words came out weak. "It's just pride, Abe."

"It is *not* just pride!" He slammed his hand on the table.

Erin jumped. The first time she'd heard him raise his voice. The first time she'd seen the pulse in his neck like that.

More quietly he said, "It's honor."

After holding still and silent for a moment, he stood and left the kitchen and turned down the hall to the bedroom.

"Abe?" Erin jumped up and went to the edge of the hall.

His eyes gazed back, white, from the shadows.

Don't ask him. Don't ask him. All that matters is Abe. Have you forgotten what it's like to be dumped by cowboys?

Abe started to leave, as though he'd concluded she had nothing to say.

"Abe, please." She came close enough to smell the horses and cows and his sweat. Close enough to see the familiar lines near his mouth and eyes, to see his long lashes.

"What?" Abe knew, suddenly, that she was going to cry. That she would use tears and maybe threats to get him to stay.

He knew, also, that he would not give in.

"Can we stay...can we stay till our wedding? It'll be after branding, and then...then, I can be married here."

With her father present.

It seemed little to ask, and it surprised him she *had* asked. She made a study of not caring what Kip did, if he lived or died or wished her good-morning.

"I have to tell him we're leaving, Erin. Once he knows, he may not want us to stay that long."

She hugged herself.

There was no more to say.

And when they lay down to sleep, they closed the night with chaste kisses. Neither mentioned Beulah Ann's request. When their love felt like walking on a roof peak, neither wanted to talk about raising someone else's child.

AT BREAKFAST, Erin knew that Abe hadn't yet had time to talk to Kip. But he was the first one in for the midday meal. As Maeve banged an eggbeater on an empty pot, Abe crouched to greet her, and Erin asked, "Did you tell him?"

"Yes." Abe didn't bother looking up. When it came to

her father, she was like Martha, begging for a scratch. But less honest. Maybe because a dog couldn't understand words like *I have just one daughter.* "After the wedding is fine with him."

He stood up and saw her pretending it didn't matter. Gazing into her eyes, Abe called her hand, the way she'd called his the first night he'd told her, "I love you." He pushed back a lank lock of red hair, touched her face.

"What?" She glanced sideways at the soup on the stove.

"I have an idea." He had his own reasons, hopes of seeing she got what wasn't his to give. Of Kip Kay's giving it. "Your book. Maybe publishers would like it better if you covered the history of two ranches. A subdivision's going in across the road. But this ranch has a past and a future."

Her eyes blinked, then glowed. The way the kids had looked at him when he twisted balloons for them at rodeos.

Abe felt his face getting hot, but he confessed, "I even thought of a title for you. *A Tale of Two Ranches.*"

Her arms strangled his neck, and Abe hugged her back. He knew, from Erin's trembling, that she must be asking herself the same thing he was.

When it came down to recording history, would Kip Kay tell the truth—or choose to keep his lies?

ERIN WAS WASHING the supper dishes that evening when Kip came in to refill his coffee thermos for the night shift. He missed a beat when he saw her there, looking like Jayne, as always.

Well, it wouldn't be happening for too much longer, Kip told himself. Just till after branding, till after she married Abe in June. Then, Abe said, they would go.

Chaley had come by that afternoon. Seeing her, seeing that she wasn't really happy in Gunnison, that she was despondent and seemed to miss the ranch, had reassured Kip about his own decisions. He'd made concessions enough to Erin and her child. What he'd done was fair. If it wasn't enough for Abe, well…maybe it was best that they left. Maybe it was best.

Hearing a sound from the dining room, Kip peered around the corner. In her playpen, the baby fit rings over a cone.

The water went off. "Oh, Kip."

He spun.

Erin pushed back her bangs self-consciously in a gesture of Jayne's. "I wanted to ask you something. Actually, a couple of things."

"Yes?"

"I…studied history at the University of Nevada. Anyhow, I've been recording the history of the Cockburn ranch." Her eyes watched him like they were afraid of a BT, a booby trap. "I'm putting together a book, and I'd like to balance the history of a ranch that ends up as a subdivision with a picture of a working ranch that's surviving. So I wondered if you would be willing…to share the history of this ranch."

Strings of tension pulled tight through his body. The Kay Ranch had a history. It included a soldier coming home to bury his daddy and a wife who wouldn't stay. Erin hadn't just studied history; Beulah Ann had told him she had a doctorate. *She's so smart,* Beulah Ann had said, as though her own smarts didn't measure up. Damn that Lane.

Erin waited with those big Jayne-eyes, the way Jayne used to look when she was afraid of him. *You ought to be afraid, Erin. Because we both know how smart you are and just what you're doing.*

"No," he said. He didn't want to hurt her, just be firm, as he would with Chaley. Being careful to keep his voice kind, he asked, "Now, what else can I do for you?"

Her chin shook. Kip reminded himself that Chaley had looked the same way when she'd said she was leaving the

ranch. *We all have wrecks, Erin.* And like Chaley, Erin was
getting up. Standing tall. Talking.

To Erin it barely felt like talking. Just like making it to
the next moment, which she hoped wouldn't be another
pencil-holder moment. Obviously, he wanted to say yes to
something, to make up for that no. "I have some money,"
she said, "from my mom's estate. If I wanted to buy some
cows, is there any way I could work out leasing pasture or
something like that? Just till we go, of course."

His eyebrows tried to form one line. "You don't want
to buy cows and move them so soon. Trucking them will
cost you money. You should wait till you and Abe settle
somewhere."

The way her throat felt signified nothing. Being honest
didn't mean crying. You cried when you were dumped, and
she was wanted by the best damned cowboy ever was born.
"They're a wedding present for Abe. I really want
them..." Chaley had a herd of her own. Why shouldn't...

That was the difference between being Kip Kay's
daughter and the wife of his foreman, Abe had said.

"Give them to him on paper. Then have them shipped
where you go. That's the thing to do."

"Yes. You're right," Erin said, her eyes bright. "I didn't
think of that."

He filled his thermos while she resumed washing dishes.
As he turned to go, Kip saw her reflection in the window.
Jayne's face wet with tears.

He steeled himself. *Nothing to do with me. She knew
how it was when Abe took the job. Abe knew, too.*

He left the house, closing the door quietly behind him.

"What's happening?"

The voice startled Kip, coming out of nowhere that way.

It was Abe, who had been standing in the shadows of
the deck. Doing what, Kip couldn't imagine. Except waiting.

Kip pushed his hat tighter on his head. "Number 618

was looking close half an hour ago. I'm going out to check her again."

In the dark Abe tried to read his boss's face. "Why is she crying? Why is the woman I love crying?"

It came out like a line from a bad movie, and Kip's long sigh was the finest of insults.

Abe's hands itched.

In the black corridor outside the rectangle of light from the window, the rancher walked past where he stood. Walked past and did not look back.

He's an old man. He's your sweetheart's father, your daughter's grandfather. Don't do it.

Abe followed him down the steps.

At their foot the rancher waited, facing him expectantly. *Do you have something else to say?*

"Maybe Erin and I shouldn't go. Maybe we should stay here and fill this ranch with your descendants until you can see right from wrong."

"Suit yourself."

"More of my father's grandchildren. Are you ashamed to have the same grandchildren as my father? He was proud of Maeve."

"I know." Kip's pale eyes were eternally calm, like the eyes of some Buddhist monk. "And I know how casually you fathered that child. Just like your brother fathered Beulah Ann's."

With the same instinct that told him when to dodge a bull, when to vault, Abe knew just what to say. His heart clenched just a little as the words came out. "Erin sure was easy."

His back slammed against the edge of the deck, hard enough that he would have a long narrow bruise the next day, and hands grasped his throat. The hard breaths of his attacker, the pressure on his windpipe, scared him, and it took will not to resist, to keep his own muscles slack. It helped that saying the words had shocked him, made him sick. He could only gaze at Kip's eyes, and the rancher's were waiting for him, his face twisted. Abe stayed limp, just looking at those blue eyes.

They changed. From anger to a realization that was like fear.

Eyelids the shape of Chaley's came down, and the powerful hands that smelled like leather released Abe's neck. One slid to the shoulder of his Carhartt and rested there, like Kip was an old man catching his breath, leaning on someone younger. Abe could only see his hat, not his face, before the rancher withdrew his hand and walked away.

Abe waited, motionless, till the lights of the ranch truck went on and the vehicle drove past. The next seconds were like seeing an empty bottle of rye and realizing he'd drunk it all.

He'd been stupid and now he was sick.

Abe had wanted to make Kip Kay admit that he loved Erin, loved her like a daughter. He had wanted to win.

He'd won.

And he stood against the deck in the dark, seeing Erin's face and reliving the night they'd made precious Maeve, till Martha came around asking what was wrong.

ERIN WAS IN BED when Abe came in that night, but she wasn't asleep. "I've decided about Beulah Ann," she said.

Beulah Ann.

I know how casually you fathered that child. Just like your brother fathered Beulah Ann's.

Abe stripped off his clothes and eased between the sheets.

"We should say no," said Erin.

"Why's that?"

Erin couldn't tell him. He was Abe, who smelled like the animals. Abe, who knew her father had never wanted her. But she couldn't say she'd spent her life being dumped by Lane, and it had happened again that same night in the kitchen.

"Erin?"

There were other things to say on the subject. Erin picked one. "Okay, no one's ever paid me the compliment she has, and I would love to raise my cousin's baby." It was a naked truth, calling Beulah Ann her cousin out loud. The blushing silence was brief and perfect, and during it Abe's fingers threaded through hers. "But when it comes down to it, she'll want her baby, and she should have it, and I wouldn't take that from Beulah Ann."

"You can't know what she wants."

"Yes, I can. And your brother's not fit to look at her."

His hand released hers. "Watch what you say."

Erin remembered about Annabelle, and she remembered her father's love letters to Jayne. And that dumped could be a two-way street and a busy one.

To Abe her quiet felt like the silence women used to make men feel knee-high to a grasshopper. Closing his eyes, he saw Lane's birthday bottle of rye. *Use some sense.* But sense hadn't mattered in Reno. It was using no sense that had made Maeve. God, Maeve. He had to see Lane, had to talk to him. Had to look into his eyes and...

He saw Kip Kay's blue eyes in their fury.

Shame spoiled the victory.

Lane would be the same story told a different way. Lane might be persuaded to go to the birth, might see the baby, might even fall in love with his offspring in his own way. Might marry Beulah Ann.

But in the end he would leave. As their mother had left him.

And there would be a baby....

He didn't want to think about Beulah Ann, who became mixed up with Erin, Erin who'd borne Maeve. Erin he'd called easy.

We have to get out of here.

It would be good to leave the place where he'd called her easy—and where there were more stars than anywhere else and where water ran in ditches the two of them had cleared. To leave these mountains and never look upon the Skyline Ranches subdivision.

He remembered Rado, his barter from Josh Tanner a lifetime ago. He was tempted to tell Erin the Paint was for her, to cheer both of them. But Rado would be her birthday present, a surprise. So he told her only about the trade, that he'd acquired a new horse, and then he ran out of other talk.

"Abe?"

"Yes."

"Are you going to tell your mom about Lane?"

His mom.

"No." That was for Lane to do.

"She might come to see him. If you called her. Say you just said, 'Lane needs you. He doesn't know it, but he really needs you. Could you please go to whatever rodeo and watch him and spend time with him?' Say you—"

"No." Her turnaround made his head spin. *You're a good woman, Erin.* Easy was Taffy, so eager to lick his feet that he tripped on her. Easy was Martha's brown eyes gazing up at him.

Easy was giving it all.

When he wouldn't go away, Erin had said, *Can you dance, or are you just a public nuisance?*

"You don't have to tell her what's going on."

Lane again. Still. "My mother doesn't go to rodeos. She explained to me one time in Kentucky. I didn't get it till last fall. You know why she left?" He propped himself up in the moonlight. "She left because after Busy died, she figured she could love her children less if she lived apart from them. And if she loved us less, she wouldn't have to be afraid of something happening to us. So she decided not to love us anymore."

"She said that to you?"

"In a nicer way. She apologized for it, said she regretted it now. Said she loves us both. But Lane got the first message loud and clear. And he can't hear the second."

"Maybe if she said it to his face, he'd hear. Gosh, Abe, they're both alive. Your dad and my mom are dead, but your mom is still alive. She and Lane could make their peace."

Abe didn't miss the echo. Erin was saying to him what he'd said to Kip. About Kip's relationship with her.

Kip hadn't listened.

Would Annabelle?

"Oh, I love these wildflowers in this dear land of ours,
The eagle I love to hear scream,
I love the red rocks and the antelope flocks,
That graze on the mountaintops green."

—"Home on the Range,"
written by Dr. Brewster Higley, 1873

CHAPTER FIFTEEN

IN THE MORNING, fresh storm clouds rolled in from the southwest, and Erin stood by the cold frames wondering whether to keep things alive or let them die. The chicks had to be fed of course. Just as Taffy had to be disciplined for killing one. But the seedlings just starting to pop up green...were they worth the effort?

"Do it. Save them. I'll lend you the warmer for my car."

It was Lucky, ambling past from the bunkhouse.

Erin laughed. "I think they'll weather the storm without it." No reason to confess that she'd actually been deciding whether or not to water. Whether to let the little green things shrivel up and die because she wouldn't be there in August to freeze or can the vegetables, to fill pitchers with cut flowers. "Maeve, where are you going?"

Maeve wobbled after Lucky. "Horse!"

Lucky had sat her on his horse a few days earlier, for just a minute, holding her in the saddle so she could get the view.

Picking up the baby, letting the hand go on to work, Erin stared at the clouds reflected in the cold frame's glass, trying to see a crystal-ball future. Abe would find a job on another ranch. Probably not such a pretty one, surrounded by mountains and forest. But he would continue to cowboy and she would go with him. She imagined another trailer, set in a sagebrush landscape, maybe near those adobe foothills she'd seen between Grand Junction and Delta, a desert out of *Star Wars*. She saw a uranium-era house in Nevada or Utah. She saw saguaros in Texas, blizzards in North Dakota.

And the lanky cowboy, her Abe, was always there.

"Wa-wa," said Maeve, who wanted to help pour water onto the soil in the black plastic flats. Good enough reason to do it.

While Erin held Maeve and let the baby dump too much water onto the soil, dislodging seedlings, they heard horses' hooves and saw Abe coming back from the pasture, driving the Percherons and the flatbed that was used, in good weather, to haul hay for the cows.

"Horse!" Maeve wanted to get down, to run to the flatbed, but instead, Erin brushed off a crate near the cold frame and sat holding the toddler. Abe waved as he drove past.

"Wave to Daddy."

"Da-dee."

He stopped the team at the corral to the south, beside the hay shelter and the equipment shed. When he began to unhitch the horses, Taffy scurried around his feet until he yelled at her. Erin called the cocker spaniel, but she ran away, chasing birds.

Then the day froze. Kip came from the barn, striding toward the equipment shed to give Abe a hand with the horses.

He was the hoarder of history, but she'd been silly to cry over not having cows for Abe on his wedding day. There were finer wedding gifts for a rancher's son.

"Let's go to the trailer, Maeve."

INSIDE, ERIN HUNTED the local telephone directory. What was Jack Draw's place called?

Soaring Eagle Ranch.

The number was listed and she dialed it.

"Hello?"

"Yes, this is Erin Mackenzie calling. I understand Mr. Draw sold his property, and I was wondering what's happened to the brand?

"The brand? I wouldn't know about that." The woman sighed. "Hang on a minute."

Coming back on the line, she said, "I have no idea. We don't have anything to do with that."

"Could you give me the number of someone who could help me?"

"Just a minute."

After another twenty minutes on the phone, Erin had spoken with three people, none of whom knew anything about the triangle-E brand. The last shot was the realtor, who wasn't in his office. Erin left her number and put down the phone just as Abe banged open the door. "Erin, I'm taking Kip to town. He just broke his leg."

He left as fast as he'd come, running back across the yard in his insulated work overalls, under the charcoal sky.

Grabbing Maeve, Erin rushed after him. He was moving his truck to the equipment shed. Leaving it idling, he leaped out and dashed to the other side to help Kip to his feet. When she reached the men, Erin saw that Abe had immobilized the injury using an old wooden snowshoe and nylon webbing from a frayed halter. Obviously no one had considered 911.

"What happened?"

"Cocker spaniel." Kip gritted his teeth, sweat gathering in the pockets beneath his eyes.

"Taffy got under Marty's legs, and he reared," Abe explained.

One of the Percherons. Taffy must have startled him.

The two men made their way to the truck, Kip leaning on Abe. Abe said, "Get the door, okay?"

Erin opened the passenger door of the vehicle. Shivering, she wished she'd stopped for a coat. She bundled Maeve close. "Where's Taffy?"

No one answered.

"Is she all right?"

"Ran off," said Kip as Abe helped him onto the seat. Eyes clouded with pain, he inched back on the seat till he bumped into Maeve's car seat.

"Erin, move that thing," said Abe.

Setting down the baby, she raced to the other side. As she unbuckled the car seat and dragged it out the driver's side, her father said, "Thank you, Abe. Ah. That's fine. There…" Abe supported his splinted leg, lifting it into the truck, and Erin stood breathing, holding the car seat in the cold.

As she caught Maeve up in her arms again, she told herself she'd been silly.

For thinking that somehow Abe would have caused her father to break his leg. That maybe he'd been trying for something worse.

STARTING DOWN THE ROAD, Abe fought the urge to take every bump at thirty-five.

"Go to Gunnison," the rancher ordered, eyes shut. "Cheaper."

"They have all those ski doctors in Alta," Abe pointed out. "If you break a leg, everyone says go to Alta." He thought they should go to Gunnison, too, but someone should play devil's advocate. Especially since they had so much time to decide, slowing down and steering around every bump on the road.

"Want some music?" Abe thought Lane had an old Metallica tape in the glove box.

Kip was shaking his head.

Too bad Martha wasn't along to share the cab. She would *try* not to crowd his leg, being such a smart dog, but she did get excited....

"Ow! Watch your driving."

"Sorry. I'm doing my best."

The time till they reached the highway was like time for reflection in church. Counting sins and four regrettable words. The first snowflakes hit the windshield.

At the highway Kip said, "Wonder what Jack Draw's going to do with those cattle."

So here's where we pretend it didn't happen, thought Abe, *like we pretend Erin's not your daughter.* He didn't want to answer. But what did Kip care about Jack Draw's cows? "Thinking of crossbreeding?" He was kidding. Kip Kay lived and breathed Herefords and Angus, like sensible men.

"I'd take those Normandies if the price was right." Kip winced as he said, "Think I'll pass on the hairy ones."

Abe didn't feel much like chuckling or he would have.

Conversation lapsed and the snow kept on.

In the fuzzy thinking of agony, Kip replayed the night before. Erin's requests—and her secret. Wanted to buy cows for Abe. That morning before breakfast, he'd caught her looking through sale books in the kitchen. Well, if she asked his help buying cows, he'd give her that much.

As for what had happened outside... Grabbing Abe Cockburn by the throat was something he'd wanted to do for a long time. But now that it was over, he felt sheepish.

No, worse than that.

Why is the woman I love crying?

Raising Chaley, living with Lorraine, Kip had learned that women often cried—well, just because they felt like it. Hormones. Erin had wanted cows to show Abe on their wedding day. Good grief, he would have made room for a few more head. But it made no sense to haul cows around when you didn't have to.

As for the ranch history, that was manipulation.

But Abe had said too much.

"Kip, what did Beulah Ann do to go to prison?"

Kip blinked alert. He breathed through the pain in his leg. Beulah Ann. "Well, that's up to her to say. She's paid the penalty."

Abe avoided a pothole on the road. Kip was right. Strange how Kip could do some things right—and be so wrong when it came to Erin.

They were nearing Guy Loren's place, which had been his home for eight years. He'd given up bullfighting to come work on Kip Kay's ranch.

He told you what to expect, Abe. You're the one who shook on a bad deal.

Except it wasn't. The foreman's job was sweet.

The bad deal was that the boss wouldn't admit he had a daughter named Erin or a granddaughter named Maeve.

The bad deal...

The fifth wheel grew closer, and it said, *This is the best you were, after your daddy lost his ranch. Till Kip Kay gave you a break.* Slowing to check out Loren's stock, Abe felt Kip watching. But neither spoke, then, or for the rest of the drive.

Snow lay two inches deep on all the cars in the hospital parking lot. It had collected on the hood of Abe's truck, too. He parked at the emergency-room door and went in to tell them he had a man with a broken leg.

When Kip was loaded into a wheelchair, ready to be taken inside, Abe wanted to tell him that he was going to Stockman's and that Kip should call him when the surgery was done.

But you didn't do that to your fiancée's father.

Even if the father wouldn't admit that he was.

Instead, you sat in the waiting room and hoped he didn't die on the table. And you pretended you'd never considered one main reason the deal was bad. That no part of Kip

Kay's thank-you-God-I-love-this-ranch spread would ever be yours.

KIP HATED to be laid up, and within twenty-four hours of breaking his leg, he thought he'd go mad. He couldn't even drive his truck. The best he could do was ride in the cab of Abe's while the foreman made his rounds. And after a morning of that, Abe said the horses needed exercise, and Kip was stuck in the house. With all the ice from snowfall the night before, he could barely negotiate the steps to the deck; he'd break something else if he wasn't careful.

And in the house...

Well, there was Erin. Cooking and cleaning downstairs, though she'd never once ventured upstairs. But thanks to his injury, Kip was stuck in the downstairs guest room.

On the evening of the day following his accident, he broke down and called Chaley at her apartment. She wasn't home, so he left a pathetic message mentioning that he'd broken his leg. Then he grabbed his crutches to make it out to the den. As he left his room, a small toddling personage came down the dark hall toward him. "Mama?"

"Hi, Maeve. I don't know where your mama is." Erin never left the child alone that he'd noticed, and as soon as he spoke, Kip heard the door bang. She must have taken out the trash.

"Maeve?"

Turning her teetering body around, Maeve walked toward her mother's voice. "Mama?"

Kip's heart twisted strangely. What *would* be the harm in accepting Erin as his daughter? Having to give in somehow? To say that what Jayne did was all right? Having to own up to his own hurt pride at coming in from the cows and finding his wife gone?

Or just simply having to face Chaley.

Chaley, who was out somewhere tonight.

Well, there were other problems. This leg. It made him

feel weak, and in weakness he had to rely on Abe to run the ranch. Abe had tried to twist his arm, planning to leave. Just yesterday morning, Abe had said, *I'm afraid, if that's how you feel, we need to leave.* That night, he'd insulted Erin.

A man did not give in to extortion.

"Do you need more coffee?" Erin asked someone in the kitchen. "I just put on a fresh pot."

Kip had scarcely moved from the doorway where he'd seen Maeve. He couldn't tell who was in the kitchen with Erin until Abe spoke.

"Thanks."

"Abe, is everything all right?"

At first Kip imagined a dead cow; it was snowing cats and dogs outside. Then he realized the question was personal. Were the two of them having problems? *Was* Abe bluffing the other night? Or was he capable of saying the kind of things to Erin that he'd said to Kip? *That's just what he wants you to wonder.*

"When are you quitting tonight?" Erin asked.

"Midnight."

"Are you staying warm?"

"Sure."

Kip thought he should creep back into his room, not eavesdrop, but the conversation troubled him. Especially when he heard the door shut again. Abe leaving. No kiss for Erin.

Chaley had always complained that Abe wouldn't give up rodeo. And Kip had seen the way he'd looked at Loren's stock the day before. Rodeos, they got in a man's blood. When Abe quit here, would he go back to bullfighting?

That would be bad for Erin and Maeve. A man couldn't make a living that way. And it was hard on marriages.

Maybe even engagements.

In two seconds Kip thought it through, then leaned on his crutches and started out to the kitchen. Erin was tossing

Maeve's toys into a big bag she brought over to the house each day, while Maeve chewed on a stuffed bunny.

When she saw him, she immediately straightened. Her hair was still damp from being outside. "Oh. Hi. Can I get you anything?"

She was like that. Always thinking of others' needs. If she tried half as hard to please Abe, he should be the happiest man alive.

And she *was* trying, wasn't she? With that wedding gift.

Looking after his own herd could keep a man too busy for rodeo.

"I have an idea for your cows," said Kip.

Erin stood there, unmoving, and Maeve gazed up at her grandfather with big dark eyes.

Damned, he thought, if she wasn't about the most beautiful child he'd ever seen. Abe should thank his lucky stars for such a pretty little girl. *Maybe we should stay here and fill this ranch with your descendants until you can see right from wrong.*

Thinking his broken leg was making him soft and sentimental, Kip nonetheless said what he'd come to say. "You might look at Jack Draw's cows. He's sold his place to a developer. The cattle won't be going with it. If you bought some, we could just drive them over here. You wouldn't have to pay for trucking. If you'd like, I'll call his foreman, and you and I can go over and look at them."

Erin hated herself for feeling like he'd just shared the truth about cowboys, for feeling like he'd just handed her the damned grail. It was Abe who'd given her that. But her father was going to help her buy cows! Her father.

"Oh, thank you!" she exclaimed. "Thank you."

Kip smiled and nodded and turned away, and she listened to the whisper of his aluminum crutches as he blended with the shadows in the hall.

IN THE TRAILER at the same moment, Abe held the telephone in the bedroom to his ear, listening to it ring a thousand miles away. He'd planned it out while mending fences the day before, but tonight had decided him. *Abe, is everything all right?*

Everything might be all right in a world where fathers always claimed their babies. And a man never spoke out of turn.

"Hello?"

"Mom, it's Abe."

"Abe! Is everything all right?"

He heard that jump of fear in her voice. She knew it wasn't Lloyd this time. Which left him. And Lane. And Maeve, if she cared about a child she'd never seen. Abe still hadn't sent a picture.

Is everything all right?

Just like Erin.

"Everything's fine. Kind of." Taffy flopped down near his feet. The delinquent had shown up the night of Kip's accident, slinking to the porch with her tail between her legs. "Erin and I are getting married in June. The twenty-first. Will you come?"

"There?"

"Yes. On...the Kays' place."

"Oh. Well, yes. Of course I will. The twenty-first? I'm writing it down."

What kind of woman had to think so hard about whether or not she would come to her son's wedding?

"You can see Maeve then, too. Why I'm calling is, I want Lane to be my best man, and he's on the road, and I can't go track him down. Kip broke his leg, and I can't leave."

"Well, why don't you write to him? Isn't there a rodeo secretary or something like that?"

Abe smiled at his mother's version of the rodeo secretary. It was true he could get mail to Lane one way or another. Even have it hand-delivered by Guy Loren. That wouldn't accomplish his goal.

"We had a little falling-out." Lane's disappearing for Lloyd's funeral qualified. "I don't want to ask him in a letter. And—" he tried to remember what Erin had suggested two nights before "—Lane's going through kind of a rough time. I think he needs you."

"What are you talking about?"

Martha came into the room and he reached down to pet her. The bedroom was dark, and he could pretend he wasn't there, doing this. He could pretend to his mother, too, that all of this was casual. "Seeing you is just what he needs. If you came here, went to one of his rodeos, spent some time with him—that would be the thing."

"Abe, I don't go to rodeos. You know that. I just can't."

Abe wondered how he could look into the eyes of a charging bull and jump over it, how Lane could climb on the bull's back and ride it, yet Annabelle couldn't go *watch* a rodeo. If he played music for a living, would she come hear his band? If he raised cows, like his daddy...

"What if I send him a plane ticket to come here?" she asked.

There had been plane tickets before. They had come too late.

"Lane is having a problem with selfishness," he said. "And something's happening where he needs to think about other people, and he's not doing it. So, I think you should set an example for him." Wincing, he pressed a hand to the bridge of his nose.

"Abe, just what has your brother done?"

Martha, look how you're looking at me. You're still in love with me, aren't you? "I have to get off the phone. I have to go back to work."

Annabelle sighed. "Do you even know where he *is*, Abe?"

Martha kissed his hand. He let her kiss his face. "I have

his schedule. I can send it to you. I will. I'll send it to you. And—" he remembered his story "—the wedding won't be the same unless he's there."

"Don't put that on me, Abe. I didn't agree to anything. I have to think this through."

"Okay. I love you. Good night."

"Good night, Abe."

He hung up, and Erin was in the doorway.

"Is she going to do it?"

"No telling."

Erin came in and sat on the bed. "Why aren't we making love?"

Time to swallow the burden of what he'd said to her dad. And to remind himself that he'd fallen in love before he knew her birthright was the Kay Ranch. *Cowboy up, Abe.* "Where's Maeve?"

"Asleep."

She must have gotten her down quietly.

They touched. Lay on the bed together.

"Tell me what's wrong."

"Nothing's wrong. Feel this."

She touched him, made fast work of his sterling belt buckle, unzipped his fly and opened it, releasing the pressure. With her hands on him, he dragged her closer, unbuttoning her shirt. "That night," he said. "I'd never been in love before that night when I saw you."

"THERE HE IS," said Kip, leaning on his crutches at the kitchen sink the following afternoon. He and Erin had been waiting for Abe to come back in his truck so that they could use Maeve's car seat when they drove over to Jack Draw's.

"Good. Oh, he must have gone to get that horse." Slinging her tote bag and camera over her shoulder—she planned to photograph the aspen at the ranch—Erin reached down for Maeve's hand. "Walk?"

Maeve lifted her baby hand up to her mother's larger one.

"What horse?" On crutches Kip made his way to the door. While Maeve slowly toddled the length of the mudroom, he clapped on his hat, zipped his coat.

Erin told him about Abe's trade with Josh Tanner.

Kip only grunted in answer.

After holding the door for her father, Erin led their slow progress across the deck. She'd shoveled a path first thing that morning. With the way from the house cleared, Kip had spent a good part of the day over by the corral and the barn, giving advice to the hands.

By the time Erin, Kip and Maeve reached the bottom of the stairs, Abe was unloading the Paint, who snorted and shied and generally gave him trouble. Taffy raced to Erin's feet and stood barking, then charged across the yard and behind the trailer.

"Maybe she'll go in with the bulls," Kip muttered. The two ranch dogs were watching her from beside the barn with what could only be described as dismay.

While Abe calmed the Paint and stood holding him, Kip limped closer, his crutches sinking in the mud and snow. "That's a showy animal. For Erin?" He couldn't think of another good reason Abe would have done the trade. For the money he would've made from Josh Tanner, Abe could have bought two decent cow ponies.

Abe's eyes went keen—in a way that made Kip nervous. An ace up his sleeve? Not likely.

"He's kind of snorty. Hasn't been ridden much." Abe smiled at Erin. "Erin likes Noon just fine."

Erin's eyes dropped a little, though Kip could see she was nodding, agreeing. It was the answer of a woman who wanted a horse of her own, and Abe was the man to give it to her. Under the circumstances, Kip was a little surprised Abe had acquired another horse for himself, especially one so green.

Ignoring both Kip and Erin, Abe led the Paint toward the barn.

Erin gazed after it. The Paint was beautiful; no wonder Abe had agreed to the trade. She and Maeve would visit the horse in the barn when they returned from Jack Draw's, she decided as she opened the passenger door of the truck to get the car seat.

"Shall we take this truck? I can get Abe to unhitch it."

"We'll take mine," Kip said. "You drive." He whistled to the dogs, and the border collie and blue heeler came running, eager for a ride.

Distantly Erin observed that it was one of those firsts in life that she'd never had. Driving her father's car.

They were all loaded in, and Erin was turning the truck when Abe came out of the barn and gave her a "What gives? Where are you going?" look.

"Tell him you're taking me to see some cows," Kip said.

Erin threw him a smile, and Maeve giggled, almost as though she understood the conspiracy.

"You like that, do you?" the rancher said.

Erin rolled down the window, and Abe came near.

"I'm taking my— I'm taking Kip to look at some cows."

It was one of those slips that everyone noticed. For a heartbeat, no one spoke. At last, half-turned away, Abe said, "Have fun." He headed back for the barn, undoubtedly to see to his new horse.

He's right about Noon, she thought. *Noon's plenty of horse for me.* Watching uneven spots in the road, Erin eased the truck forward.

"Noon's a good horse," said Kip.

"I really don't need a horse of my own. I don't ride enough. And I'm probably not a good enough rider to have a more spirited horse."

"Buy Back's got a good dose of Thoroughbred in him. You handle him fine."

It took a second to answer. What with driving. "Thank you."

Puffs of dust plumed from the road ahead. A silver-blue mini pickup came toward them.

"There's Chaley. Pull over."

She did and rolled down the window. As her pickup stopped alongside Kip's, Chaley did the same. Her hair was in one braid, and she tossed it as she gazed past Erin at her father. With a smile that was affectionate and miffed in equal parts, Chaley asked, "Forget I was coming?"

Kip ducked his head. "Afraid I did."

"Going into town?"

"Actually we're going to look at cows."

"Whose cows?"

Erin flattened herself against the driver's seat so Kip and Chaley could see each other better and talk over her. In seconds the conversation subtly changed. Chaley hinting that her father should abort the trip, reschedule for another day and visit with her, instead. Kip not offering to do so.

It was not about her.

"We won't be more than an hour," he said. "We're just running over to Jack Draw's." He added, "You could follow along."

Chaley's eyes settled on the third occupant of her father's pickup. Abe's daughter. "No, thanks. I just came by to see your leg, see how you're getting along. It looks like you have plenty of help, so I'll see you later."

With that, she put her truck in gear and drove off, leaving Kip in the silent aftermath of her bad manners. He felt Erin glance over at him. Even from the corner of his eye, it was hard not to notice how pale she looked. Pale as the ground outside, spring trying to get through the snow.

Suddenly exhausted, Kip said, "Keep driving."

Neither of them spoke till Jack Draw's, where Kip said,

"This man's got more money in his fence than I've got in cows. Now they'll tear it all down."

Erin drove under the stockade gate. Afternoon clouds hid half the mountains to the east, but their gray couldn't hurt the Soaring Eagle Ranch. "It's sickening to think of this subdivided," she said. She should photograph the stockade gate, the fence, the new buildings, as well as the old.

"Glad Lloyd's not alive to see it." The next words fell over those, as though he was pretending the first hadn't been. "The foreman here said he'd meet us at his house. It's that ski-condo thing over there. Good God, what people will do. That foreman lives better than I do."

Jack Draw's foreman was older than Abe and dressed in a good canvas shirt, a new pair of jeans and good Justin ropers. His coat was all sheepskin, his hat one-hundred-percent beaver fur, custom-made. He introduced himself as Randy and said, "You want to talk cows. We'll be having a sale June thirteenth. Want to take a drive? And you wanted to take photos, you said."

Erin nodded. "Thank you."

The foreman's extended cab pickup made it possible for them to ride together. They stopped for Erin to photograph the aspen and the old homestead and Jack Draw's mansion. Twice Kip suggested places on the ranch she should capture on film. *Now, the view from this rise is right pretty. Randy, drive over there. Let's see if your boss has replaced that old sign by the forest-service fence.*

Several times Kip got out with his crutches and inspected some short-haired white cows with brown and yellow-red spots. The second time he returned to the vehicle, Erin, in the back seat with Maeve, asked, "What about the Scotch Highlanders?" She liked the shaggy cows best of all. Though *The Cattle Raid of Cooley* was an Irish legend, she'd always pictured the Donn Cualigne as large and furry. A Scotch Highlander bull would be worthy of Queen Maeve's raid.

Kip's head didn't move.

Randy said, "Yeah. He's selling those, too. Calves, after they're weaned, will probably go for about five hundred, the mamas seven."

When Erin had her photos, the foreman drove them back to the barn. Kip angled his crutches to get out the door. "Well, thank you, Randy. We'll be in touch." He maneuvered out of the cab, wedged his crutches under him and shut the door.

As the foreman started to open his door, Erin asked, "Randy, what happened to Jack Draw's brand? Did he sell it?"

The foreman turned around, met her eyes and nodded. "Yes, ma'am. He sold it to me."

"If you speak the truth, have a foot in the stirrup."

—Turkish proverb

CHAPTER SIXTEEN

WHEN KIP AND ERIN and Maeve left to see the cows, Abe returned to the barn. Kip had been easy to read today. He thought Erin should have a horse of her own. He wanted his kin well treated, though he wouldn't admit the kinship.

It made a man wonder, and while Abe wondered, he tried a few notes of "Home on the Range" on his harp. The Paint was receptive, calm about it.

There just weren't a lot of jobs in this area, and Abe couldn't move away while he owed Josh Tanner work. Anyhow, moving would cost money, and that would be the end of his savings and the start of debt.

Or taking money from his wife.

He stowed the harmonica and petted Rado. *I'm going to give you to the woman I love. And my love for her will always be pure, because her daddy will never give her part of this ranch.*

"My dad's sure taken to your new fiancée."

At the voice Abe jumped, startling the Paint. In slow movements he rubbed the horse's shoulder before he left the stall and joined Chaley. Martha, appearing at the opened barn door, trotted inside to say hello. Patting his leg for her to jump up so he could scratch her ears, Abe said, "Really?"

"Well, she's driving him around."

They must have gone to look at Jack Draw's Normandies. Abe didn't believe Kip would buy any—he was probably just killing time on that broken leg—but you never could tell.

Martha sniffed Chaley's boots and Chaley said unenthusiastically, "Hi, Martha."

Why had Chaley come around? They had nothing to say to each other. Except— "Your dad tell you we're leaving?"

"No."

"Well, we are." Abe started toward the barn doors, and Martha tagged after. He wanted to ride the Paint, but other things came first. He hadn't seen any of the hands since he'd returned from Josh Tanner's. They had guests now, three sisters from New York, and George had them out riding fence.

"Don't leave on my account," Chaley called after him.

Abe stopped walking. "We're not."

She caught up with him just outside. "Look, what I came to say is…all of this hurts. I really… I'm just admitting to myself that I… Well, it's my own fault. I got you drunk and dangled this ranch in front of you, and then I told my dad we were engaged and…I apologize. It was a bad thing to do to you. I've just…always really liked you. A…a crush, I guess. I'm trying to grow up and get over it. Obviously you have this thing with her."

"Erin," Abe prompted. *This thing* didn't cover Maeve or till-death-do-you-part, but he let it go.

Chaley's eyes darkened sullenly. Her arms crossed her chest, hands holding the opposite elbows. "I just wanted to say I'm sorry. And I've accepted that you don't love me, that you never loved me."

She·was bringing back days he didn't want to think about. He'd been a different man the night she'd proposed. Back then, nothing was for keeps, and he'd had no faith in his own power to turn dreams into cows and grass.

You still don't, Abe. What in hell are you going to do when you leave here?

A truck was coming down the drive, probably Kip returning with Erin. Martha stood alert, then headed away to greet it. Abe said, "I'm sorry, too. And I'm trying to grow up, too."

Chaley latched on to him, hugging him around his coat, and Abe waited a polite period before trying to step back.

As the truck's engine shut off, they both turned to glance at the occupants of the vehicle.

It was Lane.

"Well, look who's here," said Chaley. "The deadbeat dad." To Abe's dumbfounded expression, she explained, "Dad told me why Beulah Ann left—he didn't have to say who. I think I'll leave you two virile sires and go back to my little apartment."

That was Chaley. Abe was glad to see her saunter away, with only a brief wave for the man in the pickup. Lane made no move to open his door.

Let him get out. Let him come to you.

It was tempting to walk back into the barn. But if he did, his brother would wheel around and leave. End of story.

Slowly, as Chaley spun a U-turn and spewed gravel on the trailer and the bull pens, Abe approached the truck. Through the windshield, he saw his brother's eyes, first meeting his, then dropping.

Abe came over to the driver's side. It had just been a month, but Lane looked different. Less like a rookie, more like someone who'd ridden some bulls and won some money. He wore the look of a full-time drifter, like he was already gone, present just in body.

But manhood hadn't settled yet.

"Bet you're pissed."

Abe didn't know what to say. That was a first for him with Lane. "What are you doing in town?"

"There's bull riding in Delta. Professional Bull Riders Association."

Abe changed the angle of his hat, lowering the brim to keep the low-slanting sun out of his eyes. Martha had finished sniffing his brother's tires and sat down at Abe's feet to scratch.

"I also wondered," Lane said, "if you're going to do what Beulah Ann asked."

Rubbing his chin and his jaw, Abe couldn't even look at Lane. *He's a kid. He's still a kid.* For the first time it occurred to Abe that Lane really wasn't ready to raise a baby.

He fathered one. He better get ready.

"I don't know." Abe leaned on the driver's door. *Do you have anything to say for yourself, Lane?*

One of those questions adults ask children when there's no answer. Thinking it, Abe felt like an asshole. His brother wasn't a child, but he was in a mess. He found a better question. "Are you asking me to do that? Not Beulah Ann. You?"

Lane's jaw was jumping, his mouth pressed shut. His pale-lashed gray eyes stared away from his brother's face, then back. "Why do you have to be so perfect, Abe? How come, when you screw up, it all works out easy for you, and you come out smelling like a rose? Beulah Ann says Kip made you foreman."

Abe backed away from the truck.

"Yeah," Lane said. "I'm asking."

"And I'm thinking." Perfect. Smelling like a rose. *You don't know what's going on with me.* "And while I'm thinking, why don't you think, too? Why don't you think about someone besides yourself for a change? Change. There's an idea. Why don't you *change,* Lane. You can come out smelling like a rose, too. If you stop acting like a pig."

He saw the words hit Lane. Sink in. Then his brother's

clenched jaw gave an almost audible scrape. Firing up the engine, Lane spun the vehicle back so fast that Abe was knocked away from it and almost fell. Knocked far enough away that when he heard the yelp, he also saw Martha's body tossed away from the truck. She convulsed, out of anyone's control, then lay still.

"WELL, I'M NOT SURPRISED," Kip said as Erin turned onto the highway, leaving Jack Draw's place. She had just told him about Randy's buying the triangle-E brand. "You could see that about him. People want the damnedest things. Now, Abe... I can see Abe or Lane wanting that brand bad enough to pay thousands of dollars for it. But someone else? If it's not your family brand, a brand is a brand. That was a sweet thing to want to do, though. Abe would have liked it."

Abe would have loved it.

"Charlie Cockburn picked out that brand for his wife, Elizabeth," Erin said. "She used to call everyone to dinner with a big iron triangle. It's hanging in the trailer."

"It's something," remarked Kip, "that your name starts with an *E*, too."

Outside, green shoots were trying to penetrate the snow.

Stretching in his seat, Kip said, "Well, old Jack Draw will have his sale, and you and I will go buy some cows, Erin. You and Abe can pick out your own brand together. Might mean more that way, anyhow."

Erin couldn't imagine that. One night when she'd been working on the ranch history, Abe had said the same thing about her name—the coincidence of its starting with an *E*.

ABE AND LANE drove into the ranch just before supper, and Lane went straight to the trailer. In the kitchen Abe told Erin that Lane had accidentally hit Martha. They'd taken her to the vet, where she'd undergone two hours of surgery for internal injuries. She had to spend the night at the animal hospital.

Lane would be staying at the trailer, although he begged off supper. Didn't want to see Kip, Abe figured, and didn't blame him.

That evening Abe didn't go back to work after supper, leaving the cows to the care of the hands. While Erin made chocolate-chip cookies, he played the harmonica for Lane, then entertained Maeve and talked with his brother. Like Kip, Lane wouldn't say why Beulah Ann had been sent to prison, and Abe liked him better for it.

While the cookies were baking, Maeve went into her room and came out pulling a waddling wooden goose that quacked.

"It's Mother Goose!" said Lane. "I remember her."

Erin and Abe were motionless as he sat down on the floor with his niece.

Seeing that someone had come to her level, Maeve walked unsteadily to the edge of the room and brought back a small wooden wagon with blocks in it. She dragged it to Lane, and soon he was building towers for her to knock over.

From the broken recliner near the TV, Erin could see Abe's face. He was watching Lane the way you looked at someone who didn't know he was dying.

"Lane," asked Erin, "where's Beulah Ann?"

He set an alphabet block on top of a stack of blue square blocks. "She's in East Texas with a girlfriend."

"Why isn't she with her family?"

"She and her mom don't get along too good."

That was news. And here was Lane in Colorado playing with blocks and preparing to ride bulls and broncs the next day.

On the other hand, maybe he was practicing entertaining a baby.

And rodeo was how he earned his living.

Lane stayed only through the night. He left in the morning before breakfast, and that afternoon, while Maeve was napping, Abe brought Martha home from the vet.

The Australian shepherd's rear leg had been broken and was now splinted, and her abdomen was shaved and bandaged. Abe had to lift her up the steps and into the trailer.

While Martha and Taffy curled up together on an old Boy Scout sleeping bag of Lane's and Taffy licked her friend's paws, Erin and Abe lay together on the couch, like spoons, and she asked him what he thought about Lane.

"I'm thinking hard about doing what they asked. He tries, Erin. But he wants to rodeo more than anything. I was never like that with bullfighting." His mother wouldn't even have had time yet to get the rodeo schedule and pictures of Maeve and Erin that he'd sent her. They'd taken a whole roll on a disposable camera purchased at City Market.

"That's fine for Lane. But what about Beulah Ann giving up her baby? Maybe Beulah Ann could come live with us. Then you could be a male role model for the baby."

"Thank you, Erin. I always wanted a harem."

"You better not."

He squeezed her, got up and sat on the floor to pet Martha. He sang "Old Corrals and Sagebrush," and it was all for Martha, who deserved better than him. Whenever he tried to walk, he kept falling, and he wondered how his brother could think he came up smelling like a rose. He'd apologized to Lane at the vet.

There was nothing he could say to Martha.

ABE WANTED to invite the Lorens and a few rodeo friends to the wedding, but that was all. Erin wrote to some friends in Reno but knew they wouldn't come. That left family and the hands on the Kay Ranch and Ella Kelsey from the museum—and Josh Tanner. Ella liked the idea of a children's room at the museum and of Erin's running afternoon workshops; together they schemed on Tanner. A mountain wedding was perfect for introductions, they decided, for chatting up money.

Her father would be there of course, watching like any other guest.

Erin reread his letters to her mother.

He only had to get up in the morning to be a hero.

And Jayne should not have left.

Almost every day Abe made certain she got out riding. She knew the sun lighting dewdrops on new spring leaves, the slant of the same sun through the needles of the evergreens. And it wasn't just in riding that she'd become part of the ranch. She knew the black roll of clouds past the kitchen window and would never forget the sound of the dinner bell, the feel of ringing it. Her seedlings crowded the glass of the cold frame, running out of room.

The truth about cowboys had vanished and become life, where Abe raised Herefords and she raised prize-winning vegetables for the county fair. Honesty was pouring her father coffee in the morning. Honesty was a blank line on her birth certificate.

When she and Abe took Martha to have her stitches out, Erin made him come shopping for wedding clothes. In a high-dollar Western-wear store, which at first he wouldn't enter, they bought him a thigh-length black coat, a satin waistcoat, a white shirt, a black string tie and a new black hat. The whole set reminded Erin of Charlie Cockburn's wedding suit, but as they left the store, Abe said, "I'm wearing my own jeans and my own boots, if you don't mind. If you want to spend all your mother's money on wedding clothes, you'll have to do it without my blessing."

"I have my wedding dress already."

But you didn't wear an artifact that could stir painful memories in the living. Not without asking.

Kip's cast had been replaced by a splint, and he was managing with just one crutch. When Erin suggested barbecue for dinner, he had volunteered to get the coals going. Sunshine hit the deck at four. Maeve was playing with blocks and boxes in her playpen on the deck, and Erin waved at Abe as he rode in on Rado.

To Erin, Kip remarked, "That Paint has shaped up into a good horse."

"Yes."

"You must have done some riding in Reno." The grill smoked—the breath of summer nights.

Erin told him about making A's and getting six weeks of riding lessons each summer. "It was a lot of money for my mom. She told me once that she gave up her cable subscription for my lessons."

"No great loss." He studied the coals, stirred them with a poker. Before Erin could remember how to get mad, he said, "Your mama still like Joni Mitchell?"

She knew he couldn't say, *Did she.* "Yes."

Her father became like an old man searching for a memory, and it was "Both Sides Now."

Erin knew every word, and they sang that song until Jayne was there on the deck with summer's keenest smell, picking up her granddaughter and rocking her. Smiling at Maeve's grandpa.

They could not look at each other, and Erin watched Abe, instead, carrying the Paint's saddle to the barn.

"I'm going to wear her wedding dress."

Kip's eyes darted up from the grill, as though he was hunting a cooking implement, but the poker was in his hand. It was Erin he found. When she looked, his eyes tilted in a too-bright smile, that look of spilling-over emotion Erin had seen in other men who'd been to that war and suffered in the jungles of a strange and seductive land. He was beautiful, too, like they were; he was one of the channels for the deepest feelings of humankind, as he said, "I think that would please her, Erin."

They heard Abe on the deck stairs. He went to Maeve in her playpen first thing and lifted her out.

"How's that Paint on cattle?" Kip asked.

"Fair to middling. What is it, Maeve?"

She wanted to show him her bunny, the birthday present he'd given her.

"Yes, that's your bunny." Kip sure had a thing about that horse.

Calves were calves, as Lloyd had said. And Kip had come near to killing him for calling Erin easy. So why were they leaving?

He'd never have a ranch of his own. The cattleman's life was packing its bags, moving to history. Kip had a June-twelfth hearing in court, to fight Denver for water. And now that summer was coming, the town of Alta was screaming about grazing rights again, trying to outbid the rancher for rights that were his. Someday the town would win. Money always did.

His dreams were fading with the light, but Erin kept hers. They were thin green plants she coaxed straight. They were curtains for the trailer. On her birthday he would make one of her dreams come true, and this place would be sweet, though it would never be his.

Once Erin had gone inside to cut vegetables for supper, Kip said, "I hope you won't feel I'm prying. But is there some reason you two can't afford rings?"

They had picked out bands in Gunnison. "Doesn't seem necessary." When Kip started looking like bad weather, Abe said, "You can't imagine what it would mean to Erin to know that you care so much about how I treat her."

The rancher hauled around from the grill, pointing a hot poker at Abe. "I *don't* want to hear it again. We've had this discussion."

Hit him again. Hit him again. "Fine. Tell Erin I can't

stay for supper. I'm going to work." Abe left the deck and strode down to the corral and deliberately provoked Kip further by spending several minutes with the Paint. When it occurred to him, he went into the tack room and dug up one of the few currycombs on the ranch and went out to groom the horse.

Kip glowered from the deck and Abe was singing "Eighteen Inches of Rain" as he climbed into his truck to drive out to the north pasture. This wasn't calling Erin easy. It was just foolproof mischief, guaranteed to help Kip see what Erin meant to him.

But the land took away his fun. There was a pile of twigs clogging one of the ditches. Abe got out to clear it, and his eyes ached over the grass and a bluebird on the barbed wire.

"Old Paint's a good pony, he paces when he can,
Goodbye, old Paint, I'm a-leaving Cheyenne."

—"Goodbye, Old Paint,"
traditional cowboy song

CHAPTER SEVENTEEN

ABE BAKED her birthday cake the night before, and even Martha was more herself and chewed on a rawhide bone he'd bought her. He and Erin played albums on the stereo, walking after midnight with Patsy Cline, sharing "XXX's and OOO's" with Trisha Yearwood, and they took turns dancing with Maeve and rocking her as Lloyd had on a long-ago night. When the baby had gone to sleep, Erin opened a bottle of Jack Daniel's, and she and Abe passed the bottle and danced some more and made love on the couch.

In the morning Kip would watch Maeve so that the two of them could ride in the mountains together. Abe hadn't told a soul he was giving Rado to Erin, but he had enlisted some help. During breakfast Lucky would saddle the Paint and Buy Back, putting the saddle Erin always used on the Paint. Maeve's gift was a new bridle. A new saddle would have to come later; Abe wanted Erin to choose it herself. At lunch when she opened the saddlebags he'd packed, she would find Rado's papers.

It was midnight before they went to bed. "This is the best birthday I've ever had, and it hasn't started yet."

"Well, this is all you get, so I hope you're satisfied."

Abe was almost asleep by the time she answered. "That's what he says. Without words."

It woke him up all the way.

The world had never seemed uglier. And suddenly leaving was a black-and-white matter again.

HER FATHER DIDN'T SAY, "Happy birthday" to Erin the next morning, just, "Morning, Erin," as she poured his coffee. Abe dried the breakfast dishes, and as they finished up, Kip hobbled in from outside. "All right," he said. "Where's my charge?"

Maeve was in the dining room in her playpen. Erin and Abe both hugged her and told her they'd be back later, and as they left, Kip was lifting her from the playpen, a children's book under one arm to read to her.

Abe helped Erin into her spring coat, a blanket-lined denim jacket. They put on hats and gloves and went out.

Lucky had tied the horses to the corral fence. Buy Back wore Abe's saddle. Beside him stood a polka-dot Appaloosa, cream-colored with brown spots, a horse Abe had never seen before. The tooled saddle on his back wore a large pink bow.

Erin gasped. "Abe!"

"Don't look at me."

She ran down the steps, then crept toward the horse as if she couldn't believe it.

That made two of them. Abe trailed after her.

Emerging from the barn, Lucky gave Abe a puzzled shrug. "Boss took over."

Which must have seemed odd to Lucky. Not to Abe. Kip had given her an Appaloosa. Same as he'd once given Chaley.

It was as good as saying Erin was his daughter.

The manila envelope with the papers stuck out of the saddlebag. Erin watched her hand reach for them, open the envelope. *This doesn't happen in my life. What happens in*

*my life are riding lessons six weeks a year. It doesn't
happen that a cowboy wants to marry me and my father
gives me a horse. This is Walt Disney, this is a Kodak
moment, and it's not true.*

A sheet of notebook paper was on top.

Happy Birthday, Erin.
Enjoy him.
   —Kip

She looked toward the house, and Kip stood in the
kitchen window with Maeve, watching her. Her legs were
water.

A few feet away Abe checked Buy Back's girth.

Erin read the papers.

His name was Wish.

Holding Buy Back's reins, Abe said, "That is about the
best-looking horse I ever saw."

Erin touched the horse's neck. Living flesh. Her fingers
threaded through its mane. A part of her thought, *Too late.*

Erin gave the papers to Abe and walked toward the
house. The steps were long. *You missed the second-grade-
class play, when I was Dorothy. I couldn't give you the
pencil holder I made for Father's Day. I'm twenty-seven
years old, and I've never had a dad.*

When she came inside he was in the den, reading to
Maeve in his easy chair. *Green Eggs and Ham.*

Seeing her, he frowned, all bluff, teasing. "Aren't you
supposed to be out riding with Abe?"

She had read his letters from Vietnam, and sitting there
in that chair, he was a man with eyes that held too much
emotion. This was who he was, and he'd given her Wish
with the broken heart he had. In an instant she crossed to
being his caretaker and protector, without his ever having
been a father to her.

This was his moment, his kind of healing, his gesture of love.

She would not say what she'd come in to say—the times he hadn't been there. She would thank him and try to make him feel like it was Disney, like she was a mermaid and her father had given her legs. "I've always wanted a horse of my own," she said. "Thank you."

CHEER UP, ABE. Kip didn't do this on purpose. It wasn't anybody's fault.

Except, of course, Abe's own.

Erin's going inside gave him a chance to retrieve Rado's papers from one of their lunch bags. Abe wished he had left them loose in the saddlebag; he'd been afraid they would shift position during their ride and Erin wouldn't notice them. Unfortunately this way, Kip had missed them, too. If he'd seen them, he would have withheld his own gift.

No. It's better this way. Rado couldn't make her as happy as this gift from her dad.

An Appaloosa. The Paint didn't even come close. The more Abe thought about it, the more he was embarrassed by his own gift. A horse he'd happened on by accident. A horse he'd traded for.

Wasn't even paid for in labor yet.

It's her day, Abe. Just help make it special.

Wish was a seven-year-old gelding. Abe wanted to insist on riding him first, to make sure Erin could handle him. Kip sure hadn't ridden the animal with his broken leg. But he would have bought him from someone he trusted.

When Erin returned to his side, he said, "Let's see how those stirrups look. Why don't you put them where you want them, and we'll check the fit?"

Her fingers combed the leather of the saddle again before she assessed the stirrups. "I think they're right. I'm going to try them."

Abe saw she wanted to do everything herself. She untied the reins and mounted up, then reached forward to stroke Wish's shoulder.

When she turned the horse, he responded easily and well, but Erin found she had to hold him, too, that he had some go. She was suddenly in heaven. This was her own horse. Dammit, she had a horse of her own.

She grinned at Abe, and he grinned back, tightly, but she chalked it up to his quick glance at the deck. Kip leaned on one crutch, holding Maeve in his free arm and watching.

Abe mounted up.

They walked the horses past the house, heading for a trail that led up into the national forest. The rancher waved.

Trying to improve his frame of mind, Abe held a silent conversation with Buy Back, full of profanity and well-expressed opinions about Kip Kay. And finally it came down to one word. *Shit.* He had no gift for Erin, just a Paint he never wanted to see again. Wish had come with complete tack, and even the bridle from Maeve was now useless.

If Abe didn't watch it, he could feel that way himself.

HE'D PLANNED that they follow the Alta Mine Trail up into the national forest, but there was no way he was going to take a young horse he didn't know up anything that steep. Instead, he chose the four-wheel-drive Alta Road. Wish behaved well, though Abe kept a distance between the two horses and advised Erin to do the same. When they'd gone a mile, they stopped to let the horses breathe.

Erin took off her hat, then reset it on her head and sighed as Wish nipped at grass near the tree where she'd tied him. "Want to ride him, Abe?"

He had to smile. "I'll take you up on that."

Abe wanted to satisfy his curiosity, and he did. The Appaloosa was a damn fine horse, so good Abe felt some envy. Kip Kay must have given Erin a horse he would have liked for himself. There was no more generous gift.

And Abe suppressed the thought that in Rado, he'd thought he'd chosen a horse that was right for Erin and would make her happy. That the Appaloosa was too much horse. But it was sour grapes. The truth was, beside Wish, the Paint could not measure up.

THEY HAD BIRTHDAY CAKE that night after supper and everyone sang ''Happy Birthday'' to Erin, and Kip winked at her across the table. When the time came to blow out the candles, she wished happiness and peace on Beulah Ann. It was only as she and Abe took Maeve back to the trailer that Lucky, yards behind them, cleared his throat and said, ''Would someone please tell me what is going on?''

Abe snapped his head around.

Lucky bent nervously to scratch the blue heeler, who was probably after dinner scraps.

The starry night shone on the four of them, the family of three and Lucky, and Erin realized there were no answers. That she'd never be able to say that Kip Kay was her father.

''Erin's birthday,'' said Abe, and he put his hand on Erin's back and kept it there all across the yard. She was shaking, and his hand felt warm and good.

Inside he said, ''Sit on the couch and close your eyes.''

Ah. The gift. She'd had the certain feeling he planned to give it to her on their ride, but what had happened was sex on a Navajo blanket next to Alta Creek, sex on scratchy wool under a blue sky, with the sound of water beside them. She'd said, *I just lost my virginity, Abe. Thank you.*

He said he'd never made love outside, either.

Now, eyes shut, Erin heard him say, ''Here, Maeve. Give it to Mommy. Go give it to your mama. That's a good girl.''

A large lightweight box was set in her lap. Maeve's little fingers plucked at Erin's jeans. "Mama."

Erin lifted her up to the couch. "Will you help me unwrap it?"

While Martha stretched out at her feet, Abe took the seat on Erin's free side. It wasn't much of a gift, he knew, but a shopping trip to Alta had yielded nothing except a Lorrie Morgan CD he'd tucked under her pillow. Nothing could measure up to that horse. Everything he found smelled like last-minute purchase. This...well, it was something real, anyhow. Erin had said how she would feel about having it. And Chaley was facing what their engagement had been— and realizing that his relationship with Erin was much more.

And if Kip noticed it...he'd interpret it his own way. Which might be good. *He'll think I'm cheap. He'll think I'm mistreating her. He'll squirm over it. And maybe...*

It wasn't outside the realm of possibility. In fact, the gift of the horse was another sign that things were going in the right direction. If, for instance, the news reached Chaley that her father had given Erin a horse...Chaley would ask questions. Kip must know that.

Erin had unwrapped the red paper and lifted the lid from the box. She pulled out the tissue and newspaper he'd stuffed inside, and Abe saw her growing more puzzled.

She'll find it.

She did. Unearthing the black velvet-covered ring box, she said, "Mmm," with a speculative smile.

Maeve was tearing apart a piece of tissue paper.

Erin opened the box. The ring was shaped like a twisted branch, and the diamond was its fruit. She had seen the ring before, on Chaley's hand; now Chaley would see it on hers. The thought made her tense, but Abe laid his arm over her shoulder, drew her close.

"It belonged to my dad's mom. It's important to me. Like Grandpa's woollies." Softly he admitted, "I let

Chaley wear it because I didn't have any money. I want you to wear it because I love you." He made himself look into her cavern eyes, and he touched her face, her white skin. Pretty didn't matter, but they didn't come prettier than her. "Erin, I'll understand whatever you decide. But I would feel honored if you and Maeve would take my name."

Her lips were curving, smiling, and he saw behind her eyes that she knew Cockburn family history, that she understood about the triangle-E brand. "I never thought of doing anything else."

She held the box out to him.

Taking the ring from it, Abe remembered their imaginary ring. Then he slipped on her finger the ring that Chaley had worn, too.

KIP NOTICED the ring the next morning at breakfast. He said nothing, but Abe knew the minute he saw it. His mouth tightened and Abe felt like a jerk.

Like a real clown.

He was going to get rid of the Paint the first chance he could. Return him to Josh Tanner, if Tanner would take him.

Abe could scarcely eat and left breakfast early, giving Maeve and Erin a quick kiss. He saddled Bo, his father's horse, and set out to mend fences. By noon it was warm, and he came back for his truck and a shovel and torch and spent the rest of the day working on the ditches so the water would flow as it should. He worked hard, and the work taught him who he was and who he wanted to be. It taught him what Lloyd hadn't been able to, with words or the example of his life.

Branding in two weeks. More dudes would be visiting. Chaley would probably come home to help, and she would ask about Erin's horse....

He was sweating at six-thirty when Erin rode up on

Wish, bringing his supper in an old lunch pail that had been Lloyd's. She looked good on the horse, proud of herself, but Wish didn't stand as she dismounted. Abe caught the reins and held them.

He'd been right. The Appaloosa was more horse than was good for her. "Erin, be careful riding him. He's got some spirit."

She took his words seriously, which helped. For some reason she still saw him as the man who had the truth about cowboys. They tied Wish to the gate and sat in the truck together while Abe ate the fried chicken and rice pilaf.

"Give me some pointers," she said.

So they talked about riding and Wish. The weather changed as they sat in the truck, charcoal clouds banking over the mountains from the southwest. Watching their progress, Abe said, "Erin, when your daddy gave you that horse, he had to know Chaley would ask why. You know what this means, don't you?"

She twisted his grandmother's ring on her finger and saw the storm coming and the darkness chasing shadows from the pasture, everything disappearing in blue-gray. "I know what I think *you* mean. What are you getting at?"

Abe didn't know what he was getting at. His feelings changed as often as the weather. The night before her birthday, he was sure they had to leave. The horse made a difference. And in the past twenty-four hours, he'd learned something elemental, the kind of thing you learned when you'd hit bottom.

"I'm saying I love this country," he told her, "and I can put up with your dad if you can." There was more—things he'd tell Kip at some point. What he needed to tell Erin was different. "At first, when I found out about Maeve, I was set on our getting our own place, something to give to her. But maybe people won't be raising cows in twenty years. Even on this place, the water is a fight every season. It seems better—it seems more right—to stay and help your dad.''

Erin stilled. The land. This land. Her father had given her Wish, and now Abe was reading the future. It didn't have to be awkward to say so. "You think he might give us part of the ranch someday?"

It was a fair question, thought Abe. She suspected him fairly. But there was no answer. He couldn't say that the pain of not being able to give her Rado had taught him to be a better man. That the pride of having his own spread wouldn't make him finer, the secret Lloyd had always known.

He opened his mouth to tell her he didn't care about her father's land. When he couldn't say it, he understood that wants burned away slowly, even after you knew what was right.

There was no shame in the truth.

"I love this land. I love you more."

They looked at each other and her eyes watered. "I'm sorry."

Abe gazed toward the weather. "My mom had this saying when we were growing up. 'Where there's heart room, there's house room.' I feel that way, Erin."

He'd shifted topics, but she followed. Next he was going to say that he would look out for his kin; it was right.

You're looking out for Lane, she thought. *What about Beulah Ann?*

"She should keep her baby," said Erin.

"If she doesn't?"

It was a request.

"Okay." Her lips pressed together.

Abe knew the way she loved Maeve, knew she was scared of loving Beulah Ann's baby that much and giving the child back to her mother someday. Because Erin would give her back, if Beulah asked.

"As a niece or nephew," she said. "No lies."

"No lies." They were holding hands.

"Shall I write Beulah Ann?"

"Lane's my brother. I think I'll ask your dad for a few days off." He squeezed her hand and released it. "You better get that horse back to the barn before we see some lightning."

Thunder rolled overhead, and Erin peered out the window at Wish's ears. "I think I'll lead him. In fact, Abe…"

The dark brown eyes asked, *Please?*

He kissed the cook, then tipped his hat to her. "Yes, ma'am." Climbing out of the truck, into the wind, he sang:

"Foot in the stirrup and hand on the horn,
I'm the best damned cowboy ever was born.
Com-a ti-yi youpy, yippy yay, yippy yay;
Com-a ti-yì youpy, yippy yay."

ERIN MADE IT BACK to the house first. Kip had brought Maeve outside. He stood at the foot of the steps, leaning on his crutch, keeping a sharp watch on the baby and eyeing the road.

When she slammed the truck door, he said, "Abe bringing Wish in?"

"Yes." Erin was embarrassed.

But Kip's nod was one of satisfaction as he saw the cowboy riding the Appaloosa down the road. Thunder rumbled. As Erin scooped up Maeve, who wore her red corduroy hat, Taffy emerged from around the corner of the house and stared at the approaching rider. When she recognized Abe, she took off toward him.

"That dog hasn't got the sense God gave little green apples." Rain plopped on the brim of Kip's hat. "You'd best get your baby inside."

"Thanks for watching her." Maeve was only wearing

overalls and a T-shirt, and it was getting chilly, so Erin carried her toward the trailer, calling to Abe, "I'm taking Maeve in."

He nodded, then nearly tripped over Taffy. "Go!" he said to the dog. "Go on!"

Taffy put her tail between her legs and charged through the corral, past Bo and Buy Back and toward Erin's garden. The trailer door shut behind Erin.

On his crutch Kip hobbled a short distance to see around that trailer. The dog was not above harassing his bulls, and she was too dumb to look out for herself, especially without other dogs around; Lucky had taken the ranch dogs into town, and Martha must be nursing her aches in the trailer.

Thunder cracked overhead, and the rain wet his shirt. Abe had Wish's saddle and bridle off and let him into the corral.

Kip made his way over to Abe. "What do you think?"

Of the horse.

"You made Erin real happy." Abe stood holding the saddle and tack. He needed to talk to Kip. About going to find Lane. About coming back to stay.

"What's wrong with him?"

"Likes to do things his way. He'll get over it."

"What would you have put her on?"

We're not standing in the rain to have this conversation. He couldn't undo yesterday and no longer wanted to. "A horse you gave her."

A distant yelp distracted the rancher. "Where is that dog?"

"Getting what she deserves." Shaking his head, Abe turned for the barn.

Kip maneuvered through the corral rails, limped past the Paint and Bo, then ducked through the rails again, getting cold and wet. That long-eared cocker spaniel was just the kind of dog Jayne would have owned—an animal without sense. She'd owned a declawed Persian cat when they were married.

Jayne had been murdered. He couldn't right that wrong, and so he worried that this dumb animal would sooner or later be stepped on by something with hooves.

Erin's garden, behind the trailer, was edged by a fence of chicken wire, crates and scrap lumber, all stuff she'd found around the place. It was a good fence, and her rows were neat. She'd gotten her root crops in already, and he could see green poking through the dark earth spotted by rain.

Where was Taffy?

The bulls stood in the rain, two Angus in the closest pens, others penned beyond. And there was the dog, whimpering in a heap as Black Jack, the bigger of Kip's bulls, prepared to hook her right out of the pen.

Something had already happened to that muddy mass of golden fur, and Kip didn't think twice before he wedged himself between the rails of the pipe corral. Black Jack looked up, eyes caught by the familiar.

"Hi, Jack," Kip said. "I'll just take this nuisance out of your way." He left his crutch, to make less stimulation for the bulls. The other Angus watched lazily as Kip limped through the mud to the whimpering dog.

He'd just picked up Taffy and saw her leg bent funny and the blood on her belly when his own sense returned. Thunder banged almost simultaneously with a lightning flash.

Black Jack lowered his head, and Kip knew he couldn't run fast enough. But he damned better try, and he did, knowing that breaking his leg again would beat dying. The suddenly pouring rain took him to other places, monsoon season under a triple canopy. His feet felt wet although they weren't. *And this is how I'm going to die—rescuing Jayne's dog from my favorite bull.*

His boots slipped on manure, and he went down and felt

the bull coming as he sensed something flying through the air nearby. A pair of battered ropers landed feet away, spraying him with mud, and Kip was never so glad to see a crazy bullfighter.

"Hey, Black Jack! Come and get me. Let's play."

Heart pounding, still under the giant trees along the Nam Nim, Kip held the whimpering dog and tried to drag himself up with his screaming leg. He'd never been wounded, but he'd seen men crawl away for their lives. He had to crawl while Abe played with the bull in the rain.

White lightning blinded him, illuminating the Colorado mountains, home for a cowboy. He dragged himself through the mud and manure toward the fence. A short spiral of barbed wire, lying where it shouldn't, poked out of the mud beneath the lowest rail. A wreck waiting to happen. The wreck was in his mind. The wire. Some things never went away. He saw again what he'd found in the wire after the sappers came. Jayne's dog was warm soft fur in his hands, smelling comforting like a dog. Her big brown eyes made him think there were things to live for.

Mud clung to his eyelashes, hanging before one eye as Abe turned that bull, had Black Jack chasing him in the mud and manure. Boots, instead of cleats. Kip dragged himself for his life and rolled under the pipe rail, tangling in the barbed wire, and then Abe was out of there, springing over the fence and landing beside Erin's garden. Kip saw him coming around the corral while Black Jack slammed into the fence, shaking the rails, rolling his eyes and pissed off. Shaggy wet father of the herd. *You're a damned good bull*, thought Kip.

Trying to get his good leg under him, he hunted for something to grab. A post. If he could just balance... But he couldn't let go of Taffy.

A young man reached beneath his arms, lifting him, and gave him his crutch. Kip felt weak and mean as he gripped the crutch, holding the dog, knowing he was a step from sliding in the muck again. It was all over him.

He still had his hat, anyway.

Taffy's eyes went wide at the burst of white flashing all over the yard, and Abe put out his hands for the dog. "I'll take her to Dave." The vet. "Let's get you to the house."

"Take her now," growled Kip. He'd risked his life to get her this far.

With a breath Kip heard, Abe adjusted his hat and walked away, strong and able, carrying the dog. A truck started in the storm.

Aching, Kip made for the house. And on the way he saw the pretty Paint that would never be a great cow pony. Not like the Appaloosa.

A horse you gave her.

"Oh, shit," he whispered.

HE WAS IN THE LIBRARY with his leg up, drinking whiskey, when Abe returned from the after-hours visit to the vet. Erin and Maeve were in the trailer; he'd talked to Erin, told her his plans and kissed her good-night. She'd asked how Taffy was, and he'd wondered what Kip had told her.

Now Kip didn't say a word.

"She'll live to cause more trouble," said Abe.

Kip nodded, took a drink.

There was something off about the sight. Abe didn't think hard about it, just sat on the edge of a chair and said he wanted to find his brother.

No response but another slim nod.

Abe thought he'd wait before he said anything about staying on. He left.

HE KISSED ERIN AWAKE to tell her he was leaving, and they held each other for a long time in the dark.

"Drive carefully. I couldn't stand it if something happened to you."

"I'll come home." He promised Martha, too, and she wagged her tail and wanted to go with him. The trailer was quiet; a draft reached under the door and chilled him. "Take care of Erin and Maeve, okay?"

He'd never left Martha behind until now. He wasn't sure why he was doing it, except that he would be apart from his family for the night.

Outside he loaded the Paint. He'd called Josh Tanner while he waited at the vet, and Tanner was sorry they "didn't need" the horse. Just bring him by, put him in the barn. They'd go back to cash payment.

Abe sang "Goodbye, Old Paint," and rubbed Rado's withers.

Wish had been skittish in the rain. He'd have to spend some time on that horse; Erin alone couldn't do what the Appaloosa needed.

"You're a good horse," he told Rado, loading him in the trailer. He secured the butt chain, backed out and closed up the trailer.

Abe climbed into the cab without ever seeing the figure on the deck, spying in the dark.

*"They say I drink whiskey; my money is my own,
And them that don't like me can leave me alone.
I'll eat when I'm hungry, I'll drink when I'm dry,
And when I get thirsty I'll lay down and cry."*

—"Jack o' Diamonds,"
Confederate drinking song

CHAPTER EIGHTEEN

IN THE MORNING, Erin lugged a box of Cockburn-ranch research material to the big house. Today was baking day; while the bread rose, she'd work. Maybe a subsidy publisher was the answer for her book. Self-published books on Colorado history did well, and Ella Kelsey had encouraged her. She said they would sell the book in the museum gift shop.

As she crossed the yard with Maeve, the door of Mears Cabin opened, and a man stepped outside and waved to her. It was the judge from Denver; he and his wife were the ranch's only guests this weekend. *They get up early.* They'd want coffee, so the minute she was inside, Erin filled the coffeemaker. The kitchen light was on, and Kip's hat still hung on the hook, but all was quiet.

Maeve tottered into the dining room and lifted her arms to be put in the playpen with her toys. "Mama!" When Erin set her inside, the baby immediately picked up her cube that had holes of different shapes for putting blocks in.

Starting to leave, Erin saw something from the corner of her eye and jumped.

A man in pajamas cowered beside the far credenza. Erin smelled whiskey from where she stood. She'd never seen her father when he hadn't shaved.

Slowly she inched her arms back down to the playpen. "Spider."

The word made her look. His face was crumpled in fear and horror; he was wide-eyed, seeing something Erin couldn't. Except that she knew Spider. Spider was the Master of Bingo, Spider wore a peace sign on his helmet... Spider was in her father's letters. There was a sound outside on the deck, and Kip started wildly and screamed, "Incoming!"

The shout froze her as he dashed, awkwardly dragging his bad leg, to the playpen and grabbed Maeve, held her and dropped to the floor.

Heart pounding, Erin reached down for Maeve's soft body in her little overalls and turtleneck. Words wouldn't come. "Give me..."

Guests entered the kitchen and Kip's eyes darted toward the noise. He scrambled to his feet, clinging to the oak table, but still had Maeve, who was startled but quiet. Someone said, "I wonder if we can talk Erin into an early cup of coffee."

Her father beckoned with life-or-death urgency and held tight to Maeve. Limping silently, he stole across the dining room and down the hallway leading away from the kitchen. Erin rushed after him and her baby, unable to utter a sound, unsure what sound was right.

The ranch office held filing cabinets. There was a military orderliness to it. A desk. A picture of Chaley. A university degree on the wall. Erin had dusted the room. It was the ranch office, for her.

For him it was someplace else, and he shut the door behind her. The alcohol smell of his body blended with his sweat, a person unwashed. He was the only scent in the room.

"Get down!" he whispered. "Dammit, get down!"

"Maamaa." Maeve reached for Erin and kicked her feet, trying to escape. She was going to cry.

Erin held out her arms for the baby, and her father seemed to see her for the first time. His face changed, the lines going slack, and he all but furrowed his brow.

"Jayne?"

He was scary, Erin. I couldn't control him.

But he let her take Maeve, and her daughter's body was soft against her shoulder, soft and safe, and Maeve's cries subsided.

Erin felt her mother's presence in the room. A wave of Jayne.

Mom, help me. Help him.

The voices in the kitchen were muffled, faraway. Erin almost opened the door and yelled to them. But the guests shouldn't see the ranch owner like this. *He won't hurt us, will he, Mom?*

As the back door closed, Kip squinted at the sound. Slick perspiration coated his face and forehead, even his ears. He glanced down, and when he saw his own bare feet on the oak floorboards, when he saw the fabric of his striped pajamas, the panic left his face. He looked almost himself.

Erin tried to hold him in this world. "Dad." The deliberate choice felt accidental and natural. And good. "Want some coffee?"

His head shot up, and his window to the here and now had shut. "Jayne." His eyes fixed on Maeve. "Let me hold her, Jayne. Please."

"She'll cry."

"She won't." He stood, tall and newly confident in some other, younger persona.

Erin held her daughter, held one of her tiny hands in one of hers. *We're going to be fine.* "Can I call Chaley, Kip?"

"I just want to hold her! Please."

He was angry. Too intense. Afraid of what he might do if she didn't let him, Erin said, "Here's your grandpa, Maeve."

His hands shook the way hers had the first time she'd handed him Maeve, in the barn. He acted like a man with his firstborn, afraid of dropping her.

A place behind her eyes was suddenly too hot, as though a blinding light shone there.

"Look at you," he said to Maeve. His forehead creased, his mouth half-open, he lifted her to his shoulder and rested his cheek against Maeve's soft curls. "She's beautiful, Jayne. She looks just like you."

The tears seeped from Erin's eyes and hit her cheeks. *Stop! Stop. Please.* She was in the presence of the grail, and it shone too bright. It was the truth about cowboys, and it resided where darkness met light and became love, and now she was here, and it was stronger than she'd ever known. The truth was too strong.

She tried to make it go away.

"Kip. I'm Erin, your and Jayne's daughter. That's Maeve, your granddaughter."

He seemed not to hear.

"Kip, she's hungry. And I need to make breakfast. There are a lot of people who need breakfast." God, she shook, like him. "Here, Maeve."

Erin reached for the baby.

Kip hugged the child a moment more, with his eyes shut, then relinquished her. Holding Maeve tightly, Erin opened the door and went out into the hall. On rubbery legs she walked through the dining room toward the sunshine coming through the kitchen window, streaming in the doorway like a white glow at the end of a tunnel.

ABE FOUND LANE in Cortez, where he was supposed to be. His brother was sleeping under a new camper shell in the bed of his pickup at the campground near the rodeo arena. Abe parked and bedded down in his own truck. Long before dawn his eyes opened wide, and he saw Kip as he'd last seen him.

In the cold night, he banged on the back window of Lane's shell. His brother got up, and they drank coffee in the dark at a picnic table and pretended it was normal that Abe had shown up.

There's no hurry; this shouldn't be rushed. He shifted his feet in the sand and tried to see the desert. Somewhere coyotes yipped. He was five hours from home.

He pictured Kip.

Lane said that the Cortez rodeo wasn't big, not that much money. He was chewing, and he spit a stream of tobacco juice into the sagebrush.

"Trying to keep women away?" Abe asked.

"Right. Have to fight 'em off."

The summer constellations twinkled above. Morning stars. *Say it and go.* "Lane, if you and Beulah Ann both want it when the time comes, I will be a father to your child."

Lane removed the plug from his mouth, discarded it and leaned back on his hands, staring at the bumper of his truck.

After a minute he said, "Thank you."

There was no need to rush off, Abe told himself again. Martha was at home with them. Still, he shifted on the edge of the bench, wanting to be gone, as he asked Lane, "You ever seen Kip drink?"

SHE COLLIDED with Lucky in the mudroom and thrust Maeve into his arms. "Kip's been drinking and is having war flashbacks. Take Maeve to the trailer and call Chaley and tell her to come. And just watch Maeve, okay? I'm going to get breakfast on."

The hand peered past her. "What's Chaley's number?"

Erin didn't know. It must be coded on the kitchen phone,

the ranch phone. "I'll call her. You watch Maeve. And try to keep the guests out of here till breakfast is ready. I'll try to do something about him."

As Lucky took the baby outside, Erin grabbed the telephone receiver and read the list of frequently called numbers. *Lloyd* had been changed to *Abe*. She found *Chaley-H,* Chaley at home. She pushed 3, and the number was dialed. The phone rang until an answering machine came on.

What could she say to an answering machine?

She hung up and tried 4. *Chaley-W*. An answering machine for the vet's clinic. *Saturday*. They were closed. Where was Chaley?

The house was quiet. She went through the dining-room door, and the sunlight from the kitchen window surrounded her and reached beyond her, making a tall black paper doll for her to follow.

Erin didn't mean to creep. She didn't fear a man who held a child so gently, who was a good father to his own daughter, Chaley. It was for his sake that she walked silently, to give him peace in the morning.

She returned to the office with her giant's shadow.

Breath was the first thing she felt, his in her face, accompanying the crack of her head slamming against the wall of the hallway, jarring her eyes, bringing tears. "Dad," came out of her. Then, there was only pain and no way to breathe or scream with his hands squeezing her throat. Sweat ran in the sun cracks around his wide and staring eyes, and the stench of whiskey filled her nose and mouth as her arms flailed upward, grabbing his hands.

His eyes blinked, and the pressure on her throat lessened minutely. She tried to pull his hands away, tried to draw breath.

The back door banged. "Erin!"

She hadn't heard the truck.

"Erin!"

She pried Kip's fingers from her throat, and as they went away, her breath burned and her windpipe felt bruised, and she knew she would never be the same. The truth had many shades and she hadn't been there, she hadn't been there till this minute.

A cowboy cast a long shadow.

Erin watched her father study the new shape, the man and the hat outlined on the oak floor where it met wainscoting.

The shadow moved, and it was the only time Erin had heard boots in that house.

Abe said, "Everything all right?"

The unshaven man in sweat-drenched pajamas turned, saw him and was suddenly present. And defeated. Dragging a hand up the damp skin of his face, Kip said two words.

"The Paint."

ABE HELPED HIM bathe. Kip had broken his leg again yesterday in the bull pen and didn't know it. *I've had worse hurts.*

They didn't talk, besides that, for many minutes. Abe passed him towels in silence, gave him his crutch. Pretended there was no weakness, as he would want Kip to do for him.

When he was half-dressed, Kip sank onto the edge of the bed. "Did you find your brother?"

"Yes."

Abe stood near the dresser in the guest room while the rancher buttoned his shirt. *Those hands tried to choke Erin.* You couldn't hurt a man for mistaking his daughter for the enemy. You couldn't lose control yourself, the way Abe thought he might. He tried to see Kip as he would a temperamental horse, like that gelding Rowdy, an animal who couldn't help being what he was.

When Erin knocked and said she'd brought them

breakfast, Abe opened the door. There were bruises on her throat. "All right?" he said, taking the tray.

She nodded. "Everyone's eaten." Her voice was hoarse. "I'm going to the trailer." Looking past him at Kip, she said, "Chaley's coming. She should be here any minute."

Abe set the tray on the dresser. There was a small folding table against the wall, and he opened it, set it in front of Kip and arranged Kip's breakfast and coffee on it. Then silverware.

When he looked up, Erin was gone.

Without lifting his eyes, Kip picked up a piece of French toast. There were two thoughts in his mind. Erin. And the Paint. The horse had set him drinking. Abe was a fox and a devil. That damned Paint.

Well, he'd had his moment of weakness. Now it was time to cowboy up and make things right again.

If he could.

The pictures came, the pictures of Spider and of other things, and he remembered that Abe was there in the room, Abe in his hat. He stared until he could see Abe's ropers. It was a trick he'd been using this past hour to take the images out of his mind.

Abe saw him wipe his hand across his face.

"Dad," said Chaley, in the doorway. She came to her father's side and bent over and hugged him.

He hugged her back, his eyes unfocused. When she straightened up, he said, "Abe, why don't you go see how...she's doing. Chaley will help me pack and take me into town. I'll be gone a few days."

"I'll take you," Abe said. "Send Chaley to the trailer when you're ready."

Too tired to fight him, Kip watched the foreman collect his plate and go. He listened to Abe's footsteps reach the kitchen. It was a long time before the back door shut.

Immediately Chaley asked, "Are you going to the VA?"

"Yes. But there's something I have to tell you first, Chaley. Sit down, honey."

She took a seat in the room's one armchair, one of those chairs none of them ever used, the guest-room chair. She looked as tired as he felt, and he saw that she had no inkling. She had always been the sun of her own universe. And of his.

It was his job to teach her to see beyond her own light.

"Chaley..." Ah, this burden, this secret could leave him now; the truth could come out. He took a breath. He saw Spider. He blinked and saw her eyes. "Chaley, you have a half sister. Her name is Erin."

ABE FOUND HER on the floor playing blocks with Maeve or, rather, pretending to play. Just an hour ago her father had half choked her. Since then, she'd fed the crew and cleaned up afterward. Now she was trembling. But the first words out of her mouth, in that same rasping voice, were, "Where's the Paint?"

He shut the door of the trailer and crouched to get a kiss from Martha, to pet her. "I'm so glad to see your tail wagging again."

Strands of red hair fell across the side of Erin's face as Abe sat beside her, put his arm around her.

Knocking over a tower of blocks, Maeve giggled. "Daddy."

"Hi, Maeve. I gave the Paint back to Tanner. Thought we could use the money, instead."

She didn't seem to hear. "I forgive her," Erin said. "I forgive her now."

Her mother. Abe didn't ask about her father, if she forgave him, too. He touched her throat and pressed her head against his chest. A lump rose from the back of her skull, and he asked her about it.

"He threw me against the wall." Hoarse shaking voice.

If he'd seen it, Kip would be dead. "Do you still want to stay here?"

She shook her head. "I want my horse. I want the Paint."

He held her away from him and saw she'd been crying while he held her. The bruises on her throat left no room for why. Why she wanted to leave. But everything had changed for him, too, that morning. It had to do with helping her father bathe and the fact that Kip Kay had a broken leg and hadn't noticed. The fact that he could mistake Erin for the enemy—and that Denver wanted his water and Alta wanted his grazing rights.

And that he was her father.

Abe kept quiet. If she wanted to go, they would. But where?

AFTER HE TOOK KIP to the hospital, Abe went to Josh Tanner's. He brought home the Paint, and Erin saddled Rado with the saddle Kip had given her. While Abe watched Maeve, she rode toward the north pasture, past the heifers. The Paint was gentle; she felt none of the anxiousness she had with Wish, none of the sense that she was not in charge. With the Paint, she could concentrate on her riding, and her eyes memorized the shades of his coat, the patch of black in his mane.

Here was none of the needy feeling, the desperation of something given too late, that she'd experienced from her father's gift. The Paint was like Abe's love for her, secure and dependable.

She breathed the mountains through her aching throat, tried to ignore the throbbing from the back of her head. Bluebirds, magpies, sparrow hawks, meadowlarks, red-winged blackbirds...they flew over the fields, landed on the barbed wire. To the west she spotted a pair of red-tailed hawks soaring. Rocky Mountain irises edged the road, and crimson and blue columbine grew beneath the fences. The cool air smelled of evergreen.

Her father would have wanted her had Jayne stayed. He would have adored her, as he'd adored Maeve in those moments of confusion, when he'd mixed everyone up. As he loved Chaley.

Do you want to stay? Abe had asked.

It didn't matter. She had received the thing for which she had come. She had gotten all of it, and after the wedding she and Abe could take their cows and go.

And Kip, she thought, would not drink again, would not be driven mad by the presence of someone who carried him back where he shouldn't have to go.

Pete was in the north pasture, and the sound of his harmonica reached Erin before she saw him. He was sitting under a tree playing "Amazing Grace." She listened hard, tucking the moment, like the smells and the land and the lowing of a cow, into her memory. She would collect these memories to take with her when she left, and the pencil holder would be full.

KIP RETURNED from the hospital five days later. Chaley brought him home in the afternoon, but when she opened the mudroom door for him and saw Erin she said, "I'll see you later, Dad."

"Thank you, honey."

From the kitchen table, where she sat polishing silver, Erin heard him kiss her half sister and heard Chaley say, "I love you. Call if you need anything."

Erin trained her eyes on the paper that lay on the table, the second chapter of her book about the Cockburn ranch. Maeve was playing on the floor, trying to fit the halves of plastic Easter eggs together.

Remembering the eggs when she saw her father's crutches and his new cast, Erin got up. "Let's make a path, Maevey, so he can get through."

The lie hurt her tongue.

He.

We will leave, she thought, *to end the telling of lies. The use of pronouns to avoid specific words, like "your grand-father."*

"She's fine," said Kip. "I'll be careful. What have you got there?" Still in his coat and hat, he leaned over the table, and Erin let him read. After a moment he stepped back, with his crutches, watching out for Maeve. Balancing on one crutch, then the other, he shed his coat and hat and hung them up.

He made his way around the baby, and Erin ignored his progress down the hall. She tried to concentrate on words. They swam before her. Rubbing hard with the rag, she hurried to finish the silver.

Footsteps creaked overhead. The sound of a drawer.

What was he doing upstairs on that twice-broken leg?

Erin rolled her eyes. "Cowboys," she said to Maeve. She put the silver away, twisted the lid on the polish, glanced at the clock. An hour to weed in the garden before she had to start supper.

The stairs, down the back hall by the den, creaked. Well, he was her father. He was a veteran, and he'd been wounded rescuing Taffy from a bull, and she would take care of him. She left Maeve and walked down the hall. As she rounded the corner, she saw him struggling down the last six steps, carrying a boot box and a cigar box and his crutches, clinging to the railing.

"There you are," he said. "Get this stuff, will you?"

She came to take the boxes, to help him situate his crutches. Slowly he descended the last steps.

"In your room?" she asked.

"Oh, let's go out in the kitchen."

The boxes. What was in them?

Her heart raced, and she wished it wouldn't. It was like when he'd given her Wish; she hated it that she cared so much. She pressed a hand to her forehead. Was there anything to say?

He was cheerful.

Erin walked ahead of him to the kitchen, set the boxes on the table and picked up Maeve, pretending the boxes didn't matter. One had once held Justin Boots, the other Havana cigars. She carried Maeve to the window to look out. "Do you see Daddy?" There was Abe, back from riding fence with three guests.

She watched one of the guests try to tip him. He shook his head.

The crutches made their muted sounds behind her. Kip was lifting the lid off the boot box. As though satisfied that it contained what he thought, he replaced the lid and said, "You're welcome to this stuff. Look it over and use what you can."

Maeve wanted down, and Erin let her squat to find an egg that had rolled under the edge of the counter. She approached the table and opened the lid on the boot box. Photos and letters and news clippings. The one on top was about him coming home from the war.

She shut the box as though it was Pandora's. This was his way of saying she could write the history of the Kay Ranch, and it was just like Wish. It was everything except someone to give a pencil holder to. "Thank you," she said. "I'll enjoy looking through that. And I'll let you read whatever I do."

His callused brown fingers—the fingers that had choked her—had lifted the lid on the cigar box and were digging through trinkets.

He pulled one out and leaned on his crutches to face her. The crutches helped his balance as his workingman's fingers plucked the cape yoke of her Western blouse and prodded the pin through.

"I never knew you were decorated."

His look was like when he'd told her he had just one

daughter, like nothing mattered. He'd finished with the pin and grabbed the hand grips of his crutches again.

He's going to say something—he's going to say something that will make everything right and end the lies.

"Now, you are." Kip closed up the cigar box and tucked it between his forearm and the crutch. Then he wheeled around Maeve again and hobbled down the hall to his room.

IN THE BARN, Abe touched the Silver Star. "Does it change anything?"

"We're not leaving because I'm afraid of him. I'm not afraid."

So she thought her father had acknowledged her valor. Maybe he had. Abe thought it more likely he'd apologized the best he could.

Maeve waddled toward the blue heeler, who had seen her, too, and was fleeing. Martha herded the toddler back to her parents.

"You changed your mind about staying the day he attacked you. I thought you were afraid. Or angry."

She shook her head. "I called him Dad. It changed...everything."

"You can call him that."

"I can't!"

Her shout startled Martha and made Maeve cry. Abe understood the reason for it—and that it was something he couldn't fix. Because of what her father had said to her and never taken back. That he had just one daughter.

As she gazed absently toward some hay bales, her hand against the medal on her shirt, he picked up Maeve. "Erin, it's going to be hard to find another place this good. You don't have to stay here and spend your life putting up with Kip. But if you want me to talk to him, I will."

"It won't help." Her face was white, her eyes two dark holes. "It has to come from him, and it never will."

He couldn't stop himself. "What happened to his being your hero?"

She shoved his chest with both hands and left the barn crying. He had to chase her to the trailer, carrying Maeve. Inside it was dark, and he put Maeve in her crib with some toys.

When he lay on the bed with Erin, not taking off his boots, she said, "Don't make me feel small. Before, I thought it was enough. But he tried to kill me, and he can't say the words 'I'm sorry.' Maybe he's not. I can't stay here."

Kip's hands had been around Abe's throat, too. *He tried to kill me, on your behalf.* He and Erin were strong enough together that she could hear it; she knew how he felt about her. He held her tight against him, so tight she wouldn't be able to see his face. "I need to tell you something that happened between him and me."

He crushed her in his arms while he told her that he'd just wanted to get her father's goat, that he'd just wanted to win. And what he had said and what Kip had done. Only then did he let her go, and her eyes weren't the same.

It was like the first time. It wasn't worth it.

"I didn't mean it," he whispered. "I fell in love with you the night we met. I had to have you."

She kissed him and got out of bed, like it didn't matter.

And the last thing he saw before he went back to work was Erin at the trailer's kitchen table, looking through the box of things her father had shared. Her fingers touched his Silver Star, pinned to her shirt, as though to make sure it was still there.

ERIN HAD NO MAID of honor.

She'd hoped for Beulah Ann, but Beulah Ann had not responded to her letters, sent to the Texas address Erin had gotten from Lane. At least Abe's mother had said she'd be there on the twenty-first without fail; they'd reserved Mears Cabin for her.

By branding time, the weekend before Jack Draw's cattle sale, Erin had nearly settled on Ella Kelsey as a matron of honor. Erin had spent a few afternoons volunteering at the museum. They liked each other. Surely Ella would agree.

But she'd also wonder why Erin didn't have someone closer to her.

Because of Maeve, Erin couldn't participate in the roundup and branding. So she watched from outside the corral, with the heat and smoke from the fire stinging her eyes, mingling in her nose with the scent of burning cowhide and manure.

Abe roped the calves from the saddle, and Lucky and Pete dragged the animals to the fire. There, the calves bawled and dropped manure as they were branded, inoculated and castrated. They had all been treated with dehorning paste after birth to prevent horn growth.

Twenty calves had been branded and cut when Chaley's silver-blue pickup pulled into the yard.

Erin saw her father notice the truck. From his position just inside the corral, he gazed over the fence rails. But when Lucky and Pete dragged over another calf, he focused on that.

As Abe roped another calf, Erin took Maeve off the top rail where she'd had been holding her and set her on her feet to walk toward the trailer. Chaley was part of the lies. If Erin didn't see her, she didn't have to live them.

Chaley headed for the corral, leggy and athletic in her cowboy hat and jeans, and Erin coaxed Maeve around to the garden behind the trailer. The root crops and beans were bushy, the peas almost ready to pick.

While Maeve found her spade and pail, Erin attacked the bindweed, in a peace removed from the corral. The bawling calves and the men laughing and shouting to one another seemed faraway.

"Hi."

Chaley had let herself in the chicken-wire gate. The sinking sun cast part of the garden in shadow, and Erin's own shadow ran into Chaley's form.

"Hi," Erin said.

Her half sister crouched farther down the row from Erin and absently pulled a few weeds. "Be sure to watch the weather every night," she said. "The surprise frosts will really get you up here."

Erin knelt in the soil and sat back on her heels.

Chaley's eyes were just like Kip's. Blue, with heavy, almost serpentine lids. "Dad told me."

Maeve dumped dirt onto a carrot top, burying it.

A calf bawled, protesting his fate.

This is it, then. He told Chaley I'm his daughter. He said I'm his daughter.

It was flat, with something missing. There was only this strange distance between her and Chaley, and nothing to say.

But her half sister didn't seem to notice the absence of a reply. She was staring at something. Erin didn't know what until Chaley said, "Did Abe mention that ring's kind of been around?"

"Of course. It doesn't bother me. I just tell myself..." Why did she always have to be the nervous one, always the one afraid of getting hurt, of being a fool, of being the intruder? She finished, anyhow. "That my sister wore it."

Chaley's look was ironic.

I hate this. I'm going to leave. I'm going to pick up Maeve and walk away. Why did I ever want to get married on this ranch? Why did I ever say we should stay this long?

"He's changed," Chaley said suddenly. "I always wanted him to settle down and be like he is now. But he wouldn't. He must really love you."

Standing, Erin brushed off her jeans. Nothing could get

worse with Chaley. This woman hated her, and Erin had nothing to lose except a dingy pride that had been beaten down to a pebble. "Chaley, are you going to come to our wedding?"

"My father would never let me forget it if I didn't."

My father...

Erin breathed through it.

"Since you're going to be there, anyway, would you consider being my maid of honor?"

Her half sister choked. Dragging her fingers through the soil, she made a sound of exasperation. Still squatting, she stared off at the bull pens, then over at Maeve.

Erin waited for her to say something worse than no.

Chaley pushed herself to her feet and met Erin's eyes with no enthusiasm whatsoever. "If I can pick my own clothes."

Not sure whether to feel relief or misgiving, not sure this denouement was even a good thing, Erin said, "You can wear whatever you want."

"We never made love," said Chaley.

Erin answered, "I know."

*"We arrive at truth, not by reason alone,
but also by the heart."*

—Pascal, *Pensées*

CHAPTER NINETEEN

THAT NIGHT, there was a barbecue and a dance on the narrow lawn alongside the house. The ranch had eight paying guests, and neighbors came, and Chaley stayed; Kip had hired a three-piece band from Alta. The hands had built a fire, and the guests stood near it, drinking beer when they weren't dancing.

When Maeve got sleepy, Erin kissed Abe and told him to have fun. She walked back to the trailer, thinking about Chaley, about her father confessing to Chaley. Abe knew, too; when Erin explained, he'd hardly reacted.

He'd already told her there was nothing to stop her from calling her father Dad again.

I can't. It's not enough.

She was a small girl walking home from summer camp, stuffing a pencil holder rolled in a paper bag into the outside trash can so Jayne would never see it. Jayne, who'd fled a man who mistook her for the enemy.

In the trailer she put Maeve to bed with her bunny, then set up at the kitchen table, to pore over the contents of the Justin Boots box, her treasure trove. She'd seen everything. Letters from her grandparents to various people. News articles about the ranch. Photos of relatives she'd never known she had.

Outside at the party Abe had smiled by the fire, laughed with the hands. He was happy here.

Erin opened the door of the trailer so she could look across the yard. He was coming up the steps, handsome in a red work shirt and new jeans and a new summer hat.

When she opened the screen, he grabbed her. "I missed you."

"Don't let the bugs in."

They shut the doors, shut themselves inside.

Erin opened her mouth to tell him they would stay.

And could not.

JACK DRAW'S CATTLE SALE was Friday the thirteenth, and on the twelfth Kip went to court to defend his water rights. When he returned that night for supper, he said, "Have to go back tomorrow." The kitchen was full—Lucky, Abe, Pete and Maeve were about—and he didn't catch Erin's eye or look at her.

She washed vegetables in the sink as though she hadn't heard.

So she had to go to the cattle sale alone. Her father's situation was unavoidable; this wasn't his fault. He had to defend the ranch's water rights.

At dinner food had no taste.

I'll go alone. And I'll talk to that foreman about the brand. Everyone has a price.

But the foreman, Randy, had been making good money with Jack Draw. His price might be more than she could afford. Or he might just refuse to sell.

After dinner, while Maeve played on the floor, Abe helped her with the dishes. These June nights he spent with her, quitting work early. Tonight, though, Erin wanted to talk to her father without Abe, to get advice about the sale.

Unfortunately Kip retired to the den and Abe didn't leave. When the dishes were dried, he poured a cup of coffee. "We need to tell your dad when we're going. He said Chaley's moving home. But he needs to fill two jobs, yours and mine. And, Erin, I haven't found anything. We have to stay in this area till I finish working on that Paint of Tanner's. And we haven't heard from Lane or Beulah Ann. If they want us to take their baby... We could do worse than stay here, Erin."

The door to the den was down the hall and around the corner. Was it open? Could her father hear?

As Abe watched her over the rim of his coffee cup, she felt like hiding. It had happened a lot lately.

Leaning against the counter beside him, she folded her arms across her chest. "What?"

He spoke close to her. "Maybe you should talk to him again."

Her chin shook. Abe scalded himself with the coffee and set it down. She was crying, and he held her.

"We can stay," she said. "We'll just stay, all right?"

Giving in, like he'd given in after Lloyd died.

"Fine," he said. "And what you call him is your business. But starting right now, to our daughter that man is Grandpa."

"All right." She tore away from him, ripped a paper towel from the roll by the sink.

When Abe turned, Kip Kay stood in the doorway.

He came in on his crutches and helped himself to a coffee mug from one of the hooks. Erin kept her back to him, wiping her eyes.

"We're staying," said Abe. "If you don't mind."

The rancher rested on his crutches to pour his coffee. "I don't. Be glad to have you."

Abe crossed one ankle over the other. "And I'm sure you agree that it wouldn't be respectful for Maeve to call you anything but Grandpa."

"You're her parents. I'm sure you know best." Kip took a drink and glanced at Erin, then set down the mug. "Erin, would you give me a hand with this? I'm going back to the den.''

Abe smiled a little. He wasn't wanted, which was good. Maeve had wandered into the dining room and was crawling after a ball under the table; he went to get her as Erin carried her father's coffee down the hall.

"I'M SORRY about tomorrow," was the first thing Kip said as he settled into his easy chair. Through the open door Erin heard Abe talking to Maeve in the kitchen. "You should ask one of the hands to go with you. Pete or George.''

"All right." Abe had told him they were staying. Now was the moment to be true and honest. To call her father Dad again, now, when he was in his right mind. She could not. She said, "Good luck in court tomorrow.''

"Need plenty of that." Nodding, he said, almost to himself, "I'm glad you're staying. Chaley's coming back, too.''

And Erin knew he was thinking about the ranch. That he needed Abe.

She left him drinking his coffee.

THE NEXT DAY at noon she saddled Wish. She'd begged Abe to baby-sit so she could "take a ride.''

While Erin mounted up outside the corral, he said, "I wish you'd ride the Paint if you're going far." He grabbed Maeve, swinging her up onto his shoulder before she could wander in with the horses. The sun had brought out freckles on his nose. In the heat, the ranch smelled like dust and pine sap.

"I won't learn to handle Wish any better by not riding him." Today she would ride the horse her father had given her. Because they were staying and she needed to convince herself of his caring.

She slapped at a fly on her neck.

"Be careful." Abe stepped closer and lifted his face for a kiss, and she bent over and kissed Maeve, then him. Leaving her family, she wheeled Wish around and started down the road to Jack Draw's.

Chaley's truck was coming at her, raising sun-filtered dust clouds for a quarter mile behind. Erin turned Wish toward the side of the road and held his reins, made him stand although he wanted to go.

The pickup slowed and stopped. "Dad around?"

"He's in court again."

Her half sister's eyes studied the horse. "Where are you going?"

"To Jack Draw's cattle sale. I'm buying cows for Abe for a wedding present."

"You're kidding." Chaley smiled, as though Erin had done something endearing.

Wish shifted under her and lowered his head to try to eat. Erin kept his head up. "It's a secret." *Oh, hell, why not?* "Want to come?"

Chaley pondered it for two seconds. "Sure. Let me go get Mouse."

Erin trotted Wish on the road while she waited for Chaley, and soon she saw her half sister riding toward her on Mouse. She was wearing a white hat. Her braid flapped behind her and her horse kicked up dust as she rode.

The two Appaloosas walked side by side in the noon heat.

"How many head?" asked Chaley.

"I think about forty." She chewed her lip. "I want the Scotch Highlanders."

Her half sister stared straight ahead over the dusty washboard road, then laughed.

"What?"

Chaley shrugged. "People say they have a lean beef. That's good."

I'm glad I asked her to come.

But Erin didn't tell her about the brand.

Not then.

The road lay clear as far as they could see. Chaley asked, "Want to lope?"

Erin applied a gentle leg pressure to Wish's sides, and he broke into a trot, then a lope. No joy could compare to this; it was unique. This horse was hers, and she could ride him tomorrow, too. Later, as she and Chaley rode up to Jack Draw's barn, where numerous pickups were parked, the cowboys stared at their horses.

They dismounted and loosened the horses' girths and went to look at the penned stock and at Draw's remuda. Inside, the auctioneer's voice was already going, and soon they ventured through the doors into the place filled with men in cowboy hats.

It was Erin who made the bids, but Chaley coached her, and together they bought forty heifer calves. Randy, the foreman, was busy with sales, and Erin wouldn't get a chance to talk to him about the brand unless she stuck around. She dawdled outside with Chaley, discussing the calves. "I want to have them brought over the day before the wedding. Maybe send Abe to town or something."

"Is Dad in on this?"

"Yes."

"Let him take care of it," said Chaley. "He likes shenanigans."

There was a break and people streamed out of the barn. They would be selling the horses next, and Chaley said, "Let's get out of here."

Erin saw Randy and waved to him.

"Oh, did you have to do that?" Chaley muttered.

The foreman was making a beeline for Chaley, but he stopped a few feet away and stared at Wish. "Not for sale, is he?"

"No," snapped Chaley, untying Mouse.

Erin said, "Maybe."

"THE GUY TOOK A HORSE?" Kip asked, when she explained that night. While she washed dishes, Abe had taken Maeve out to the barn to look at some new kittens. Kip had spent a good day in court; the ranch's water was safe this time. He was eyeing a seat on the water board now. He and Abe and Chaley would have to talk about it, divide up the civic duties. Erin could do her share, too. That was quite a coup she'd pulled off today. "Well, I'll be damned."

He rubbed his jaw and faced the kitchen window, and Erin wondered if she'd hurt him. But he turned and smiled with a watery-eyed brightness and said, "That was a nice thing to do. Now let's see how we're going to move your herd."

Relief freed her tongue. "I cried riding him home." And Chaley had said, *I can't believe you did that.* Erin and Randy had shaken on the deal. He would do the paperwork and they would make the trade on Friday.

"Well, I think your Rado is a fine horse. Let's talk about those cows." Kip said he would send Abe to Grand Junction on Friday, and he'd have the hands move the cows then. The guests could help, too. "You can drive me over so I can see what you got. We'll help get 'em across the highway."

Erin had spent the day riding on the land. It had made her feel strong. She wanted to bloom, brave as the starry columbines. She could imagine Abe's arms around her, and if her father hurt her feelings, she could walk out to the barn and Abe would hold her.

But her voice wouldn't go above a whisper. "Thank you, Dad."

He winked at her, his eyes beautiful, like the eyes of someone who felt too much. The kitchen clock ticked, measuring the patient moment.

When she moved he asked, "What do you hear from Beulah Ann?"

"Not a thing. I've written her four times."

Kip went back to gazing out the window, which really meant seeing his own reflection, because it was dark. "That was a good trade you made. I'm glad you did it." He laughed and said, "Good for you."

SUNDAY WAS Father's Day. Chaley came for breakfast and brought doughnuts from City Market and a sterling silver bolo tie for her father. Erin gave him an unsentimental card—*Happy Father's Day*—signed only *Erin*. He said, "Thank you," and took it with him to his room.

With Erin's help, Maeve gave Abe a card with her handprints on it. He put it on their dresser. But from the way he smiled, not quite with his eyes, Erin knew he was thinking of Lloyd. When she brought him his supper in the south pasture, his eyes were red.

They sat in the truck bed to eat, and a cranky cow who thought they were threatening her calf tried to climb in with them. When they moved into the cab to escape her, Abe said, "I didn't get him anything last year, and neither did Lane."

Maeve, in the car seat between them, touched Abe's hand. "Daddy," she said and lifted her arms. "Up!"

ON THE NIGHT before his wedding, Abe took his other girl with him to Grand Junction to buy a new lawn mower. He asked Martha repeatedly why Kip Kay had to have a new lawn mower today; the rancher had insisted he wanted Lucky to mow the lawn in the morning. "And why not Gunnison? Why couldn't I buy a lawn mower in Gunnison? Sometimes, Martha, I feel just like a slave."

It was ten when Abe got home, and finally dark, if you could call a full-moon night dark. Tomorrow would be the longest day of the year. Following habit, he did not park until taking a turn through the ranch to see if anything had changed in his absence. He trawled past the corral and the barn and the guest cabins.

It was time to go up to cow camp, in the high country. He would play the harmonica there, nights around the fire, and love Erin and Maeve, love having his family with him. But Lloyd would be missing from the circle.

Cows grazed in the pasture behind the guest cabins, and he slowed to see the stock in the full-moon light. It illuminated the barbed wire and everything beyond.

He braked.

Stared.

Leaving the truck idling, Abe got out and let Martha out, too. He spread the barbed wire and stepped through. With an eye on the cows and their calves, he headed for two shapes different from the rest.

No, there weren't just two. Ten…twenty…thirty?

They weren't keen on his coming near, either, and he wondered how a person was supposed to read a brand on the things.

But the calves had been recently branded.

With a triangle E.

A heifer calf peered at him from under shaggy bangs.

"You're not a cow at all." Good grief. He headed for the pickup to drive the rest of the fields, then back to the barn, to see the horses.

Wish was gone.

Not in his stall. Not in the corral.

"Come on, Martha," he said. "Let's go find Erin."

HE EXPECTED to find her waiting up, but only the light over the stove was on, and she didn't come out of the bedroom to greet him. Only Taffy showed up, wagging her tail and jumping on him like he was the only man in her life. "Yeah, I know who you love best," said Abe.

Kip had even been known to let her in the house.

Papers sat on the kitchen counter, held down by an unopened bottle of Jack Daniel's. The setup seemed like an invitation, addressed to him, and Abe stopped to read.

Then he opened the bottle of Jack Daniel's and took three long swallows.

Erin. Oh, Erin, sweetheart, you did good.

Mostly. Lord, had Kip had anything to do with this?

No, Kip wouldn't have let her do it.

On the way to the bedroom Abe stopped in Lane's old room.

Maeve slept on her tummy in the crib, her bottom sticking up in the air. She'd lost all her covers, and Abe put them over her and put her bunny right next to her tiny hand.

When he stepped into their bedroom, the room that had ceased to feel like Lloyd's, he thought he could smell Erin's skin. He could also smell faintly the scent of sex, of when they'd last made love.

Abe sat on the foot of the bed to tug off his boots and she sat up, the covers falling around her white chemise. He said, "Hi."

Erin studied him in the dark. He was smiling. When he came to her, naked, she smelled the Jack Daniel's.

"Is it all right?" she asked. Her father's chin had fallen to his knees that afternoon when he'd seen the calves. *You bought Highlands?*

Chaley had said innocently, *They have a lean beef. This ranch needs some innovation.*

Pete and George had smirked as they moved the herd.

"What? Getting our brand back?" Abe hugged her, messed with the sheets, figured out how to get on the same layer. Ah. There she was. *Oh, Erin.*

"The calves."

"You mean," he said against her skin, "do I mind being the sole owner of forty baby heifers of unusual breed?"

"Yes."

The Jack Daniel's had helped him adjust to the notion. Her body was also helping him adjust. "I love them. They're the cutest cows I ever saw."

"George laughed. He said they looked like walking wigs."

Abe had to take a breath. "No one around here," he said when he could talk, "is going to make fun of my herd." *Or my wife.*

She would be his wife tomorrow.

"How did you get the brand?"

"It's your wedding gift, Abe. It's not polite for you to ask how much it cost."

Wish's stall had been empty. "How does Kip feel about it?"

"I think," she said, "he's proud of me."

"So am I. I also have an attraction to you that will not quit." He went about showing her what he meant.

Much later Erin was almost asleep when he said her name.

"Hmm?" she answered.

"I really love my herd."

THE BEST MAN was absent.

The ceremony was scheduled for eleven in the morning, and by nine Lane still hadn't arrived. Abe loaded Buy Back and Rado into the trailer with the saddles and other equipment for the three days he and Erin planned to spend at the line cabin near the meadow where they would be married. There was a corral for the horses, and he and Lucky had brought feed for the animals and food for the people. Terry Loren, Guy's wife, and Ella Kelsey from the museum were handling the wedding refreshments. George would man the grill. When the horses were loaded, Abe and Lucky caravaned up to the meadow and set up the chairs and unloaded a big charcoal grill.

Once the chairs were arranged and the horses put in the corral, it was time to go home and change. If Lane didn't show, Abe decided, he'd ask Kip to stand up with him. Right now Erin's father was minding his granddaughter.

And Erin was dressing in the big house, hiding out with Chaley.

Chaley. Abe hadn't got over gritting his teeth when he heard her name. Her smile at breakfast was Chaley-smug, and so was her self-defense. *It was Erin's idea. She said she wanted Scotch Highlanders. Anyhow, they've got good cold-weather tolerance. With all that hair.*

Back at the trailer, Abe stayed outside as long as he could, playing with Martha and watching the road. So far the people he was most counting on, most needing to see, were no-shows. Lane was working on a perfect track record of missing funerals and weddings.

And Beulah Ann...

Come on, Beulah Ann. Don't let me down.

But finally he had to go in and dress in the clothes he and Erin had picked out.

"Ah, Martha." Abe adjusted his string tie in the mirror over his father's old dresser. "I'm glad *you* could make it."

THE PERCHERONS' HOOVES made a soothing clip-clop on the graded road, but the borrowed buggy gave a bumpy ride. Chaley, at the reins, said, "Did you ever read those Laura Ingalls Wilder books? Didn't it sound so romantic when she and Almanzo would go riding in a buggy? But it felt like this."

Teeth-jarring.

"Well, the washboards on the road probably weren't so bad," Erin pointed out.

"But the roads were worse."

Chaley had dressed as a stage driver, in men's clothes with her hair in a long ponytail. Erin felt small beside this grand gesture of Chaley's, this buggy ride. She knew that it wasn't all generosity, that it was also Chaley's way of holding up her head. And maybe a way of apologizing for not steering her clear of shaggy cows.

There was dust on the road, so Erin clasped a lap robe around the tiered skirt of her mother's lacy dress. The country style, with a full sash and leg-of-mutton sleeves, had been popular when Jayne and Kip were married. Ella Kelsey had decorated Erin's ivory cowboy hat with flowers. And she'd worn sensible shoes, tan lace-up ropers, because she and Abe would be riding away after the ceremony.

She'd pinned her father's Silver Star to her dress, though she wasn't brave enough to ask for what she wanted or even to dream it. There were some things that meant nothing if you had to ask.

"There they are," said Chaley as the meadow came into view, filled with chairs and guests.

Abe, in his black coat and hat, held Maeve as he spoke with the minister. As Chaley drew the team to a halt, Kip walked toward the buggy. Coming over to Erin's side, he offered her his hand.

A lump in her throat, Erin took it, let him help her to the ground.

KIP JOINED ABE in front of the chairs in the shade of the trees. Like Abe, he watched the road, severely put out with Lane. If Lane didn't show, he'd have to stand up with Abe.

Oh, well, it would work.

Now Chaley was messing with the boom box, making sure the tape was set to the right place. He'd offered to hire live music, but Erin had said, *The hands want to play after the wedding.* George had a banjo and Pete would play his harmonica.

Kip had gone ahead and slipped money to Terry and Ella for the food.

Chaley checked her watch, said something to Pete and hurried to the area behind the chairs, back where the food was arranged, near the aspens.

The minister asked Abe, "Ready to start?"

Abe's eyes searched out Erin and he spotted her speaking

with Chaley. Beautiful Erin, one of the aspens against the meadow grass. He'd thought she was a city girl when he met her. But Reno was a cow town with casinos, and she had a country heart.

No Lane anywhere.

Exchanging a look with Kip, he killed a mosquito on Maeve's arm. Bloodthirsty things were everywhere. "Maeve," said Abe, "it's time to go sit with Lucky."

"Mama."

"You'll get to see Mama in a minute. She's right back there."

"Mama."

Chaley came up the grassy aisle between the chairs. "I'll take her, Abe. We have someone to watch her."

Someone was blond and pretty and smiling big as Chaley brought Maeve over to her.

Beulah Ann.

Before he could go back and say hello, the music started. The minister said, "I guess this is it."

Where's my best man? Kip had left his side and gone to the back of the chairs, with the women.

Abe's heart knocked strangely.

Kip wasn't even looking toward the front but was staring at some latecomers. As the two figures made their way behind the last row of chairs, the rancher stepped aside to give them room.

They turned up the aisle.

The best man had arrived. On his arm was a beautiful woman with smooth light brown hair. She beamed at Abe.

Oh, Lane. Oh, Lane, you done good.

The best man, with the slow bow-legged stride of one who's ridden too many broncs and bulls, escorted the mother of the groom to her seat in the front row.

Then, to the tape-recorded "Wedding March," came Chaley in her stage-driver clothes, bearing a bouquet of wildflowers. Abe gazed past her, at Erin.

As SHE LISTENED to the music, Erin's heart and breath kept uneasy pace with the butterflies in her stomach. Chaley was already halfway to the minister and Abe. And Beulah Ann had taken Maeve around the seats and up to the front.

Erin moved toward the opening between the chairs. *Abe.*

Close by, someone cleared his throat.

Erin had noticed him there earlier. She couldn't pretend she hadn't. This meadow was the most honest place she'd ever been, and she couldn't pretend, just bite her lips together hard.

Because he was still there, in his suit and vest and bolo tie, gazing down at her with eyes that felt too much, that brimmed with the deep feelings of the heart.

"I wasn't there for your first steps, honey, or your first words. But I'm sure as hell glad to be here today." Kip looked down at her face that was part his and part Jayne's, looked into her eyes just the way he did Chaley's to make sure she understood. "I hope you'll do your daddy the very great honor of letting him walk you down the aisle and give you to your husband."

Erin nodded.

Kip offered her his arm, and she took it, held it.

And they walked through the meadow grass toward Abe.

When they reached him, Kip put Erin's hand in Abe's, clasped the joined hands firmly together and stepped away.

And Erin, whole, looked into the gray-green eyes of the man she loved most. "Cowboy," she said, "you're mine."

"Anyone can see we may not be raising cattle here in twenty years, that the world might not let us. But these ranches weren't built on the prospect of defeat. And, one way or another, I hope my grandchildren will grow up working this land."

—Kip Kay, quoted in
A Tale of Two Ranches,
by Erin Cockburn

EPILOGUE

KIP HAD TOLD Beulah Ann he'd clean the line cabin after the honeymooners returned to their trailer. It wasn't from a sense of proprietorship—just a wanting to be back in that place, where he and Jayne had honeymooned, too.

Gus and Call, the ranch dogs, followed Rowdy up the road, running off to sniff trees and scrub oak. Damned blue heeler would probably end up with a nose full of porcupine quills.

A helicopter chugged overhead, and Kip lifted his eyes to the shape, spinning back, seeing a Huey. His knees hugged the horse, and he was grateful to be riding even a widow-maker like Rowdy. The shadow of his own hat on the ground reassured him, and soon he saw the cabin through the aspens. Rowdy picked his way over a fallen trunk, and Kip led him through the widest slots in the trees until he came staring-close to some newly stripped, newly carved bark. He reined in the horse.

"Well, I'll be damned."

When Kip had left the meadow at sunset on Saturday, the sound he'd heard as he departed was the mournful wail of a harmonica from the porch of the cabin, Abe playing "Home on the Range."

Ah, you'll be good to this land, thought Kip, reading the inscription in the broken tree bark, left for history:

THANK YOU, GOD. I LOVE MY WIFE. ABE COCKBURN, 1997.

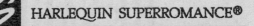

HARLEQUIN SUPERROMANCE®

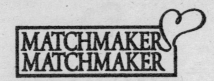

When love needs a little nudge...

SWEET TIBBY MACK
by Roz Denny Fox

Tibby Mack is, at twenty-seven, the youngest resident in Yaqui Springs, a retirement community near California's Salton Sea. The folks there have become her family, her friends...her matchmakers. But what chance do they have of finding Tibby a husband when the youngest man in town is sixty-six?

Then Cole O'Donnell arrives. *Age:* 30. *Looks:* good (make that great). *And* he's inherited his grandfather's property in Yaqui Springs. He's the answer to their prayers. Not Tibby's, though.

But the matchmakers know that these two should be in love and that once in a while, love needs a nudge....

Watch for *Sweet Tibby Mack* (#746) by Roz Denny Fox

Available in July 1997 wherever Harlequin books are sold.

HE SAID

SHE SAID

Explore the mystery of male/female communication in this extraordinary new book from two of your favorite Harlequin authors.

Jasmine Cresswell and Margaret St. George bring you the exciting story of two romantic adversaries—each from their own point of view!

DEV'S STORY. CATHY'S STORY.
As he sees it. As she sees it.
Both sides of the story!

The heat is definitely on, and these two can't stay out of the kitchen!

Don't miss HE SAID, SHE SAID.
Available in July wherever Harlequin books are sold.

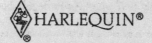

It's hot...and it's out of control!

Beginning this spring, Temptation turns up the
heat. Look for these bold, provocative,
*ultra*sexy books!

#629 OUTRAGEOUS
by Lori Foster (April 1997)

#639 RESTLESS NIGHTS
by Tiffany White (June 1997)

#649 NIGHT RHYTHMS
by Elda Minger (Sept. 1997)

BLAZE: Red-hot reads—only from

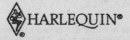

He changes diapers, mixes formula and
tells wonderful bedtime stories—he's

Mr. Mom

Three totally different stories of sexy, single
heroes each raising another man's child...
from three of your favorite authors:

MEMORIES OF THE PAST
by Carole Mortimer

THE MARRIAGE TICKET
by Sharon Brondos

TELL ME A STORY
by Dallas Schulze

Available this June wherever
Harlequin and Silhouette books are sold.

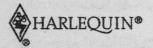

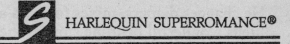

HARLEQUIN SUPERROMANCE®

SISTERS

A trilogy by three of your favorite authors.

Peg Sutherland
Ellen James
Marisa Carroll

A golden wedding *usually* means a family celebration.

But the Hardaway sisters drifted apart years ago. And each has her own reason for wanting no part of a family reunion. As plans for the party proceed, tensions mount, and it begins to look as if their parents' marriage might fall apart before the big event. Can the daughters put aside old hurts and betrayals...for the sake of the family?

Follow the fortunes of AMY, LISA and MEGAN in these three dramatic love stories.

April 1997—AMY by Peg Sutherland

May 1997—LISA by Ellen James

June 1997—MEGAN by Marisa Carroll

Available wherever Harlequin books are sold.